PASSION PLAY

PASSION PLAY

BETH BERNOBICH

A TOM DOHERTY ASSOCIATES BOOK
NEW YORK

PASSION PLAY

Copyright © 2010 by Beth Bernobich

Maps by Jennifer Hanover

A Tor Book
Published by Tom Doherty Associates, LLC
175 Fifth Avenue
New York, NY 10010

www.tor-forge.com

Tor® is a registered trademark of Tom Doherty Associates, LLC.

ISBN 978-0-7653-2217-3

First Edition: October 2010

Printed in the United States of America

0 9 8 7 6 5 4 3 2 1

ACKNOWLEDGMENTS

It took me many years to write this book, and along the way an army of friends and strangers have generously offered me their criticisms, suggestions, and encouragement. I am grateful to them all.

Teresa Nielsen Hayden at the Viable Paradise Workshop showed me where to start the novel. Lois Tilton deftly pointed out where to stop. Sherwood Smith read draft after draft, giving me feedback on prose and plot and characters, as I fumbled toward the story I really wanted to tell. My wonderful editor, Claire Eddy, was an expert at asking all the right questions so I could see myself how to clear up the murky parts. Kristin Sevick patiently guided me through the production process. My very thorough copyeditor, Jane Herman, saved me from all kinds of inconsistencies and infelicities. Many thanks as well go to my agent, Vaughne Lee Hansen at the Virginia Kidd Agency, for taking me on, and to Gardner Dozois for introducing us.

My special debt of gratitude goes to my husband, Rob, and my son, Matt, for all their understanding and support.

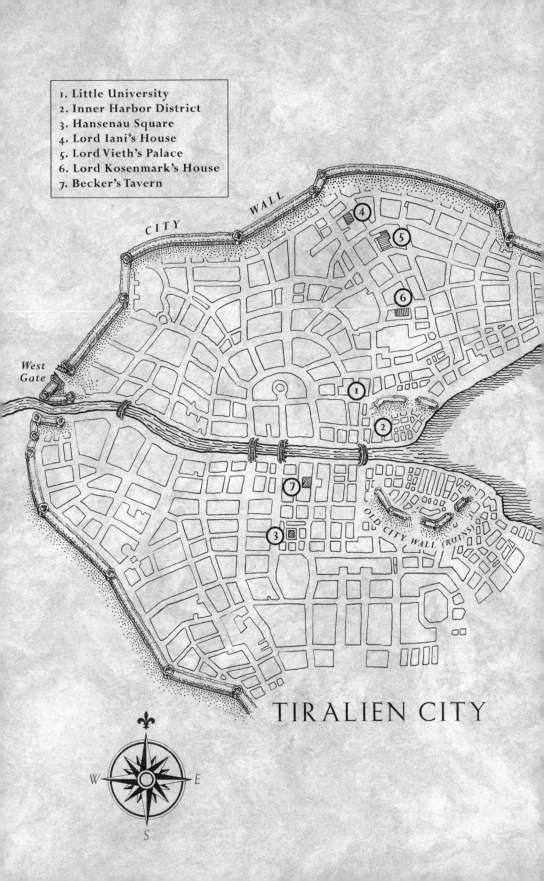

1. Little University
2. Inner Harbor District
3. Hansenau Square
4. Lord Iani's House
5. Lord Vieth's Palace
6. Lord Kosenmark's House
7. Becker's Tavern

CITY WALL

West Gate

OLD CITY WALL (RUINS)

TIRALIEN CITY

W · E
S

PASSION PLAY

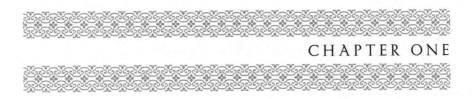

IN THE GAME of word links, a large vocabulary was not always an advantage. Words indeed were necessary—the game consisted entirely of words given back and forth, and each response had to connect to the previous one. The good players possessed a quick mind and the ability to recognize patterns. Those who could see the unexpected connections, however, inevitably won.

A simple game with endless strategies and unexpected side effects.

Therez Zhalina watched Klara's face intently, waiting for her friend to turn the miniature sand glass and start the next round of their game. It was a late summer's afternoon. The two girls sat in a seldom-used parlor on the third floor of Maester Zhalina's house. The maids had opened the windows, letting in the warm salt breeze from the harbor, less than a mile away, and a hint of pine tang from the hills and mountains that circled the city to the north.

Klara held the sand glass lightly between her fingers, tilting it one way, then another. She appeared bored, but the look did not deceive Therez. She knew Klara's style. Her friend would start with something innocuous, like *chair* or *book*. Then, at the crucial moment, she would throw out a word guaranteed to fluster her opponent.

I shall have to use her own strategy upon her first.

"Lir," Klara said, and flipped the glass over.

"Toc," Therez answered at once.

"Stars."

"Eye socket."

Klara choked. "Therez! That is *not* fair. You deliberately chose a horrible image."

Though she wanted to laugh at Klara's expression, Therez did not let her attention lapse. "No more horrible than yours, the last round," she said. "Besides, the link is perfect: *And Toc plucked out his eyes to make the sun and moon for his sister-goddess, Lir.* Come, the round is not over. A word. Give me a word, Klara."

"I'm thinking. I'm thinking. What about— Ah, love-of-the-ocean, the sands have run out. Are you certain this wretched device runs true?"

"The glass came with a guild certificate from the artisan."

"Damp," Klara said grumpily. "Just like everything else in Melnek."

"If the sands were damp, they would run slower not faster." Therez poured a fresh cup of chilled water and stirred in a few spoonfuls of crushed mint. "Here," she said, handing it to her friend. "You sound like a marsh frog—a very thirsty one."

"Oh, thank you." Klara drank down the water. "How delightful to know that my voice is like that of some slithery bog creature. Do you think the young men will appreciate me more, or less, for that virtue?"

Therez smothered another laugh. "Oh, much more. Think what money you could save them on entertainment. No more fees to musicians when you are about."

"Hah. There speaks a true merchant girl."

"No more a merchant girl than you," Therez said. "Here. We'll play one more round. Unless you're tired of losing."

"Make it a double round," her friend said. "And promise me you'll turn the glass without delay."

"Agreed." Therez reversed the timer. "Duenne."

"Empire."

"War."

"Treaty."

They each rapped out answers as quickly as the other spoke, the words connecting through all the facets of life in a trade city on the border between Veraene and Károví. *Guild. Taxes. Caravan. Freight. Scales. Fish.*

"Lev Bartov."

"Klara! He's not a fish."

"He looks like one. Come, give me a word or make a challenge."

"Very well. No challenge. My word is *shipping*."

"Port."

"Melnek."

"Home."

"Hurt. No, wait. I meant to say *winter*."

The sands ran out in the silence that followed. Unwilling to meet her friend's gaze, Therez turned the sand glass over in her hands. Its graceful wooden frame, carved from rare blackwood, made a swirling pattern against the luminescent sand, and the artisan had painted fine gold lines along its edges, reminding her of sunlight reflecting off running water.

"When do you go?" Klara said at last.

"Next summer."

"That late? I thought it was—"

"Next spring? It was. My father changed his mind."

And he might again, Therez thought. After a long tedious lecture about expenses, Petr Zhalina had agreed that Therez's brother, Ehren, would resume his studies at Duenne's University. After longer discussions and several invitations, he gave permission for Therez to spend a year with their cousin's family, who also lived in the capital. But so many *ifs* and *maybes* lay between now and next summer. Their grandmother's illness. Their father's uncertain health and the state of his business . . .

"Do you want to play another round?" she said.

Her voice was not as steady as she would have liked, and Klara's eyes narrowed, making them appear like quick, narrow brushstrokes against her dark complexion. But her friend only said, "No. Thank you. May I have another cup of water?"

A welcome deflection, Therez thought as she poured chilled water for them both into porcelain cups. Her father paid extra to have ice blocks transported from the nearby mountains, and stored in his cellars. Her brother said the ice reminded their father of the far north, and Duszranjo, where he'd once lived. Therez didn't know if that were true. She only knew that her father's whims on what he spent and what he saved made little sense to her.

"He must have been so very hungry," she murmured, half to herself. "Starving, for more than one life."

"What was that?" Klara said.

Therez roused herself. "Oh, nothing. I was just thinking of . . . past lives."

"Ah, those." Klara's black eyes glinted with curiosity. "I must have been a marsh frog at least once. Though marsh frogs seldom care to become humans. What about you?"

Therez shrugged and pretended to study her water cup. But she could sense Klara's attention. Her friend might pretend indifference, but she was watching Therez closely. "Oh, a scholar," she said lightly. "I remember ink stains on my fingers. I had a lover, too. Another scholar. I remember us wandering through a library filled with books about everything in the world. About history and poetry, about Lir and Toc. About . . ." About magic and Lir's jewels, gifts from the goddess to Erythandra's priests in ancient times, she thought. She had been a scholar more than once, but she didn't want to tell Klara that part.

Klara, however, was smiling thoughtfully. "Scholar," she said softly. "That I can believe. Do you remember how it ended, your time with your lover?"

Which one? Therez thought. The answer was the same for both. *In the darkness, running from a man I'd known years and lives before.* But who her lover was, or who the other man was, she still did not know.

She turned her head away. "It ended badly. That's all I know. What about you?"

"Ah, mine." Klara smiled pensively. "Mine are little more than vague dreams—shadows in the night, as the poets call them. But this I do remember—how in all of them I always had friends. It gives me joy to think that."

Some of the ache in Therez's chest eased. "And so it should."

A brisk knock startled them both. Klara arched her eyebrows. "It cannot be your father," she whispered. "He never knocks."

"Klara, do not make a joke, please—"

She broke off as the door opened to a liveried boy. "Mistress Therez," he said. "Your mother would see you at once in her parlor."

Klara immediately stood and shook out the folds of her loose summer gown. "A summons, I see. Then I shall not detain you a single moment." She leaned close and whispered, "We shall continue our talk tomorrow, my scholarly friend."

I should not have told her anything, Therez thought as she escorted her friend down the stairs. That was the danger of the word-linking game. Admit one secret and the rest come spilling out. It had nearly happened when her mother first mentioned the cousin's invitation. She'd wanted to cheer or laugh, both of them inappropriate reactions. Both guaranteed to convince her father she ought to stay home. Oh, not that she had any true plans. Just hopes and wishes that a twelve-month at Veraene's capital city would let chance show itself. That she might meet a poet or a scholar— anyone who was not a merchant's son.

Or even a merchant's son. As long as he is not like my father, I shall not care.

She parted from Klara at the next landing, and turned into the family's private wing. All the house was quiet, except when Petr Zhalina held meetings or dinners for his colleagues, but the silence here was deeper, and the air lay heavy, thick with the scent of crushed herbs. Therez drew a deep breath, wishing for a cleansing northern wind, then hurried onward to her mother's rooms.

She found her mother surrounded by a handful of servants who were laying out pens and ink bottles, parchment, drying dust, and packets of sealing wax. A tray with cups and two carafes occupied the center of the table.

Isolde Zhalina turned at her daughter's entrance. "There you are, Therez. I'm sorry to have interrupted your visit, but we have much to do. Your father has decided to hold a dinner party next week, and you're to help with the arrangements. I'm sending out the invitations today."

"Next week?" Therez asked. "Why the hurry? Papa said nothing before."

Her mother glanced briefly toward the servants. "Why ever the hurry? Therez, don't ask such questions."

So there were business matters afoot. Therez obediently seated herself at the table and poured herself a cup of tea. She waited until her mother had dismissed the servants before she spoke again.

"What is the matter?" she asked. "Can you tell me now?"

"Business," her mother said, taking her own seat with a heavy sigh. "Your father decided to start contract negotiations early this year. He's anxious. So is Ehren."

Late summer brought the annual contract negotiations when merchants settled with the caravan companies and shipping guilds for next year's transportation. Other guilds often set their contracts as well—the silk guilds who provided raw silks, or woven fabrics, or finished goods; the miners' guilds who specialized in marble and granite and gemstones; the sundry smaller guilds and artisans who commissioned merchants to sell their wares. The season's negotiations made for tense conversations at dinner. Still, that did not explain the urgency in her mother's voice.

"Your father is fretting about losing influence," her mother continued. "The City Council didn't invite him to the debate on caravan tolls, and even though they apologized, saying they thought him too ill to attend, I cannot believe the oversight was entirely accidental. Then there are the rumors about higher taxes, talk about closing the border . . ."

"We heard those rumors last year."

"Yes, but the rumors are louder this year. Much louder. I didn't pay attention at first, but Ehren says he heard the same reports in Duenne. The king is anxious, and because he's anxious, he wants more taxes, more fees, and stricter controls between all Morauvín's cities and Károví. And if the king *does* close the borders, we shall have to depend on smugglers or forgo our trade across the border. Your father would dislike that, especially after he's invested so much time and money in opening those routes."

She poured herself a cup of black tea from the other carafe and stirred in a spoonful of honey. The pale sunlight, filtered through the room's smoky glass, was not kind to her delicate features. Therez could plainly see faint lines crisscrossing her face, and silvery strands glinted from her neatly dressed hair, like frost upon the mountains. Her mother's troubled look was not new, not since her father's illness last spring, but this volubility about taxes and trade was a marked change.

"That's not all, is it?" Therez said softly.

Her mother glanced toward the door. "No," she said in a low voice. "I don't know what you've heard, but Maester Galt has taken charge of the shipping guild, and he's proposing changes to the fee structure. Talk says he's already given the best terms to Maester Friedeck and his son. Your father thinks . . ." Another beat of hesitation. "We do not know if Ehren can return to the university, or if you can make your visit."

Therez's chest squeezed tight in sudden distress. It took her a moment before she knew she had her voice under control. "Ah, I see. I had no idea how difficult the year had been."

Her mother shrugged. "We are not in danger of poverty. But you know your father."

"Yes, I do." Therez fell silent. Her tea stood cooling, hardly touched, but she no longer had any desire for its delicate flavor. She had always told herself that her plans might be overturned, but she had not realized how much she had depended on them. Her thoughts flicked back to her word game with Klara. Melnek. Home. Hurt. The sequence was not far from the truth. If only she could live a year—or even two—away from home, perhaps she could determine if hurt was a necessary part of life.

"May I see the guest list?" she asked.

Her mother handed her a sheet. Therez read through the list of names, written in her father's plain square handwriting. Galt, the head of the shipping guild, of course, and various other guild masters. Maester Gerd Bartos, the current head of the City Council, whose eldest daughter was contracted to marry Galt. A dozen of the most influential merchants and liaisons to the City Council, Klara's father among them. The list covered an entire page.

"Papa's invited half of Melnek," she commented.

"Yes. We must extend ourselves more than usual." Her mother called up a brief unconvincing smile. "Though it won't be all work. We shall have music and special dishes and dancing afterward. You are to pick the musicians yourself."

She took back the list of guests and went through Petr Zhalina's orders for the dinner, which were more exacting than usual—not only whom to invite, but also how many courses to serve, how much to spend on musicians and decorations, how long the dancing would last. It was unnecessary for Therez's mother to emphasize that Petr Zhalina wished to make a good impression. The length and detail of these instructions were evidence enough.

Therez absorbed all these implications for a moment. One dinner could not ruin their business, but clearly any future success would build upon its outcome. Every guild head invited. Every leading merchant—

Then it struck her. "I didn't see Maester Friedeck's name on the list. You might want to add him. Or no? What's wrong?"

The habitual crease between her mother's eyes deepened. "No. When your father heard the news about Maester Galt and Maester Friedeck, they . . . quarreled."

Therez bit her lip. Suggestions were a delicate matter, even with her mother. "Could you convince Papa to change his mind and invite him? Maester Friedeck, I mean."

Her mother dipped her pen in the inkwell, still frowning. "Why?"

"Because if the rumors are true, Papa will want Maester Friedeck as an ally, not a rival. He could use this evening to win his goodwill, if not his support. And if the rumors are false, and we snub him, then Papa would needlessly antagonize an important man. You did say this dinner was the key to next year's success."

Isolde Zhalina studied her daughter a moment. "Yes," she said slowly. "I can see why Maester Friedeck should come. But let us have Ehren make the suggestion. That will do better."

She nodded firmly. That, too, was out of character, Therez thought. A sign that all was not well in this household.

It never was.

Be quiet. It can be.

Still arguing with herself, Therez wrote down the name of a prominent musician. She immediately drew a line through the name, unhappy with her choice. Her pen hovered over the paper. When was the last time her mother had laughed or smiled without care? How had she looked, nearly five and twenty years ago, when Petr Zhalina courted her? Had he promised his love and all his heart? Had she, like Lir, laughed with delight? Or was theirs a marriage of gold and politics, even from the beginning?

The scratching of her mother's pen ceased. She was staring at the guest list and frowning harder than before.

"A problem?" Therez asked.

"No. But I always find it hard to pick the right words. Especially for certain guests."

Ah, so the list was not the complete list. Somehow this did not surprise Therez. "Who else is coming?" she asked.

Her mother wrote a line, paused. Her glance flicked up and back down to the parchment before her. "Baron Mann, if he accepts," she said at last. "A few others."

Therez exhaled softly. Baron Josef Mann had recently come from a season at Duenne's Court. Her father must have special plans indeed.

"Paschke," she said. "We must engage Launus Paschke for the evening. With him and his company, we won't need any other musicians."

"Paschke would indeed make a favorable impression," her mother murmured. "I only hope—"

She broke off and frowned again. Therez reminded herself that a failure meant more than disappointment for herself and Ehren. Failure also meant a lecture from Petr Zhalina to his wife, delivered in a soft monotone that would wash all emotion from her mother's face. And he would not drop the matter after one or two days—or even a week, Therez thought. That anyone could endure. But her father would bring up the subject weeks and years later—small pointed reminders of his wife's failings. Strange how a whisper could wound so deep.

It would come out right, Therez told herself. They would dazzle their guests, her father would secure his contracts, and she would see her own plans to fruition. But every detail must be perfect.

BY LATE AFTERNOON, Therez had planned the wines and most of the decorations. She had written to various artists for advice with the finer details; she had also sent a letter to Launus Paschke, asking to meet and discuss hiring his company. In turn her mother had completed the invitations and given them over to Petr Zhalina's senior runner for delivery.

"We are done for today," her mother told her. "Go and visit your grandmother. I know you want to."

Therez did not wait for her mother to repeat the suggestion. She ran to her rooms to store away her notes, then hurried down the corridor to the lavish suite where her grandmother lived alone. Naděžda Zhalina called these rooms her empire, and there she had once ruled with vigor. But in the last year, age and illness had overtaken her—the empire had shrunk to her bedchamber, invaded by nurses and maids and companions. Therez came into the richly ornamented sitting room that formed the outer defenses of that kingdom.

A maid sat there, mending stockings.

"Is she awake, Mina?"

Mina shook her head. "Sleeping, Mistress. Very lightly."

The sleep of very old people. "What about her appetite? Did she eat today?"

"Three bites, Mistress."

Therez glanced through the half-open door. The rooms beyond were dark, but a faint light edged the bedroom door. "I'll just look in, then. I won't wake her."

She glided through a second, smaller sitting room, which was given over to dozens of porcelain figures, through the dressing room, to her grandmother's bedroom door, which she eased open.

Bowls filled with fresh památka cuttings were set about on tables, the pale white blooms like candle flames in the semidarkness. Her grandmother had carried away a handful of seeds from her old home in faraway Duszranjo, in Károví, decades before. After they arrived in Melnek, and her son purchased this house, she had planted beds of them in their formal gardens, over his protests. Now that she was ill, she had the flowers brought to her. Off in one corner stood a thick crude figure of a gnarled bent woman. Lir, as the crone. She had another name in Károví, in the old days, but the goddess was still the same.

Another maid, Lisl, sat in one corner, knitting by the light of a shaded lamp. Therez signaled for her to remain still and tiptoed to her grandmother's side.

Her grandmother lay with her head turned toward the window, snoring softly. She looked old, Therez thought. Old and frail. Her ruddy-brown skin was mottled, and her once-black hair lay scattered thinly over the pillow. Under the loose pouches of skin, you could just make out traces of the strong old woman from six months before.

Therez's grandmother stirred. "Therez," she whispered. "Hello, my sweet. Come closer."

Therez touched the old woman's cheek. "Are you well?"

"Dobrud'n. Good and not good, as they say." Thirty years in Veraene had not erased her strong accent. "I was hoping you would visit." She tried to sit up. Her face crumpled and she sank into her pillow again with a muttered curse. "I hate it," she whispered angrily. "I hate sickness and— Ah, you didn't come to hear my complaints."

"I came to visit. If you'd rather complain, then I'll listen." Therez gathered her grandmother's hands in hers and gently kissed them. She could feel how light and fragile the bones had become. The surgeons had warned them to expect her grandmother's death within the next few months.

Already her grandmother had closed her eyes again, and her breathing turned soft and raspy, a sound like that of paper sliding over paper. Lisl's knitting needles resumed their regular clicking. Therez gently withdrew her hands, thinking to let her grandmother sleep, when the old woman's eyes fluttered open. "Tell me about the dinner party," she whispered.

Therez suppressed a start of surprise. Of course her grandmother had heard. Probably from Lisl and Mina. "If you already know, Grandmama, what can I tell you?"

Her grandmother laughed softly. "Impertinent child. Tell me what these silly girls don't know. What has your father planned?"

"He's planned everything," Therez said drily, which provoked another laugh from her grandmother. "But he's left a few choices to me and my mother. We shall have Paschke for our music, if he has no other obligation, and I've written to Mistress Sobek, the theater artist, for advice on the decorations. I can tell you already that there will be flowers and sweet candles, dancing, and three courses of the finest dishes Mama could decide upon."

"And the guests? Who are they?"

"Friends. Neighbors. He's invited nearly all the chief merchants and anyone with a voice in the City Council." She hesitated. "He's even invited Baron Mann, if you can believe it."

"Friends," her grandmother said. "Those are not friends. Those are allies, rivals, partners. Sometimes I think your father— Well, never mind what I think. It should be an interesting evening. I wish I could watch. Pity. And with you the chief of everything. So big since last year. Soon you will find a husband."

Not until Duenne, Therez thought, but she only smiled. "I'd rather wait another year, Grandmama. Sixteen or seventeen is old enough."

A brief spasm passed over her grandmother's face. "I was seventeen," she whispered. "Saw your grandfather in his shop in the marketplace. He was young then, quieter, but that day he was laughing. Such a bright smile. Oh, I fell in love so quick, it hurt."

Therez stroked her hands, not liking the quaver in her grandmother's voice. "Maybe we should postpone the dinner party. It's not right. Not with you so . . . tired."

"Bah. Don't be foolish. I'll see more dinner parties. I dream of them sometimes. Strong dreams, too, and all of them in the same palace. And always in winter, far to the north. About scrubbing, if you can believe it. Floors and walls. Tin plates. Silver plates. Once a platter of gold that I polished until it gleamed like the sun. I did well, they said, for someone so young. I almost told them I knew the work from lives and lives before, but I didn't. I knew they wouldn't like it."

Therez's skin prickled at her grandmother's words. Strong dreams were always life dreams, the scattered memories of previous lives. Even those who dreamed faintly would find their life dreams more vivid as death approached. "Don't talk like that," she said fiercely.

Her grandmother made a tch-tch sound. "Ne. Not to worry, sweet. I only meant that I dreamed sometimes." Another pause while she recovered her breath. "Therez, why is your father holding this dinner party?"

Therez blinked, startled by the question. "Business, my mother said. The autumn contracts." She didn't want to mention the part about Ehren's studies, or her own trip to Duenne. That would only provoke another argument between her grandmother and her father.

But her grandmother was already muttering. "Business. Always business. Money. Contracts. Deals and trade. Sometimes I think your father forgets the famine was thirty years ago. Not yesterday."

"It could happen again tomorrow," said a voice from the doorway. "Or have your forgotten how easily wealth turns into poverty?"

Petr Zhalina stood in the doorway, a tall narrow shadow against the gloom. Only a white band showed where his shirt emerged from his dark gray vest and coat. With a wave of his hand, he dismissed Lisl, who vanished into the outer rooms.

Naděžda Zhalina opened her eyes; her expression turned wary. "Dobrud'n, my son."

"Good afternoon, my mother."

Her mouth twitched. "Such a diligent son. Have you come to wish me farewell?"

Petr Zhalina lifted his chin. His lips thinned even more, if that were possible, and the angles in his cheeks grew more pronounced. "I came to see about your health. Therez, please leave us."

Therez turned toward the door, but stopped when her grandmother lifted a hand. "Come again this evening, sweet."

"She comes if her duties allow," said her father. "Therez. Go."

Therez hurried out the door. She heard a low murmur from her father and a brusque reply from her grandmother. She paused, wondering what the new argument was about, but both voices quickly sank into whispers.

A shiver passed through her—a reminder of death and the coming winter—and she fled to the brightly lit halls below.

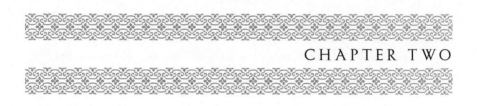

CHAPTER TWO

EIGHT DAYS LEFT, then three, finally none. All the guests had accepted their invitations, including Baron Mann. Paschke had rearranged his schedule at Therez's request. They would bring both plucked and hammer-stringed instruments, he told her, as well as a complement of oblique and transverse flutes, and even a water flute, which only a master could play with any success. In the dining room, the steward had arranged flowers made of perfumed silks and gossamers and faille in the latest fashion from Duenne. Therez's mother seemed cautiously pleased.

That afternoon, Therez sat by her grandmother's bedside, watching the old woman's chest rise and fall as she slept. *I'm so tired*, Naděžda Zhalina had whispered. *So tired, and yet I cannot sleep. Tell me a story, sweet. One about Duszranjo.*

And so Therez had, repeating all the old stories and folktales her grandmother had once told her—about ghost soldiers who haunted the mountain passes, about the famine her grandparents and father had survived, about the near-immortal king who ruled that northern land of Károví. The longer she spoke of long ago and faraway, the more easily she could forget the whispers and the tensions of now. How her mother would suddenly fall silent and tremble. How her grandmother and father conducted a silent war of determination. How her brother seemed more distant now than when he first left for university.

Her grandmother stirred restlessly. "Him," she murmured. "Always him. He never changes."

She was dreaming again, Therez thought. Were these more life dreams? Or simply the wanderings of an old weary mind?

Outside, muted by thick walls, the bells rang five long peals. Two hours until the dinner party. She ought to go. Gently, she eased her hands from her grandmother's and rose. She'd dismissed Lisl before, telling her to take a free half hour. The girl ought to be back soon.

Her grandmother gave a breathy moan. Therez hovered anxiously. She laid a hand over her grandmother's forehead, which felt clammy to her touch. Her grandmother twitched away and started to mumble in Károvín—something about a palace and a king. *The* king. The only king.

Leos Dzavek. Now she understood. *He* was the one who never changed, not since he'd stolen Lir's jewels from the emperor, almost four hundred years ago. Emperors and kings had died since then. The empire itself had broken apart. Only Leos Dzavek remained unchanged, wrapped in magic even long after the jewels themselves had vanished.

"So strange," her grandmother whispered. Her shivering grew stronger, in spite of layers of woolen blankets and the abundant fire in the fireplace. Therez chafed her grandmother's hands gently. The soft loose skin felt chilled to her touch.

She deserves better, Therez thought angrily. *My father has money enough to hire any mage-surgeon he pleases. If he pleased.* Magic might not save her grandmother's life, but at least a surgeon trained in magic could ease her passage from one life to the next. Her mother had dared, once, to make the suggestion, but her father had dismissed it with an abrupt gesture. Magic, he said, was a useless expense.

Her grandmother muttered again. Therez heard her own name amid a stream of garbled words. She bent over her grandmother. "What is it?" she whispered. "What are you saying?"

"Ei rûf ane gôtter . . ."

A chill washed over Therez as she recognized those words from history books—*I call to the gods*—the first words in any invocation of magic, the language of old Erythandra.

I wonder if she heard them from Leos Dzavek himself. I wonder . . .

"Ei rûf ane gôtter," she whispered. "What comes next, Grandmama?"

No answer. Just a faint wheezing. Therez repeated the words slowly. She'd read so many history books that talked about magic, and more books about languages, but none of them had contained any true spells. All she could remember was that the old tribes of the northern forests and plains had brought their language with them when they migrated south to Duenne, conquering as they rode. Centuries later, the priests of the empire used the same invocation to call upon Lir and Toc, to summon the magic current for their rites.

"Ei rûf ane gôtter," she repeated. "Ei rûf . . ." Now a few more words came back to her. "Ei rûf ane gôtter. Komen uns Lir unde Toc."

She felt a fluttering in her chest. Was that magic?

She drew a long breath and repeated the words, her thoughts pinned upon each syllable, upon the moment in between.

The air went still and taut. Therez could still hear the fire hissing in its grate, but the noise was muted, as though a veil had dropped between her and the room. She felt a faint breeze against her cheek, smelled the scent of new-mowed grass.

. . . she knelt on the hard flagstones of the landing, scrubbing the floor with her brush where some fool of a serving girl had dropped a plate of berries. Those stains might never come out of the mortar, never mind the white stones that showed any dirt at all. Her hands ached. Her knees were stiff and sore. And the cold. You would think a grand palace would be warm, but it was never warm in the north, not even in summer . . .

It was a life dream—she recognized the intensity at once—and she was part of it. Then her thoughts dipped again into her grandmother's. She saw a vast white staircase curving above and below her, felt the cold hard stones against her knees, and heard . . .

She heard footsteps ringing off the stairs. Hurriedly she dragged the bucket into the corner and wiped the stones dry. Just in time for the man—he looked like a starving bird with great black eyes, she thought—to round the corner. A young woman dressed in layers of robes followed him. She wore an emerald set in her cheek, a blood-red ruby in her ear. It was the younger prince of Károví and his betrothed. They never notice us, she thought. Invisible is what we are. She liked that.

The young woman paused. Her gaze dropped to the old woman's.

And within her grandmother's thoughts, Therez felt a shock of recognition. I know her.

"Therez!"

Therez jerked her head up. Isolde Zhalina stood in the doorway. Her face was hard to read in the dim light, but her stance was rigid, her voice anxious. Behind her flitted the shadow of a maid—Lisl or Mina. "Therez, what are you doing here?" her mother said. "It's late."

Only now did Therez hear the bells ringing—much louder than before. The air in the room had turned chill—the fire had died—and there came to her the scent of cold ashes, overlaid by a stronger, greener scent. An hour had vanished without her knowing it. "I'm sorry," she said. "I forgot about the time. I—"

"Never mind. Dress and come downstairs as soon as you can. I'll talk to your father."

Therez brushed a hand over her grandmother's forehead. In her mind's eye, she could still see the berry-stained flagstones, the wash of pale sunlight over the walls, which were as white as a snowdrift. Then she was running to her own rooms, stumbling because her legs were cramped and stiff. *Hurry, hurry, hurry. Do not give my father an excuse for anger.*

Four maids waited there, along with her mother's senior maid. As soon as she appeared, Asta called out orders to everyone, including Therez, urging them all through the preparations: The scented bath. The powder applied to Therez's skin and then dusted off. The layers of clothes, from the stockings and linen undershift to the silken gown that fell in pleats from the high ribboned waist. Therez felt more like a puppet than a girl as she obeyed polite requests to tilt her head this way and that, or to hold perfectly, perfectly still while a maid stitched an errant pearl back onto the lace of Therez's overgown. Another maid applied perfume and the merest dab of color to her lips. All the while, her veins buzzed with excitement.

Or was that the magic?

"Nearly ready, Mistress Therez. Margrit, I need— Ah, good, you have them."

Asta plucked a long shimmering ribbon from the hands of a waiting girl. Deftly she wound it through Therez Zhalina's loosely bound hair, while another maid slid the dancing slippers on Therez's feet. The air smelled of lightly spiced perfume, of fresh wildflowers, and a cloud of steam lingered from the bathwater. One of the maids hummed softly as she tidied up.

"Another length of ribbon, Margrit. Eva, set out the pearls."

Asta swiftly fastened the pearls into Therez's hair. "All ready."

Therez stood, ready to run downstairs, but Asta stopped her with a gesture. "Stop," she cried. "Take one look before you go. For good luck."

Therez paused and blinked at the long mirror. At first she saw only a swath of colors—the silken gown the color of ripe apricots, the pale golden lace of her overgown, her long black hair gathered back with ribbons that matched her gown. Pearls glinted in the lamplight when she moved her head. Only when she blinked again did she see herself clearly. A small slim figure, very much like her mother in that, if nothing else. Everything else belonged to her father—her dark eyes, canted above full cheekbones, the same coppery-brown complexion of the borderlands of Veraene and Károví. She felt the brush of cool air against her cheek, though her rooms were warm and close, and a rippling sensation beneath her skin that excited and unsettled her at the same time. Magic, lingering in her blood.

"You look like a shining jewel, Mistress," Asta said softly.

I look like a gift, wrapped and tied with decorations.

But she only murmured a thank-you for the compliment and hurried from her rooms. Immediately, she ran into her brother, who took her hand. "What took you so long?" he said. "He's waiting."

"Is he angry?" she asked

Ehren hesitated. "Anxious."

Which meant he was more than angry.

They sped down the stairs and through the public salles. Streamers bedecked the galleries; the woodwork and tiles gleamed from polishing. Paschke and his musicians stood together in a corner, tuning their strings to their song pipes. A singer stood apart, eyes closed, doing her breathing exercises. Therez wished she could stop to speak with Paschke, but her brother beckoned impatiently. She tore herself away, hoping that her father did not blame her mother.

Too late. They arrived at the entry hall to find Petr Zhalina standing close to their mother, delivering a swift intent lecture in undertones. Therez could not hear his words, but she saw her mother's blank face, the footman with his gaze averted. She hurried forward ahead of Ehren. "Papa, I'm sorry—"

Her father broke off his lecture. He turned abruptly around to face Therez. She shrank back, but he said nothing more than "Thank you for your promptness, Therez."

He would say more later, she thought. He always did.

To her relief, the bells began to ring the hour. Ehren went to his father's side. Therez took her position by her mother. A quick touch of fingertip to fingertip brought a brief smile to her mother's face. Then the footman was opening the doors to admit their first guest—old Count Hartl, whose mansion stood opposite theirs. Soon after came an official from the silk guild, followed by Klara's father and mother, along with Klara herself and her several brothers. Klara took Therez's hands in hers and leaned close to whisper, "I have some news to share. It was just decided today, and my father says—"

"Klara," said her mother. "Save your gossip for another time, please."

"Find me later," Therez whispered back.

Isolde Zhalina led these first arrivals into the salon. Over the next half hour, dozens more arrived, and between the many polite greetings, Therez found she could breathe more easily. It would be a good evening, a successful one. Her father would be pleased. There would be no obstacle to Ehren returning to his studies, or her spending the year in Duenne. No whispered accusations to their mother.

"Baron Mann," said the footman.

Baron Mann sauntered into the entry hall. "Maester Zhalina," he said. "Young Ehren." He turned toward Therez, just as she rose from her curtsy.

She had a swift impression of jewels and silks and darkly handsome looks. "Maester Zhalina's beautiful daughter. Greetings." He caught hold of her hand and kissed it.

"My lord," said Petr Zhalina. "We are honored."

Mann smiled blandly. "Indeed."

A dry chuckle caught Therez's attention. A newcomer stood in the doorway, a stocky man of medium height and dark hair, frosted with silver. Therez recognized him immediately—Baron Rudolfus Eckard, once a member of the King's Council. A cool breeze accompanied the baron's entrance, penetrating the thin silk layers of her dress. She shivered.

Father must have promised the world to lure this man into our house.

Petr Zhalina bowed. "Baron Eckard."

Eckard smiled pleasantly. "Maester Zhalina. Thank you for the kind invitation. You've rescued an old man from a dreary evening alone."

"Liar," Mann said, with evident amusement. "Your house is never empty, Rudolfus. But come, shall we join the others?" He relinquished Therez's hand and gestured toward the next rooms.

"Gladly." Eckard turned toward Ehren Zhalina. "Maester Ehren, would you join us in the salon? I hear you spent last year in Duenne. I'd be grateful for any recent news."

Mann grinned. "He wants a more dignified report than mine."

Baron Eckard mildly observed that they were blocking the entry hall. He and Mann departed with Ehren Zhalina for the salon, with Mann immediately embarking upon a story about recent court doings. Therez was wondering why an influential baron would ask Ehren's opinion, when the outer doors opened again, and the footman announced, "Maester Theodr Galt."

Theodr Galt, the newly elected head of the shipping guild, strode inside. Like Mann, he was dark, but tall and powerfully built, with his long black hair tied into a loose braid, such as the more conservative nobles wore. He wore a suit of wine-red silk, patterned in subtle diamonds. When he moved through the light, the cloth seemed to shimmer and change. He was a rich and influential man, destined to become even richer and more influential with his new position and his approaching marriage. But for all his advantages, Therez thought he appeared dissatisfied as he made his bows to her father.

"Maester Zhalina. How fares your business?"

"Never so good that I could not wish it better. Perhaps we could discuss matters after dinner."

"Perhaps."

They exchanged guarded looks, then Petr Zhalina motioned to Therez. "Therez, please escort Maester Galt into the salon. Tell your mother that I shall stay here to greet the last of our guests."

Galt offered his arm to Therez, who laid her hand on his sleeve. He smiled, and covered her hand with his. As soon as he did, a strange prickling ran up Therez's arm and down her spine, and she felt a sudden tightness all along her skin. Within came the sensation of a string drawn to its limit, a barely subdued fury. Without thinking, Therez recoiled from his touch.

"Is something amiss?" Galt asked in a cool voice.

"I—" She gulped down a breath. Her pulse was thrumming in her ears, and she caught a whiff of an intense green scent, as though someone had crushed a handful of grass under her nose. *It's just my imagination,* she told herself. She managed a weak smile to Galt and her father. "My apologies, Maester Galt. Nothing is wrong, just a moment of faintness. Please, let me escort you inside."

To her relief, the sense of overwhelming tension faded. She escorted Galt through the doors to join the other guests.

The salon was crowded with all of Melnek's richest and most influential families. Merchants and guild masters, City Council members, and minor nobility. A group of older merchants had gathered in one corner; Therez turned in that direction, thinking Maester Galt would like their company.

"No."

With a slight pressure of his hand, Galt steered her between the many guests, toward the center of the room. Several younger couples played word links. Near the musicians, she spotted Klara next to her cousin Lev Bartov. Another, older group of men were talking politics. Rumors of war. More troops sent to northern garrisons in Ournes to quash the faction demanding a separation from Veraene. Talk about closing the border in Morauvín and the next province over, even though that would mean a disruption of trade for Melnek and the other big trade cities. So the rumors were true, she thought. And after her father had worked to establish a new liaison with those Károvín merchants.

"What are you thinking?"

"War," she said.

"An odd subject for a young woman."

She smiled and felt renewed pressure of his hand over hers.

"Why are you smiling?"

Therez glanced up, then down. His gaze unsettled her. "No reason."

"No?"

It was going badly. She could think of nothing to say to this man, and she knew she must not displease him. Therez glanced anxiously from side to side, looking for someone Galt might find acceptable. She sighted her brother near the windows, still engaged in conversation with Baron Mann and Baron Eckard. Galt followed the direction of her gaze. An odd expression flickered across his face. "Do you know them? Those men with your brother?"

"We've been introduced," she said cautiously.

He nodded. Taking that as a request to join them, Therez gratefully led him toward the barons and Ehren.

Baron Mann saw them first and greeted Therez with a smile. "Ah, Mistress Therez. You've already abandoned me for another. Have you come to make amends?" His eyes brightened with interest when Therez gave Galt's name, and his smile took on a curious tension, though his manner was utterly polite as he exchanged greetings.

Therez allowed herself a silent sigh of relief. The musicians had not yet begun their next piece, and she could just hear the word-linking game above the general murmur of conversation. Word. Letter. Love letter. Marriage. A predictable sequence, but the players evidently found it amusing. Then she saw Klara emerging from behind the Leffler family. She was heading toward Therez with look of barely suppressed excitement.

Ehren leaned close. "Go and talk with Klara. I'll take care of our guests."

She smiled in thanks and hurried toward her friend. Even before they met, Klara was already speaking swiftly. "You will never guess, Therez. Never, never. My father— Wait, let me recover." She made a show of fanning her face. "So. My news. I am going to Duenne next summer."

"Duenne? Next summer?"

Klara laughed. "Now you sound like my pet mynah. Yes, Duenne. Yes, next summer. My brother is going to university a year early, to study magical jurisprudence, whatever that might be. Imre explained the terms to me a hundred times, but they still make no sense. Anyway, the important thing is that our beloved father believes the connection will help our business. And because he is going, it was merely a question of convincing my mother, who convinced my father I would learn better manners by accompanying Imre to the capital. Of course I did not disabuse either of them of the notion."

"I would not have you any different. But a season together! That means we shall have dances and theater outings . . ."

". . . and visits and shopping. If you consider mucking about those dusty booksellers to be shopping. Now do not glare at me. We shall spend alternate days shopping for books and paints. Visit me tomorrow and we shall start the plans for our triumphs. Speaking of triumphs, who are those men with your brother?"

"Baron Mann and Baron Eckard."

"Ah. Interesting. Very interesting. And who— Goodness, it's Maester Galt." Though no one stood close enough to overhear, Klara bent close to whisper in Therez's ear. "Did you hear the rumors?"

"No, what happened?"

In a breathless tone, Klara told her. "His marriage contract. Broken off yesterday. The father insisted, even though he shall have to pay oh so many penalties. And you can be sure that Maester Galt will not offer Maester Bartos any advantages in shipping contracts for the city. So it's odd, very odd. No one knows why he did it. Maester Bartos, I mean. And no one has seen Marina Bartos these past three days."

Therez shivered at all the implications. That explained Galt's dissatisfaction, the unnerving tension in his voice and manner. It also explained why Maester Bartos had sent his regrets that morning. She wanted to ask Klara where she'd heard the rumor, but her friend had drawn back.

"Beware," Klara murmured. "They are coming toward us—all of them— even Maester Galt."

"Telling secrets?" Mann said as he approached.

"My lord teases," Klara said. "We are both too young for secrets."

"Then I shall have to help you both collect more," Mann said with a laughing glance at Therez.

Ehren smiled. Eckard shook his head. Galt was studying Mann with an odd, restrained expression on his face, and Therez wondered what their conversation had been. She wondered even more when the steward announced dinner, and Mann immediately held out his arm to her. She and Klara exchanged a glance.

"Casting about for a better partner?" the baron murmured.

Her cheeks warmed. "Of course not, my lord."

Mann's answer was a soft laugh. Shaking his head, he escorted Therez to her seat. Her father had decided to rearrange the seating himself, and to her regret, Klara was placed too far away for easy conversation. Instead, she had both barons across from her, as well as Theodr Galt.

Her father took a seat next to her.

Therez suppressed a shiver. Marina Bartos and her mother were to have sat in these two seats. *Breathe,* she thought. *And listen.*

Happily, the servers were filling wine cups and handing out the first course, a dish of aromatic rice balls, flavored with rare spices from Pommersien, in the south of Veraene. The music had started again, but softer, with just the water flute and a descant flute in minor harmonies.

"We were discussing art," Mann said to her father. "Most interesting. Maester Galt here prefers sculptures and painting. What are your preferences, Maester Zhalina?"

Therez's father shrugged. "My time is taken up entirely by my business, alas. I make a poor judge in these matters."

"What about you, Mistress Therez?"

Therez shook her head.

"A quiet, secretive girl," Mann said. "You must tell me later when we dance. Maester Galt, I meant to ask, before we were called to dinner, why such a decided opinion against theater and song?"

Galt flaked his rice, as though picking through various responses. "Perfection," he said, half to himself. "Once your artist carves his flawless statue, nothing can spoil his work. Unlike with theater or song, his patrons do not depend upon such vagaries as the actors' moods, or the lighting, or whether the audience itself might disturb their enjoyment."

Mann's lips parted in a strange smile. "So, you are a collector."

Galt sent him a keen glance. "Call it what you like, my lord. Those are my tastes."

"Tastes are born of our nature," Mann replied. "Myself, I prefer variety and spontaneity. Whereas you like your treasures immutable. Predictable. Controlled."

His voice was pleasant, but Therez detected a tension in the air, and she held her breath. Why was he baiting Galt? Had he heard the rumors about him? Did he know something more? In the background, Paschke's water flute played its rippling silvery melody. Galt studied Mann a long moment; however, he said nothing more than "As my lord wishes."

Mann smiled again, a more predatory one than before, then applied himself to his plate.

"Was my son helpful to you, my lord?" Petr Zhalina said to Baron Eckard.

"Very helpful. He's convinced me that little has changed in Duenne in the past three years."

His tone piqued Therez's curiosity. "How long did you live in Duenne, my lord?"

Her father shot her a swift look, but Eckard smiled pleasantly. "Thirty years, Mistress Therez. Thirty long and interesting years."

"A city of a thousand opportunities," Mann said musingly. "Some worthy. Others . . ."

"Others we shall not mention," Eckard said with a pointed glance that Therez found intriguing.

"Is that why you left, my lord?" said Galt. "Because you disliked the opportunities there?"

Eckard shook his head. "Opportunities change, Maester Galt. I served Baerne of Angersee until his death. Like any new master, Baerne's grandson wished for new advisers, and so you find me here."

"But what of the old king?" said Lev Bartov, who had remained silent until now. "I heard that he had become most peculiar in his latter days. In fact, I heard—"

He stopped at Eckard's level glance. "Baerne ruled well and long," Eckard said quietly. "More than that I would not hazard saying. Nor should you."

A brief silence followed, after which Petr Zhalina asked Baron Eckard for his opinion on trade matters with Károví. Eckard answered politely, and the conversation turned to more ordinary topics.

Therez picked at her food, half listening to the baron's views on various treaties, but she hardly tasted the roasted venison with its honey glaze. Her thoughts remained on Eckard and Duenne. A city of opportunity—exactly what she hoped for, though she knew her ideas to be very different from those of an ex-councillor in the King's Court. Perhaps she could ask him later about the city?

The servants cleared away the last course; the guests proceeded into the larger salle for dancing. Baron Mann claimed Isolde Zhalina's hand for the first dance, while Petr and Ehren Zhalina took Lavena Friedeck and Mina Hess as their partners.

Quite unexpectedly, Therez found herself facing Baron Eckard. "My dear," he said. "Will you honor me?"

Whispers rose and fell around them. Aware of the audience, Therez could do no more than murmur a yes. Eckard led her onto the floor as the music sighed into life. Palm against palm, he stepped to the left, and she to the right. Then he lightly clasped her hand and spun her into the first movement of the dance.

He danced well, was her first surprised thought, as he guided her through the intricate turns and sweeps. He was older than she had guessed, with deep lines etched into his weathered face. Thirty years at Duenne's famous court. She tried to imagine him as a youth, dancing at the king's balls. She could hardly picture such a scene or such a place.

"You are thinking hard," he observed.

Therez recalled herself with a blush. "My apologies, my lord. I was thinking about Duenne. And the King's Court. And, well, what the city is like."

"Ah, that is right. Your brother mentioned your plans to visit a while. Next summer, no? Have you alerted all the booksellers?"

Therez dropped her gaze. "My lord teases."

"Not at all. It's rare to find a young woman who reads seriously. Or perhaps I'm being unfair to young women in general. Tell me . . . what kind of books do you prefer?"

"History. Legends. Poetry."

"Then you must certainly know about Tanja Duhr."

Ehren must have mentioned her love of poetry. But it was true, Tanja Duhr was her favorite poet, and she welcomed the new topic. With Baron Eckard taking the lead, they talked about the woman's poems and how language had changed in the four hundred years since she wrote them. Then, because Duhr had witnessed the empire's final years, they talked about the old emperor and his many heirs, all executed for treason, except the youngest daughter. About Leos Dzavek coming to court as a young prince. About his theft of Lir's jewels, the downfall of the empire, and the founding of Károví. About magic and war and times of great change. There were no constraints, no examining every word before she spoke. It was like breathing for the very first time.

All around, the dancers flowed between the beribboned columns, and Paschke's music spun through the air.

"Duhr wrote what she witnessed," Eckard said. "Both the larger events and those small intimate stories of lovers and grief and trust and betrayal. And we, who come after, are made richer for her works. But then, I believe we all carry a book within our hearts. Our dispositions. Our ambitions. Our secrets. It takes great trust to let another person read that book."

"Have you found such a person?" Therez said.

His mouth curved into a pensive smile. "Yes, I did. We loved. We married. We had children, and then she died. What about you, Mistress Therez? Have you a favorite book?"

He had phrased the question so she could answer either meaning. Even so, she found herself tongue-tied a moment. "I don't know yet, my lord. I enjoy so many different books, but to choose one . . . I don't know," she repeated.

The dance was drawing to a close. Baron Eckard spun Therez around but before he released her hand, he bent close. "When you do choose a favorite book, if ever you do, remember to choose for friendship above anything else."

He was gone before she could reply. Therez turned and came face-to-face with Baron Mann.

"Mistress Therez. Will you honor me with the next dance?"

She hesitated, but a glance to one side showed Theodr Galt approaching. "Gladly, my lord."

Mann's mouth tilted into a smile. "A quick-thinking girl. No wonder Maester Galt treasures your company."

So he had seen Galt, too. Therez lowered her gaze, keeping her eyes and mouth under control. Mann liked to flirt. And he liked to provoke other men.

Baron Mann kept up a stream of light compliments throughout the dance. Therez would have found his conversation diverting, except for the look she had noticed on Galt's face when they passed in the dance. Mann had seen it, too, for he made an offhand comment about avid collectors. She wished she could tell Mann's character better, but he was like a book with latches and locks, its ornate cover deceiving. Whomever he did allow to read his pages would find the contents interesting, she suspected.

As she expected, Galt claimed Therez for the third dance. "Mistress," he said.

"I am honored," Therez said with a curtsy.

His hand was warm, his skin as smooth as her father's. He spent his time in counting houses, she thought, or at elegant affairs such as this one.

The dance's first notes floated through the air—a slow-moving traditional dance, where the partners circled each other in wheel patterns. As more couples joined the dance, the smaller patterns joined in a single, larger one. The steps required all her concentration, which gave her an excuse for keeping silent. It was just as well. Galt's dancing was polished and assured, but more constrained than Baron Mann's, and his expression less inviting than Baron Eckard's.

"Your father tells me you were your mother's chief assistant in planning this evening," he said unexpectedly.

Therez nodded cautiously.

"Do you often do so?"

She nodded again and felt his fingers press against her shoulder. She glanced up, startled, and caught a brief tight smile on his face. It was not a happy smile.

"You talked more with Baron Eckard," he observed.

So that was the difficulty. "We talked of Duenne. I hope to visit next summer."

"I'm surprised your father would allow you to travel so far alone."

I don't know if he will, she thought, but she had no wish to talk about her father.

"You like books, I heard," Galt said after a moment. "Do you have a preference in authors, or are you simply an enthusiast?"

"I . . . I find it hard to say which."

"Because you are young? Or because you do not trust your opinion?"

Because I do not trust you, she thought. Galt seemed to catch something from her expression, because he did not repeat the question. With a firm hand, he spun her through the couples in a breathless rush. When they reached the farther side, he brought her to an abrupt halt and held her close. For a heartbeat, it was as though they were alone in the hall. His scent made her think of winter fires. Against her will, she felt the first stirrings of attraction.

"You see," he said softly, "I can dance as well as any baron."

And then they rejoined the dance as though nothing had happened, only Therez found it difficult to follow his lead or answer his questions. Her pulse beat too hard and too fast. So did his, but whether in attraction or anger, she could not tell. That she could not tell bothered her nearly as much as Galt himself. What *had* happened between him and Marina Bartos? No, she didn't want to know. She only wanted the dance to end so she might get away from him and his jealousies and his strange intent gaze.

To her relief, Lev Bartov danced with her next. They chatted about markets and trade and the weather, and he asked her opinion of music. After Lev came an interlude of song. The dancers paused while Paschke's lead soloist performed an old ballad, accompanied only by a drummer, softly keeping time. Therez noted how Baron Eckard smiled, and how Baron Mann himself appeared different, so entirely absorbed in the music. A secretive, misleading book, indeed.

When the dancing resumed, Therez partnered first with Willem Leffler, then Klara's brother Imre. Therez half expected Galt to approach her again, but he had disappeared, apparently. She saw him much later, walking with her father from another room. Both looked pleased. That could only mean they had reached some key agreement. Perhaps even the shipping contracts . . .

I am a merchant's daughter after all, she thought, and laughed to herself.

Well after midnight, the guests began to take their leave. Eckard, one of the first to depart, spoke graciously to her parents and her brother. Pausing by Therez, he took her hand and bowed low. "Pleasant reading," he murmured.

Mann followed shortly after, offering pretty compliments to Therez and her mother and the promise of a visit to her father. Once he had left, the other departures came faster, and Therez's attention was consumed by the exchange of compliments and the final good-byes.

The last person to go was Theodr Galt, who lifted Therez's hand to his lips. "Mistress. A delight to make your acquaintance. I look forward to our next encounter."

His lips were warm, and he held her hand longer than absolutely necessary. She felt a tremor run through her, and a lingering frisson of magic. *Danger,* said her instincts. *Whatever this man gives comes at a price.* It was with relief she saw him turn to her mother and father.

At last the hall was empty. Therez breathed a tired sigh and wished her parents and brother good night, but when she turned toward the stairs, her father raised a hand. "Therez, come with me. I have something to discuss."

Therez exchanged a surprised look with Ehren. Her mother shook her head. A warning? Had something gone amiss? But there was no time for questions. Her father gestured impatiently for her to follow him. Just as she passed through the salon doors, she glimpsed Ehren leaning down to listen to something their mother said.

Petr Zhalina led the way back through the parlors and the dancing salle, and into the wing where he kept his offices. At his private study, he unlocked the doors and motioned for her to go inside. With growing apprehension, she took the seat in front of her father's desk. The scent of roses and violets drifted through a partially open window. Fainter still a whiff of památka flowers.

Her father set the lamp on a high shelf, where its light reflected from the dark windows, and from the large sand glass that occupied one corner of the room. He took a seat behind his desk. He was about to give her bad news, she could tell. The autumn contracts in suspense. Ehren's return to university delayed, and her trip to Duenne canceled. But she had thought he looked so pleased earlier, when he and Theodr Galt had reentered the dance salle.

Her father ran a hand over his eyes. He did look tired, with shadows beneath his eyes, as though he had not fully recovered from his illness last spring. Then with a shake of his head, he reached for pen and paper. His hands, long and slender like Ehren's, moved with swift assurance as he dipped the pen into the ink, tapped away the excess, and wrote. Therez saw the name Theodr Galt written in small square letters.

"I've come to a decision," he said. "You remember the talk we had last winter."

She nodded. Petr Zhalina had summoned his daughter into his office to discuss marriage, or rather to deliver a dry summary of his expectations and her obligations. Even so, he had explicitly said that such duties would come after she turned seventeen.

"I'm pleased to say that the opportunities I foresaw have arrived, and sooner than I calculated. I've made my choice for your husband, Therez. Theodr Galt. Tomorrow we negotiate the terms and sign the papers."

Reaction was swift and unthinking. "But Papa, you said—"

Her father struck a line through Galt's name. "You dislike my choice?"

"I . . . I don't know him well enough to like or dislike."

He waved a hand to one side. "You will. You have no reason not to."

Point decided, no argument, said his tone. Therez let her breath trickle out. "I expected to spend the next year in Duenne. You surprised me."

"Galt surprised me, to be blunt. He said he didn't need to mourn the loss of his former marriage prospects. The girl had disappointed him. So had the father. But their foolishness didn't erase his need for a wife to manage his social obligations, and you impressed him this evening." Her father wrote out Galt's name again, then a series of numbers after it. Habit? Or did those numbers have a significance?

He blotted the paper neatly—a methodical gesture. "You are young, I told him. He argued that you will turn sixteen next month—not an uncommon age for marriage in some parts. You might continue your education in his household if necessary. He offered generous terms." That last was said almost as an afterthought.

He sold me. Theodr Galt named a price and he agreed.

Mann's comment about avid collectors went through her mind. Her skin went cold and she had to suppress a shudder. What did Mann know about Galt? Or had he simply guessed at the man's nature? "What about—" She stopped herself before she mentioned the rumors. Her father would not pay any attention to them. Instead, she asked, "What did Grandmama say?"

At that, her father looked away, but only for a moment. "Your grandmother has no say in this matter. Come, Therez. Fortunes are directed and planned for. They are not found like a treasure by the roadside. I will not argue the point. Tomorrow I hold the formal interview and we sign the contracts."

"The shipping contracts?" she said impetuously.

Spots of color appeared on her father's cheeks. "Do not be stupid, Therez. We are signing all the necessary contracts that touch upon this family. More you need not discuss."

But I am not an entry in your ledger. I am not a crate of stone or wood, to be signed for and delivered.

Therez held her hands tightly together, willing her pulse to slow, her face to remain a blank. Her father was watching her closely, his gaze bright and rapt. He would lock her in her rooms tomorrow if she did not show a proper gratitude. He had done it before.

"What did Baron Eckard discuss with you?" he said. "Look at me when you answer, Therez."

She met his gaze steadily. "Books."

Petr Zhalina frowned. "What kind of books?"

A pause. "History books."

"Interesting." He looked thoughtful. "Did he show you any attentions? No, never mind. His days of influence are past." He released a sigh. "You may go, Therez. If you like, you might want to talk with your mother. I told her to expect you."

Dismissed. Therez hesitated, but her father appeared fully absorbed in writing columns of numbers. Still, he was observant, she knew from experience. She rose and curtsied, as an obedient daughter should, and though it took all her effort, she kept her expression fixed in a pleasant smile. *Turn around*, she thought. *Leave the room. Do not lose control.*

She walked steadily through the business wing, back through the public dining room, where the chambermaids were still at work. The steward greeted Therez in passing. She answered automatically, she hardly knew what, and kept on walking until she reached the stairs.

She stopped and leaned heavily against the newel post, forehead resting on the smooth wood. Tomorrow. Marriage next week or next month. It all depended on the contract her father signed. Her stomach lurched at the thought.

It took several moments before she could recover herself enough to climb the stairs. Numb, she passed through the familiar rooms where her mother entertained. A small parlor. A gallery decorated with paintings and other artwork. A library with rare first editions. It was a rich man's house, built from luck and skill and determination. Her father had come to Ver-aene from Károví with nothing more than a cargo of rich furs, which he traded for shipments of marble, which he then turned into his first profit in gold. Therez thought she had understood him, had admired him for his intelligence and fortitude, even if she feared his temper.

It was quiet in the family's private wing. No voices disturbed the hush; no shadows except hers moved across the walls. Therez came to her mother's suite. Lamplight edged the door. Isolde Zhalina waited, as ordered, for Therez to visit and discuss the news.

What advice could I ask her? How to hide your thoughts? How to breathe without giving offense?

How to be a prisoner, not a wife and partner.

No, no, no. No, I cannot give up yet.

She turned away from her mother's door and passed onward to her brother's door. Ehren was awake, too, apparently, because she heard the soft notes of his flute. He had long ago given up regular lessons, but now he was practicing, which he did whenever he wanted to soothe his nerves.

She knocked. Almost immediately the flute went silent. Ehren opened the door. "Therez." He looked wary, she thought. But not surprised.

"Ehren, do you . . . do you have time for me? I have a problem."

He stood aside. "Of course. Come in."

As she entered his study, she realized she had not visited her brother's rooms since he came home from university. Her distracted gaze took in the shelves overflowing with books, the letters on his desk, neatly stacked and waiting for his attention. One of the letters, addressed to Ehren, carried the device for Count Beckl's house. Another envelope, in a more ornate hand, had a name she didn't recognize. More signs that her brother had changed without her noticing.

"Therez, what's wrong?"

Therez opened her mouth, closed it. It took another moment before she could frame the sentence. "Father told me I would be married. He's negotiating my betrothal."

Ehren nodded. "Mother told me. You must have been surprised."

She thought her voice would shake. Instead, she found herself saying calmly, "It's too sudden, Ehren. Far too sudden."

Again that wary look. "You mean the business with Maester Bartos."

"Of course I mean that. Don't you think it strange that Maester Bartos broke off the marriage? He must have had a reason. And besides—" Her voice had scaled upward. She broke off and tried again. "I've heard rumors. Nothing definite, but nothing good. And no one has seen Marina Bartos for three days. I want to know what happened to her."

But Ehren was shaking his head. "Gossip. That's all you've heard,

Therez. There is nothing wrong with Marina Bartos except an attack of the vapors. Galt counts himself lucky to have discovered the truth about her character before their marriage took place."

"You heard from him, but not from her family."

"I don't need to. Theodr Galt is a respectable man. He wants a suitable wife to handle his social affairs, not someone who takes to their bed at the least contradiction or correction. And he's not the only lucky person. You are, too. With Galt as your husband, you will have money and status, everything you could want."

And you and Papa will have favorable terms on the shipping contracts.

She ought to nod obediently. Ought not to protest. It was, after all, what all the good families expected of their children. But Galt frightened her. It was how his lips paled when he saw her dancing with Mann. It was his tone, when he did not like her replies, and the look on his face when he took possession of her hand. The fury she sensed running just beneath the surface. Magic had made it plain to her, but once detected she thought it obvious to anyone. The rumors only confirmed what she already knew. Theodr Galt was a cruel man.

Ehren took her hands in his and smiled. "Therez, you're just reacting to the surprise. I'll attend Father's meeting with Galt tomorrow. I promise to look out for you."

Hope, quickly followed by doubt. "What if you find he was at fault with Marina Bartos?"

"I told you. Those stories are just rumors."

"But what if those rumors are true?"

Her brother made an exasperated noise. "I tell you they aren't. Besides, Papa wants to expand the business, and with the trade embargoes, Maester Galt can help us with new routes."

"Us? Aren't you going back to university?"

He hesitated. "I don't know."

So our father has snared us both.

Slowly she nodded. "I understand."

"You do?" Ehren gazed at her anxiously.

"I understand perfectly."

Still he hesitated. "You sound . . ." He paused. "Empty."

She smiled. "I'm just tired, Ehren. I think I'll go to my rooms. Thank you."

In her own rooms, a maid had waited up for her. Therez dismissed her, saying she would undress herself. A grateful look flashed across the maid's face. She dropped into a curtsy and left Therez to her solitude.

Therez extinguished the lamps in her outer rooms one by one. Methodical—that was the key to self-control. She proceeded into her bedchamber where a single lamp burned. She took off her dress and laid it carefully over a chair. Next came her stockings and her jewelry and undergown. Dressed in her shift, she removed the pearls from her hair and unbound her long braid.

Tomorrow Galt and my father will negotiate the terms and sign the papers, she thought, brushing out her hair. *They might even announce the betrothal in public.*

Therez shivered. She had the sudden vivid image how Theodr Galt had looked, clasping her hand, when he said good night. But now all perspective had changed. She was shrinking, her figure dwindling to the size of a gem, which he picked up and gazed at with satisfaction, before placing her in a box and turning the key.

I can't marry him. I can't. I'll end up just like my mother.

But what could she do? Her father and brother did not care. Her mother had no influence. And her grandmother was dying—whether in a week or a month. She could not help Therez. No one in her family would do what Maester Bartos had done for his daughter.

Therez stood and moved swiftly to her dressing room. She flung open her wardrobe, pushed aside the dresses and gowns, and, reaching into the back, pulled out a riding skirt. It was plain and dark, made of sturdy wool. An armful of warmer tunics and shirts came next, then a pair of low boots. Knitted stockings and underlinens came next. From the linens chest, she dug out three thick blankets.

Money. I need money.

She gathered up the clothes and blankets, carried them into her bedroom, and tossed them onto her bed. Then she pulled out a small locked box from another closet. She unlocked the box and poured out a heap of coins. Twenty gold deniers. Fifty-odd silver deniers. Was it enough?

Her strength unexpectedly left her. She sank to the floor, dizzy. "Where am I going?" she whispered. "Where can I go?"

She stared around her bedroom. What could a privileged girl do outside her household? Outside marriage? She knew sewing and embroidery. Beyond that, she was accomplished in writing and sums.

Her heart beat faster. Writing. Yes. A thousand opportunities exist in Duenne. Both barons had said that. And she could write. She knew about trade and business. With that kind of training she could . . .

"I can go to Duenne just as I planned," she said out loud. Not exactly.

She would have to earn her keep—as a scribe perhaps, or an assistant to a merchant. That would be far better, she thought. Then she could make her life as she wished.

Working swiftly, she changed into the plainest of her traveling clothes. She located a bag for her belongings and packed her clothes and blankets. After a moment's thought, she added a knife her brother had given her years before, then a handful of bracelets and necklaces. The jewelry she could keep hidden, then sell once she reached Duenne. But no silk stockings or skirts. Nothing fine or obviously expensive. She must not call attention to herself.

She looked at her shelves, which were crowded with books—poetry books, volumes of essays, texts on history. One shelf alone held her old lesson books, with notes scrawled in their margins. If only she could take one—just one book for her exile.

The quarter-hour chimes sounded, followed by two gongs from the hour bell. No time to choose, she could buy more once she reached Duenne. Quickly, she stuffed her money into a leather purse. She paused, thinking of robbers, then removed her money, divided it into three heaps. One share went into her boots. She wrapped a second portion in a handkerchief and tucked it into her shirt. A third went into the bottom of her bag along with her jewelry. She slung the bag over her shoulder, and with a last survey of her room, she left.

Outside, the corridor was still and dark. She glanced down the hall, toward her grandmother's suite. But there could be no visit nor farewells, even silent ones—not if she wished to avoid notice.

Good-bye, she thought. *I love you. Remember me.*

She glided through the hallway and down the stairs, finding her way by touch. When she rounded the last turn and came into the silent entry hall, she hesitated. Ten more steps to the door. It took her several long moments before she could bring herself to take the first of those ten.

I will never see this house again. I will never see Klara or Ehren. Or my grandmother.

She drew a long breath. Her pulse was beating fast and hard, but her hands were steady as she unbarred the doors. A cool breeze blew against her face as she stepped outside.

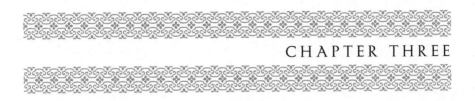

CHAPTER THREE

THICK FOG SWIRLED around her, and a green grassy scent, like the fragrance of new wildflowers, drenched the air. Somewhere to her left, a torch burned. By its light she could just make out several figures moving about. They were little more than flickers and smudges against the eerie white blankness. From a distance came the muted whuff of a horse, footsteps, and numerous voices speaking in low tones. She couldn't make out what they were saying, but she recognized the soft, slurring lilt of a northern Károvín dialect. Everything else was muffled, as though wrapped in cotton. The fog, of course.

It was the fog that caused them to lose their way in the hills. An unnatural fog, called up by the king's mage-trackers, who led these soldiers directly to her and the young man from Veraene's Court. He had died messily. Remembering, her stomach lurched. She swallowed the bile in her throat and pulled against the ropes binding her to the stake. They did not budge.

A rough hand took hold of her chin and raised her head. It was Ferda Krecek, a captain recently assigned to castle duty. Leos's dog, the men called him. He examined her dispassionately, his eyes narrowed to dark slits. The torchlight gave his brown complexion a ruddy cast.

I did not expect to catch you so easily, he said.

I should have learned more magic, then, she said breathlessly.

Ah, defiance. He did not appear impressed.

Not defiance, she said. A chance for peace, for honor—

He stopped her with an abrupt gesture. There is no honor in treason.

"Shit, shit, shit! You damned idiot!"

"Damn yourself, you piss-faced son of a whore."

Therez scrambled to her feet, slipped, and fell against a door's framework. It took her a moment to take in her surroundings—cobblestones and men's voices arguing, smoking torches that reeked of tar, and dawn's gray light seeping across the sky. Not far away stood Melnek's western gates, closed until daylight.

She located her bag and checked her belongings. Money safe. Clothing just as she left it. She rubbed her hands against her skirt. They stung where she'd barked them against the door frame.

"I tell you it wasn't my fault."

"Lying bastard."

Two men faced each other, not ten steps away. Both were stocky and red-faced, their hair tied in sweat-soaked braids. A blocky shadow stood beyond them—a wagon with two horses.

One man pointed angrily at a shattered crate, its load of salted fish strewn over the cobblestones. "You," he growled. "You lost me a week's pay."

The other man swore. "That I never did. You're the bastard who dropped his end. Dropped it like a limp prick."

"Stop it, both of you." A third man shoved his way between the two. "We're late. What's the dust-up?"

"Balz fucked himself up last night."

"Fah! That's a lie, Dag. He saw this chit—"

Dag shot an angry glance at Therez. She shrank into her doorway, but he only muttered a curse about whores in the streets. Still cursing his crew for their stupidity, he ordered them to clean up the mess and load the other crates.

Therez caught up her bag and slid around the corner into the alley. *It was an accident. It wasn't my fault.*

Dodging the crowds, she circled around the square. Despite the early hour, teams were already at work, making ready for departure. Men and boys darted from one task to the next. Some carried torches and held them aloft for others who were loading crates and sacks into the wagons. Dogs and sheep milled about, adding to the noise and confusion.

She stopped by a fountain and washed her hands and face. An old worn column rose from the center, carved to show Lir in her three aspects. The maiden was hardly more than a suggestion of youth and grace, and only a trace of the mother showed—centuries had obscured her face. But for the crone, the artisan had caved strong deep lines. It was from her upraised hands that the water flowed. An old statue, carved in the style of those centuries before the empire absorbed Morauvín, before the Erythandran priests gave the name Toc to Lir's unknown consort, with whom she disported during her season of love.

Therez drank a second handful of water and scanned the square. She would have to act soon. The gates would open before long. She knew from listening to her father and Ehren that caravan masters often sold seats in their wagons, when space allowed, and kept the money for themselves. Even if she couldn't find a caravan bound directly for Duenne, she could take passage across the hills to the next trade city and wait for one that did.

Of the three or four caravans, she dismissed the two smallest. Those had only two or three wagons apiece, and no other passengers she could see. A third caravan had a dozen wagons, with several families gathered around. Therez circled a group of apprentices, chatting about their new posting in Kassel, and approached a woman nursing her baby. "Excuse me," she said. "Can you help me?"

The woman looked up. She took in Therez's rumpled clothing and her eyes narrowed. "What do you want?"

"Could you tell me where this caravan's bound?"

The woman's expression remained wary. "You look fair young to be alone."

Therez drew a shaky breath. "I'm fifteen, almost sixteen. Old enough to lose my parents."

"Ah, well." The woman's mouth relaxed. "I'm sorry."

"So am I." Therez brushed a hand over her face. With hunger and weariness, it wasn't hard to feign distress. "I'm going to my aunt in Duenne. I need to find passage today."

"Well, this one's bound for Strahlsende and then south to Klee. You'll do better with that other caravan. The caravan master is just over there." She pointed toward a heavily built man who leaned against a wagon, his arms folded, watching his crew at work and occasionally snapping out orders. The man's face was a dark brown, tanned even darker by the sun. He looked as rough as Balz, but with a shrewd expression in his black eyes.

Therez hesitated.

"Go on," said the woman. "He won't bite."

The man glanced in their direction. Seeing their interest, he smiled—a quick wolfish smile that showed yellow teeth against his dark face. He turned his head and said something that made the nearest man laugh.

Therez felt the blood rise to her face. She thanked the woman and started across the square, skirting the muck and puddles. The caravan master continued to watch, his mouth quirked in a faint smile, as though he enjoyed observing her fastidious progress.

"Are you the caravan master?" she asked, when she was close enough to make herself heard.

"I am." He had a low, raspy voice. Close up, she could see that his trousers were stained and patched. He wore a coarse brown shirt, unbuttoned to show a thick muscled neck.

"Are you— Is your caravan going to Duenne, sir?"

"My name's Alarik Brandt, not sir. And yes, it is."

"I need a passage to the city," she said as confidently as she dared. "How much do you charge?"

The caravan master flexed his hands and stared at Therez with a long, appraising look. Just when she thought she would have to repeat her question, he nodded. "Three denier for the passage. Gold ones."

Three. That was far more than she expected. "What if I don't have that much?"

The man shrugged. "Then you get no passage from me. At that price, it's a favor I'm doing you."

Before she could say anything, a commotion broke out nearby. Two boys were wrestling with a balky horse, which had become entangled in its harness. Without another glance at Therez, the caravan master started toward them. "Damned fools," he muttered.

"Wait," Therez called out.

Brandt paused, his back to her.

"I have the price," she said.

He turned back, his face unsmiling. "You do?"

She nodded.

More noise broke out as a half dozen men stopped their own tasks and went to help the boys with their unruly horse. One or two stared at Therez but the caravan master gestured at them sharply and they turned back to their tasks.

Brandt folded his arms. "Well, girl, show me you have the money."

Therez dropped her bag onto the ground and rummaged through her clothes for the purse, which she'd stowed underneath. Her neck felt hot under the man's amused gaze, but at last she untangled the purse and rooted through its contents. Finally she separated three gold denier from the rest. She shoved her purse back into her bag and stood up.

The man held out one hand, and Therez placed the sum into his callused palm. His hands were as dark as his face, the skin pebbly, and a crooked scar twisted the flesh around his thumb. Unexpectedly, her thoughts veered back to her father's hands, as smooth as the bales of silk in his warehouse, and to his voice, which never rose above a thin whisper. This man was as unlike her father as she could have wished.

"That was the price of a seat," he said. "If you want meals, that's two more denier."

Gold ones, his tone said. The price *was* too high, but she had no more time. Another hour and her mother would discover her absence. "Two for meals," she said, as matter-of-factly as she could. She dug out two more coins from her pack.

He took them with a grin. "I like a girl who pays her debts."

She nodded, not knowing how to answer that. At her silence, Brandt grunted and waved a hand toward another wagon. "Take a seat in that one. Oh, and if you want a bite, ask Ulf, the cook, for some bread and coffee. Tell him Alarik sent you."

"Where is the cook wagon?"

"Ask." He was already moving away.

Therez released a shaky breath, still unsettled by the transaction. Liberty at the cost of five gold coins. Fair or not, she would have paid twice that.

One of the smaller boys pointed out the cook wagon for her. Ulf had packed most of his gear, but he poured her a cup of thick black coffee and hacked off a generous slab of bread. "Best I can do, girl. Alarik should have sent you earlier. Here, have another cup of coffee. You look worn out. Bring me the mug when you're done."

The bread was tough, the coffee bitter and thick with grinds, but the meal filled her empty stomach and revived her strength. Therez brought the mug back to Ulf, thanking him. Ulf's glance snagged momentarily on her face, curious. "Going to Duenne?"

"To stay with my aunt." The lie came more easily this second time. "My parents died. My aunt said she can find me a posting. At least I hope she can."

Ulf grunted, indifferent to aunts and dying parents, and turned back to his duties. Therez hurried back to her wagon and squeezed into a gap between the tightly packed crates, directly behind the driver. Nearby, a scholar in his black robes perched in another wagon, reading from a small book. A troupe of tumblers practiced their tricks in the small clearing between. Soon one of Brandt's men came by, shooing them to take their places.

Alarik Brandt mounted his horse and started bellowing out orders. The crew was furiously loading the last few boxes, while mounted guards circled the wagons. A drover's herd of sheep streamed past, bleating, with dogs nipping at their legs. Dust choked the air. Somewhere a child was sobbing. The noise rose until Therez thought she would go deaf. Then a voice called out from atop the city walls. Others, whom she could not see, pushed the gates open.

"Wagon first, start forward," Brandt called out.

One by one the wagons rolled through the gates. Therez's teeth clacked together at the first jolt, and her head knocked against one of the crates. The driver grinned. "Hold on, girl."

Outside the city, they passed a stretch of grasslands where goats and cows grazed, followed by scattered workshops, then a village. Keeping one hand on the wagon to steady herself, Therez rose to her knees for one last look at Melnek's rust-red towers and walls. She could just make out the governor's palace and the chief bell tower near her father's house. A faint echo of chimes sounded in the air. One. Two. Three quarters. Six deep-throated peals for the hour.

The last time she would hear these particular bells. Therez's throat squeezed shut. She felt a peculiar emptiness inside, even as she told herself that she was glad, so very glad, to finally be quit of Melnek, of her father's house. Oh why, then, was she crying? Stupid, foolish tears. She wiped her eyes with the back of her sleeve. *I'm just tired. That's all.*

As the sun climbed higher, Therez pillowed her head on her arms. Before long she fell into a doze. This time, no dreams broke her rest. No voice whispered threats. When the wagon hit a deep rut, she woke with a stifled cry.

Melnek had disappeared from view. Sunlight glanced over the open fields, where farmers swung their scythes, bent to the ground, and straightened once more. To the north, Veraene's border hills and mountains blended with low clouds, making a wall of dark blue shadows.

Therez sucked in a deep breath of air that smelled of dust and fresh-cut hay. She twisted around to see their direction. Ahead, the caravan stretched out with riders to either side. Brandt himself was in the lead. Even as she turned back, he bellowed out new orders to his crew. "Volker, Brenn, you miserable get of a gang-fucked bitch, I wanted you forward now!"

Someone laughed, but it was a muffled sound, calculated not to carry forward. A moment later, one of the outriders passed Therez's wagon. He looked young, with smooth round cheeks and a patchy beard. Catching her glance, he grinned.

"Volker, you piss-drinking whoreson. I said now."

Therez flinched. The boy simply shrugged and urged his horse forward. Another rider followed. He looked a few years older than his partner. His dark brown face was leaner, and his eyes canted more, but she saw the resemblance between them. Both carried knives and clubs in their belts, but no swords.

By late morning the hay fields gave way to a stubbled expanse, then to green-gold meadows bordered by stands of dark-blue pines. Not long afterward, the caravan halted by a clearing to rest the horses.

Working in unison, Brandt's crew swiftly unhitched the horses and tied them in pickets beside the road. Others had unloaded cooking gear, while Ulf, the cook, and his boys lit several fires. Mugs of hot coffee and slabs of bread toasted with cheese were the fare. Therez carried her portion to one side, where she found a seat on the grass.

Therez nibbled at the chewy bread, studying her new companions, crew and passengers alike. Most had settled around the wagons for their meal. A few, like Ulf and his assistants, still busied themselves with chores, eating as they worked. As Therez watched, she tried to guess where each one came from. Most, she could tell, came from the central plains—thick black hair and round, dusky brown faces. A few had the same borderland features and accents she was used to. Several more had the much darker coloring typical of men from Fortezzien and the other southeastern provinces; they spoke with a lilt and wore their hair tied back in complicated braids. Ah but that man over there, with the pale brown eyes, was clearly from the kingdom of Ysterien in the west.

Whatever their origins, the men who belonged to the caravan were mostly lean, their whipcord muscles hardened by years of hefting barrels and crates onto wagons. Some, like Volker and Brenn, were hardly more than boys.

The other passengers had collected into small groups, talking among themselves over their breakfast. The scholar sat by himself. Nearby was another solitary man, carving a stick of wood into pipes. Therez saw the tumbling troupe with their colorful tunics and knitted hose of southern style. The four or five families—she couldn't quite tell them apart—looked like farmers on their way to Hammenz or Kassel. She would have to be careful. If asked, they might remember a solitary girl traveling to Duenne.

Volker was walking toward her, carrying a mug of coffee and a plate. He gave her a sunny, infectious smile. "Hello. I saw you this morning."

She smiled back. "You rode past my wagon."

He grinned. "You mean Otto's wagon." With his mug, he indicated the spot next to Therez. "D'you mind some company?"

She shook her head. With practiced ease, he settled onto the ground, sitting cross-legged with his plate on his lap. "So what's your name?"

"Ilse," she said, somewhat quickly. "My name's Ilse."

She had chosen the name while sitting in the wagon. A pretty name. Different from her own. It sounded odd on her tongue, but Volker didn't seem to notice. "I'm Volker, in case you missed what Alarik was saying. Alarik Brandt—he's the caravan master. Or did you talk to Niko? He's the second. That's him over there, by the piebald mare."

He pointed toward a lean man in dusty brown trousers, who was wiping his face with his shirt. Before Therez could answer, the second outrider she'd seen earlier came up behind Volker. "She talked to Alarik. I saw her while you were busy with the horses." He nodded at Therez. "I'm Brenn," he said. "Volker's my brother. Where are you bound?"

"Duenne . . . to my aunt's house. She promised to find me work."

She saw them exchange a glance. Was it her accent? No, Brenn was looking at her hands. "What kind of work?" he asked.

For that she had an answer, too. "Lady's maid, if I'm lucky. I can stitch and sew and read a little."

Again the brothers looked at each other. "We wondered about that," Volker said. "You talk so pretty, like you don't need to work."

"Ladies' maids talk pretty, too," Brenn said quietly. Unlike his brother, he was studying Therez with a thoughtful expression.

Volker nodded. "So they do."

Therez pretended an interest in the state of her skirt. "I need the work badly enough. My father and mother died, and, well, my aunt said she could keep me long enough to find a posting, no longer. Said I was old enough to earn my own living."

Volker laughed. "Our da said the same." He drank down his coffee and wiped his face with the back of his hand. "Say, I hope you didn't let Alarik bully you into paying too much."

"But don't argue with him," Brenn said. "He doesn't like that. He—"

A string of shouted curses interrupted their conversation. Brandt was shouting to his crew, orders mixed with blistering threats. "Break's over," he barked at the riders. "Trim your tongues, stuff your pricks into your trousers, and get those wagons moving."

Brenn and Volker shrugged, and with muttered good-byes they ran to their posts. Therez handed her cup to the cook's boy and reclaimed her seat. Within a short time, they had retaken the road.

THE CARAVAN MARKED a dozen long dusty miles that day. With every one, Therez breathed more easily. So many hours for the maids to discover her absence. Another frantic hour while they searched the house and grounds. Some undetermined interval before they reported the matter to Therez's parents. The questions, the accusations, the weighty silence of her father's anger. She had difficulty imagining what came next. He might spend the day in isolation, working over his accounts. He might order a wider search. He might do nothing at all, consigning her to her fate as he would a cargo of spoiled goods, but she could not depend on that.

"How many weeks until we reach Duenne?" she asked Brenn that evening.

"Ten," Brenn replied. "Maybe twelve. Depends on the rain."

"That long?" She had calculated half the time.

"We start off fast, but then we slow down," Brenn said. "From Kassel on it's stop here, unload those crates, pack up new goods, restock the supplies. And we make an overnight stay in Strahlsende, because that's one of the main stopovers."

He went on to describe how Melnek's fish traded for Kassel's combed wool, which traded for lumber from Strahlsende's forests, which in turn traded for rare furs trapped in the Gallenz Valley. He was describing the interior plains when Volker joined them. "You like traveling?" he asked Therez.

"Well enough." She nibbled at her plate of roasted beef, which was salty and tough.

"Have some ale," Volker said.

Mutely, she shook her head.

"Not fine enough for a lady's maid?" Brenn said. He was smiling, but Therez stiffened.

"Don't tease," Volker said to his brother. "But speaking of fine . . . did you see the carnival girls?"

Brenn shrugged. "They look nice."

"Not as pretty as Ilse," Volker said. "But they promised to show me their magic tricks later."

Brenn covered his laugh with a cough. He muttered something to Volker, who turned red. "That's not what I meant."

"It is."

"Is not. That's your blood talking."

"Fah! Your blood you mean."

They spent the rest of their break trading insults, until Brandt's second, Niko, ordered them off to first watch. Therez finished her meal slowly, picking at the meat. She knew what Brenn meant by blood. *Desire.* Galt had desired her. The memory of his proximity made her cheeks turn hot. Other memories—how his mouth thinned when she danced with Mann, his cool precise voice as he spoke about perfection in art—drove the blood away. She shivered and closed her eyes. When she opened them, she saw one of the horse boys, just glancing away.

That night she slept under her wagon, with her knapsack as her pillow, wrapped in all her blankets. The ground felt cold and hard, and a trace of frost sharpened the air. Gazing between the wagon spokes, she counted the stars glittering in the night sky—the Crone's Eye, Toc the Hunter, Lir's Necklace. A milky expanse overspread the western horizon.

The old tales spoke of a dark void, filled with stars, which lay between this world of flesh and the magical plane called Anderswar. Except the stars were the souls of the dead, launched in flight to their next lives. It was part of what linked each soul to Toc, who had himself died and was reborn. *And what links us to Lir,* Therez thought. *She who grieved through the winter, thinking that her brother-lover was no more.*

Were they grieving for her at home? Was her grandmother already part of that cloud?

I had no choice, she told herself. *If I had stayed, I would be in Theodr Galt's house even now. I would not see my mother and grandmother again, except for rare visits. Because a collector does not like to lend his possessions to others.*

Even so, tears burned her eyes. Do not think about home or family, she told herself. Think about Brenn and Volker and the tumbler girls. Think about tomorrow and the next day, with a new life and a new name. *I'm not Therez any longer. I am Ilse. I can write my own future.*

DAWN CAME EARLY, announced with the rattle and crash of pans, and a steady monologue from the cook as he cursed his boys, the crew, and the uncooperative firewood. Therez sat up stiffly and rubbed her eyes. The sky was muddy gray, streaked with red from the still invisible sun. A large fire in the middle of the clearing sent up plumes of smoke and cinders. Scents of coffee and grilled meat filled the air.

Therez rubbed her scalp and briefly wished for a hot bath. What she got instead was a curt order from Brandt's second to hurry with her breakfast or she'd get left behind.

Niko went off to rouse the other passengers. Therez joined the line for the latrines, and then to the stream, well opposite, where she made do with washing her face and hands in cold water. Her clothes already looked filthy. She brushed away the dirt, scrubbing out the worst stains, and finally gave up. Still shivering from the water, she untangled her braid with her fingers, shook out the dust, and rebraided it. No comb. No washcloth. What else had she forgotten?

Breakfast consisted of bread and grilled beef, with coffee to wash it down. Scolding her and all the other passengers, Ulf retrieved the mugs and plates and set his boys to washing, while he repacked his gear. By this hour, the caravan looked nearly ready to depart. The caravan master was making the rounds, barking out orders to hitch up those horses, fill in the latrine, move faster or he'd dock their wages. His gaze passed over Therez, before he stalked on to the next hapless member of his crew.

When Niko passed by again, Therez lifted a hand to catch his attention. "Excuse me."

He swung around. "What, girl?"

"Do we have time for . . . ?"

She meant to say *for bathing*, but Niko interrupted with a yelp of laughter. "Sure we have time, girl. Piss quick, or you get buried in the latrines."

He strode away, leaving Therez flushed and stammering. Three of the crew grinned at her. Her cheeks burning, Therez caught up her bag and jogged back to the stream. A glance showed her that she was alone. She pulled off her tunic, unbuttoned her shirt partway, and splashed water over her face and neck and body. The cold water brought goose bumps to her skin. She gritted her teeth and scrubbed fast, hoping to finish before someone came by.

Loud hoofbeats made her jump and clutch her shirt together. One of the outriders, she told herself. Then a man called out, "Ho, caravan master!"

It was Váná Gersi, her father's senior runner.

Therez ducked behind a screen of bushes. Gersi. Here. Within a day of her escape. *He must be checking with all the caravans,* she thought, as she rebuttoned her shirt with fumbling hands. *I have to hide. Run away. Before Brandt tells him about me.*

She scanned the wilderness of trees and bracken and scrub extending away from camp. Now that her first panic had passed, it registered that she had no food and no shelter other than her blanket. What if she hid until the caravan left? She could follow the highway to the next village and find lodging there.

She slung her bag over her shoulder and turned around.

Volker stood just a few feet behind her. He was holding a pair of empty water buckets, and he was grinning. "Ilse. What're you doing?"

Therez bit her lip. "I was thirsty."

He continued to stare at her so pointedly that she glanced down. Half her shirt was unbuttoned; the other half was crooked. She flushed and turned to fix the buttons. Taking a quick step closer, Volker caught her hand. "Can I help?"

He kissed her on the lips, his other hand going to her breast. Therez pushed him away. "No."

Volker wiped his mouth, no longer smiling. "You mean, not yet."

He snatched up the buckets and stalked to the stream. Keeping his back to Therez, he refilled the buckets. When he swung around, she shied away, but he only muttered a warning not to be late and marched back to camp.

Therez let out a breath.

"Hey, girl."

Alarik Brandt stood in the shadow of an oak tree. His smile was a bright flash against his dark face.

"Teasing my boys?" he asked. "Or didn't he offer enough?"

She gulped down a breath. "I . . . I was thirsty."

"As you say." He nodded back at the camp. "Business with that rider is over. We're heading out, with you or not. Coming?"

Still smiling, he tilted his hand, palm upward. It was an ambiguous gesture, one that might be equal parts invitation and demand. Her pulse gave an uncomfortable leap. Had he guessed that she was the reason for Váná Gersi's search? *He doesn't know,* Therez told herself. *He won't unless I betray myself.* With her pulse still beating far too fast for comfort, she dropped her gaze to the ground and headed back toward camp. As she passed Brandt, she heard his soft laughter, felt his warm breath graze her neck. It took all her control not to run.

CHAPTER FOUR

GRADUALLY THEREZ RELAXED into the pattern of her new life. She rose early and ate breakfast alone. She learned to do without warm water and regular bathing. She borrowed rags from Ulf, the cook, and hiding behind his wagon, she washed herself bit by bit. She learned how to scrub her clothes with sand and cold water, hanging them near the fire at night to dry.

Volker soon forgave her, as he put it, and joined her for supper, along with Brenn. The two brothers had made friends with the tumbler girls, and by the second week, they all spent their evenings together, trading stories while Therez listened. The girls did know magic, she discovered, and often delighted the caravan crew with their tricks. They traced silvery lines in the air. They called up brightly colored globes from nothing and sent them flying aloft, like soap bubbles. They made Volker's hair stand on end, much to Brenn's delight.

"I know about magic," Volker told them afterward.

Lena, the older girl, laughed. "What kind of magic?"

He grinned. "Tricks. I could show you later."

She shook her head, her eyes bright with glee. "No, thank you. I know your kind of tricks."

Brenn rolled his eyes and exchanged a look with Therez. "The only tricks Volker knows are ones that get him into trouble. Now me, I wish I knew real magic, the kind mages study in Duenne. Like the magic they use to fight wars, or see into the past."

"Then do it," said a man's voice. "Leave the road and find a teacher."

It was the scholar Therez had seen the first day. Until now, the man had kept apart from the other passengers, reading his books. On the longer stops he sometimes walked beyond the camp perimeter, returning only after the campfires were banked.

"Do *you* know magic?" she asked.

In answer, he lifted a hand and curled his fingers, murmuring in a strange tongue. Erythandran, Therez realized with a rill of wonder, recognizing the words. But unlike her own poor attempt two weeks before, there was no doubt of magic's presence. She felt a pressure against her skin and the faint tattoo of another pulse. The scholar spoke another phrase and a sharp green scent overlaid the camp smells of horse and wood smoke. It reminded her of hot sunlight, of fresh-cut hay and summer fields. When the scholar opened his fingers, a light bloomed within his cupped hand.

"Touch it," he said to Therez.

Warily, she stood and approached him.

He was tall, with a bony face and the ruddy-brown coloring that marked the borderlands around Károví. The cuffs and hem of his robe were frayed, and the black dye had turned a rusty brown in places, but in his eyes she read assurance. At his gesture, she touched her fingertips to the light. Something tickled her skin. "Steady," the man said. "Almost."

He spoke another phrase in old Erythandran. Her fingers turned transparent. Where her blood flowed, threads of light gleamed.

Therez let her breath trickle out. Magic. Inside her. It was . . . it was far more wondrous than she could ever have imagined.

"Try it yourself," he said. "Look at something tiny—a nail, a stone, a freckle. Good. Now breathe slowly. Find the point between inhale and exhale. When you think you've found it, repeat these words."

Ei rûf ane gôtter. Komen mir de strôm.

The words rolled through her mind. Magic echoed against magic, and she sensed the possibilities unraveling from that one phrase. Healing. Fire. Illumination of the soul. If only she had known these words two weeks ago, when she bent over her dying grandmother.

Suddenly afraid, she plucked back her hand. "You must have studied for years."

His mouth tilted in a wry smile. "Hardly. I know a little. I'm going to Duenne to learn more. Maybe you should join me, instead of working as a maid."

"I can't," she said quickly.

"Why not?"

Therez opened her mouth, closed it. "I don't know."

And she didn't. She no longer lived in her father's household, where magic was not precisely forbidden, it was merely discouraged, labeled a useless distraction outside of a few practical applications.

Except it's hard to break the habit of nearly sixteen years.

But the scholar was smiling, as though he had expected such an answer. "Maybe you should think about it," he said. "We have a few more weeks ahead of us. Talk to me before you leave the caravan, and maybe I can find you a place in Duenne that better suits your talents."

Therez stared after him as he walked back toward the main campfire, where Ulf was handing out coffee to the next perimeter watch. Magic. He thought she ought to study magic. The idea so distracted her that she didn't hear what the others were saying until Brenn tugged on her arm. "You're from Melnek. You must know."

"What should I know?"

"About Károví's King Leos—the man who traded his heart for magic. I thought all the people from the borderlands knew those stories."

Therez shook her head. "They're just folktales, Brenn. They're not true history."

"History!" Gabi laughed. "I'd rather have stories."

They insisted until Therez finally relented and told them the folktales she had learned from her grandmother. How Lir and her consort (sometimes called Toc) had created a lake of fire called the Mantharah and, from it, the rest of this world. How Lir took a handful of fire from the Mantharah and squeezed hard to make a single white jewel, which she gave to the first emperor of Erythandra. How centuries later a traitor sent a thief to steal the jewel so he might take the throne himself. The emperor's chief mage had used powerful magic to divide the jewel into three pieces, and hid them in three secret places within the palace. But in the latter days of the empire, a prince of Károví named Leos Dzavek had turned thief himself and took all three jewels so he could gain eternal life.

"The old kings never dared that," Therez said. "Their priests would not allow it, saying that Toc himself had died and was reborn, and so no ordinary man should refuse what the gods themselves endured. But some claim that King Leos was the chief mage reborn. They say he bargained with Toc to win his life and the jewels as a mark of the god's favor, so he would never have to die again."

"Then the gods took back their favor," Gabi said softly.

"Not the gods, but a wolf," Therez said. "A giant wolf, who led King Leos through the paths of the dead. But this time, there was no bargain. This time, there was no victory. The wolf buried the jewels forever and King Leos returned without them."

The crescent moon was sliding behind the trees when Therez finally said good night to her friends. She picked her way between the wagons until she reached Otto's. A movement in the trees caught her attention. One of the caravan guards? The mysterious scholar?

Alarik Brandt emerged from the shadows. He held a short club in one hand. His other hand rested on his knife hilt. He paused and glanced at Therez. His teeth bared in a smile.

He wants to frighten me.

She smiled back to prove she wasn't afraid. (Even though she was. Could he sense how her pulse beat faster? Could he see her shiver from all that distance, through the night and shadows?)

Brandt's smile widened. He gave her a mock salute and continued on his way.

THE CARAVAN MADE its first stop in Hammenz, where two passengers disembarked, and the crew unloaded barrels of salted fish. A few days later, they turned off the main highway for a smaller road that cut southwest through the hills. More stops punctuated their journey, just as Brenn predicted, and their progress slowed. One in Venner to deliver crates of sea salt. Another two days later to pick up leather and hides. Several families disembarked in Kassel, and the tumbler troupe, along with Lena and Gabi, left the caravan in Strahlsende. Soon the only passengers who remained were Therez and the scholar, both of them bound for Duenne.

Nearly a month after leaving Melnek, Alarik Brandt called for an overnight stay in the trade town of Mundlau. Therez stayed close to the wagons, not liking this loud rough town. She could hear the crew excitedly discussing how they would spend their brief hours of leave. Brandt would dock anyone who caused trouble, but apparently there were many ways to define trouble, and many more ways to evade punishment. Even Brenn and Volker talked about the brandy they would drink, and the women they would bed.

By late morning, a sullen, subdued crew returned to work, loading crates and bundles that had arrived earlier from the local merchants. As Therez waited to reclaim her seat, she saw Brandt approaching from the agent's offices, across the square. To her surprise, he was heading directly toward her.

"Wagons are filling up," he said without preamble. "I'll need two more denier from you, if you want to keep your seat."

Therez started. "But I already paid for my passage."

"So you did, but goods come first." He plucked a knife from his belt and ran its edge underneath one ragged fingernail. When Therez said nothing, he looked up with narrowed eyes. "I need an answer, girl. Pay up, or stay behind. Which is it?"

Her first inclination was to tell him no. But they had passed fewer caravans on the road than she expected, and she disliked the idea of waiting
here, in this ugly town, until another happened by. Swiftly she calculated
what money she had left and what she expected to need. If she paid Brandt,
that would leave her thirteen gold denier, plus the silver and copper, and her
jewelry. It would be enough, she decided.

"Two deniers?" she said reluctantly.

"Two. And give them now. I've work to do."

Two more coins left her pouch for Brandt's weathered palm.

After Mundlau, the caravan passed into a long stretch of wilderness blan-
keted with pine forests. There would be no more stops until they reached the
Gallenz Valley, Brenn told Therez. There they would meet up with the main
highway running between Duenne and the port city of Tiralien. The caravan
would also make a longer halt, for supplies and other goods, before the final
stretch to Duenne.

"Five weeks to Gallenz. Three more to the city herself," Brenn said.

Therez was thinking of Duenne, and how she might find employment,
as she took inventory of her belongings that night. The task had become
part of her routine, and her fingers deftly sorted through socks and shirts
and linens, as she mulled over her future. Then her hands paused, and a chill
went through her.

My money. My jewelry. They're gone.

With shaking hands, she searched the pack again. She took out every
item and shook them one by one, searching for even a single coin or bracelet.
Nothing. The money in her boots and the small bag she kept underneath her
shirt were still safe, but the main portion was gone, and so was her jewelry.

She stuffed her belongings back into her pack and hurried back to the
camp. She spotted Alarik Brandt, leaning against a wagon wheel as he supervised a crew digging the fire pits. He had his knife out and was whittling a new
tent stake. Therez pushed through to stand in front of him. "Someone robbed
me," she said in a low voice. "They took my money and— They took all of it."

Brandt frowned as he sliced a long flake of bark from the new stake.
"My men don't steal."

"I didn't say that—"

"You did. Girl, I'm not your nursemaid. If you lost your money, that's too
bad."

Therez trembled, from anger and a cold abiding panic, but she turned
away, knowing it would do no good to argue with the man. *It's not the end,*

she told herself. *I paid for meals. I won't starve. I'll just have to find work faster once I get to Duenne.*

"One thing more." Brandt raised his voice, causing a few of the men to pause in their work. "I'm needing a bit more money. Goods and profit and all that."

Therez stopped. "I can't pay anything more. I—" She bit her lips on her next words. She didn't want to mention she still had money. If he knew, he would take it. "I can't pay you," she said again.

"Can't have that either."

His voice had gone flat, making the skin on her neck prickle. She turned around to see him watching her with a steady, unblinking gaze. The knife lay in his palm, its blade glinting in the red light of sunset.

"What do you mean?" she whispered.

"Credit," he said, closing his fingers over the hilt. "I'm thinking you have a rich family back in Melnek. They'll pay the bill for a runaway."

It took all her effort to keep her voice steady. "I'm not a runaway."

"Then why did Petr Zhalina send his lackey after you?"

Therez blinked, but his expression didn't change.

"Do you have anything else to say, girl?"

"No," she whispered.

She kept her face under control as she walked back to the campfire. The cook offered her a mug of coffee. She accepted it without thinking and carried it to the fire, where she crouched, her bag shoved between her feet.

I have to get away.

But how? The caravan had left Mundlau nearly a week ago. Between here and there lay only wilderness, and the nights had turned raw. She would surely starve or freeze. If she did nothing, however, Brandt would send her back to Melnek, where her father would starve and freeze her soul.

Therez drained the mug. She returned the mug to the cook's boy and demanded bread and cheese. "Stew's ready inside of an hour," he told her.

"I can't wait that long."

The boy hesitated. Something in Therez's expression must have decided him, because he looked around furtively. Ulf was occupied. The other two boys were away, fetching water. The boy quickly hacked off some bread and a thick square of cheese. "Don't tell anyone," he muttered.

Therez nodded. She packed away the bread and cheese, then slung the bag onto her shoulders. Go now, she thought. Everyone is too busy to notice one girl. If I walk fast, I can make at least a mile before nightfall.

She had just passed the sentries, when one called out to her. Therez walked faster. She heard footsteps hurrying after her. Panicking, she broke into a run, but her pursuer overtook her and grabbed her braid.

Therez hit the ground with a thump. Her vision sparkled. When she could see again, she saw Alarik Brandt standing over her. His face was flushed, and his eyes were bright with anger. "You silly bitch. I told you to stay."

"You have no right—"

He slapped her across the face and hauled her to her feet. "Rope," he called out. "Tie this bitch to her wagon. And search her for money. She was thieving from us."

He shoved Therez into the arms of the closest man. Therez kicked, but the man twisted her arms behind her back and wrestled her to the ground. "That's better, sweetheart. Now for the money." He called over one of the horse boys. "Look in her bag," he told the boy.

The boy tossed out her belongings piece by piece. "Nothing here."

"Then we look a bit closer." The man thrust his hand underneath her shirt and discovered Therez's bag of silver coins. "Huh. Alarik was right."

"That's mine," Therez said.

"Where'd you get it?"

"Home."

"Thought your parents died. Thought you had to work for your bread." He spat on the ground. "Let's make sure we've got everything," he said to the boy.

They pulled her boots off, which uncovered the knife and the rest of her coins. Still not satisfied, the man pulled up her skirts while the boy felt around for more contraband. At the urging of their audience, he felt underneath Therez's shirt again, grinning at her fury. She ought to have fainted from the humiliation, except she was too angry.

"Nothing else, I guess," he said, withdrawing his hand.

Brandt returned in time to observe the end of their search. He took the knife and money and counted through the silver and copper denier. "Good enough," he said. "I'll keep these to pay for my trouble."

"Thief," Therez said.

Bending down, Brandt smacked her face twice. "You are the fucking damned thief," he said, each word like another slap against her face. "You stole from my passengers, you little whore. I plan to report you in the next town."

He spoke loud enough for everyone in camp to hear. Before Therez could argue back, he gave her another, harder smack that made her head ring. "Tie her to the wagon," he said to the crew. "If she behaves, she gets supper and a blanket."

They bound her wrists and tied her securely to an axle. Therez slumped against the wheel. Tears leaked from her eyes, stinging the cuts on her face. Her head still ached from Brandt's slaps and her lips bled freely.

My father will lock me away. Tie me up with silk and ribbons. Lecture me with whispers. Then he'll barter me off in marriage.

But not to Galt, who had to know of Therez's defection. Or maybe Galt wouldn't care. He might like a reason to punish her as well. He might even like her better this way. He might use the knowledge like a bit and chain to keep her tamed. The thought made her dizzy.

"Hey. Hey, Ilse."

Brenn crouched beside her, Volker stood a few steps behind. Brenn had a pan of stew in one hand. A thick fragrant steam rose from the stew, which had thick chunks of bread floating in it.

"I brought you supper," Brenn said. "Alarik said it was all right. Ilse, please look at me. It's not my fault."

He motioned for Volker to fetch the water. When Volker returned, Brenn held the water skin to Therez's mouth while she drank.

"Alarik's cussing like a storm cloud," he said indifferently.

"What'd you expect?" Volker said. "Course, sometimes that means he's in a good mood."

"Sometimes." Brenn wet a corner of his shirt and wiped the tears and blood from Therez's face. "You should eat," he said. "At least, while it's hot. Makes it taste better."

She shuddered. "I have to get away."

"You can't," Brenn said gently.

"I have to. Didn't you hear? He wants to sell me back to my father."

"Ilse, hush. Listen to me. You have to play along with him. It's easier that way—"

"No!" She was breathing hard now. "I won't go back. He can't make me."

"He can," Brenn cut in. He glanced toward the campfire, a dozen feet away. "Ilse, he likes his money, and he doesn't like girls talking back. He won't let you get away, not now."

"So does my father. That's why I left. I couldn't—"

"Couldn't what?" asked Volker.

Therez shivered, sick at the thought of home. Brenn stroked her hair, murmuring comfort. Volker lay on his stomach, staring at them. "Maybe," he said. "Maybe we could help."

Therez stared, hope rising within her. "You could?"

Brenn's fingers twitched back from her hair. "Are you mad? Alarik would kill us. He knows how you've been looking at her, Volker."

"He won't know," Volker insisted. "Not if we just get her a knife. She could wait until dark and cut the ropes. He won't ever guess. At least we could if she—"

He broke off. A look passed between the brothers, and Therez's mouth went dry. "If I do what?"

Volker dropped his gaze. "It's like Brenn said," he said slowly. "Alarik won't like it if we help you. He's got a temper. I was thinking we could make a trade. Something for you. Something for me and Brenn."

With a faint shock, Therez realized what he meant. A trade. That kind of trade. "You want a lot."

Volker looked up, his expression calculating. "So do you."

Therez looked from one brother to the other. Volker's eyes were bright with anticipation. Brenn was flushed with embarrassment, but she could see the change in his face, too.

"No," she whispered. "I won't do it."

Volker shrugged and got to his feet. Brenn hesitated a moment, then he stood, too, and turned away. Therez hardly cared. It was too much, what they asked.

She tugged at the ropes, but the crew had tied the knots securely. She bit and chewed at the ropes. No good. Therez blew out a breath in frustration. If only she could beg someone's mercy, but the crew would not dare to confront Brandt or Niko, and all the passengers had left the caravan a week or longer before.

All except the scholar. Her heart lifted momentarily with hope when she remembered him, remembered how he had treated her kindly and spoke of finding her a place in Duenne. Surely he could stand against the caravan master—

No, she thought bitterly. *He is one man, with just a few small magics. He could not stand against several dozen.*

There was no one who could help. Except Brenn and Volker. And they wanted a fair trade.

So make the trade, a part of her whispered. *It's only your body, lent for a few moments, a half hour. Then you can walk away free.*

Over and over, from one side and the opposite, she argued with herself, all the while aware that Brenn and Volker had not moved far away. As if they knew she was desperate. As if they knew she had no choice. She wrenched away from the rope and twisted her wrists, only to have the rope bite deeper into her skin. With a curse, she collapsed onto the wet ground and bit her lips to stop the sobs from breaking free of her throat.

Stay and let Brandt sell her back to her father. Go, make the trade, and walk free.

She closed her eyes, felt her heart thumping against her chest. So hard and fast, as though she were running a race. *Perhaps I am,* she thought. She drew a long breath. "Brenn?" she whispered softly. "Volker?"

Volker knelt beside her in a moment. "Changed your mind?"

Her throat had closed, she could not speak. She nodded.

He whispered something to his brother, who whispered back. A moment later, Volker crawled underneath the wagon and beckoned to Therez. Awkwardly, she crawled to his side and lay down. Brenn sat with his back to them, shielding them from view.

Volker unbuttoned Therez's shirt and untied her bandeau. The cloth fell away, and he laid a hand over her breast with an ah of pleasure. The night breeze brought goose bumps to Therez's bare skin, but she didn't mind. She didn't mind anything now, she told herself.

"Roll over," Volker whispered. "Quick. Before Alarik walks by."

Yes. Get it over with. Therez lay on her back. Volker unbuttoned his trousers and knelt between her legs. He shoved her skirt high around her waist. Her underlinens thwarted him only for a moment. He cut through them with his knife and tossed the pieces to one side. All the while he told her what to do, but Therez found it difficult to attend, and so she was unprepared for the sharp stab when he made his first thrust. She bit her lips as Volker pushed harder, grunting with the effort. Something broke, finally, and he slid fully inside her.

She lost track of things then. It was hard to breathe, hard to keep from crying out against the insistent pain. Volker was panting in her ear—little grunts and moans of pleasure. Finally, when she thought she could bear no more, Volker collapsed on top of her, laughing softly. "Oh, that was good. Now it's your turn, Brenn."

The cold night air washed over her a moment, then Brenn took his brother's place. "Not how I wanted it," he muttered. "But it'll do."

Brenn was bigger and heavier, and the pain went on much longer. Volker took up the pan of stew and lay next to them, eating and watching. Therez met his gaze once. He was grinning.

With a hard jerk, Brenn finished and rolled off Therez. She lay there, numb and aching and sick. A sweetish smell filled the air, underneath it the distinct scent of blood.

"Ilse?" Brenn touched her hair.

She recoiled from his touch. Awkwardly, he pulled her skirt down and buttoned her shirt, but she refused to move. Volker had already left—she heard his voice from a distance, excited and merry. Finally Brenn muttered a farewell and crawled out from under the wagon to rejoin his brother. She was alone, just as she wanted.

MUCH LATER, NIKO came by and tossed a blanket to Therez. Brandt circled the camp a few times, talking with various members of his crew, but did not speak to her again. Slowly the camp settled into quiet. Ulf banked his campfire and sent his boys to their tents. Guards took their places along the perimeter for the first watch. A few passed the wagon on their way to the latrine ditches, but no one glanced in her direction. Then, just when Therez thought the boys had forgotten her, Brenn slowly came past. He, too, visited the latrines. On his way back, he knelt and fiddled with his bootstrap. When he stood, Therez saw a flash of metal from the newly risen moon.

My knife.

She waited until there was no one in sight. Her hand closed over a wooden handle, still warm from Brenn's touch. It was a short paring knife from Ulf's stores.

Footsteps brought her pulse leaping. She went still, the knife held close to her chest. It was Brandt and another man. They were talking about the crew's mood—which was sullen from boredom—and how the stopover in Mundlau had only worsened it.

"We'll take a longer break at Donuth," Brandt said. "That runner said we could find Zhalina's agent there."

"Won't the old man make trouble?" the other man said. "About hiding the girl?"

"But I didn't," Brandt said. "The girl showed up later, on foot. Maybe she rode with another caravan. Maybe she ran off with a boy, and the boy abandoned her. Besides, what matters is that Zhalina promised us gold for any word of his daughter. We did better and found the daughter herself. That should be worth something."

A grunt and a laugh. "So she's not a thief."

"Oh, she is, or I'd have to give back the money. Right?"

The pair moved on. Therez waited until the camp fell silent once more. With her pulse thrumming in her ears, she braced the knife between her knees and began sawing at the ropes at her wrists. It was painfully slow. Twice she cut herself on the blade. But at last she sliced through the last strand.

With a few strong slashes, she cut the rope tying her to the axle, then pulled on her boots and tucked the knife into one. She wrapped the blanket around her shoulders and emerged from under the wagon.

In starts and stops, Therez crept between and around the wagons, into the forest beyond. Moonlight filtered through the branches, casting blue shadows over the undergrowth and forest floor. She could make out a dark trench that marked the latrines. Farther on, to her right, a stream glittered.

Two shadows, moving between the trees, sent her into a crouch. The perimeter guards. They made frequent rounds, she knew. She would have to time her escape carefully.

Once the guards passed by, Therez counted to ten, then rose to her feet and slipped from tree to tree. Leaves whispered and stirred beneath her feet, no matter how lightly she trod. In spite of the urge to run, she paused every few steps, hoping the guards would think her a forest animal.

She had just reached a point beyond the horse picket, when her foot sank into a muddy patch. Without thinking, she jerked her foot free, stumbled, and heard a sudden noise, like that of men startled into movement.

"Who's that?"

Therez bolted.

"Grab her!" a guard shouted.

"What's going on?"

"Alarik's girl. She's got loose."

Therez dodged around a tree, fell over a half-buried root, picked herself up, and kept going. The blanket flapped loose from her shoulders. She let it fall, not even slowing down. More shouts sounded from the camp. Therez glanced back and saw lamps flaring into life. Then she heard Alarik Brandt's hoarse bellow.

Faster. Faster. Faster.

Her pulse beat in time to the words. She plunged into a dense thicket, jumped over a rivulet, and dodged between tall oaks and bristly pines. Thorns and branches tore at her clothes and face. She broke free, stumbling, only to pitch over the lip of an unexpected bank.

She hit the ground with a thump and kept falling, tumbling over rocks and branches, finally crashing against a massive tree trunk at the bottom. The tree had fallen over, and she could see the hollow underneath, veiled by roots and dirt and leaves. Therez scrambled inside and lay still.

Just in time. Footsteps thudded heavily down the hillside. The men, three of them, circled the clearing, whispering and muttering to one another. One paused by Therez's shelter, his boots just inches from her face.

"She's not here," he said.

"Probably got away," said another one. "Damn. Well, there's no use tripping around the dark. Let's go back and tell Alarik."

"He won't like it."

"Don't I know that."

They walked off, expressing their disgust by kicking the branches and leaves. Therez heard their noisy climb back up the slope. Quiet returned, but she counted to a hundred, then another hundred, before she crawled from her hiding place. By now, the moon was well up, and the sky was clear. It was cold, but she could survive. *All I have to do is walk.*

She turned and froze. A man stood before her, outlined by moonlight. Therez spun away, but another man lunged at her and threw her to the ground. When he tried to contain her arms, she fought back, biting and clawing and screaming, until he stunned her with a hard blow.

"Don't break her face," the other man commented. "Alarik wants that fun himself."

"Right." His companion hauled Therez to her feet, twisting her arms behind her back. She sobbed in pain and terror.

The third man came sliding down the bank. "That was easy." Then to Therez, he snapped, "Quiet. Alarik's fucking angry enough without you howling."

The camp was awake and filled with tense activity. Ulf had relit the fires and was handing out coffee. Brenn sprawled over a log, held down by two guards, while Niko beat him with a knotted rope. Volker leaned against a wagon wheel. He looked dazed and sick, and his face was bleeding freely. A dark figure moved in the shadows—the scholar. Therez caught a glimpse of his face, but his expression was unreadable.

Alarik Brandt stalked into view, one of the sentries at his side. He glanced at Brenn's back, covered with bleeding welts. "Put him to bed and give the other one six cuts."

"Dock 'em?" Niko asked.

Brandt nodded. "Ten days for both. Scut work from now to Duenne."

He swung around and saw Therez. His lips drew back from his teeth. "You."

Therez shrank back. Brandt seized her arm and propelled her past the circle of wagons, to a point near the horse pickets. A smaller fire burned here, its light casting a ruddy light on Brandt's face. He still had that feral smile.

"You've whored my men," he said in a low voice. "You bribed them to disobey me. I don't like that."

She licked her swollen lips. "I had to."

"Had to? You stupid bitch. Don't you understand? I'm getting good money for you."

"No," she said in a low voice.

Brandt made a guttural sound. "What do you mean no?"

She forced herself to meet his gaze directly. "I mean no. You can't send me back. Not after what I did."

He laughed softly. "Is that what you believe? I can. And get your father's thanks and reward. Think on that, girl." His eyes narrowed as he studied her. "Unless . . ."

His gaze traveled down her body. His expression changed from rage to one colder and more speculative. She swallowed, her mouth hot and dry, and tasting of blood. "Unless what?"

"Unless you want your freedom more."

"What are you saying?"

"I'm saying the choice is yours. Go home to your family. Or make it worth my effort to keep you. It's a favor, wench. Say the word."

A trade.

She felt a curious tightness in her belly. She had no name for this emotion. It wasn't desire, nor was it panic. It was like standing on a lofty cliff and staring into the abyss. Not six feet away, the outriders and drivers and sentries were talking. A few openly watched, and she heard their muttered laughter.

I have no choice, Ilse thought. *Unless you call it a choice to let this man sell me back to my father. I shall have to pretend and hope he believes me. And pretend that I believe him.*

She lifted a hand to her shirt. Brandt tensed, then relaxed as Ilse slowly unbuttoned her shirt and dropped it to one side. Boots and socks followed. She unbuckled her belt and let the skirt slide to the ground. Stepping from the puddle of cloth, she stood before Alarik Brandt, with as much grace as she could muster.

Cold smote her back. A wave of heat billowed from the nearby fire: its light gilded her copper brown skin and reflected from Alarik Brandt's bright eyes. He watched her, lips parted, the pulse at his throat beating faster. After weeks on the road, he stank of sweat and horse, but so did she.

Ilse took his hand and pressed it against her breast. His fingers tightened. She forced herself to smile. "I will do whatever you like. Tell me what you want."

Brandt told her, and she obeyed. "Good bitch," he said roughly, midway through. "Very good. The boys gave you a first lesson, eh? Softened you up. Made you ready for me. Oh no. I'm not done yet. Not nearly. Good, sweet bitch. Oh yes."

It lasted longer than she had hoped. When he finished, Brandt called Niko over. "You're next," he said, casually lacing up his trousers. "Choose three more after you. That'll be the routine—four a night not counting me. More when she gets used to the work. We want this one to last."

Niko flashed a grin and nodded. When Brandt was gone, he ran his fingers along Ilse's throat. He was a raw-boned man with knotted muscles from hefting barrels, and his hands were rough and callused. "Pretty," he said. "Never had one so pretty like you." His hand dropped from the skin of her throat to her breast, already sore from handling. Ilse winced, and the man laughed deep in his throat. "I like that, too."

He gave her to the second man, the third, the fourth. Afterward one of Ulf's boys came with a bucket of water and rags and a rope coiled over one shoulder. "Clean up," he said. "Alarik's orders." She dunked a rag and wiped her face. The boy had not moved. He was there to watch, she realized.

She washed herself thoroughly, shivering all the while. The water was frigid, its waters born in the nearby mountains. Water from Duszranjo's glaciers. From her father's homeland. Taking up another rag, she scrubbed her body clean.

CHAPTER FIVE

HER NEW DUTIES became a part of the caravan's routine, no different from breaking camp or resting the horses at intervals. When Brandt judged her used to the routine, the four men became six. Sometimes he offered her during rest breaks, as a reward for work done well. Otherwise they kept her bound, and when the caravan passed near settlements, he ordered her gagged and hidden behind the pots in Ulf's covered wagon.

She lost track of the days, but she remembered other details. The curses the men used. The taste of their skin. The weight of their bodies atop hers. She remembered whether they took her fast and brutally, like Niko, or used her slowly, like Alarik Brandt.

"Open your mouth," Brandt said. "Make it soft, like a peach. Good."

Pretend, she told herself, opening up her mouth to his. Brandt's manner was different this night. He had ordered her to strip. Now he kissed her slowly, as a lover might, and ran his hands over her bare skin in a light caress.

Pretend.

Murmuring softly, Brandt kissed her throat, her shoulder, the crook of her elbow, the inside of her wrist. He'd unbuttoned his shirt; she saw a number of scars—a long jagged one near his shoulder, a semicircle of small ones like tooth marks above his left nipple. His rough gray hairs tickled her skin, and his mouth felt hot as he bent to suckle her breast. Slow. Insistent. He gave a groan and slid up to kiss her full on the mouth, inserting one hand between her thighs.

"Good," he whispered hoarsely. "Now do the same with your other mouth, wench. Makes it easier, eh? Almost feels good, right? Yes, now grip tight, tighter."

I chose him. I chose him.

She never knew why her body betrayed her—whether she had worked so hard to pretend that she had crossed an invisible boundary—but when Brandt slid his fingers inside her and caressed her with skill, she unexpectedly moaned in response.

Brandt smiled. "I knew you could. Now do it again."

That night he would not yield her to the next man until she had cried out for all to hear.

HE SET NEW demands on her and watched to see that Ilse complied. Yielding wasn't enough. Consent wasn't enough. He wanted her willing participation.

I can pretend anything, she told herself.

No matter how shameful the act, she never resisted, knowing that Brandt watched sometimes, when she coupled with the other men. His presence was like the night breeze upon her skin, or the salt taste in her mouth. With Brandt himself, she had entirely lost her defenses, it seemed, because when he caressed her, she moved, and when he entered her with his customary skill, the tightness in her belly relaxed into warmth. She had never meant to make a trade like this. She would have wept, except for Brandt's dark eyes that studied her so closely.

Four weeks passed. Ilse never saw Volker, except at a distance. Sometimes she caught Brenn glaring at her. She didn't blame him. She didn't blame any of the men. Not Ulf, who was always glad for his turn. Not the horse boys. Not even Niko, who liked it rough. Blame was too easy.

The fifth man for the night had just left. Ilse was wiping her face with a dirty cloth, thinking she had just one more obligation for the night, when a soft voice said, "My turn."

Brenn pointed from her to the blanket. She obeyed and lay back with her skirt pulled up. He unlaced his trousers and took her quickly, not bothering with kisses or talk, the way some did. When he finished, he rolled off to one side with a groan. "Alarik has plans," he whispered.

Ilse started. "What do you mean?"

"He says he's done with you. He wants the money your father offered."

"He can't," she whispered. "He promised."

"He will," Brenn insisted. "He'll hand you over to your father's agent in Donuth. He'll get a reward and be gone inside a week."

"My father will have him jailed."

Brenn shook his head. "He'll say he found you on the road. Niko will back him up. If you talk about whoring, Alarik can say you started it yourself."

"That's not true. I—"

"Ilse, everyone heard what you told Brandt. You did ask for it."

Cold swept through her. She had. By Lir's mercy she had asked Brandt to make her a whore.

I pretended too well.

Brenn pulled her close and kissed her on the mouth. "One more time," he murmured. "Pretend good for me, Ilse."

So Ilse slid her arms over his back and kissed him with feigned passion, whispering all the words Brandt had taught her. She moved her body in time with his, urging him with every caress to finish quickly. Only when his breath came ragged, and she knew he was on the point of his climax, did she turn her head away, too weary at last to pretend. There, just beyond the circle of fire-light, stood the scholar.

THE NEXT THREE days passed in a chill gray blur. The late autumn rains had commenced, a cold steady downpour that soaked their clothes and turned the hard-packed dirt road into sludge. Brandt's mood, never good, turned as foul as the weather. He drove the men harder, ordering longer marches. The horses slogged through the mud, heads down, but their progress slowed to a few miles each day. Campfires served only to make wet clothes into damp ones.

By nightfall of the fourth day, the rain had subsided to a heavy drizzle. Mist rose from the wet ground; above, a veil of clouds obscured the half moon. Ulf tried in vain to light his campfires and succeeded only in burning his fingers. The scholar used magic with greater luck, but the wet logs smoked more than they burned. In the end, Ulf handed out cold beef wrapped in flat bread.

Tired and miserable and damp, Ilse finished her meal and drank her coffee. It was bitter stuff, thickened with bark, and hardly warm enough to ward off the cold. All that was left of her was an emptiness, a pervading chill and damp, and not only from the rain. But if she thought too long on that, she found herself weeping helplessly, and so she would not let herself dwell on Brandt, or her condition, or how she had once hoped for freedom. Even when Brandt summoned her, she obeyed but could not bring herself to pre-tend. Another week in servitude remained to her. Then a term locked up in Donuth. Then her father. After that, she would be just another kind of prisoner.

Brandt leaned against a wagon. He grabbed Ilse's hair with one hand. With the other, he pushed down on her shoulder. She knelt and opened her mouth. She was used to this routine as well. Her mind wandered. She let it, wondering idly if Brandt would increase her duties next week, or if he had set a limit.

We want this one to last.

Brandt pulled her head back and looked down at her face. Firelight cast blue shadows over his eyes, making her think of the fiends in her grandmother's stories.

"You're daydreaming," he observed.

She licked her lips and suppressed a tremor. "I'm tired."

His free hand circled her throat, fingers resting lightly against her pulse. "From sitting all day?"

Nervously, she nodded.

Brandt studied her, running one thumb along her jaw. "Go to bed. It's a wet night. You can make it up in the morning."

Niko led her to her bedding and made her ropes fast, grumbling all the while that Brandt had cheated him and the others. "He says tomorrow," Niko said, half to himself. "But I know him. He'll start us early, damn it, and me without a turn in three days." He gave a last tug to the ropes, then tossed several blankets to her. "Keep warm for me, sweet."

Ilse wrapped herself in the blankets and lay down. The ground was cold, and the air tasted of winter. In Melnek, there would be snow on the streets and tracings of frost on the windowpanes. Her mother would have ordered the heavy curtains hung and the fires constantly lit throughout the family and servants wings. Home. Did they remember her? Was her father still searching? Was her grandmother alive?

"Dobrud'n," a man whispered. "Are you awake?"

She recognized the scholar's voice.

"I am," she whispered back in Károvín.

He squatted beside the front wagon wheel. "I heard what the boy told you. About Donuth and your father. I have something for you. Here."

Uncertain, Ilse reached toward him. Their hands met, and he laid a hard round object in her palm. It was rough and gritty, flat like a disk, with sharp edges—a stone, shaped into a cutting blade. Ilse detected traces of magic beneath its surface, calling up images and textures that reminded her of the scholar's hands and face and voice.

"Wait until moonset," he whispered. "Use it to cut your ropes. When you get past the perimeter, head east, then south. That should take you into Gallenz, into the valley and away from Donuth."

The valley was a week's ride from here. Did he mean to give her food and a tent?

It seemed he had thought out everything. "Dig a hole to keep warm at night. Cover yourself with leaves and dirt, if you have to. Look for pine nuts and groundnuts. Carrots and thistles and cranberries if you can find them. Drink from running streams."

He poured out a flood of details, things to remember, which foods to avoid and which to hunt for, how to build shelters and traps with just a knife and her own strength. Ilse listened hard, knowing she would forget the half of what he told her, but trying to remember just the same. In passing, she wondered where he had learned all these skills, or if he had read them in a book.

"Your best chance is to find a village," he said. "There have to be dozens in these hills. Beg for food. They won't refuse you, not these people. They know what it's like to starve. Once you reach the highway, you can go west—to Jassny, even Duenne."

"Not Duenne," she said quickly. Not with Alarik Brandt heading there. And surely her father would expect her to go to Duenne.

"East, then. Tiralien is closest. It's a big city. Girl like you can find work." He paused. "I'm sorry I did not come to you sooner. I— I didn't want to take a wrong chance and hurt you worse than before. No, that wasn't it. It was because—"

Because he was afraid. Just as Brenn had been afraid. As she was now.

"It doesn't matter," she whispered. "I understand. And thank you. Thank you, thank you, thank you."

He stopped her with a gesture. "Do not thank me. Please." Then his hand brushed her cheek. "You remind me of my sister," he murmured before he crept away.

ILSE WAITED UNTIL Ulf had banked the fire, and the guards had dispersed to their first watch. She would not forget herself this time. Gripping the stone blade between her knees, she rubbed the rope over the sharp edge. Back and forth. Back and forth. Her hands went numb from holding the rope taut, but she kept going. Once the watch changed. She paused until the new sentries had taken their posts and the old watch had retired, before resuming her work. Her wrists were bloody from pulling against the ropes, but she was nearly free. Just a few more strands.

The last strand snapped. Ilse, taken by surprise, pitched forward and nicked her chin on the blade. She pressed her hand against the cut. Her hand came away sticky. She wiped her chin again before it came home that she was free of her bonds.

Free.

Her chin stung, but she was grinning. The first victory was hers.

She wrapped her skirt around the knife and cut through the remaining ropes, then hid the stone in her boot. She rolled up the bulkiest blanket and draped a second one over it. It cost her something to give up the blankets, but unless someone checked, the guards would think her still asleep.

She crept from underneath the wagon. The trees were little more than dark blotches against the gray mist blanketing the camp. Nearby, the horses shifted about restlessly. The horse pickets lay toward the sunrise, she remembered. She crawled in that direction. There was a danger that Brandt had posted an extra watch over the horses, but the horses themselves made enough noise to cover hers. If she were quiet and quick . . .

A man coughed, not six feet away. "Damned rain."

Ilse froze. That was Niko's voice.

"Go back to your tent then," said Otto, one of the drivers.

"Not yet. Gimme another swallow."

She heard a gurgling, then Niko smacked his lips. "Ah. That's better. One more, and I'll go."

"You must want a headache."

"Already got one 'cause of the damned rain."

"You been sick a while. Did you catch something from the girl?"

"Nah. Gave her something else, though."

Otto wheezed with laughter. "Well, if you didn't give to her, then I did. If Brandt doesn't get her back to Papa soon—"

"Doesn't matter. Brandt's got it all worked out. Gods, she's a sweet fuck. I told Brandt to keep her. He says no, we can always get another one."

They both took another swig from the bottle. She was lucky about that—all the guards were drinking hard these past few days—either from boredom or bone-deep weariness, or just because they could not bear the endless damp and cold. Alarik Brandt's bitterest threats made no difference, except to force the guards to keep their liquor hidden.

Niko took one last drink, then shuffled away toward his tent. Otto remained by the horses. He was one of the rougher men. He'd pinch Ilse hard enough to leave bruises, and sometimes took her during rest stops, when Brandt wasn't looking. If he caught her . . .

Her heart beating fast and hard, Ilse edged around the pickets, toward a ridge of boulders that lay just beyond the camp circle. The going was difficult. The rain had stopped, but the ground was soggy, and she feared the squelching mud would give her away. Twice, she paused, thinking she heard footsteps or voices from the perimeter guards, but once she passed the latrines and the trash pit, Ilse breathed more easily. The land ahead was covered in mist, with trees appearing as vague dark lines that reached upward to the darker sky, veiled by clouds.

She glanced back to the camp. The campfire sent up a dull gleam from its coals, throwing one of the wagons into relief. She thought she could pick out Otto's figure, standing somewhat apart from the horses with his legs planted wide apart and his head thrown back, a misshapen shadow against the drifting fog.

She rose to her feet and started walking.

SHE WALKED UNTIL dawn, then dug a pit beneath a stand of oaks and buried herself. For just a moment, she breathed in the scent of dust and decay, a rich aroma like that of magic, before sleep overtook her. Nothing broke her rest until the midmorning sunlight filtered through the dirt and leaves. She jerked awake with a cry, half-forgetting what had happened.

No Brandt. No bonds or guards. She was free.

And alone.

Once she might have feared the solitude, but now . . .

I laugh and hear its echo in my heart.

Ilse set off with Tanja Duhr's poem running through her thoughts. She did not stop until she encountered a running stream, where she drank until her stomach was swollen. The scholar's advice remained vividly clear, but she had no idea how to find pine nuts or groundnuts, or where carrots and thistles grew. She told herself stories as she walked to distract herself from the ache in her stomach.

Her stubbornness lasted until late afternoon, when her legs collapsed beneath her. Ilse propped herself against a stump, staring blankly at the trees around her. *Pine nuts,* she thought. She swept the ground. Her trembling hands met needles and pinecones and the typical detritus of a forest floor. Wherever pine nuts were to be found, they weren't here.

Later, she wasn't sure how, she stood up and walked on. The forest gave way to a meadow—she had climbed up a ridge without knowing it—and from here she could see the land falling away to the north and west. Somewhere out there, Brandt and his caravan were climbing through the hills toward the Gallenz River and its highway.

It was cranberries she found first, a tangle of bushes half-hidden under a boulder. They were dried and bitter to the point of making her ill. She ate them anyway. In the same field, she discovered rosebushes from which she plucked the hips to eat raw. Gradually, she learned to see more provender in the fields and underbrush. Wintergreen grew in the pine forests, wild onions on the open slopes. Pine nuts and grapes, raspberries and thistles. There were days she went hungry, but she always gathered enough to survive.

For ten days, she marched through the empty wilderness. The only voice she heard was her own, when she sang or wondered aloud. At first she reveled in her isolation, but when the nights turned cold, and her throat ached fiercely, she wondered if she would ever reach a village, or if she had accidentally wandered off the map of the known world. She could die of hunger or sickness or accident, she realized with a sudden pang, and no one would know.

On the morning of the eleventh day, she stopped. Ahead, a dull gray stone tower poked through the blue-green expanse of pines. A village at last?

"Hello?" she called.

No answer, except for a bird rousted from the brush. Cautiously Ilse approached the building. It was large, built of rough-cut logs and covered with creeping vines. Her first excitement faded when she realized it was not part of a larger village.

She edged closer, ready to bolt if necessary. Someone had dug a fire pit in the yard. It was cold, its ashes scattered with only a few charred sticks at the bottom. Closer to the lodge, she found a broken leash and a rusted knife, its blade chipped but still sharp. She picked that up, and holding it blade out, she pushed the door open. "Hello?"

No one answered. She ventured inside.

It was a hunting lodge, with just a single room and a stone-and-mud chimney. A few benches stood off to one side; straw pallets lay beside the empty fireplace. Most likely the owners used it in the autumn and winter, but visitors had come fairly recently—she found a stack of leftover firewood, three metal pans stacked in one corner, a net hanging from the rafters, with a cache of shriveled onions and smoked beef. Spare blankets and a carrying satchel had been stowed in one corner. It was the mantel above the fireplace that yielded the most valuable treasure.

A tinderbox.

She laughed, a breathy soundless laugh. With this she could boil water, brew hot tea, scrub herself clean. She could get *warm.*

That night, she built a fire and roasted slices of meat for her supper. Once she filled her stomach, she chopped up more meat and the onions, and set that mixture to simmer in the coals. She washed out another pan and brewed tea from raspberry leaves.

The night was fair, the moon full, and the skies clear. Ilse gazed upward into the violet expanse as the stars winked into life. "Ei rûf ane gôtter," she whispered.

At her words, the air stirred, and a green scent, like that of pines, drifted past her face. She thought of the nameless scholar who had painted her fingers with magic. She hoped he was safe and wished him well.

CHAPTER SIX

ILSE STAYED THREE days in the lodge. She slept, she foraged, she spent hours staring across the undulating hills, until her muscles unknotted, and the ache in her throat faded. But she knew she could not remain here through winter, and so, reluctantly, she packed her newly acquired gear into the satchel, along with blankets and as much food as she could gather, and moved on.

She resumed her steady march through the hills, which changed over the miles from pines to stands of oak and beech, with their leaves a shimmering mass of scarlet and incandescent yellow. The autumn days were bright and clear, but cold. Ilse wrapped the blanket around her shoulders, and bent her head against the sudden bursts of wind, which plucked the leaves and sent them spinning round her.

By the end of two weeks, she came to the southern edge of the hills. Below, the land fell away in pleats and folds toward a broad sluggish river—the Gallenz River. To the east, she could make out a golden blur. That had to be the port city Tiralien. Beyond it lay the dark blue band of Keriss Bay, whose waters also touched Melnek's docks and quays.

Within the day, Ilse reached the highway beside the river and turned east. Six more days to houses and inns, she told herself. Six days to people and work and living inside. People. It had been a month since she'd spoken with another human being. The thought made her mouth turn dry.

She had the road to herself for a day. Then, late the next morning, Ilse heard the tramp of footsteps behind her, then grunts and squeals. She plunged into the brush and lay still, her breath coming fast. It was a drover, herding swine, nothing more. Once he passed, she retook the road, cursing herself for being a coward, but she did the same when a caravan of mules passed, and again, to avoid a farmer's wagon.

On the third morning, she stopped to soak her sore feet in the river. One toe had a new blister. The heel was bruised from where she stepped on a rock. She would have to stuff more grass into her disintegrating boots. She had started to pluck some, when she heard a harness jingle. Ilse snatched up her boots and satchel, ready to dart across the road—

No.

She would not run away.

Ilse sat down by the riverbank, taking quick looks to the side as the two wagons approached. The horses were dusty and shaggy and broad-chested; they trudged steadily as though plowing fields, head down. Three men, and a woman. Farmers, most likely. None of them were young. It was the woman who held the reins of the lead wagon. Like the men, she wore a patched brown tunic and loose trousers, tucked into old scuffed boots. A yellow scarf covered her hair, making her square face stand out. From time to time, she tossed back a comment to her companions in the other wagon. Ilse's pulse beat quickly, but she continued to stuff grass into her boots.

A rattling snort made her jump. It was the lead horse, leaning toward her as though to nip.

"Hey, Graysmoke." Reins slapped against the horse's flanks, bringing out another snort, and a shake of its head. "None of that." Then, "Did that monster hurt you?"

Ilse shook her head. She edged back from Graysmoke, who eyed her from beneath his shaggy gray forelock. The woman slapped the reins again. The horse sidled, then took a few reluctant steps forward. "Stupid horse," the woman muttered.

"What is it?" called a man from the second wagon.

"A girl," the woman said. "Graysmoke playing his tricks." She turned her attention back to Ilse. Narrow black eyes took in Ilse's dirt-stained clothing, the worn-out boots with burst seams, the satchel and blanket. But all she said was, "You look tired, sweet."

"I'm . . . I'm fine," Ilse said. Her voice sounded rusty. "He just startled me."

The woman tilted her head. A smile sent creases spreading outward from her eyes. "Glad to hear that. Where are you going? Tiralien? Or one of the little towns betwixt here and there?"

"Tiralien."

"Want a ride?"

Ilse shook her head. "I've no money."

"Neither do I. I'm going to Tiralien to get some. Me and the family, that is. You can ride a ways in our wagon—we've room enough for one skinny girl. Besides, you look as though you walked clear from the westlands. My name's Nela, if you want to know. Those are my cousins, Gregor and Maxi and Uwe. What's yours?"

"Ilse. They call me Ilse."

Nela nodded. "Pretty name. So, will you come along with us? We have some sandwiches and ale, if that makes a difference."

Kindness. Kindness and food. And a ride. Overcome by their generosity, she almost couldn't speak at first. "I'd like that. Thank you."

Nela leaned down and held out a rough hand, to help her into the wagon. "Gregor, she's starving. Give her your sandwich. You've already had four."

"I was hungry," Gregor protested, but he handed her the sandwich with a wink and a smile.

Ilse bit into the sandwich and nearly cried with delight. Smoked beef, soaked in oil and vinegar and smothered in cheese. It was the most she had eaten at one time in a month. While she ate, she listened to the drivers talking among themselves as they discussed where they might eat supper that night, if Becker's tavern still served that special autumn wine, and if Maxi's brother might join the business next year. The caravan was small, its two wagons packed with crates that smelled strongly of vinegar and straw.

"We take the spoiled grapes from summer and turn them into vinegar," Nela told her. "The fish markets like it for pickling."

To their questions, she explained that her parents had died, and her aunt was unable to keep her. She was looking for work. "Any kind," she said. "I don't like begging."

"What were you thinking of?" Nela asked. "Work, I mean."

"Chambermaid," Ilse said. "Or helping in kitchens. Whatever I can find."

Nela gave her a long considering look, but said nothing. The others offered names of families she might apply to, though they had no guarantees. Business was off, they said, what with taxes and gossip about war with Károví.

It was late afternoon before they reached the city gates. Tiralien was a big city—far larger than Melnek—spreading across both riverbanks and climbing some distance into the nearby hills. As they waited in the queue of wagons, Ilse listened to the drivers trading news. It was more of what she had heard in Melnek—ships practicing maneuvers along the coast, troops moving along Károví's border in response, and the endless speculation of what next year might bring for crops and profits and trade.

Once through the gates, Nela and her cousins guided the wagons across the main square to a fountain, where Ilse climbed down from her seat. "Thank you," she said, hoisting her bundle over her shoulder.

Nela shrugged. "You made the trip shorter. Are you sure you won't stay with us? We're here a few days at least."

Ilse shook her head. She'd heard how they were sleeping in the yard with their horses and wagons. There wouldn't be room enough for another person, no matter how small. "You've done me favors enough. I can manage."

Gregor grinned. "I bet you can. Remember what I said about the fish markets. Talk to Uwe's brother-in-law. He might want someone for this and that."

"Or the inn near Becker's tavern," Uwe said. "They always need chambermaids."

Ilse accepted one last gift of a sandwich, then made her way through the crowds toward a large avenue that branched from the square and led east. Just as Gregor told her, she came to a large plaza with a wide opening at the opposite end that marked the avenue's continuation. Several smaller lanes and alleys branched away at various other points. Ilse took the third lane to her right. Here the crowds thinned out as the markets gave way to government offices and counting houses, most of which looked deserted.

Across the square. Down a broad avenue. Left into a narrower lane. Ilse counted five cross streets to her next turning, only to discover the lane blocked by a gate. She took the next one, hoping to find a cross street, but that one took an unexpected detour in the opposite direction. Before she realized it, she had come to a small courtyard lined with taverns and wine shops. Several men and women leaned against the walls, drinking from bottles and playing dice. She paused, uncertain.

"Hey, darling." One man looked up from the game. "You're new. Come with me and we'll have a drink."

Ilse stepped back. "I'm not thirsty. Thank you."

"Oh, a fine-talking girl." He tried to kiss her.

Ilse pushed him away. "I said no."

"Leave her alone," said a round-faced woman with hair loose about her shoulders. She slid between Ilse and the man, and slung an arm around Ilse's neck. "Come with me, girl, and I'll show you how it works on the streets."

"Watch out, girl. Etta's got quick fingers."

Etta winked. "You're just jealous."

Ilse twisted away from Etta. Etta grabbed for Ilse's arm, but caught hold of her satchel. Before Ilse could wrestle it back, the man tried to snake his arm around her waist. He was laughing, Etta was shrieking, the rest of the crowd urged them to fight. Ilse wormed free of them both and pelted back down the lane, her satchel flapping against her legs. She heard shouts and laughter, Etta's high-pitched squeals. A pot tumbled from the satchel, bouncing and rattling over the stones. Another. Ilse did not dare to stop. She veered into the next alley, which led south and east until it met a wooden fence. Dead end.

She fell to her knees, breathing hard. They would have robbed her. Taken her worn-out blankets. Or worse.

Gradually her breathing slowed. She had lost at least one pot, she remembered. With trembling hands, she checked through her possessions. Worse and worse. The blankets, tinderbox, and knife were gone, too. And Gregor's sandwich. All she had left were a dented pan and a waterskin.

She wiped tears of frustration from her eyes. Grit and soot streaked her hands. Now what could she do? She ought to find her way back to the main thoroughfare. If she hurried, she might find Becker's tavern and the inns around it. But the skies were darkening, her clothes were filthy, and she didn't think she could face an interview tonight.

She found a drier patch of ground, where the fence tilted inward. The satchel helped only a little. Cold mud soaked into her skirt, and the heavy salt tang mixed with the reek of urine. Ilse curled into a tight ball and closed her eyes. "Ei rûf ane gôtter," she whispered. A few more words came back to her. "Komen mir de strôm.

The air thickened around her. A whiff of green, like the rich tang of pine, washed away the alleyway's stinks, leaving only its own fresh scent, reminding her of the fresh cold winds of Melnek, blowing down from the mountains. For once, the memory of home did not hurt. Gradually her muscles unlocked, and the terror bled away. She felt as though a vast hand cupped her inside it, keeping her safe. *Tomorrow*, she thought. *Tomorrow I will find work. And a home. I will make my own life.*

Overhead, a pigeon cooed. A dog whined, then fell silent. With the sky turning dark, and a breeze fingering her hair, she slept.

SHE WOKE TO the early-morning sunlight. Rain had fallen during the night, and gray clouds promised more that morning. Ilse stood and brushed the mud from her clothes. Working by feel, she untied her braid and worked out the tangles, then plaited it neatly. After some consideration, she decided to abandon her satchel and the few remaining items it contained. It would only make her look shabbier than she already did.

Several streets over, she came upon a market square with a fountain. She dunked her head in the fountain and splashed more water over her face. Yesterday's last meal with Nela and her cousins was only a memory, and she felt the first growl of hunger. Perhaps a new employer would feed her before he set her to work.

First she had to find the places Gregor and Nela named. The market square was nearly empty, but a few vendors were already at work setting up their stalls. One, an older man dressed in a worn jersey and stained trousers, eyed Ilse suspiciously as she approached. "Don't want any," he said gruffly, and turned away, dismissing her presence.

Ilse paused, her cheeks going hot. "I'm not what you think."

The man shrugged and continued to arrange his stacks of baskets and cups and bowls. The baskets were woven from reeds; the cups and bowls were carved from a dark wood. Plain wares for plain folks.

She took a deep breath. "Please. I'm looking for work. But I'm a stranger to the city, and I've lost my way. Could you help me?"

The man stared at her, hands on hips. "Long way from home?"

She nodded.

"What about family?"

"Not anymore."

"What kind of work?"

His voice had lost its first hard edge. She met his gaze, which was neutral. "Kitchen work, scrubbing floors, anything," she said. "I've some places to look, but no guarantees."

He regarded her silently. She read doubt in his expression, but all he finally said was, "You're a pretty girl, even underneath that dirt. Maybe too pretty. And you come from money—I can tell by your speech."

"Why should that matter? I need the work."

"I believe you. But others might not. They might think what I did."

She made a helpless gesture. "It's a chance I have to take."

In the end, he gave her a roll from his breakfast and directions to Becker's tavern. He also told her where to find Tiralien's better neighborhoods. "If you don't have luck with the taverns, try the mansions near the governor's palace. They always want new hands in the kitchen or stables."

Within the hour she found the place. She peeked inside, where two girls were sweeping the floors, supervised by a dull-faced older woman. No customers. No sign of Nela or her cousins. Disappointed, Ilse withdrew and continued to the inn Gregor had mentioned.

She came inside the entryway, treading softly. A tall gray-haired man popped out from a side room. "Who are you? What do you want here?"

"I was looking for work. I heard you wanted a chambermaid."

The man surveyed her clothes and face. He shook his head. "Sorry, but you won't do."

She drew a sharp breath at his tone. "Why not?"

"For any number of reasons, girl, but first because you aren't a chambermaid—I can tell by the way you talk. Besides," he pointed at her clothes, grimacing, "I run a clean inn, not a pigsty."

Ilse rubbed her hands over her skirt. "I'll work hard."

"Maybe. Maybe not. I can't take the chance."

It was no different from any obstacle she had encountered in the wilderness, she told herself, after he shooed her out the door. Or those first days without food or warmth. She glanced around and saw the man watching her through the half-open shutters. He made a pointing gesture: *go*.

More shops and inns lined the street. She tried them all. Each time, she met with a rebuff. Too young, said one. Too dirty, said a few others. "You've no experience and it shows," said one grim-faced woman. "First thing I know, you'll get tired of the work and flirt with the men. One of them will tumble you. I've seen it happen too many times. Makes a bad impression with some of the customers."

By late morning she had retraced her steps to Becker's tavern. Drovers and sailors and a few guardsmen were drinking ale in the common room. Serving girls threaded between the tables, delivering platters of roasted meats, grilled fish steaks, and stewed vegetables. Ilse ventured inside until she came to one of the girls. "May I speak with your mistress?" she asked.

The girl looked her up and down. "Back in the kitchen."

Ilse made her way into the kitchen where a red-faced woman was berating another woman and waving a wooden ladle to make her points. At Ilse's approach, she broke off and rounded on Ilse. "No beggars. Out. Out of my kitchen."

"But I—"

"Out." She seized Ilse by the arm and dragged her through the kitchen to the back door, where she shoved her into the alley. "And stay away."

Ilse rubbed her hands over her face. Even here in the alleyway, she could smell cooked meat and spices and bread from the kitchen.

I can be a scullion. I can scrub floors and tables. I can carry out trash.

All the words she meant to say—meaningless if no one let her speak.

She left the wharf district for the wealthy neighborhoods the vendor had suggested, but Tiralien's various quarters were like a patchwork quilt— ordinary ones alternated with finer ones—and she spent the afternoon wandering through streets and knocking on back doors. A dozen times over, she began with her speech, "Please, I just came from the country, and I'm looking for work. Do you have anything—anything at all?"

The rebuffs continued. Some were kind, but most were blunt. "You aren't country-bred," they said. "You're lying already. Get out."

She changed her story, using as much of the truth as she dared. "I lost all my money. I need work. Please."

"Work?" said one chambermaid. "You don't sound like you need work—not with that accent. We don't need spoiled brats, even if you have learned to stink."

At the last house, the cook gave her bread and warm tea, though she refused to let her inside because she had just mopped the kitchen floor. "We're not a big house," she said. "We don't have room for more help. Have you tried Sedlhouf quarter? It's where the rich merchants live."

Ilse shook her head. "I don't know. I tried. Everywhere, I thought."

The woman smiled briefly. "For how long?"

"A day."

"Not so long, except when you're hungry. There's more houses in Tiralien, some of them very fine." She paused and studied Ilse's face. Her own was plump, a genial, comfortable face. "You're from up north," she said.

"Melnek."

"Thought as much. And you ran away. How did you get this far?"

Ilse swallowed with difficulty. Her throat hurt; her head felt heavy. "With a caravan part of the way. Walked the rest."

"Ah. Risky, coming all those miles alone. Why did you leave the caravan?"

"They robbed me," she whispered. "They took . . . everything. Or I gave it to them. Does it matter?"

"I see," said the cook. "You can't go back, then. But I can't give you a place here, not for pity nor praise. Master wouldn't like it."

Ilse spent the second night behind a warehouse, huddled inside an empty barrel that smelled of hops. She slept fitfully. In the morning, she scrubbed her hands and face again in an ice-cold fountain. The wind blew hard, buffeting her as it whirled around the plaza. A passing tinker took pity on Ilse, and gave her a swallow from his wine jug and a bite from his bread loaf. "Lost?" he said.

She nodded. The wine churned inside her empty stomach. "I'm looking for work. I can work hard."

He eyed her, his expression guarded. "Might be difficult."

A panicky laugh rose up in her throat. Ilse wanted to say she knew what difficult was, but she suppressed the laugh and the reply.

Her only other food that day was a discarded apple core. She gnawed it to the bitter seeds, then licked her fingers clean, begrudging every drop of juice that escaped. She found no more kind cooks, willing to part with a square of bread. She stank, said the scullions. They didn't need vagrants under the roof, said the housemaids. One stable boy tried to embrace her. Ilse slapped him and fled, while he shouted curses after her.

Throughout the next week, she begged, she stole. She lived from hour to hour, taking shelter in alleys and doorways. More than once, she thought about leaving Tiralien and returning to the wilderness. But winter had arrived, and whatever provender she had lived on before would be gone. So she remained, drifting from quarter to quarter, searching out scraps of food by day and shelter for the night. She stopped asking for employment—planning beyond the next day had become too difficult.

The tenth day found her wandering through a new quarter, on the northern side of Tiralien. The watch had rousted her a few hours before, and she had only escaped by clambering through a broken fence. Her flight had taken her into this new district, filled with shops selling fine silks, jewels, and porcelain figures—things of beauty she had once loved, but which could not feed her.

Ilse stumbled and fell to her knees. Her head spun. Her vision blurred. She needed food or she would die soon. A day or two, no longer. All because she had panicked and fled her father's house. Because she had trusted without reason. Because she was a foolish girl without any knowledge of the world.

I could have stayed in Melnek. I could have pretended with Theodr Galt. I could have—

She broke off those thoughts with a cry. Never. She could never have pretended with Theodr Galt. Even if she had tried, he would have guessed the truth. He would have punished her the way he must have punished Marina Bartos. Worse, because a wife could never escape, and if she were to try, Galt would hunt her down. Better to die now, free, than to have killed her soul outright. Ilse lurched to her feet and continued.

The street ended in a large plaza. Near the center of the square stood a fountain, its waters gleaming blue and white beneath the full moon. Beyond it, everything was dark. She would find no shelter here. Ilse turned, uncertain where to go next, when she heard a muttered curse. A second voice, louder, said something about who would get the larger share. Peering into the shadows, she saw half a dozen figures beneath the lee of a large building. The breeze shifted, carrying a whiff of smoked beef to her.

Her mouth watered. She took a step forward into the moonlit square. It was a gang of boys. She'd seen them around before, quarrelsome, laughing, rude. If they would just give her a mouthful. Just one. She would do anything, anything at all for a taste of that beef.

She must have spoken, or made a sound, because one boy jerked up his head in surprise. He hissed and tugged at another boy's arm. The other boy laughed. "It's the new whore. Whatcha want, girl?"

"Food," Ilse whispered. "I'm so hungry."

"Food, huh. How much?"

"Look at her. She's got no coins."

"Yeah, but maybe she's got something else."

Ilse watched as the gang spread out in a semicircle. If she could only be sure they would give her a few bites of meat afterward.

It's a favor, wench. Say the word.

A trade.

Four a night. Six when she learns the trade.

No. I won't. Not again.

She spun around, but the gang was upon her in moments. They dragged her into the nearest alley. She fought back, screaming and kicking and biting. One boy punched her in the face. She tasted blood, choked, and lashed out with another kick. Someone grabbed her ankle. She twisted around. A blow to her throat. A kick to her belly. Her vision went dark.

" 'S the watch. Run!"

The boys scattered. Ilse rolled onto her knees, her stomach heaving. Through a red haze, she glimpsed several tall figures striding toward her.

"Damned trash. What have they got?"

"A girl."

"We better take her in. Maybe she's part of the gang."

Ilse staggered to her feet and ran.

"Stop!" one of the guards called out.

Ilse dodged around the next corner, into a covered street. A hot pain stabbed at her belly. Her stomach lurched, and she pitched forward onto her hands and knees. *Must get away. Must not let them catch me.* The boys would beat her. The watch would lock her in prison, send her back to her father. She crawled onward, dimly aware that she had entered a maze of alleys and narrow lanes. The sharp scent of manure filled the air, mixed with the sweeter scent of fresh hay. Somewhere behind the fences, a horse nickered loudly. She came to an open gate and crawled through it into the lane beyond.

Trees and gardens stretched out before her. Beyond them, she saw tall brick walls, a courtyard with a fountain, and lighted windows. A woman's husky voice floated from one open window, rising in counterpoint to a man's deeper laugh. Soft strains of music sounded from another window. A rich family's house, she thought. Not a place for her.

She hauled herself upright and stumbled onward. Step. Pause. Press hand over her stomach. Door looming to her right. Another spasm took her. She retched and fell over. Her head thumped against the door. "Please, oh please. Oh please." She hardly knew what she was begging for. Another chance. A different future. The wisdom to make better choices.

Her heart tripped and raced forward. The quarter and hour bells rang and rang again, echoing inside her head. Voices of the city, she thought. Melnek had a solemn voice. Practical dutiful Melnek. Tiralien. Fair and bright and deceptive, offering no shelter. Duenne . . .

There was a commotion behind her. Loud voices called out. Someone was coming for her. Before they reached her, a latch clicked, and the door swung open. A pair of strong arms caught Ilse before her head hit the stone tiles.

"I'm sorry I left," she mumbled, thinking in her confusion Alarik Brandt had found her again. "I'll do what you want now."

She pulled up her skirt and reached for her new partner. Her hands encountered a smooth cheek. She stopped in confusion. A woman?

The person gently caught her by the wrist. "That's not necessary. Here, let me bring you inside."

It was a woman's contralto voice. But it was a man who gathered her into his arms—a large man with a broad chest and muscled arms, who smelled of wood smoke and cedarwood and the unmistakable scent of a man's spending.

The man did not touch her breasts or mouth. Instead he lifted her gently and stood. His shirt had parted, and her cheek rested against a smooth expanse of warm skin. No hair, not even as much as Volker's wispy fuzz.

He carried her down a hallway. Music filtered through the walls. Laughter. Then she heard another man's voice, deeper and rougher, asking questions. Her rescuer answered softly, something about fetching Hedda. Footsteps came and went. Eventually the man stopped walking and laid her on a soft, yielding mattress. A hand brushed her cheek, wiping away the tears she hadn't noticed before. From his tone, he was asking her questions, but Ilse couldn't hear much above the roaring in her ears.

"Please help me," she whispered.

"I will. I promise."

Again that voice, balanced between male and female. Ilse tried again to focus on her rescuer's face. She saw large golden eyes, inches from hers, and an abundance of dark hair. Then her vision blurred, and she slipped into darkness.

HOURS LATER SHE woke to find herself lying beneath thick cotton blankets. Someone had stripped away her bloody clothes, bathed her, dressed her in a clean warm shift, and bound rags between her legs. Her hair had been brushed smooth and lay loose over the pillow. Though her body still ached from scalp to foot, it was a dull faraway ache.

A figure approached her bed—a stout woman, with skin so black, the lamplight hardly made a difference. The woman bent over Ilse and touched her throat. She looked old, her face creased and scored by wrinkles. Silver glinted in her dark cloud of hair, and her hands smelled of magic. She studied Ilse through slitted eyes.

"Is she awake?" said another voice, whose fluting tones sounded familiar.

"Yes, and she's resisting my spells," the woman said. "Not good."

"Why not, Mistress Hedda? Resisting means she has the strength to live."

At this comment the woman laughed softly. "You would argue with Toc himself, my lord, wouldn't you? Yes, it means she has enough fight to survive."

The second person came into the circle of lamplight and stood next to the bed. It was a man, with long dark hair, casually tied back with a ribbon, and skin the color of finely drawn honey. He wore loose clothing, drifting in swathes of jewel-bright colors around his body.

Ilse opened her mouth; nothing came out except a scratchy whisper.

"Hush." Mistress Hedda brushed her fingers over Ilse's damp forehead. She spoke again, and the green scent intensified, causing the pain to recede.

"She will live," she said, as though answering an earlier question. "Despite the ill-usage. Despite losing the child."

Child?

Ilse struggled to sit up. Two pairs of hands caught her and pressed her gently back against the pillows. She caught a whiff of cedarwood before the man withdrew.

"Now you've distressed her. She must not have known."

"Impossible not to know, my lord. She was nearly two months gone—"

"Hush, I said."

A long stiff silence followed. Then the woman cleared her throat. "My apologies, my lord. So you wish her healed?"

"Of course."

"A stranger, my lord?"

The man made an impatient noise. "I found the girl outside my house and brought her inside. You would do the same."

Ilse listened as well as she could. She heard doubt in the woman's voice. The man's voice, so strange to her ear, was much harder to read. Cool and controlled, with undercurrents she could not identify.

Mistress Hedda laid her palm against Ilse's cheek. Ilse leaned against her warm hand and heard the woman's soft intake of breath. "She's a trusting girl," Mistress Hedda said. "Too trusting."

"Obviously." He said it without sarcasm, his tone thoughtful.

Their conversation dropped into a low murmur. Ilse wished she could hear more, but at her first restless movement, Mistress Hedda broke off and returned to her side. With another spell, she sent Ilse into a deep sleep, a sleep without dreams or whispers that did not break until morning.

CHAPTER SEVEN

SHE WOKE TO bells ringing from a nearby tower. Four peals, late afternoon. Sunlight poured through the windows of the small room where she lay. A cool fresh breeze stirred the room's silken tapestries; it carried a strong salt tang mixed with earth and changing leaves.

Her thoughts drifted from one hazy memory to the next. Starvation. Moonlight in the square. The boys' attack. Running from the watch. The sharp pains in her belly. A strange high voice. An old woman speaking magic words. And then a whispered conversation.

She lost the child.

She must not have known.

How could she not know?

Suddenly awake, Ilse caught her breath. How could she know?

She tried to recall her last bleeding. There'd been one shortly after she made her bargain with Alarik Brandt. The men hadn't cared. Some liked it better. Her skin growing colder, she found she could not remember another since.

Hot tears spilled over her cheeks. Stupid. Crying for the bastard get of three dozen men. Or was she really crying for herself?

The bellsong faded away. Gradually other sounds intruded on her notice. Crows chattering outside her window. The rattle of wings as they took flight. Someone in the corridor, humming softly to herself.

The door opened and a young woman, still humming, backed into the room. Her dark blue gown swirled around her legs as she turned and set a tray on the bedside table. She smiled at Ilse. "I'm glad to find you awake. It's long past time for a meal."

Her face was round and pleasant, her skin dusky brown, and she wore her hair sensibly pulled back into a tight braid. The sight of such friendliness and competence threatened to bring back Ilse's senseless tears. She swallowed them back. "I'm not hungry."

The young woman poured out a cup of tea. "Drink, then. It helps ease the pain."

Gently she helped Ilse to sit up, then plumped the pillows and held the cup to Ilse's lips. Tart and black, laced with willow extract and sweetened with honey.

"Now to eat." The young woman fed Ilse steaming mash, flavored with cinnamon and fresh apples. Summer fruits in winter—most likely shipped from southern lands or grown by magic. She had come to a wealthy household, if they did not stint at such luxuries.

"You're nothing but bones and twigs," the young woman observed. "Lord Kosenmark said to feed you well so you don't starve before the medicine takes hold."

"I won't starve."

The young woman flashed a smile. "And Mistress Hedda said you were stubborn. That's good. That means you'll get better, faster. My name's Kathe, by the way. Now to finish off a couple more spoonfuls."

Before Ilse knew it, Kathe had fed her the rest of the mash, then coaxed her into drinking another cup of tea. This time, Ilse managed to hold the cup herself.

"You look better," Kathe said thoughtfully. "Hot food—lots of it—and sleep. Another visit from Mistress Hedda, and you'll be dancing."

"That," said another voice, "is not *quite* what Mistress Hedda said."

A tall man dressed in dark blue silks leaned against the door frame. Ilse recognized him at once—it was Lord Kosenmark, the one with the ambiguous voice. "You may go," he said to Kathe as he came into the room. "Leave the tea, in case she wants more."

Kathe curtsied and retreated from the room. Lord Kosenmark fetched a chair and sat next to Ilse's bed. He was a handsome man with his honey-brown skin and full mobile mouth. When he leaned close and laid a hand against her forehead a whiff of his scent came to her, warm and personal.

Kosenmark said something under his breath. Warmth flowed outward from his hand, and her tense muscles unlocked. He smoothed a strand of hair from her face—a light, impersonal gesture. "Better?" he asked.

She nodded. He knew magic. Why then had he called in a healer?

"You must have some questions."

"Too many to ask, my lord."

He smiled. "Fair enough. Well, to save you the effort of speaking, I will offer you a handful of answers. You have a place here until your health mends. After that, I can offer you work, if you like. Wages, room, and board. We'll discuss particulars once you've recovered."

She tried to detect any hidden demands behind his offer. Though she heard none, but then, she hadn't with Alarik Brandt. "Thank you, my lord."

Kosenmark tilted his head. "I hear so many contradictory things in that cool and proper tone. For one, you do not trust me."

Because I trusted too easily before.

He must have guessed some of what she thought, because he said, "Never mind about it for now. You owe me nothing, child. Not even gratitude. Can you accept that?"

He expected an answer this time. "Yes, my lord."

"But you are still uneasy. Why?"

"Because you have no reason to help me."

He sighed. "Then think of it as charity, if you like. Do you have any more questions?"

Ilse shook her head.

"Now that is untrue," he said. "I see a hundred lurking behind your eyes."

"No more than you have questions for me, my lord. And yet you have not asked them."

At that, his mouth puckered, and she saw laughter in those golden eyes. "You are observant. And stubborn, as Mistress Hedda observed. Yes, I have questions. I shall not ask them, however, because I doubt you would answer."

Laughter with a knife's edge, she thought. The phrase sounded like a quote, but she couldn't remember the poem, or even if it came from a poem.

"If you asked me, I would answer you honestly," she said.

He was still studying her with that same expression. "Perhaps you would indeed."

ILSE SPENT THE first week confined to bed. She slept, waking for visits from Mistress Hedda, who came to renew her spells, or when Kathe fed Ilse the willow syrup and other concoctions Mistress Hedda had prepared. It was a strange house she had come to. Mornings were always quiet. Afternoons brought the muffled sounds of chambermaids at work, but it wasn't until night that the house woke, with laughter and more voices and music drifting up from the rooms below.

The second week, Ilse made a slow shuffling circuit of her room. Within a few days, she could walk unaided down the corridor. She spent her mornings sitting on a sunny terrace by the house's formal gardens, wrapped in blankets. Other houses were just visible above the trees and stone walls—dark red and copper roofs, chimneys, and farther off, a bell tower. Once or twice, she thought of home. Of Klara and her grandmother. She winced away from those memories, as from a still-tender wound. She wanted more time—months and years—before she could think upon them with any clarity.

As for today, and this strange new house . . . Well, there, too, she found herself unable to dwell upon anything more than the small surface details. The transparent sunlight of winter. The bittersweet flavor of the tea Kathe brought her. The scent of soap and sweet herbs she smelled on her pillow. Luck had brought her to Lord Kosenmark's doorstep. His kindness had rescued her from death. What came next, she had no idea. It was enough to sit quietly and let her body mend.

Kathe sometimes joined Ilse on the terrace, when her duties permitted. Ilse soon learned that Kathe's mother was Lord Kosenmark's chief cook and that Kathe was her mother's assistant. Mother and daughter had worked together for a household in Duenne before coming east to serve Lord Kosenmark, and Kathe told Ilse stories about those years, bright amusing tales that featured some of Veraene's most famous names. But for all Kathe chattered, she told Ilse nothing about this particular house, or about Lord Kosenmark.

One morning, at the end of the month, Mistress Hedda announced that Ilse was cured. Or mostly cured. "You are both young and lucky. Mostly lucky."

She poured out a thick black concoction and muttered a few words, before handing the mug to Ilse. "Drink all of it."

Ilse pinched her nose shut and drank the medicine down. In spite of the strong taste, her stomach settled immediately. A moment later, her skin tingled with warmth. "What is it for?"

"Cleansing your blood," Mistress Hedda said shortly. "If I were one of the old mage-surgeons, I'd tell you that it purges your soul in preparation for magic. Myself, I call it a strengthener. Whatever its name, you will need it for your interview with Lord Kosenmark today."

Ilse set the mug down quickly. "Today?"

"Yes, today. What's the matter? Does he frighten you?"

"Yes." She watched in silence while Mistress Hedda repacked her medicines and closed the box. "Do you trust him?"

Mistress Hedda pursed her lips. "Mostly. He's a fair man. Ah, here is Kathe, who will give you a better picture than I can. I must go to my other patients."

Kathe had brought Ilse a stack of neatly folded clothes. "We have time enough to make you presentable," she said, laying out skirts and smocks and stockings. "Luckily, we had plenty in stores."

Skirt and smock were made of dark brown cotton, and the smock had a high neckline that reminded Ilse of the uniforms worn by maids in her father's household. Ilse dressed quickly, wondering if the new clothes meant Lord Kosenmark would hire her. She had not seen him once since that first day.

You owe me nothing, he had said.

Or had she misremembered that unsettling conversation?

Once she was presentable, Kathe led Ilse down the familiar corridor, then through a sunny parlor and into a new wing to a stairwell. Up they went, three flights of stairs, past small windows, through which Ilse glimpsed more formal gardens and the stables beyond. At the top, the stairs opened onto a broad landing with a high narrow window facing north. Opposite the stairs was a massive door with carved lintels and a gleaming brass knocker.

A liveried boy stood at attention outside. Kathe ignored him and lifted the knocker herself. The knocker was padded and made a hollow thump against the polished wood. A pause followed, then the door swung open.

Lord Kosenmark stood framed in bright sunlight. "Thank you, Kathe," he said. "You may go."

He motioned for Ilse to come inside. She walked past him slowly, her heart beating too fast for her comfort. Behind her, she heard the door close, but her attention was entirely on this new room.

If she had thought him merely wealthy, her guess had fallen short. The floor was laid with wine-red tiles, set with a black marble border. Shelves lined the wall to her right. Some held books, others contained a variety of figurines in ivory or polished gemstone. Drawn by the figurines, Ilse moved toward them, taking in more details of the room as she went. A table and chairs by the fireplace. A globe made with precious metals. A vast sand glass surrounded by smaller glasses attached by pulleys and weights, the whole of which worked in unison to keep track of hours and minutes and moments. It was one of the new timepieces used in Duenne that Ilse had heard about from Ehren.

Beside the sand glass stood a huge desk, covered with more books, stacks of papers, and maps. A door at the far end was closed, but another one opened onto a rooftop garden.

Kosenmark came into the room and indicated the chair in front of his desk. "First, the long-delayed introductions," he said as he took his own seat. "At least the direct ones, since we have both heard our names from other parties. You told Kathe that your name was Ilse. Do you have another? A family name?"

She shook her head. "None that I would own, my lord."

He studied her a moment. "As you wish. Mine is Lord Raul Kosenmark."

Kosenmark. Of House Valentain. Ilse knew the name from Ehren's letters from university. *Wealth indeed,* she thought. Wealth and influence and a name as old as the empire, said her brother. Lord Kosenmark must be a younger son, or more likely, a member of a cadet branch.

"Do you know the name?" he asked.

"I've heard of it, my lord," she replied.

"What have you heard?"

His eyes were wide and bright, like a cat's. Or a hunting leopard's. "No more than stories, my lord. The same ones we heard of all the great houses."

"Indeed. So you know something of politics?"

"Nothing," she said softly.

"Ah. Good. Never claim more knowledge than you possess. Especially when that knowledge springs from hearsay and rumor."

His voice, that high unsettling voice, carried the same cool assurance Ilse had heard in Baron Eckard's voice, when he cut off Bartov's questions about the old king. Eckard had not raised his voice, but Ilse had heard the Imperial Councillor then. Wherever Kosenmark had learned it, she heard it now.

"My lord, I apologize."

Kosenmark nodded. "Apology accepted. Now let me give you a piece of information, related to the first." He laid his fingertips together. "You have come to a pleasure house. Mine. That is my business in Tiralien, whatever you heard elsewhere."

She felt the blood drain from her face. "No, my lord, I'm not—"

"I did not say you were. But you do know what the term encompasses. I wondered. For a time, I had thought someone had seduced and abandoned you."

"No one seduced me, my lord. I . . . I made a trade. A bad one."

"Was the trade voluntary?"

Her stomach fluttered. "My lord, you said you would not ask me any questions."

"I lied. Please answer me. Did you sleep with the man willingly?"

"Men," she whispered. "I slept with thirty men. More. As for willing . . ." She drew a sharp-edged breath. "The answer is yes and no. But I made the choice. The blame is mine."

"Did you end the transaction, or did they?"

"I did. My lord, why must you ask me these questions?"

"To judge your character. What changed that you first sold your body and then found the trade unacceptable?"

Her face had turned hot, from anger and shame. "I offered myself in exchange for a promise. The caravan master was about to break that promise. So I left."

"Where was the caravan bound?"

"Duenne, my lord. I hoped to work there."

"Yet you came east instead."

"We were north of Donuth when I left. Tiralien was closer and . . . I wished to avoid the caravan master. He was not willing to let me go, you see."

Kosenmark's gaze did not shift from her face. Slowly, Ilse became aware of the largest sand glass, turning within its frame in response to the weights shifting in the smaller ones. Fine silvery sand trickled through the narrow opening. As it did, she sensed the tension bleeding from the air.

"You left out some details," Kosenmark said softly. "Such as braving the wilderness alone, without weapons or shelter or food."

"I had a knife, my lord. A stone knife."

He tilted his head. "What else?"

She couldn't tell if he was mocking her, or if he was truly interested. "A blanket, my lord. Later on, I found a tinderbox and another knife. And after the first day, I learned how to forage for my food."

"Alone," he said musingly. "And for weeks, from what I gather. You were both very brave and very foolish."

Ilse made a quick throwaway gesture. "I had to leave, my lord. I had to. Someone gave me a chance, and I took it."

"I understand. Will you let me give you such a chance? One that does not involve selling your body?"

The weight against her chest eased. He did understand, she could tell from his face and voice. "What else could I do here, my lord?"

Kosenmark smiled faintly and let his gaze drift to his hands instead of Ilse's face. "My house is for entertainment. For that, I employ those who cook, those who clean, those who fetch, and those who guard these premises. Yes, some who work here do offer their bodies for pleasure—but willingly. I do not make slaves, nor do I use children the way someone has used you."

She saw how his fingers tensed momentarily. "My lord, I'm grateful—"

He looked up. "Gratitude—"

"—can prove a bitter root that does not feed the benefactor nor his charge. And yet I am grateful, willingly grateful, my lord. And that is a sweeter dish."

His gaze sharpened into curiosity, the look gone almost before she noticed. "I know the poem," he said mildly. "And so I accept your gratitude. Does that mean you in turn accept my offer? You are not obligated to," he added quickly. "You might prefer a position elsewhere. I can help there. I know of several houses in need of servants."

Choices. She had forgotten about having choices.

"You look surprised," Lord Kosenmark observed.

Ilse smothered a laugh. "My lord, I am surprised. I thought—" She broke off and pressed her hands together. "What I thought isn't important. My lord, I would like to work here, if I may."

His mouth quirked into a smile. "Indeed, you may start your work today. When you leave here, you will go to my secretary, Maester Berthold Hax. He will record your name and other particulars and will teach you about the house's routines. If you have more questions, you may ask him."

His tone was cool and businesslike, which she found easier to bear than outright kindness. Perhaps he guessed that, too.

Hax's office stood on the third floor, directly below Kosenmark's suite. It was a room very different from Lord Kosenmark's grand open space—every space stuffed with maps and books and leather-bound scrolls. A magpie's nest, but with a strange kind of order imposed over the chaos. Hax's appearance matched the room. He was an ancient man, to her eyes. His hair was white, its wisps escaping from its ribbons, and his skin was creased by folds upon folds. He wore a short indoor robe of fine-combed wool, with the cuffs turned back. He had the look of someone from the western provinces, lean and bony, with skin the color of pale sand and eyes that matched.

Hax waved her toward a bench. "Lord Kosenmark said I would see you today. Please, sit. I have a few questions and then I'll explain a few things." He looked and spoke more energetically than she expected for someone of his age. Taking out pen and paper, he said, "Name?"

"Ilse."

"Family name?"

She didn't hesitate this time. "None, sir."

He nodded. "Age?"

Her birthday had passed sometime during her wilderness trek. "Sixteen."

"Lord Kosenmark said you were young. He suggested you have only light duties at first. Later, once you're accustomed to the house, those might change according to your ability and our needs."

Hax went on to explain how much she would earn and what rules the house had. His hands were long and thin; he used them to sketch airy shapes to emphasize his words. Different servants had different hours—for example, there was always someone on duty in the kitchens, but the chief cook and her main staff worked hours centered around the house business. Ilse would be a member of that staff, and so she would be expected to work from late morning until just before midnight. As a start, she would be kept in the kitchen itself under Kathe's supervision. "Don't worry," Hax said. "We shall not overtax you."

"Yes, sir. Thank you, sir."

Hax spread his ink-stained hands outward. "You were gravely ill. We should not want any setbacks. Now, as for your training . . . Mistress Kathe has undertaken to instruct you, but your orders come from her mother, Mistress Greta Raendl. She in turn reports to Mistress Denk, the steward, who reports to me."

Who reported to Lord Kosenmark. Ilse nodded.

"And you," Hax said, "do you have questions for me?"

"None, sir."

"Really?" Hax tilted his head in a way that reminded Ilse of Kosenmark. "You have the look of someone brimming with unanswered questions."

She did have questions, and all of them began with why. Why did Lord Kosenmark bother himself with a runaway? Why did he run a pleasure house? Why had his expression gone so cold when she admitted to hearing stories about him? But she could ask none of these. She shook her head.

Hax regarded her a moment longer. "I think you will do well in this household, Mistress Ilse. Especially if you continue to mix your curiosity with discretion."

He sent a runner to fetch Kathe Raendl, who soon appeared, flushed and breathless.

"Mistress Ilse will be staying with us," Hax said. "Take her to your mother for more instructions. From there, it goes as we discussed."

Kathe's face brightened. "You agreed. I'm so glad. You'll like it here, I know. Come, we should hurry away before Maester Hax scolds us both."

Hax's mouth twitched, but he only waved them out the door. Taking Ilse by the hand, Kathe led her down to the first floor and along a complicated route through a dozen rooms, all furnished with cushioned divans and ornate tables. Ilse noted the gold leaf work, the graceful statues set in alcoves, the richly colored paintings and silk hangings. It could be any noble's house, she thought, except for the many beds and a faint musky scent throughout.

They turned onto a plainer corridor and soon came into the servants' region. Down the hall, through a chaos of runners and scullions and lackeys and chambermaids, and through a wide set of doors, into the kitchen itself.

The kitchen was enormous, with a high arching ceiling set with vents for the smoke and fumes. Three fireplaces with grates and hooks lined the innermost wall. Another wall contained an oven. The last one had racks of knives and pots and other implements Ilse didn't recognize. Scullions were swarming in and out with buckets of water. Other doors led into storerooms and a courtyard outside.

Several girls stood at the kitchen's central tables, shelling peas, gutting fish, and chattering despite the general noise. Kathe and Ilse circled around the counters to where Kathe's mother stood, supervising the activity as she mixed pastry dough. A younger, round-faced woman looked on, clearly unhappy.

Mistress Raendl nodded at Kathe, and handed the bowl to the woman. "Both of you work on the pastries," she said to Kathe. "Take that open spot on the counters, the one by the windows." Then to Ilse, "Lord Kosenmark told me you wished a position here. Do you know kitchen work?"

She had the same thick straight hair and dusky brown face as her daughter, and she spoke with her voice pitched to carry above the kitchen's din.

"A little," Ilse said slowly.

"What kind? How long? And speak louder, child. Tell me the truth. I hate surprises."

The truth. The truth was that Ilse sometimes had watched the cooks at their work when she was a child. "I don't," she said, fighting to keep her voice calm. "That is, sometimes the kitchen girls let me chop carrots or stir the sauces."

"In other words, you know enough not to lick the spoons." Mistress Raendl sighed and looked doubtful. "You came from money. Why aren't you still there?"

She had hoped to be done with that question. "You could say I left home because of money, Mistress Raendl. I have none now. And I need work."

"And we need willing dependable hands. You've a quick tongue, I'll grant you."

Ilse couldn't tell if the woman was pleased or resigned. "Then you'll have me?"

Mistress Raendl laughed, and suddenly she looked more like her daughter. "Didn't you hear me? Of course you have a place here. Lord Kosenmark promised you one. Though he would listen to my opinions if I disagreed. He listens to all of us, whether we like it or not." Her mouth tucked into a fleeting smile. "We'll start you in here with easy chores. More when you prove yourself. Now there are six other girls who work in the kitchens. Kathe will introduce you around and show you your new quarters, but that comes later."

Mistress Raendl went over the details of Ilse's new position. Kathe would tell her the rest, she said, and if she had questions, she might ask the other girls. She then gave Ilse her first task of rinsing a huge pan of rice, and came by at intervals to inspect her work. More light tasks followed—washing apples and pears and other, more exotic fruits, picking the stems from plums and cherries, setting out clean wine cups for another girl to fill.

She was given a break, which she took with Kathe in the courtyard outside. Resting on comfortable wooden benches, they drank a pot of tea and ate fresh cheese tarts and biscuits layered with spiced beef. Several of the kitchen cats made a hopeful circle around them. For the most part, Ilse fed and played with the cats, listening while Kathe chatted about Tiralien in spring and summer, when trade ships crowded the harbor and the house took so much business they had to hire extra hands. All too soon the break ended and they returned to the kitchen.

It was easy to tell when visitors began to arrive, for the pace quickened noticeably. Ilse cut and arranged the fruit under another girl's direction. After that, Kathe set Ilse to washing and drying the heaps of dirtied cups and plates and silverware. Two of the regular serving girls began loading trays with wine carafes and crystal wine cups. A few hours later the fare changed to platters of meat pastries, plates of grilled salmon garnished with peppercorn from Veraene's tropical south, poached eggs drizzled with spicy red and golden sauces.

The third hour bell that night rang before the pace finally slowed. Mistress Raendl checked over the next course of sugared confections, added another few loaves of bread to the ovens, and sank onto her stool with a sigh. "We've passed the flood tide," she said to no one in particular. "Now they'll drink wine and coffee until midnight. Kathe, take Ilse to her new rooms. I'll see to the shift change myself."

Her new quarters were on the third floor, Kathe explained as they followed yet another route through the first floor. She would share the room with the six other girls who worked in the kitchen. Other dormitories housed the runners, still others the chambermaids, and so on.

"Common room's mostly empty by this hour," Kathe said. "We've more private rooms on the second floor—dining rooms, pleasure rooms, libraries. Some of the customers like to talk."

Or entertain one another. Music filtered through the doors of several parlors they passed—a reed-pipe's breathy notes, the twang of a guitar. A man shouted out bawdy lyrics to the song, both musicians broke off their playing, and the piece ended in laughter. Farther on, she heard muffled conversations and softer moans, a woman's urgent voice babbling a string of promises, a man's abrupt groan as he reached climax. Her heart beat faster.

"How can they?" she murmured.

Kathe hesitated a moment, then said, "I asked once. Adelaide—she's the senior courtesan—said she felt like part of a theater, only with an audience in her arms and not yards away in their velvet-hung alcoves. She was a courtesan in Baerne's Court, you know. She came east when Lord Kosenmark did."

Kathe continued her explanations of the various rooms and what they were used for. Servants might enter the public rooms on errands, but they also had their own private corridors that ran beside and behind the public rooms. Some of these had peepholes set at intervals. These were for the servants, to check if a room was occupied before they entered. "You should learn the house," Kathe told her. "We have two serving girls, but at times we'll need you or the other girls to carry trays. Just remember, there are three routes to any room. Come. We turn here."

A stairwell took them directly into the servants' wing on the third floor. Ilse's new dormitory was a large room at the end, with eight beds and a large fireplace. No one had lit a fire, but there were stacks of wood and kindling. On the mantelpiece stood three half-consumed candles and one lamp.

Kathe lit the lamp with her candle. "This bed is yours," she said, indicating a narrow bed near the room's washstand. It had a plain dark coverlet and more blankets stacked at the foot. Kathe pointed to the trunk at the bed's foot. "You'll find enough clothes in there to last until we've measured you for new ones."

"But I don't need—"

"We all dress properly for our station," Kathe said firmly. "Lord Kosenmark's orders." Then her face relaxed into a smile. "I'm so glad you decided to stay. I was afraid I might frighten you off, or my mother would with her fierce looks. Speaking of my mother, I must go. I'm to supervise the next shift for a few hours. I'll come by tomorrow morning to show you where we get our breakfast."

Alone, Ilse made a circuit of the room, taking in more details. A straw broom in one corner, with a dustpan nearby. Small trinkets stood on several of the other chests, and one wall had a series of pencil sketches. Cards were laid out beside one bed, as though a game had been interrupted. Another bed was rumpled, with clothes heaped over the covers. Small clues to her new companions.

I wonder if I'll like them, was her first thought. And then, *I wonder if they'll like me.*

She felt a bubble of panic. Once or twice, Ilse had caught the other girls staring at her. None of them had talked to her, but then Mistress Raendl had kept them all busy, and whenever Ilse had a question, Kathe had immediately appeared to answer it. But she knew enough of maids and servants to realize she would have to learn fast and work hard to earn her place among these girls.

The bubble of panic subsided, but did not entirely disappear.

She went back to her bed and opened the trunk. A cotton nightgown was on top. Underneath, a couple of woolen gowns for serving in the common room, and more dark smocks and skirts for kitchen work. Caps, shifts, stockings, and bandeaus. There was also a store of new clean rags for her courses, which were due next week.

Footsteps sounded in the corridor. Ilse closed the lid and stood up, but whoever it was continued past her room.

She unlaced her dress and slid it off. Her shift followed. The cool air lapped against her bare skin. Without warning, she saw Alarik Brandt's dark eyes, staring as she undressed for him.

Stop. He's not here. He cannot hurt you.

She picked up the nightgown. A faint draft from above rippled over her body. *Softer than a lover's kiss,* she thought. Like a caress from memory that had never been.

CHAPTER EIGHT

"STOP. DON'T LIFT the blade so high."

Kathe moved Ilse's hand, which held the knife, to the correct position. "Now make tiny cuts. Pretend you are chopping up snowflakes."

She watched as Ilse carefully minced the bundle of parsley. "Better. But you need to relax, Ilse, or you'll cut yourself."

Ilse nodded. Relax. Concentrate. Try to ignore Lys and Rosel, who whispered and giggled at the next worktable. She adjusted her grip on the handle. That small change did feel more natural. Keeping the blade close to the cutting board, she made a series of tiny cuts, shredding the parsley into fine dots.

"Excellent! Now do the rest of this bundle, then start on the cabbage. I'll come back in a moment."

Once Kathe had left, Lys leaned close to Rosel. "I thought pets weren't allowed in the kitchen."

Rosel snickered. "Talking pets. Watch. I bet she cuts off her finger."

Ilse closed her eyes a moment. Knife. Sharp. Wound. Grief. Just as well she wasn't playing word links right now. She'd never be able to keep her distress a secret.

The teasing had begun the second day, after Kathe spent an hour teaching Ilse the most basic chores. Teasing was natural, Ilse had told herself. She was the new girl, after all. That night, however, when Ilse went with the other girls to the house baths, the questions had started. Dana had asked what it felt like to have mountains of gold. Rosel had wanted to hear where Ilse came by her scars. Steffi had wondered aloud why Ilse had been so sick that Lord Kosenmark had Mistress Hedda visit every day for a month. Lys said nothing, but she had watched every exchange with a calculating expression.

Ilse finished with the parsley and scooped the heap into the waiting bowl. Next came a small pile of blood-red cabbage, which Kathe had told her must be shredded into pieces no longer than her little finger. Lys or one of the other senior girls would mix these ingredients into a salad. Ilse's only concern was to cut the pieces correctly. She worked far slower than the other girls, but once she settled into a rhythm, it wasn't so bad.

Still, she was relieved when Kathe reappeared with one of the house runners trotting behind her. "I finished the parsley—"

"Good," said Kathe, but she looked distracted. "Ilse, I came to tell you that Mistress Hedda is here to see you. She comes at the worst times for us, though I guess our good times are bad for her. Ah, now I sound just like my mother." She paused to take a breath. "Never mind me. Just go with Mathes here, who can show you to her. But please hurry."

Ilse wiped the knife with a clean rag and rinsed her hands. As she followed the runner out the door, she heard a stir of whispers, and Kathe hushing the girls irritably. More gossip, she thought with an inward sigh.

Mistress Hedda waited for her in a small plain room near the back of the pleasure house. It looked more like a workroom than one used by the courtesans, and contained little furniture other than a few wooden chairs and an old desk. A small cot stood in the corner under the window, which had the curtains pulled open to admit the late-afternoon sun. Mistress Hedda sat on the cot, bent over an open trunk, sorting through her herb packets and vials and murmuring numbers and names as she did so. At Ilse's entrance, she looked up. "Good day, young woman. I've come for one last examination. Sit down here."

Ilse sat on the cot. Mistress Hedda took her left hand and laid her fingers lightly over Ilse's wrist. "A touch fast. But nothing to worry about. The fever is definitely gone. Now chin up, dear, and look over my head."

She muttered to herself, something about the flesh around the eyes looking puffier than usual. "Are you sleeping well?"

"Yes, ma'am."

"Mmmmm. So very proper. I see Greta has you trained thoroughly. Now please lie back. Stockings off, please, and legs apart. I want to make certain you've had no setbacks."

Mistress Hedda pulled the curtains shut and lit a lamp. Ilse did as ordered and stared at the ceiling while Mistress Hedda examined her, all the while asking about her dreams, her appetite, and whether she had any cramping. Her touch was both gentle and impersonal, which made the ordeal easier, and the need to answer questions helped Ilse keep her mind away from painful memories.

She sat up and rearranged her clothing while Mistress Hedda wrote down instructions for her to give Mistress Raendl. "You are much stronger, but not entirely well," Hedda commented. "You have shadows here still."

She touched Ilse's cheek, which was warm. "When I happen to see you next, I want these hollows gone and your color brighter."

Ilse tucked the slip of paper into her pocket. "No more draughts then?"

"None. I brought my physicks and my bottles for Josef today. The silly boy caught cold from sleeping with his window open. He's a southern flower and should know better."

Ilse had seen Josef in passing—he was a slender young man, often sought by the nobles, according to the other courtesans. "I thought we were in the south."

"There talks a girl from the borderlands. But Josef comes from Valentain, where the winters are hotter then your northern summers."

Valentain. So he came from Lord Kosenmark's homeland. "I wondered why he came north then?"

"An invitation perhaps," Hedda said drily. "I've heard six stories, all different, and those were from Josef himself. I believe he likes to reinvent himself each year."

They all had, Ilse thought. Josef, Nadine, even Kathe and her mother had reinvented their lives when they left Duenne's Court to serve in Lord Kosenmark's unconventional household.

"And you, what does Kathe have you doing?" Mistress Hedda said.

Ilse smiled. "Washing and drying dishes. Today she started me on mincing and chopping." She had not known there were so many terms for using a knife, nor that there were so many different knives in a kitchen. But Kathe was patient, and her mother often said she appreciated an honest effort.

"Do you like it?"

"Well enough."

Mistress Hedda's mouth twitched. "The truth now."

Ilse dropped her gaze to her hands. "I'm not doing as well as I'd like. But I certainly like it better than where I was."

"Do you get along with the other girls?"

Ilse shrugged. "Well enough."

Hedda's eyes narrowed. "I see. Well, I won't badger you, and Josef is waiting."

As she hurried back to the kitchen, Ilse wondered if she ought to have told the truth. But what was the truth? She hated the teasing and the questions, but there were times when Dana showed her the sketches she made, and sometimes Janna and Steffi let her join in playing cards during breaks. In turn, she had taught them the word-linking game, though only Janna showed any skill or inclination for it. But nothing erased the awkwardness she sensed, from shy little Hanne all the way up to Lys, the most senior girl in the kitchen. It came from her accent, the fact that Kathe spent more time supervising and teaching Ilse while the others had earned their places through skill or years of apprenticeship.

I'm a charity case, and they know it.

She came into the kitchen, dodging out of Lys's path as the other girl charged through the doors with a heavy tray. Hanne and Dana polished silverware. Janna was setting out rows of clean wine cups. Two spit boys rotated the huge beef roast that the kitchen girls would later slice and garnish. Kathe was not in sight, but off in one corner, Mistress Raendl and Mistress Denk discussed small details of the night's menu.

"Ilse! What took you so long?" Rosel said, coming up behind Ilse. "Dana needs help with the radishes. Special client for Adelaide. You need to polish these before she cuts them up." She propelled Ilse toward the cutting board, where a heap of dirty radishes waited. "Here's a rag. Don't stop polishing until you can see your face."

Ilse picked up one radish gingerly. Even she could see that these radishes were filthy and spotted, as though someone had picked out the worst from a very bad barrel. "Are you sure?"

Rosel's face was bland, but she heard muffled giggles from the others.

"Of course she's sure," Janna said. "She—"

She broke off suddenly. The other girls bent over their stations. Ilse realized that Mistress Raendl was beckoning impatiently to her. "Stop daydreaming, girl. I need a tray for Lord Kosenmark and Maester Hax—water and white wine and cups and those new rolls. Stay if they ask you. Otherwise come directly back. And throw out those radishes—they're rotten."

She turned back to Mistress Denk, and they were off again, talking about the evening's menu. Ilse threw the radishes in the trash bin. No matter how distracted Mistress Raendl appeared, Ilse knew this assignment was a test. She filled a new carafe from the wine barrel, then a second with cool water, and set these on a clean tray. The rolls came next, arranged in a pyramid on a platter. Napkins. She would need napkins and plates for the rolls.

Janna came to her side with a stack of clean folded napkins. "It was just a joke," she hissed.

Ilse started, nearly upsetting the tray. "What joke?"

"The radishes. Why did you tell on her?"

"I didn't. I—"

"You did. Now the old woman is sure to give her scut work, and it's all—"

"Janna. Ilse. Stop chattering."

Her cheeks burning, Ilse hurried from the kitchen. Hurry, hurry, hurry were Mistress Raendl's three favorite words, she thought. After two weeks of running errands, she knew most of the routes through the pleasure house. Down a connecting corridor, around through the back halls, and she came to the stairs, which she mounted as fast as she could without losing control of her heavy tray.

The runner on duty knocked for her.

"Enter," said Kosenmark's clear high voice.

Lord Kosenmark and Maester Hax were bent over Kosenmark's desk, studying a large sheet of paper that draped the entire surface. Stacks of books covered the chairs, and the table by the fireplace had another tray filled with dirty cups and the remnants of a meal. One of the smaller sand glasses turned over, causing another larger one to tilt and sound a soft chime.

"On that table," Kosenmark said, not looking up. "And pour us two cups, please."

With some difficulty, Ilse cleared off the indicated table and set down her tray. She poured two cups of wine, taking care to mix them well with water. Lord Kosenmark took his absently and drank. Hax smiled at her. "Thank you, my dear. We were growing parched and hungry from talking. Ah, could you bring me a plate of those rolls?"

Ilse fetched him the plate. As she did so, her glance fell on the paper they were studying. It was a map of northern Veraene and Károví. Blue lines radiated from the coast to mark the varying depth; green ones showed mountains and other natural features. Along with cities, the map included smaller ports and harbors. A thick dotted line and arrow pointed eastward off the coast, labeled *Lir's Veil* and *Three Hundred Miles*. That would be the magical wall of fire drawn by ancient mages three hundred years ago during the second wars to separate the island province of Morenniou from the main-land. But what caught her attention were the notations along the margins, with arrows drawn to various points on the Károvín coastline.

"Curious?" Lord Kosenmark said.

Ilse took an immediate step back from the desk. "My apologies, my lord."

He handed her his cup. "Please refill my cup. More water this time."

She did as he ordered, cursing herself silently. More than one person had warned her about undue prying. Even Kathe, with all her quicksilver chatter, rarely gave away any secrets. Keeping her gaze averted from the map, she handed the cup to Lord Kosenmark.

"Tell me what you saw," he asked mildly.

Without looking up, Hax said, "Do not tease her, my lord." He held a scrap of paper in his hand and seemed to be comparing it to something on the map.

"I'm not. I'm being curious. Just as she was."

Hax shrugged and went on studying the map. Kosenmark's attention remained on Ilse.

"I saw a map, my lord," she answered, somewhat breathlessly.

"Of what?"

"Of Károví and Veraene."

"How do you know that? Are you versed in maps?"

She met his gaze as steadily as she dared. "I come from the north, my lord. I recognized the names of cities and mountains and rivers."

"Indeed. Do you understand Károvín?"

"Dobru i nem, my lord. Good and not good."

"Dobr' velmi," he replied. "Very well indeed."

He continued to study her with that cool unnerving expression. Then Hax gave a soft exclamation. Kosenmark turned to his secretary. "What have you found, Berthold?"

"An interesting clue, my lord."

"Ah." Kosenmark waved Ilse away. "You may go. We shall serve ourselves."

Ilse curtsied, but their attention had already returned to the map and Hax's paper. She stacked the two trays together and quickly gathered up the rest of the dirty dishes. The two men were conversing in low tones, obviously still aware of her presence, but just as she exited the door, she heard Kosenmark's voice saying, "I see your point, but can we trust Benik's judgment?"

"I would," Hax said. "Interesting that Armand has also . . ."

Armand of Angersee. What did Lord Kosenmark have to do with Veraene's king? Or Károví's coastline?

Only the memory of Kosenmark's unnerving gaze kept her from pausing to listen. She shifted the tray to a more comfortable position and hastened back to the kitchen. Thankfully, the evening's preparations had already begun, and an ordered chaos had taken hold of the huge room. Kathe, engaged in measuring out coffees and spices, looked up at Ilse's appearance—a long questioning look. Ilse smiled as convincingly as she could, before turning to unload her tray and plunge into the next round of tasks.

THE FIRST RUSH had passed. Most of the girls were washing dishes, except for Lys, who kept the common room supplied with wine, and Rosel, whom Mistress Raendl had set to scrubbing the floors. Rosel's eyes were bright, as though she had been crying. "Scut work," Janna hissed in Ilse's ear. "I told you."

Ilse looked around the kitchen. Dana and Steffi scowled at her. "I said I was sorry."

"Sorry doesn't make it better."

"What if I told Mistress Raendl what happened?"

Janna's eyes widened. She hesitated, then said, "Go ahead. I dare you."

Ilse set down the plate she was washing and went to find Mistress Raendl.

The cook was just checking over a tray of sugared biscuits. She was frowning and muttering to herself, something about glazes and colors. "Yes," she said, without looking up. "Did you come to tell me the dirty dishes all disappeared?"

"No, Mistress. I came to ask—to say . . ."

"To say what, girl?"

Ilse started at her sharp tone. "I came to say that Rosel meant no harm with her joke."

"And?"

The kitchen was too noisy to hear any whispers, but Ilse could sense the other girls watching this scene. It was another prank, she thought. Or maybe not. Maybe she could do nothing to make friends with these girls, not with her accent and her manners and how she arrived at this house. *I can still try. I have to.*

"Nothing else," she said. "But I thought it was important to tell you."

Mistress Raendl pursed her lips. Her gaze flickered toward the other girls. "I see. Thank you. You may go back to washing dishes." Her voice rose slightly, cutting through the clatter. "Rosel will take no harm with her chores tonight. She might even learn some good sense."

Ilse turned back to her workstation. Dana was chewing her lips. The other girls were blank-faced and silent. She could not tell if she had made things better or worse.

She had just finished with the plates and had started on a stack of pots, when Lys came into the kitchen. Her sharp gaze took in Rosel kneeling on the floor. She frowned. With the ease of long practice, she conducted one whispered exchange with Steffi as she dropped off her load of dirty dishes, and another with Dana, while she loaded up a new tray with more wine and cups. Ilse tensed, but no one looked in her direction. She thought Lys had gone, when a loud groan penetrated the general din.

Several girls left their stations and rushed over to Lys, who bent over, clutching her stomach. "Something I ate," she announced, then clapped a hand over her mouth.

Mistress Raendl turned around with an exasperated expression. "What now?"

"Lys is sick," Janna said at once. "I'll take her to her bed, if you don't mind."

Mistress Raendl waved her away impatiently. She scanned the other girls, frowning. Ilse could almost read her thoughts—Hanne too small, Dana coming out in spots, Rosel in disgrace, Janna occupied with Lys. It would be her or Steffi.

"You," Mistress Raendl said, pointing at Ilse. "I need you to serve in the common room. Put on a fresh gown. Rinse your face and brush out your hair. Good enough. Here, take this tray and set out the wine and new cups. Clean up the table, and bring back the dirty cups and whatever empty carafes you find. We'll have another tray ready when you get back."

A runner brought a new gown from the stores, and Ilse made ready in a small closet off the kitchen. She picked up the tray and hurried to the common room, ducking between runners and other servers. Outside the doors, she stopped, her heart beating painfully fast. She could not wet her mouth.

It's just another room.

Except that courtesans entertained their clients in that room. She had never asked if the courtesans did more than sing or talk. She hoped she would not see them pleasuring their clients. She couldn't face that. Not tonight. Not ever. It occurred to her that Lys knew or guessed far more about Ilse's time with the caravan than Ilse had admitted.

She knows I'm afraid.

Ilse drew a breath to settle her stomach. Today or next week or next month, she would have to face this room. She gripped the tray firmly and went inside.

She thought at first she had stepped into a well of sweet-smelling darkness. A chandelier illuminated the room's center, but the rest was enveloped in shadows. As her eyes adjusted, Ilse saw Adelaide entwined with another woman. She skirted them, only to see Nadine and Eduard, sitting on a couch with an older man between them. Nadine was singing softly, and Eduard had just laid his palm against the man's cheek. The man rose and walked toward the staircase, hand in hand with Eduard. Nadine trailed behind, still singing.

Passion. Desire. Panic. For a long moment Ilse could do nothing but breathe, and that with difficulty. She thought about Lys. That didn't help.

She thought instead about Kathe, who had always shown her kindness and patience, and her nerves steadied.

Pretend the room is empty. Pretend you are walking through a forest.

She found an open path around the next grouping of chairs and to the central tables. She knelt and cleared out a space for the full carafes and clean cups, then stacked the dirty cups on the tray. She swept crumbs from the table into her hand and deposited those in one of the dirty cups. Though she tried to concentrate only on her task, she could hear too much of what went on around her. A prolonged kiss. An answering sigh. When a man's rough voice asked Tatiana to come at once to another room, Ilse stood up quickly with the tray. *I'll come back for the rest later.*

She turned toward the doors, only to collide immediately with a stranger. One cup went flying onto the carpeted floor and shattered. Ilse caught herself before the rest followed. She heard a gasp from someone nearby, and then a smothered laugh. The stranger, a young man, lurched against her a second time. He smiled and leaned heavily against her shoulder, breathing wine and smelling of exotic perfumes. "Pretty," he mumbled, sliding his arm around her waist.

Ilse stiffened and choked back an exclamation. "My lord. Please."

"Please. Oh pretty please." He buried his face against her neck.

The entire room had to be watching. She tried twisting away, but she could not without dropping more cups. "I'm not what you think," she whispered. "Please let me go."

"Yes. Let her go, Lord Gerhart."

Lord Kosenmark removed the young man's arms from around Ilse.

"She's pretty," Gerhart mumbled.

"Very pretty," Kosenmark agreed. "But you don't want to keep her from the kitchens."

Lord Gerhart blinked. "I don't?"

"Of course not. See Johanna waving? She wants to hear about the baron's dinner party. She told me so."

Lord Gerhart paused, swaying. When Johanna blew him a kiss, he broke into smiles and stumbled toward her. Ilse knelt to pick up the broken wine cup. Splinters of glass pricked her fingers. She wrapped her hand in a napkin and brushed the shards onto the tray, trying to ignore Lord Kosenmark's presence.

Kosenmark knelt beside her and plucked another shard from the rug. "You should not be out here," he said quietly. "Have Mistress Raendl send Rosel or Janna in your place."

Ilse shook her head. "I'm not afraid, my lord."

"You aren't? Look at me then."

He was studying her with the same assessing look he'd given her earlier, when he asked her about the maps. Ilse bore it steadily, though her cheeks were hot. "You are afraid," he said softly. "And I will not have my servants teased and tormented." He paused. "Unless you believe I would rather torment you myself."

"Ne'muj Panvíje," she said. "No, my lord. But I would like to make another try."

"Ah." Humor lit his eyes then. "Understood. As you wish."

He stood, his movement unhurried, and selected a new wine cup from those Ilse had brought. He filled it and crossed the room, where an energetic conversation was taking place between several older men. Kosenmark smoothly inserted himself into the group and the conversation. Ilse watched a moment longer, but Kosenmark seemed entirely engrossed by his companions and did not look back.

Laughter broke out in one corner. Lord Gerhart was nuzzling Johanna, who giggled and shrieked with delight. Other couples were joining in the card game. Ilse drew a long breath. Another tray waited for her in the kitchen. Another after that, if Lord Kosenmark's guests continued their thirsty mood. And she would have to expect more teasing from the girls. Lys especially liked to play pranks. If that's what it took to win their friendship, then she would try to take it with good humor. Think of that, she told herself, and not what takes place in the private rooms above.

She picked up the tray and hurried back to the kitchens.

CHAPTER NINE

AS ILSE EXPECTED, Mistress Raendl scolded her for breaking the wine cup. "Lys is sick. Janna is playing games no doubt with that boy from the stables. I'll have a word with her, too, when she gets back. I should send Steffi out, but you've got to learn the trade some time." Still muttering, she sent Ilse back into the common room with a new tray and a warning about malingering. Dana and Steffi snickered behind their hands.

The next day, however, Mistress Raendl did not send Ilse into the common room. Nor the next. The other girls noticed—Ilse could tell from their half-finished conversations in the dormitory and the looks they gave her. No one said or did anything obvious, but after two more days of silent glares, Ilse approached Mistress Raendl.

"Lord Kosenmark said one of the guests frightened you," Mistress Raendl said to her questions. "Thought you were one of the courtesans, being drunk."

"But Mistress Raendl, I told Lord Kosenmark I wasn't afraid."

Mistress Raendl eyed her with faint astonishment. "You *told* Lord Kosenmark?"

Ilse flushed.

"Tell me," said Mistress Raendl in a milder voice. "Does it bother you still? The courtesans, I mean, and what they do here."

Yes, Ilse thought, but she would not say it. Nor could she tell Mistress Raendl about the girls and how they viewed her treatment as a special favor. She curtsied, which brought an impatient laugh from Mistress Raendl, and went silently to the counters and the heaps of garlic and mushrooms and onions piled up for cutting.

I do need more time, she thought, as she fine-minced a clove of garlic. *Months or years. But however long, I will get used to seeing touches and kisses and open desire. I have to.*

"Don't chop so fast," Kathe said, as she passed behind Ilse. "You'll cut your fingers."

"And bleed all over the food," Ilse said. She had done that her first time chopping and had suffered both laughter and a scolding.

Kathe took the station next to Ilse and started paring fresh carrots into fanciful shapes. She worked quickly and deftly, the knife flashing between her fingers. Kathe liked the pleasure house well enough, she had told Ilse, but eventually she would leave for a better position, ruling her own kitchen in some other lord's household. Lord Kosenmark would certainly give her an excellent recommendation.

I wish I could go with her. It won't be the same when she's gone.

Kathe glanced up. "What's wrong?"

Ilse shrugged. "Nothing."

"What kind of nothing? A large one, judging by your face."

"Nothing at all." Ilse pressed the chopped garlic into a flat mass and began a second pass, mincing the pieces into smaller bits. She had known, once, how to hide all her emotions. It had been a necessary skill in her father's household. *We were all afraid of him, even Ehren. We learned to make our faces into masks, our hearts into emptiness, all to avoid provoking his anger. And not just for ourselves, but for each other.*

Here was nothing like Petr Zhalina's house, and Kathe was her friend, but she still wished she had kept her expression under better control. It would be too painful to explain how she had failed, how she thought it necessary to leave this house. And why.

I can stay here six more months. Eight if I need the money. Then I can go to another house where no one knows about my past.

It was a lie, she knew. Wherever she went, the other servants would guess her background and mistrust her. Still, a new house would know nothing about her time with the caravan. She could reinvent herself, like Josef, one bit at a time.

Kathe was glancing at her from time to time, her expression thoughtful. "Is there anything I can do about this nothing?"

Ilse scooped up the garlic and deposited it in a bowl. Taking up a new clove, she peeled away the papery skin and snipped off the ends. "No. It's something I need to figure out myself."

"Ah. Very well." Kathe paused, then continued in a softer voice. "But you do understand that you are as much my responsibility as Hanne or Rosel or the rest of the girls are. My mother trusts me to act for her. I hope you would trust me, too."

Ilse shrugged. "Trust is a chancy beast," she said, thinking of an old folktale her grandmother used to tell.

"One with a soft pelt and sharp claws," Mistress Raendl said. Ilse jumped, then jumped again when the cook laid a hand on her shoulder. "Leave the garlic for Kathe, since she proves she can chatter and carve at the same time. You come with me. I have a new assignment for you."

She beckoned Ilse to follow her through the kitchen's outer doors and down the wide lane used by delivery wagons. A side pathway took them into a small bare courtyard—little more than an alcove, and occupied only by a stone bench and a few trees that had shed their leaves.

"We might be safe here," Mistress Raendl said softly, scanning the windows above them. "Lord Kosenmark listens to us, you see. I told you that once, but I wasn't clear enough. He listens all the time. Through the vents, in the corridors, with spy holes and other means. He had the architect and builders take this house apart, or nearly, and rebuild it that way."

"Mistress Raendl, why are you telling me this?"

"Because he's asked for you to serve at a private supper tonight, and I need to explain more about him so you don't blunder. It's not that I expect you to say the wrong thing, but you have a very expressive face. You might look . . . disturbed. Or even just curious. Both would be a mistake. How much have the girls told you about Lord Kosenmark and what happened to him at court?"

Ilse's growing apprehension vanished at this new revelation. "Nothing. Nothing at all. Lord Kosenmark was at the King's Court?"

Mistress Raendl sent her a sharp glance. "That is where I met him. He used to visit my mistress, the Countess Hanau. When Baerne died, and then the countess, Lord Kosenmark invited me and my daughter to serve in his new household. The duke was furious when he heard. He said he wanted his heir at home, if not at court."

"Lord Kosenmark is the heir? I thought—" Ilse broke off, embarrassed.

Mistress Raendl smiled grimly. "I can guess what you thought. Yes, he is the heir. No, he cannot have children. It was the price he paid, to serve in Baerne's Inner Council. So you see why you must not let any shock, or worse, pity, show on your face."

Ever since she had first heard Lord Kosenmark's strange high voice, she had refused to dwell on what that meant. There were any number of innocuous reasons—a childhood illness, an unusual trait inherited through the family. She had not wanted to think of the obvious one.

But Lev Bartov had guessed right, and Ilse remembered Eckard's expression when he refused to speak of the matter. "The king ordered him to . . . to sacrifice himself?"

The cook nodded. "Baerne declared he trusted only men who spoke harsh truths in a woman's voice. Five Houses accepted this decree. Three of them sacrificed their second sons. Those who had none to spare were faced with bitter choices indeed."

"So they could not sire heirs," Ilse murmured. "To keep their loyalty to him and not their family."

"Yes," Mistress Raendl said. "You see the results. Lord Kosenmark has a brother, but he chose to meet the king's demands himself. He took it badly when the Baerne died and Armand chose new advisers."

Ilse hugged her arms around herself and looked upward. The walls rose straight up toward the floor where Lord Kosenmark had his rooms. How to read those blank windows that hid more than they revealed? Just so Lord Kosenmark's exquisite golden eyes told her nothing, really, even when he professed anger or kindness or simple curiosity.

"Was it by choice that he left court altogether?" she said. "Or did Armand dismiss him?"

"I don't know. I just know that three years ago he moved here and set up this house. He gave me no reason, of course. I'm his cook, not his friend."

But she knew him well enough to know this most personal history. Ilse took in Mistress Raendl's voice and manner, which was brusque, almost angry, as though she was offended by what happened to Lord Kosenmark. "You like him."

Surprise, then a soft laugh. "I do. I remember him as a page. He was a wild one, they said. That changed when the Countess Hanau took him as her friend." Mistress Raendl's gaze turned distant and she smiled, as though she saw another Lord Kosenmark standing in the courtyard.

She sighed and her smile faded. "That's all past. Today, our concern is just his entertainment. I told him yesterday what you said about not being afraid. He liked that, he said, and asked that you serve him and Lord Dedrick at their private supper tonight."

Lord Dedrick Maszuryn—Lord Kosenmark's companion and sometimes lover. The other girls told stories about him in private, punctuated with giggles and sighs. Ilse had seen him several times in the common room, but never alone with Lord Kosenmark. Lord Kosenmark a duke's heir, she thought. An exiled councillor. A man very much alive to his condition, in all senses of the word. Yes, she would have to guard her expression carefully.

"Would that bother you?" Mistress Raendl asked. "If it does, I can suggest to Lord Kosenmark that you would prefer to stay in the kitchen."

Ah, but then he would know she had lied about being unafraid. Ilse shook her head. "It won't bother me. And thank you for telling me, Mistress Raendl."

"Your thanks will be a good job. Come along. They'll miss us in the kitchen and start gossiping about nothing all over again."

Back in the kitchen, Mistress Raendl set Ilse to stirring sauces. Ilse tried to keep her thoughts on the task itself—stir with firm, even strokes—even though she kept seeing Mistress Raendl's troubled expression as she recited Kosenmark's history. Lys was watching her, she noticed, but to her relief, it was a busy night, with no time for chatter.

Two hours later, just when Mistress Raendl had ordered Ilse to make ready for serving dinner, a runner came with news that Lord Kosenmark wanted service to be set back an hour. Mistress Raendl scowled at the news. "Why?"

"Lord Dedrick sent word that he was delayed, I heard."

Mistress Raendl muttered a curse. "Very well. Not that I have any say in the matter, but very well. Tell Lord Kosenmark that we are delighted to change our schedule to suit young Lord Dedrick. We'll have to make new sauces then." Still grumbling, she dismissed the runner and gave the sauces over to Kathe with orders to use them with the spiced fishcakes. She mixed a new batch herself and gave that to Ilse to stir, muttering, "The house will eat well tonight."

Before Ilse had finished stirring that batch, the runner came back with more news. A short whispered exchange followed, then Mistress Raendl turned to Ilse, her mouth tight. "You're to go make ready."

"What's wrong?"

"Nothing much. Lord Dedrick hasn't come, but Lord Kosenmark sent word to start without him. Go dress now. I'll have the first tray ready before you return."

Ilse ran for the dormitory, where she washed her hands and face, braided her hair afresh, and then changed into her best linen gown. Last week, Janna had shown her the cosmetics provided for these occasions. Working quickly, Ilse applied powder to her face, color to her lips, and dark kohl to her eyes. It had been months since she had used anything to decorate herself, and for a moment, unwanted memories joined her in the empty dormitory room. All she needed was scent and jewels . . .

. . . *the sound of Paschke's musicians, Baron Mann's warm lips kissing my hand.*

She suppressed that thought and hurried back to the kitchen. Mistress Raendl looked over her appearance and nodded approvingly. "Well done. You look neat and pretty."

"Part of the presentation," Ilse murmured.

Mistress Raendl's mouth quirked into a smile. "Just so. Here is the first tray. Lord Kosenmark is dining in the Blue Salon. You know it?"

Ilse nodded. "First floor. The far corner on the west side."

"Excellent. Now hurry."

The tray held napkins, silver goblets and spoons, and bowls of creamed soup, seasoned with green and red peppercorns. There was also a full carafe of wine. Ilse hurried along the servants' corridors and through the more public wings, until she reached the more private wing beyond. She passed through several smaller suites, which were empty, and came at last to an arched doorway with paintings done entirely in blues and darker violet, which showed Toc's death, Lir weeping over his body, and then the resurrection. Balancing the tray against her hip, she knocked.

Lord Kosenmark's voice called out. "Come in."

Ilse pushed the latch down with her elbow and swung around to push the door open with her shoulder. She was so preoccupied with keeping the tray level, she didn't notice Lord Kosenmark's appearance until she was fully into the room.

He's naked.

She stopped in shock, then remembered Mistress Raendl's warning about showing no surprise. She took a deep breath and continued forward, keeping her gaze on the table in front of her, and not the man seated behind it.

Kosenmark made a noise in his throat. Ilse glanced up. A priceless wine cup, carved from jade, sat to one side. It was empty.

He leaned back and gestured for her to refill the cup. Ilse set the tray down, keeping the table between herself and Kosenmark. He was not naked, she saw. He wore a pair of black silk trousers, which the huge curved table had hidden from her view. A fine gold chain glittered against his smooth chest, and his long black hair hung loose over his shoulders.

She refilled his cup. When he nodded for her to proceed, she laid out Lord Dedrick's place setting. A glance showed her that Kosenmark still watched her. Her composure wavered, but she kept her hands steady. Soup. Spoons. Napkins folded just so. A wine cup that matched Lord Kosenmark's.

Done. Now Kosenmark leaned back and indicated his own place. Ilse circled around the table to arrange his setting. The napkin had come unfolded. She folded it anew, as Kathe had taught her, and set that by the plate. Kosenmark did not move but she was distracted nonetheless. He was barefoot, and now she saw that his shirt lay discarded in the corner. She caught a whiff of his scent; the smell of wood smoke and cedar transported her back to the night he rescued her. Lord Dedrick had been present then, too, she remembered.

"My guest is late," Kosenmark commented lazily.

His smiled bitterly at no one, finished off his wine, and poured another cup, emptying the one carafe. Wordlessly, Ilse replaced the empty carafe with the one she had brought. He must have been drinking steadily for at least an hour.

Kosenmark watched her, still with that same bitter smile. "Dedrick is often late," he said softly. "But I make allowances for his shortcomings, as he does for mine."

Ilse averted her gaze, then belatedly realized he might take that as disgust.

Kosenmark laughed. "You say nothing. What is there to say? Greta explained it all, didn't she?"

"My lord?"

His face was flushed, his expression was entirely unlike his usual demeanor. "I heard you when she talked to you in the courtyard. She's careful of the spy holes and vents and air shafts. She knows about the listening closets, too, I think. She was here when I had the house rebuilt. But perhaps she didn't realize how the walls carry sound upward—to the open windows."

Impossible to pretend she didn't understand. "Mistress Raendl was instructing me, my lord. Nothing more."

"Of course. You were curious, and she didn't want you to blunder." His voice was smooth, whispery like silk, sharp like the keen edge of winter. "I wondered what you thought of the story. Perhaps you'd like more details about my operation, and what spells the mage-surgeon employed to give me a semblance of manhood, without violating Baerne's decree."

She wanted to make an excuse to leave the room, but the harrowed look on Kosenmark's face made it impossible to interrupt, even if she had dared to.

"Or perhaps it's not curiosity," Kosenmark continued. "Perhaps you simply pity me. You shouldn't. I'm luckier than most. Lord Pommersien killed himself within a year of Baerne's death. Duke Sellen resigned his title to his sister and spends his days in seclusion. And Count Thorren—"

"My lord, I don't wish to know more. And I don't pity you."

His mouth rippled. "But you don't trust me, do you, Therez Zhalina?"

Above the roaring her ears, Ilse heard Kosenmark say something more about secrets. "No," she whispered. Then louder, "No, my lord."

She turned but his hand was already on her wrist. "Stop," he said. "Mistress Ilse, I—"

Ilse twisted away, but he held her fast. "No," she repeated. "I will not play your games, my lord."

Tears of anger and fright blurred her vision. She swiped them away with her free hand. She wanted to say more, that Lord Kosenmark could flog her and dismiss her, but she would not make any trades, of honor or self or—

A rapid knock sounded at the door. Kosenmark immediately released his hold. Ilse sprang away. Kosenmark made a soft impatient noise in his throat and tossed his napkin to Ilse. "For your face," he said in an undertone.

Cautiously Ilse knelt to pick up the napkin. At Kosenmark's gesture, she retreated to the far corner, out of sight of the door.

"Enter," Kosenmark said.

A runner came into the room. "Lord Dedrick has arrived, my lord. He's just riding into the stable."

"Thank you. Escort him here as soon as he is ready."

The door closed again. Kosenmark glanced toward Ilse. She quickly blotted away the tears and smoothed her hair. He held out his hand. She darted forward and dropped the napkin onto the table, then stepped back.

Moments later Lord Dedrick Maszuryn swept into the room. He was a handsome young man, with a lean dusky face and abundant dark hair scarcely contained by its ribbon. "Father detained me," he said, taking his seat. "But I brought you a gift to atone for my lateness."

He slid a narrow leather-bound volume from his shirt. A book—an old one with pages darkened by age. Just in time, Ilse stopped herself from trying to get a closer look.

Kosenmark accepted the book with a smile. "Thank you. You've been hunting amongst the booksellers, I see."

"Only for you. Because I know you like such things."

When he reached for his wine cup, his hand brushed against Kosenmark's. Kosenmark tilted his hand to meet that caress. "Tell your father that his son has quite atoned for his actions. Was he discussing the beloved familiar subject, or a new one?"

Ilse dropped her gaze, not wanting to witness anything more. But she could not help hearing Lord Dedrick's throaty laugh. "Both. He reminded me of duty and of risks."

"He's not so very wrong, you know. We are both derelict, you and I, in performing our duties toward our families."

"Now you sound like my father. He wants me to find a steady occupation for my life. I nearly told him you are my occupation."

Raul murmured something under his breath—Ilse heard the word *foolish*—to which Dedrick gave an equally inaudible reply. Ilse glanced up and saw that Raul had taken Dedrick's hand in both of his. His expression was thoughtful, and he no longer seemed angry or befuddled by drink. "We can talk about that later," he said. "Or not. Greta will be raging in her kitchen if we do not proceed with our meal."

Throughout the meal, the two men spoke of friends and colleagues in Tiralien's great houses. They discussed theater and literature and argued the relative merits of various artists. It could be a conversation between any two friends, Ilse thought, except for the warmth in their eyes, and the occasional caress. Once her gaze met Lord Kosenmark's just as he kissed Lord Dedrick's palm. His expression went from smiling to blank. After nearly two months in his household, she realized that was a clue, and she wondered what he thought behind that impenetrable shield.

After she served the dessert, Kosenmark dismissed Ilse from the room. "Stay outside until we call." He hesitated a moment, then said softly, "You were right to insist you were not afraid."

A lonely watch followed. Once Lord Dedrick came to the door with his shirt unbuttoned and asked her to fetch another two carafes of wine. On her return, she knocked but heard no answer. The salon was empty. Voices sounded through a half-closed door leading into another room, the words indistinguishable, but their tones unmistakably intimate. The book still lay on the table. Her fingers itched to look inside. Resisting the temptation, she set the carafe on the table and left.

Several hours later, Lord Dedrick departed for his father's house. Lord Kosenmark escorted him to the door. He wore a fresh shirt and tunic, and his long hair was combed smooth and tied back with a ribbon, but he was still barefoot. He was carrying the book, she noticed. "Tell Kathe to have the salon and the other room cleaned," he said in passing.

Kathe ordered Ilse and several other girls to help fetch dishes. Chambermaids were already at work when they returned to the salon. More chambermaids were at work in the private room beyond.

Janna wiped down the table, while Kathe, Ilse, and Steffi collected the plates and goblets onto trays. Both Steffi and Janna were in a good mood. They chattered and laughed while they worked, and for the first time, they included Ilse.

"Lover's nest," Steffi whispered, nodding toward the private parlor.

Janna rolled her eyes. "Any good stories?" she asked Ilse.

Ilse shrugged. She was certain Lord Kosenmark would hear if she said anything indiscreet. *He listens,* she thought, *and they don't know it. Or they don't care.* Feigning a yawn, she said, "They talked. And talked. Nothing worth repeating."

"I heard his father lectures him," Janna said. "Tiresome old man. He wants his son at home on the estates, not in Tiralien with Lord Kosenmark."

"Maybe Lord Dedrick finds it restful here," Kathe said pointedly.

Janna giggled. "I doubt they rest."

She and Steffi were both laughing, and even Kathe was trying hard not to smile. Ilse said nothing. She remembered how Kosenmark had kissed Lord Dedrick's hand and the look in his eyes when he did.

"How do you think they do—" Steffi began.

Kathe cut her off with a gesture. "It's not our business. Hurry up. We've a long night still."

With Kathe chivvying them along, they were soon done and back in the kitchen. Mistress Raendl immediately sent Steffi and Janna into the common room. "You're dismissed for the night," she told Ilse. "Lord Kosenmark's orders."

Odd how the noise did not slacken, and yet Ilse could sense the sudden break in the conversations around her. Lys coolly stared at Ilse. Dana elbowed Rosel, who scowled back. Steffi and Janna paused by the doors, both of them stony-faced. Only Hanne's expression did not change, but she was wrapped in some private grief of her own as she doggedly washed pots and pans.

Ilse thanked Mistress Raendl and left the kitchen. She wished she could explain to Lord Kosenmark that his kindness was a burden, but he would only dismiss her fears and Mistress Raendl would lecture her about questioning her master. She reached the dormitory and slipped into the room, which was still empty. She set the candle on the mantelpiece, then paused in surprise.

A letter lay upon her bed, a bright square against the dark blanket. Her heart beating faster, Ilse took up the paper. A tingling met her fingers, and she caught a whiff of magic's green scent, combined with cedar and wood smoke—Kosenmark's scent. When she broke the seal, a wave of magic rippled over her skin. She had heard of spells against prying and wondered if this was one.

The letter had no date and no signature. Just one short paragraph written in a neat elegant script:

My apologies are insufficient. Let me nevertheless offer my regrets. My coin buys your willing service and nothing more. Your secrets remain yours alone.

Ilse glanced at the ceiling and its several vents. He had deliberately sent her away early so she might read the letter alone. Was he listening now? Unnerved, she crumpled up the paper, intending to throw it into the fireplace. On second thought, she smoothed it out and reread the words. It was like a prize, awarded for courage. *Or bravado,* she thought. She stored it at the bottom of her trunk, underneath all her clothing. Only then could she snuff out the candle and pretend to sleep.

CHAPTER TEN

THE TORMENTS BEGAN early the next day. In hindsight, Ilse was not surprised. She knew how girls in Melnek's families maneuvered for social ranking, and she'd overheard enough quarrels between the kitchen girls and chambermaids in her father's house. But that first morning, she thought only about hurrying downstairs before the other girls. If she worked longer today, perhaps they would not mind the hours she had not worked the night before.

She bathed quickly and dressed, her hair and skin still damp, then raced from the baths to the kitchen. To her surprise, Janna and Rosel were already there, eating breakfast. Janna favored Ilse with a long stare. Rosel ignored her.

Ilse sighed and turned away. So they still blamed her for Lord Kosenmark's favoritism. She poured herself a mugful of coffee and added cream from the common pitcher. In spite of her early bedtime, she had spent a restless night. The private supper, the letter, the idea that Lord Kosenmark knew her identity—all those had mixed together in a series of disturbing dreams. Yawning, she gulped down her coffee.

And spewed it all over the floor.

Salt. Her stomach heaved. She pressed her mouth shut and ran for the alley door, where she threw up again. Behind her, she heard smothered laughter. Ilse wiped her mouth with the back of her hand. She'd dropped the cup, too. Mistress Raendl would scold her for that and for the mess. Likely the girls had foreseen that as well.

Reluctantly, she returned to the kitchen, where she found all the girls gathered together. Lys clucked in apparent sympathy. Dana tossed her a sponge. The others shook their heads and rolled their eyes.

So that is how it will be, she thought, sponging up the mess from the floor. Pranks and tricks and snubs. There was no way to know who had plotted this humiliation. The common pitcher was just that, common, and she doubted Mistress Raendl cared to investigate something so petty. Did the girls in her father's house act the same?

Mistress Raendl did scold her for the broken cup. She also ranted at Ilse for using her best sponge to clean the floor. "It's for crystal, girl," she said, with an exasperated noise. "I should think you'd know that by now."

Ilse sighed. "I'm sorry. I'll remember next time."

"Do that. This one is ruined. And try not to be so clumsy."

Nothing marred the rest of that day. Ilse tested all her dishes carefully before she ate, and touched her tongue to her tea before she drank. Nothing tainted. Nothing out of the ordinary. Maybe the girls had exhausted their bad humor with one prank.

The next afternoon, Kathe came to Ilse with a basket of new cucumbers. "I need these washed, peeled, and diced. Make each cube the size of your fingertip. It's for Lord Kosenmark's luncheon, and Lord Vieth is one of the guests."

Lord Vieth was the regional governor, an elegant man with exacting tastes, according to rumor. He never visited the pleasure house, but he often visited Lord Kosenmark, and Ilse appreciated the difference. "Your mother must be anxious."

Kathe grinned. "Of course. I would suggest we all strive for perfection today. Or close enough to please a finicky cook. Once you've diced these, give them to Rosel and start on the peppers. Thin curling slices. Imagine them as green ribbons."

Ilse cleared off her workstation, then laid out the proper knives. She would need water to scrub the cutting board, and more water to wash the cucumbers. She took a pail to the pump outside to fetch water. When she returned, she saw at once that the knives had disappeared.

She glanced around. All the other girls were busy. Mistress Raendl had gone off to interview a replacement for the last pastry cook, and Kathe was not in sight. Maybe someone borrowed them.

She would have to fetch another set of knives, and search for the old set later. Doubt niggled at her mind. She pushed those thoughts aside and concentrated on the task at hand. Today was the first time Kathe had entrusted her with such a task, unsupervised. Ilse wanted to prove herself useful.

She washed the cucumbers thoroughly and dumped the water in the drain outside. When she returned, she found the original knives just where she had left them.

Except now they're ruined.

She picked up one—its blade was visibly notched. Another one looked dull. The third knife had a cracked hilt and broken point.

Ilse swallowed hard. No crying. No self-pity. Besides, that's what the girls wanted. Trying to keep a calm face, she fetched another set of knives and had the cucumbers peeled and diced before Mistress Raendl came back. The interview with the pastry cook had not gone well, judging by her stiff expression, and when she found the broken knives, her eyes narrowed.

"I told you not to be so clumsy. Three knives ruined. You did well with the dicing, but those are three knives we cannot use again. It's not just the cost, girl. Chip a knife and you could put out someone's eye."

Ilse shook her head.

"Are you arguing with me?" Mistress Raendl said softly.

"No, ma'am. I'm sorry. I will be careful."

More pranks followed throughout the next five days. Vinegar added to her tea. Glasses cracked so that they broke when she washed them. Pins in her stockings. Brushes and rags and spoons that vanished from her workstation when she wasn't looking. Soon her throat hurt constantly, and her nerves jumped at every sound.

It was late one evening, when there came a lull in orders from the common room, and Mistress Raendl gave all the girls an extra break. Ilse took the opportunity to go outside into the lane. The cold would keep the others away. If they set another trick, well, she was getting used to it. She wandered toward the gardens, to the path where she had first entered Lord Kosenmark's grounds, nearly eight weeks before. The trees were bare now. Winter had arrived, bringing with it wetter weather and the hint of snow. If she walked away tonight, she would have to find shelter from the cold and damp.

One of the kitchen cats curled around her legs and mewed for attention. Ilse bent to scratch its head and took comfort in its rumbling purr. *Never again,* she thought. *Never again will I run away.*

"Ilse." Kathe's voice came from the doorway.

Ilse straightened up and the cat whisked away into the darkness. "Am I wanted inside?"

"No. We've a chance to breathe tonight, thankfully. It was just—" Kathe's voice sounded tentative, unlike her usual cheerful self. "I wondered if you wanted to tell me anything."

Of course Kathe knew, or guessed at, what happened with her crew. She was clever and observant, as well as a good cook. Ilse was tempted to tell her everything. Then Kathe would lecture the girls and . . .

. . . and I shall forever need her protection.

She shook her head. "No. I have to solve it by myself."

"So you do admit there's a problem."

"Not a problem. A puzzle."

Kathe laughed softly. "As you like. But remember, if your puzzle does become a problem, come tell me, and we can try to solve it together."

ILSE WOKE THE next morning to an unusual silence. She tensed, thinking she had overslept. Then she heard a whisper, followed by a loud crackling. "I don't care," Lys said.

What have they done now?

She wanted to pretend sleep until the others went downstairs, but she could not afford to be late, not with Mistress Raendl already annoyed with her.

But when she sat up, her stomach knotted as she took in the girls' latest prank. Dust all over her blanket. More dust in her hair. She sneezed and heard the girls laugh. The dust was nothing, however. When she wiped her eyes clear of the dust, she saw that her trunk stood open and empty, and her clothes lay scattered across the floor. Keeping her face expressionless, Ilse began the tedious task of gathering her things. Shoes in one corner. Shifts and bandeaus crammed behind the door. Hair ribbons knotted into an impossible mess. They had deliberately rubbed dirt into everything, including her best gown. Ilse brushed off the dirt as well as she could, but she knew she would have to take most of her clothes to the house laundry. As the girls watched, she put the soiled clothes to one side and folded the rest.

Only when she went to her trunk did she realize that something else was missing.

My letter.

Paper crackled again. Ilse snapped her head up. Lys sat cross-legged on her bed with Ilse's letter from Lord Kosenmark. Rosel leaned over her shoulder. Both were sounding out the words they knew, speaking in an exaggerated drawl, and snickering.

"Give that back to me," Ilse said.

Rosel grinned at her. "Why?"

"Because it's mine."

"Hah," Lys said. "You probably found it in the gutter. Or stole it. Who would write such a stupid letter to you anyway?"

Ilse shook her head. She ought to have burned the letter, but she had not imagined that anyone would search her private belongings. At least they didn't know who wrote it.

Janna glanced sideways at Lys. She looked more unhappy than amused.

So did Dana. But Lys was grinning in obvious satisfaction. "So you did steal it," she said. "I thought so. You're a thief—a thief and a whore."

"I'm not a thief."

"But you are a whore." Her voice went low and angry, and dark red patches appeared on her bony cheeks. "I heard about the night you came here, girl. You were sick, they told us. Sick from spreading your legs. I heard you even tried to fuck Lord Kosenmark, so he'd let you in the door."

Ilse closed her eyes. They will never be satisfied. Never.

"Four a night," she whispered. "More after I got used to the work. Thirty men could have me, and they did. Mornings. Nights. When they rested the horses, sometimes. And I did whatever they wanted, no matter what, no matter how much I hated it. Just so Alarick Brandt wouldn't send me back to my father. So yes. I was a whore."

She heard swift footsteps crossing the room, a scuffling sound, then a squawk from Lys. But no one answered her, not even to say good-bye as they left the room one by one. When she at last opened her eyes, the letter lay on her bed. "My badge of courage," she said softly, folding it carefully into a small unobtrusive square. "I will not let it go. And I will not run away."

SHE DRESSED IN her cleanest skirt and smock and made ready for the day. The clothes that she had been able to brush clean, she put away. The rest she took to the house laundry, where the wash girl eyed her curiously. "What happened?"

"An accident."

"You should be more careful. Mistress Raendl is a strict one, I've heard."

Ilse smiled faintly. "That she is. It won't be the first time she's scolded me. I'm nearly used to it."

The girl grinned back, shaking her head. "Well, these stocking are fairly ruined. I'll tell Mistress Denk so she can order you new ones. Are you sure you want to wear that smock today? It's all over grease stains."

Ilse hadn't noticed the stains in the dormitory. She sighed. "It's the only one I have left."

When she reported for duty, Mistress Raendl did scold her, but absent-mindedly. Reading the signs, Ilse guessed the night would prove hectic and nerve-racking for them all. She was right. Within moments, a quarrel broke out between the youngest scullion and the pastry cook. Mistress Raendl spun around to deal with it. When she did, Kathe took Ilse away and gave her a mound of dough to knead. "This should keep you busy and safe," she said softly.

Ilse settled down thankfully to her task. The other girls glanced in her direction, but no one spoke to her. She was glad. She didn't want to speak, didn't want to pretend she wasn't angry and miserable.

I forgot about envy, she thought. *And jealousy. And distrust.*

Those emotions had names and faces now. She glanced around at those faces. Fox-faced Lys. Rosel with her bright eyes and mobile mouth. Janna and Dana. Steffi. Little Hanne. Lys happened to glance up. Her gaze met Ilse's and she tilted her chin up. They stared at each other a long moment, until Mistress Raendl called out for Lys to help the servers in the common room.

Ilse punched a fist into the dough. *I will not run away. I will not. Not again.*

A lock of hair fell over her face. She blew it away. Anger solved nothing. Self-pity was equally useless. *So think,* she told herself. *Unless you want to spend the next year dodging tricks, and explaining your clumsiness to Mistress Raendl.* If Mistress Raendl didn't dismiss her long before the year ended.

She folded the dough into the center and pounded it again. Lys was the senior girl and jealous of her position—that much was clear. And Rosel took her direction from Lys. Dana the moody one would join in the pranks if her day went especially badly. Steffi was simpler to work out—she just liked a good laugh. Janna . . . Janna was harder to judge. Ilse had thought her another like Steffi, but Janna thought longer before she spoke. She wasn't afraid of Lys, but she also wouldn't challenge the other girl's status.

Then there was little Hanne, the one the rest overlooked.

"She's from up north, like you," Kathe had said. "Six brothers and four sisters. Her mother and father sent her to live with a cousin because they could not feed her."

But the cousin had died, leaving Hanne without work or a home. Kathe had heard of the girl through friends and offered her a post. Hanne worked hard, but she clearly wanted nothing more than to go home.

Ilse paused in kneading the dough. Working hard. That was the key. *I have to prove that I deserve this post.*

She considered how for the rest of the evening. After the shift ended, she waited until the others had left, then approached Kathe. "I need a favor," she said softly.

Kathe glanced around. "For your situation?"

Ilse nodded. "I'd like you to give me drudge work. The nastiest smelliest work you have. If it's not too much trouble, that is."

Kathe smiled faintly. "That is hardly a favor. We always have drudge work, and we all take turns, or we earn it by making trouble. But if you want it . . ."

"I do."

The next day, Kathe provided Ilse with several sets of plain rough clothing—jerseys and trousers and socks—and told her to wear these while she worked. Then she gave Ilse a wire brush and the kitchen's filthiest pots, the ones coated with soot, or baked with sauces that had bubbled over. "Clean these until I can see my face. That should be nasty enough."

After Ilse finished that job, Kathe set her to washing out the big trash barrels. The barrels stank from rotted foods left to ferment, and Ilse had to crawl inside to scrape out the crevices. She heaved up her breakfast the first day. The second day, she scrubbed the barrels first and then ate after taking a hot bath. After the barrels came the chore of scraping out the drain pipes that emptied into the gutters outside. Normally the lowest scullions did that chore, but as Kathe cheerfully reminded Ilse, she had asked especially for those kinds of chores.

"Have you had enough?" Kathe murmured when this state of affairs continued for ten days.

"Nearly," Ilse said under her breath. Her hands were red from the soap, and her fingernails were chipped. But she had noticed a difference. Janna now greeted her when she came into a room, and Steffi asked her more often to share her stories and folktales. Dana made a point of leaving her special hand cream by Ilse's bed, when Lys wasn't around. Even Lys herself did nothing worse than ignore her.

"Take a break from the filth," Kathe said. "I need you to deliver breakfast trays to our fair courtesans."

Ilse hesitated. "What about . . . ?"

"We ran low on pickles and vinegar and a few other things, so I sent Lys and Rosel to the market. The other girls won't tell, I'm guessing."

Ilse nodded. "Very well."

Her response provoked a laugh from Kathe. "I'm so glad you consent."

"I didn't—"

"You did," Kathe said, still laughing. "But I understand your reluctance. Hurry, though. Tatiana will be crying for her tea before long."

Ilse scrubbed the dirt from her face and hands and changed into a clean smock and skirt. It was a welcome change, she thought, after she had delivered six trays to various rooms. Her last delivery was to the common room, where several courtesans lounged. A few hours remained before the pleasure house opened for general use, and the room was filled with sunset's heavy red glow. Eduard dozed on the couch and Mareike softly played her double flute. Nadine lounged next to Adelaide, but at Ilse's appearance, she rolled into a sitting position and patted the cushion next to. "Excellent. We've had one breakfast already, but I could have three more."

"You'll get fat," Eduard said, his eyes still closed.

"Maester Schaulder likes plump women." She turned back to Ilse. "What about you? You look hungry enough for another meal."

Ilse smiled but said nothing. She laid out the dishes with food and collected the dirty ones to take back to the kitchen.

"Quiet," Nadine observed. "Steffi tells me that you know stories. Would you tell us one before you go back to the kitchens?"

"I can't. Mistress Raendl—"

"Mistress Raendl," Nadine said crisply, "ate too many prunes when she was a girl."

Ilse choked back a laugh.

"It's true." Nadine's expression was grave, but her eyes were bright with mischief. "Six, count them, six baskets of prunes, eaten in a single day, on a dare. A tragedy. We speak about it often, we courtesans. Tatiana sings of the matter to clients, when they ask for sorrowful songs."

Smiling and shaking her head, Ilse wiped down the table.

"I think you ate some of those prunes, too," Nadine went on. "Or else you would be laughing right now. Just like Eduard." She poked Eduard with the foot. Eduard grunted and rolled over, but his shoulders were shaking.

"Don't tease," Adelaide said. "It's not kind."

"Hah. She likes it. Where are you going, fair Adelaide?" she asked as Adelaide stood up.

"An appointment," Adelaide said. "Luise expects me within the hour, and I need to dress. So do you. Don't dawdle too long."

She left the room silently, her gown fluttering behind. Nadine stretched out on the couch, watching, her slanting eyes narrowed to dark lines. "Do you think her pretty?" she asked Ilse.

Calling Adelaide pretty was like saying Launus Paschke could pluck chords on a guitar, Ilse thought. Adelaide had fair golden skin and hair so black, it had tints of blue. Her face and hands and body were faultless, if one dared to use that word. Ilse could see her in Duenne's palace, entertaining kings. "She's beautiful."

"Do you like her?"

"She's nice," Ilse said warily.

"Nice." Nadine laughed. She rolled over, caught Ilse by the wrist. Before

Ilse could jerk her hand free, Nadine kissed her wrist and released her. "If you ever decide that I am nice, you know which is my room. Now go, before Greta sounds the alarm."

Ilse hurried back to the kitchen and dumped the tray with its dirty plates by the washbasin. She had picked up her washcloth when Kathe reappeared. "One last tray," Kathe told her. "For Maester Hax. Oh and try not to let Lord Kosenmark see the dishes. He and Mistress Hedda are worried about the poor man's health."

"You forgot to tell me to hurry," Ilse said with a smile.

Kathe laughed. "*You* already know that. And *I* already sound too much like my mother."

The back stairways were still quiet, but when Ilse reached the landing outside Hax's office, she found his door open and Lord Kosenmark outside. "We've no more business tonight," Kosenmark was saying to his secretary. "Leave those papers for tomorrow."

Ilse withdrew, trying to keep the tray out of sight, but Kosenmark beckoned her forward and inspected the dishes. "This is not the diet Mistress Hedda ordered," he said. Hax had ordered strong tea, biscuits and honey, and grilled fish dotted with pepper.

"Mistress Hedda would physick me with boredom," Hax retorted. "You might inform her, Lord Kosenmark, that I am used to my spices. I like them. I will not give them up."

"As much as you like your strong tea and keeping late hours. Berthold, Berthold. You are a horrible old man."

"I have you to thank, my lord, as both a model and an inspiration."

Kosenmark grinned. His glance fell on Ilse. The grin altered to a friendly smile, which she found almost as surprising, and he waved her into the room. "Serve this old man his supper, child. If he carps and whines about his indigestion, we shall feed him prunes by the barrel."

It was unnerving how he knew the doings of his entire household. Embarrassed, she went about pouring the tea, and setting out the silverware on the side table. Kosenmark left with another edged comment to Hax, who was laughing silently. "He is a terrible man," he said to Ilse. "I wonder that I tolerate him so."

She smiled but said nothing. Lord Kosenmark was right about Maester Hax, she thought. The old man looked tired, and since she last saw him, his color had turned a pasty yellow. Ilse cut several biscuits and spread them with honey, since he liked to eat as he worked, and laid a napkin ready. When

she finished, she saw that Hax was observing her. "I haven't seen you about these past few weeks," he said. "Is Greta keeping you busy?"

"Busy enough, sir."

He tilted his head. "Meaning, you do not wish to offend with your answer. Very well. Thank you for the tea, Mistress Ilse. And the fish."

No more trays waited for her. Just more dreary smelly work. Someone had left a crate of potatoes to rot in the storerooms, and the potatoes had turned to black sludge. Ilse had mopped up the worst, but Mistress Raendl wanted every groove in the tile floor scoured clean to keep out the rot. Her one consolation was that Janna had murmured her sympathy in passing.

Step by step, she told herself. *They might even forget where I came from.*

She was so absorbed in her thoughts, she didn't see Hanne huddled on the floor until too late. Her feet tangled in Hanne's skirt, and she tripped, her tray flying out of her hands. Ilse landed hard on the tiled floor and banged knees and elbows. Beneath her Hanne cried out in alarm.

"Hanne, I'm sorry. Are you all right?"

"It's all right," Hanne said quickly. "It's all right. I'm—"

She broke off with a muffled groan. Worried, Ilse knelt and peered at the girl's tear-streaked face. Hanne's face looked gray and drawn, her cheek felt warm and damp. "What's wrong, Hanne?"

"Nothing. It's all right. I just wanted to rest a bit before I—" She gestured at a tray Ilse had not noticed before—a dish with strawberries, wine carafe, and cups. One of the courtesans must have an early appointment.

"Would you like me to take the tray for you?" Ilse asked.

Hanne shook her head vigorously. "No. I can get by. It's just the pains, but they'll pass. They did last month."

Cramps, then. Bad ones. No wonder the poor girl looked so miserable. "Tell Mistress Raendl. She'd let you lie down, I'm sure."

"No!" Now Hanne looked terrified. "I don't want the other girls to know. None of them get sick and I don't want to make Mistress Raendl angry. I"— she pressed a hand against her stomach—"I'm fine."

Ilse brushed away a damp strand of hair that had escaped Hanne's headscarf. "You should talk to Mistress Hedda the next time she visits the house. She has medicine that helps. But for tonight . . . What if we trade? You can take my tray back to the kitchen. I'll take yours. Where does it go?"

The other girl appeared to struggle inside a moment. "Spider room. Second floor. East wing. For Adelaide. But I thought you didn't like . . ."

"I don't mind. And the rotten potatoes can wait a few moments longer for me to scrub them away."

Hanne called up a wan smile in return. "Thank you."

The spider room was called such because its walls were hung with silvery lacework, shaped and gathered into cloud-shaped webs. A canopy over the bed was of filmy chiffon, dotted with miniscule diamonds to reflect lamplight. Ilse arranged dishes and other items on a side table. She was nearly done when she heard a heavy tread behind her.

"We must be early," said a husky voice.

An older woman stood in the doorway—a tall, heavyset woman swathed in layers of ruby silks and gray wool. She had a strongly marked face, its deep creases emphasized by the lamplight. Ilse recognized Mistress Luise Ehrenalt, a high-ranking member of the silk weaver's guild. Behind her came Adelaide, who glided into the room and laid a hand on Ehrenalt's arm. "Come, Luise. The girl is just leaving. And we've your favorite—strawberries."

Luise laughed. "You are my favorite, sweet. Or weren't you listening to me?"

Their attention on each other, they ignored Ilse, who took up the now-empty tray and withdrew. When she had offered to take the tray for Hanne, she had not thought about seeing the courtesans or their clients. Now, as the door closed, she heard Luise's throaty laugh and Adelaide's murmured replies. How did Adelaide manage it? Was it truly as she told Kathe—that she saw Mistress Ehrenalt as just an audience? But Ilse had heard genuine affection in the courtesan's voice, and now . . . now it did not sound as though she were acting.

I have to see how she does it.

Her heart beating faster, Ilse passed through another room and into the servants' corridor, which ran between and around the private rooms. Kathe had mentioned spy holes her first day. Since then, Ilse had learned which rooms had them and how they were concealed. She checked in both directions and saw the corridor was empty. She set the tray on the floor and rose onto her toes to peer through the spy hole.

The spider web's filmy hanging made everything hazy, but Ilse could make out two shadowy figures. Adelaide, taller and slimmer, was feeding strawberries to Luise Ehrenalt, caressing her face as she did. Luise caught her hand and kissed it. The next moment, the two moved swiftly to the bed.

Luise sank down. Still standing, Adelaide drew her tunic over her head and let the filmy cloth drift onto the floor. Lamplight accentuated her

muscles as they slid beneath her radiant skin, reminding Ilse of Lord Kosen-mark and how he moved. A royal courtesan. Some said she had pleasured Baerne of Angersee himself. And yet she had abandoned such a position to come here, to Tiralien.

Adelaide untied her skirt and let it drop to the floor. Ilse held herself still, hardly breathing. She had to see Adelaide's face at the moment of pas-sion. Did she pretend, as Ilse had? Was it possible to tell?

"What are you looking at?"

Ilse spun from the spy hole. Lord Kosenmark stood one pace behind her in the corridor, his face half-hidden by the dim light. Quickly, she knelt to pick up the tray. "My lord. I'm sorry I was dawdling. I didn't mean to—"

Kosenmark stopped her with a gesture. "You're weeping."

She hadn't known, couldn't recall starting, but her cheeks were wet. More tears spilled when she jerked her head away, falling like stars. Kosen-mark knelt in front of her, still a safe distance away. "What happened?"

"Nothing, my lord. I was . . . watching."

"Why?"

Ilse hesitated and saw him frown. Gulping down a breath, she said, "To see how Adelaide managed it, my lord."

"Because of what happened to you?"

She nodded. "I tried pretending. I said . . . I said I was willing. Once I even—" Her voice failed her then.

Kosenmark touched her arm. "Come with me," he said softly, his tone entirely different from before. "I'll have someone notify Greta where you are. Never mind about the tray."

With a gentle pressure against her back, he guided her to the stairs and up to his office. There he paused and spoke briefly with the runner, who dis-appeared down the stairs. Ilse continued to weep. She could not stop seeing Alarik Brandt's face, feeling him inside her, hearing herself cry out. She was dimly aware that Kosenmark had opened the door and was leading her inside.

He led her to the nearest chair. "Sit."

She sank into the chair. A green light flickered at her right, a hint of magic's scent curled through the air, then a brighter yellow halo sprang into life. No voices filtered from the rooms below. No music drifted up from the common rooms, which surely were open by now. Only the hiss of the sand glass as it turned to the next hour broke the hush.

Kosenmark pressed a cloth into her hands, a handkerchief, which smelled faintly of cedarwood. She blotted away the tears until the handkerchief was soaked. He took away the cloth then and held a wine cup to her lips. "Drink. Slowly."

It was wine mixed with water. She tried to take the cup herself, but her hands were shaking badly. Kosenmark wrapped his hands around hers to steady them. "Please do not drop it," he said mildly. "That is my favorite pattern."

He was smiling. She tried to smile back, but she was sobbing too hard. Stop it. Stop it. Stop it, she told herself, then realized she was saying the words out loud. Kosenmark appeared unperturbed. He helped her to drink the wine, then took the cup away and sank onto the floor at her feet.

"Tell me," he said, "was I right? Is your name Therez Zhalina?"

Ilse closed her eyes. "It was. Not any longer."

"And your father is Petr Zhalina."

She tensed and nodded.

"I've heard his name," Kosenmark said. "He's spent a fortune, they say, sending out messengers, offering rewards for news of what happened to you. Why did you leave?"

"My father wished me to marry. His choice, not mine."

"And you disliked his choice?"

"I did. I met the man once. He frightened me, my lord. I can't say why."

"But your father didn't listen."

She opened her eyes. Kosenmark's expression told her as little as his voice. "No, my lord. He said he would sign the contracts the next day. And there was no one who could argue with him."

"I see," Kosenmark said softly. "Who was the man?"

"Maester Theodr Galt. He controls the shipping contracts."

Kosenmark's only reaction was a sudden thinning of his mouth. "I know that man." Pause. "Let me guess what else happened. When you discovered no one could help you, you packed a satchel with plain clothes and a few other belongings—whatever you could find in a hurry. You took some gold, and with it, you bought passage to Duenne."

She blinked in surprise, and he smiled sadly. "Let us say that I was once faced with a similar choice. Similar but not the same. I had chosen my future, and my fears were those of second thoughts. In the end, I decided to stay. The following morning it was too late to undo that decision."

He was talking about the night before they gelded him. It could be nothing else. "My lord . . ."

Kosenmark lifted a hand. "What plans did you have for Duenne?"

She covered her confusion by drinking deeply. Even watered, she could

tell it was a fine vintage, this wine—light and golden, with hints of summer pears and lemons. A man who bought such wines would find her plans
childish.

But he was waiting, patiently, for her answer. "My plans were very bad
ones, my lord."

"Possibly. Tell me, anyway. I promise not to laugh."

So he guessed that as well. "My last night in Melnek, my father had a
dinner party—the one where he introduced me to Maester Galt. A man
named Baron Eckard was there, too. He talked about his time in Duenne, at
court and in the city."

Kosenmark gave a soft exclamation, but motioned for her to go on. She
nodded, wet her lips with the wine. It was hard, painfully hard to recall that
evening. How she had hoped its success would mean her chance to escape
her father's household. Laughter fluttered against her ribs. Oh, yes. It had
been a success, and she had escaped, only not in the way she expected. But
Kosenmark was waiting for her answer.

"We talked, my lord," she said. "At dinner, dancing. He and Baron Mann
both said that in Duenne there were a thousand opportunities."

"I shall have to warn Rudolfus about dangling such allurements in front
of young girls. Why did you not ask him for help then?"

"My lord, why would he give me help? Besides, I didn't hear of my father's plans until after the dinner. My father said he would sign the marriage
contract the next day. That was when I remembered what Baron Eckard
said about Duenne. I was to go there in the summer, you see, to visit my
cousin's family. They couldn't take me in, of course, not without telling my
father, but I thought I might find a place as someone's scribe—I write well
and I know about trade and arithmetic and prices and goods. You do, if you
grow up in a merchant's family."

He nodded. "Good plans so far. What happened to your money?"

"Someone stole most of it. Then the caravan master told me he knew
my name. I tried to get away, but they caught me. The caravan master said
he would send me back, unless I gave him a good reason to keep me." Her
breath came short at the memory of that exchange and its outcome. She
swallowed and went on. "I couldn't go back. Not to that house. I said I would
do anything he asked."

"I see. What was the caravan master's name?"

Her mouth had gone dry again, just thinking of his name. "Alarik
Brandt."

Kosenmark said nothing. He appeared to be turning over her story in his thoughts. Ilse cradled the cup in her hands, watching his face but seeing nothing beyond his abstraction. Without looking up, he said, "I know your father by reputation, Therez. He would take you back, if you wished."

"No." Ilse flinched, spilling the wine. "No, my lord. Please. You don't know what he's like. Please, no."

Kosenmark offered her another handkerchief. Still shaking, she dried her hands. "It was only a suggestion," he said. "You have my promise that I will not force you to leave here."

He crossed back to his desk where he poured wine for himself. When he returned, he sat in silence for a while, his expression thoughtful. "I have another suggestion," he said at last. "Would you consider a change in your duties here? You said you wanted to work as a scribe. You could serve Maester Hax as his assistant."

Ilse looked up, startled. "Why, my lord?"

"Because Maester Hax is growing old. Because I need someone with your skills in writing and language. Because whatever your father's failings, he did educate you, which makes you a better scribe than a cook's helper. Or do you prefer washing out pots and barrels?"

So he knew about that, too. She touched the minute cracks in her work-roughened palms. "But my lord, you don't know me. How can you trust me?"

"I know you well enough. I've heard what Kathe and Greta say of your character, and I've observed you myself. The offer is not charity," he added in the face of her continued silence. "I have more concerns than just this house, and Maester Hax needs someone to handle the everyday correspondence, so he can concentrate on more intricate matters. And you would not be running away, Mistress Ilse. Not this time."

It made her skin prickle to hear her private thoughts spoken out loud. "How did you—?" Comprehension came at once. "You heard."

Kosenmark shrugged. "You might as well say I spied on you. Yes, I heard, both the situation and your solution. You are not running away, Mistress Ilse, but moving on to the next challenge. Besides, it will give you money enough for Duenne, should you decide to go."

He set his wine cup aside and held out his hand. After a moment's hesitation, she took his hand, which encompassed hers easily. His palm was callused, the rest smooth and warm to her touch. She felt a trace of magic's current. Within came an easing of long tension. The sensation was painful, as though hope were a physical thing, too long kept imprisoned inside its cage, and only now unfolding after a very long time.

I have a choice. I can choose—not a new life entirely, but a next new step toward it.

Briefly, she thought of Lys and Rosel, and felt a twinge of misgiving. They would not take this new favor well. But then, she shook away the thought. "My lord, I am grateful . . . with the sweetness of true gratitude offered freely."

A smile lit his face briefly. It was like a flare of sunlight on an already bright day. "And as freely returned. Now I remember you also like Tanja Duhr's poetry. I shall take that as proof I chose well. Come. We begin tonight."

CHAPTER ELEVEN

KOSENMARK WENT TO his inner rooms for a few moments and returned with a damp cloth and a comb, so that Ilse could make herself presentable. When she had finished, Kosenmark studied her with an appraising look. "Well enough. Now to Maester Hax."

They arrived at Hax's office just as he was clearing off his desk for the night. Hax paused and glanced from Ilse to Lord Kosenmark. "Are you paying a visit for pleasure or business?"

"Both," Kosenmark said. "I've brought you an assistant."

"Ah." Another expressive glance. "Have you found my services lacking, my lord?"

For the first time, Kosenmark looked uneasy. "Do not argue with me, Berthold."

"Why not? You like a good argument, or so you claim."

"A worthy one, yes."

"Which means you will not listen to my opinion."

"I will. But not here, and not now."

Ilse began to wish herself back in the kitchens with the rotten potatoes. She stirred, uneasy, and Hax glanced in her direction. "My lord, you are right. Not here and not now. Would you grant me an interview tomorrow morning? I find it's easier to arrange my thoughts when I'm fresh."

"You mean easier to argue back. Very well." To Ilse, he said, "You will have a difficult master, you see."

"Like student, like teacher," Hax said under his breath.

"You see how he does not give up? Not really. He will argue with me for weeks now. Understand, it will have nothing to do with you, or how well you perform your duties. It will only be that he hates to lose. What was that, Berthold?"

"Nothing, my lord. Only that we ought to inform Mistress Raendl of the change."

"Good. I thought you were beginning to repeat yourself. A sign of old age."

"A sign that my lord has turned deaf. If you will excuse me, I should like a few words with my new assistant."

"Then you agree?"

Hax smiled, but it was a stiff unhappy smile. "In form, if not in essence, my lord. Yes, I agree."

Kosenmark shook his head and murmured something about needing to see to his visitors below. Hax watched him go with a long considering look. "Interesting," he said. "And unexpected, though not surprising. So you asked for a promotion, Mistress Ilse?"

"No, sir. Lord Kosenmark offered one, and I accepted."

"Hmmm. How did he come to make that offer?"

Out of kindness and pity, she thought. "Maester Hax . . ."

Hax waved a hand. "Never mind. You are being discreet. A good trait, especially in your new position. I would encourage it." He paused and seemed to consider his next words. Ilse expected him to talk about her new duties, but Hax was shaking his head. "It will be very different, with you as my assistant. A challenge for us both, I believe. Very well. Report to me after nine tomorrow morning."

A clear dismissal. Ilse curtsied awkwardly, not knowing what was correct. Hax seemed not to notice. When she glanced back from the foyer, he was staring off into a corner, his restless hands still.

SHE SLEPT BADLY and woke early, just as the bells began to peal the eighth hour. A floor above her, the large hour glass for Lord Kosenmark's complicated timepiece would just be turning over, its chimes softly echoing those outside. The other girls still slept—they had worked hours longer than her, and would not wake for some time.

Moving quietly, Ilse padded over to the washstand. *I'm not running away,* she told herself as she scrubbed her face and combed out her hair. *I'm going on to the next challenge.*

And yet it *was* too much like her escape from home, or from Brandt's caravan, both undertaken in stealth. The practical side of her said that the girls wouldn't thank her for waking them just to say good-bye. Besides, she wasn't actually leaving the household.

Bedclothes rustled. Hanne sat up, rubbing her eyes. "Ilse? Where are you going? What happened?"

Ilse came to her bedside and whispered, "Nothing happened. Go to sleep, Hanne. It's early."

"But you never came back from the spider room. Then a runner came from Lord Kosenmark, and we heard you were never coming back. Lys said Lord Kosenmark dismissed you, but then Lord Kosenmark came and Mistress Raendl and Mistress Denk went off and didn't come back for hours and . . ."

"I'm to work for Maester Hax now," Ilse said.

Hanne stared. "Maester Hax?"

"Writing letters," Ilse said, though she wasn't certain what duties Maester Hax might give her, nor how much Hanne would understand of a secretary's duties. She smiled and brushed the hair from Hanne's forehead. The girl's color was much better and she no longer felt fevered. "You know how much I like reading and writing and books. Did you ask about seeing Mistress Hedda?"

"Kathe gave me something. She said I was silly for not asking, and she was stupid for not seeing. But Ilse, it doesn't make sense. How—"

"She found a better bed, Hanne. That's what happened."

Lys was sitting up in bed, hair tumbled around her shoulders. Ilse felt her stomach twist into a knot at the girl's satisfied grin. *You knew this would happen,* she told herself. *You expected it.* Still, it took all her self-control to keep her expression bland.

"It's true," Lys said. "Isn't it? You finally spread your legs wide enough, and someone fell in. Well, I'm glad to see you go. We all are."

"Lys . . ." Dana groaned from her bed.

Ilse stood up, sat back down by Hanne's side, and took the younger girl's hands in hers. Running away would not solve anything, especially not with her staying in the same household. Janna rolled over and muttered something about late nights should mean late mornings, but by now Steffi was sitting up and demanding to know what the trouble was.

"It's her," Lys said, pointing at Ilse. "She's the trouble."

"Oh shut up," Janna said. "You're just jealous."

"Jealous? And you're not? Since when?"

"Since she did her work. Why are you so afraid of her?"

Lys spat out an ugly curse and launched herself at Janna, who scrambled from the bed. Ilse grabbed at Lys and caught the girl's wrists. "Stop fighting. Both of you."

Lys wrenched free and slapped Ilse across the face. Janna shoved Lys away. "Do that again and we'll tell Mistress Raendl."

"You would, you sneak."

"If I'm a sneak, you're a bully. I know why Steffi's sister left. And I know why Hanne jumps when you come into the room. Pinch and punch and badger and bully. That's you, and it's not right."

By this time, all the girls were standing around them in a circle. Rosel looked as though she wanted to join the fight, but didn't dare. Dana and Steffi were whispering to each other. Only Hanne, silent and pale, had retreated toward the door.

It's not enough to keep from running away, Ilse thought. She stepped between Lys and Janna. "Leave her be," she said to Janna.

"So you'd rather fight me?" Lys said.

Ilse faced her. "I don't want to fight."

"Coward."

Her dark face was blotched with anger; tears gleamed in her eyes. Strange how Ilse felt a sudden rush of pity for the girl. "Call me whatever you like," she said. "I don't care. But stop making trouble for everyone else."

Lys jerked her chin up. "Why? Who made you the queen?"

"No one. No one made you the queen, either. Even if they did, they might change their minds unless you treat them better."

Lys lifted a fist, as though to strike. Abruptly her expression changed and she dropped her hand, still clenched. Ilse glanced back. Janna and Steffi and Dana stood behind her, hands linked together. Lys's gaze shifted from face to face as she took in the situation. "Like a damned princess," she muttered.

Janna grinned. "'Smatter, Lys? Don't like to see someone else wearing a crown?" She turned to Ilse and held out her hand. "Come on. We can have one last breakfast together."

Ilse squeezed Janna's hand. She found she was smiling. "Yes, I'd like that."

THE BELLS WERE just ringing nine when she arrived at Maester Hax's office. Kosenmark opened the door to her knock. "Good morning," he said. "We were just discussing your new duties. Berthold, come to my office later, and we can review the latest dispatches."

Maester Hax motioned for Ilse to sit, then poured two cups of tea. "Are you ready to begin?"

"As ready as I know."

He seemed amused by her answer. "True enough. So let us begin."

For the next hour, Ilse drank tea and listened intently, while Hax talked and talked about those expectations. He was so kind and patient, she could almost believe she had misunderstood his mood the previous night.

"You will run errands," he told her, "for me and Lord Kosenmark. You will handle tasks the runners cannot, accepting items that come for Lord Kosenmark or me and securing them, handing off items to the couriers we use, arranging for delivery of packages, writing out fair copies of letters, and writing to his dictation. You will keep track of our supplies and order more through Mistress Denk. Mistress Denk can also assist you with dispatching the letters. Some correspondence travels with the governor's post, some by private courier, others by merchant caravans and the like. Are you following me?"

She nodded, thinking Hax must have worked wearying hours doing all these tasks, as well as the others Lord Kosenmark had alluded to. *The more intricate concerns of my household,* as he had phrased it.

They had drained the first carafe of tea, and Hax rang for another, which Janna delivered. Ilse noticed a self-satisfied expression on the girl's face and wondered what else had happened after she left the kitchen, but Hax was already talking again, his long expressive hands sketching out patterns in the air as he explained how he preferred the accounts to be kept. Ilse had some notion of accounts, but apparently Lord Kosenmark required very particular methods for tracking his investments and expenditures, and some of those methods left Ilse puzzled and shaking her head. Still, she made an effort to understand and remember.

"But all that is secondary," he said at last.

"Secondary," Ilse murmured faintly.

Hax smiled at her dismay. "Of course. All these duties come second to Lord Kosenmark's correspondence."

Lord Kosenmark received numerous letters from all over the kingdom, he told her. Letters from his family, from old colleagues in Duenne, from the inhabitants of his father's duchy in the southwest. Her initial task was to separate the letters into three categories, depending on the sender. Those from Lord Kosenmark's family or from the duchy of Valentain went into the first.

"Also a limited number of other correspondents," Hax said. "Here are their names."

He handed her several sheets of paper. Each page contained three columns of names. Lords. Dukes. Merchants. Scholars. The names and addresses ranged throughout Veraenen society and its geography. "What shall I do with letters that don't match the list?"

"Those you bring directly to Lord Kosenmark. Do not use the house runners," he added, touching his hands together briefly. "For the most part, these will be important documents for his investments, and he wishes to handle them himself. If Lord Kosenmark is not available, you bring them to me. If I am not available, you will lock them in my office in a certain letter box I will show you."

"And what if the letters have no names?"

"Those belong to the third category. Bring them to Lord Kosenmark as well, but separate from the rest—it will save us time. Again, if Lord Kosenmark and I are both absent, place the unmarked letters in the letter box."

Once she accustomed herself to that task, Hax said he would give her more details on how to subdivide them further. "You will learn the names that interest him most. Are you overwhelmed yet?"

She nodded, thinking that Lord Kosenmark attracted a huge amount of correspondence for a man dismissed from court.

"No matter," Hax said. "We shall not expect you to remember everything the first day. Now . . ." He took a bunch of keys from his belt and removed one. "I had mentioned a letter box, which I keep in my office. Here is the key. Keep it with you at all times."

Ilse turned the key over in her hand. It had a long notched blade and large octagonal bow stamped with a leopard. When she closed her hand over it, she felt the buzz of old magic.

"You must also have keys for my office and Lord Kosenmark's," Hax went on. "I shall send for the locksmith to make copies."

"Is that enough?" she asked. "I mean . . . if Lord Kosenmark is anxious about his papers, would a lock suffice to keep out thieves?"

Hax kept silent long enough that she worried she had trespassed on a forbidden topic. "We have anticipated that," he said slowly. "It comes from living at court, where there are no secrets except those fiercely guarded. We have magic safeguarding the doors and windows of both our offices. The same holds true for the strongboxes, which Lord Kosenmark had specially built by a friend. That key you hold opens the outer lid. You may then drop letters through the slot, but you cannot retrieve them. Neither can I. Only Lord Kosenmark can."

Magic. She felt a ripple of anticipation. "Does Lord Kosenmark know that much magic?"

"More than most lords. Not as much as the King's Mage, certainly. But he has made certain areas of magic his specialty, and he has friends who assist him. Are you bothered by that? Lord Kosenmark said your father originally came from Duszranjo."

Ilse shook her head. Briefly she thought how she would always need to explain how not all Duszranjo followed the old laws, only the most remote villages in the southern end, those who remembered the wars between Károví and the empire, when mages from both armies scorched the borderlands. *And they weren't laws,* she thought. *Only the natural response of someone once burned by fire, who starts at any spark or flame.*

But like anything else about Duszranjo, the legends were more powerful than the dull shadings of truth. "I was born in Veraene," she said finally. "Nothing about magic bothers me."

Hax's only reaction to that was a shrug. He then went on to explain the procedures for contacting Lord Kosenmark in emergencies—not mentioning what those emergencies might be—and how his schedule usually worked. Eventually the explanations came to an end, and Maester Hax took her across the foyer to her new study.

The room was smaller than Hax's but comfortable-looking and furnished with a writing table and several chairs. Shelves lined the wall behind the desk. Most were empty, but the lower ones held boxes of writing supplies. Maps and charts hung from another wall; a long narrow table stood underneath. Like the one she had seen in Kosenmark's office, the maps contained densely written notations in their margins and cryptic marks next to cities and ports. The third wall had a fireplace flanked by more shelves. Lamps hung from the ceiling above both the desk and the table. Someone had already lit the fire.

"You might make a list of your needs," Hax said. "Tables. More comfortable chairs. Mistress Denk can help with ordering those. Kathe will come by to show you your new quarters. Ah, my lord. I thought we were to meet later."

Ilse started. Lord Kosenmark had appeared, as silent as a prowling cat, in the doorway. "We were," he said. "Jez arrived."

That enigmatic reply meant something to Hax, evidently, because his lips parted in obvious surprise. "So soon. I had not expected—" Then he seemed to remember Ilse's presence because he glanced at her with an troubled expression. "Mistress Ilse, I must leave you to your own supervision. Write out that list of supplies and wait for me to return."

He hurried after Kosenmark, who was already mounting the stairs.

Ilse let her breath trickle out. Very strange. Very, very strange. Maybe they would tell her more later. For now, she had her first assignment.

She surveyed the room again. A short examination of the lower shelves yielded a complete set of writing materials, including pens, penknives, ink pots, and reams of inexpensive paper suited for note-taking. A small box held more expensive paper and parchment. She selected what she needed and sat at her new desk.

The chair proved sturdy and comfortable. The desk had several scratches, and its sides were badly dented, but the writing surface itself was smooth enough. All the furniture looked worn and used, and she had the impression

that everything had been assembled in haste. It gave the room a temporary feel.

Never mind. It was better than pots and pans.

She sharpened her pen, dipped its point into the ink pot, and tapped
away the excess. The blank sheet of paper tempted her with possibilities. It
could hold a list. A poem. A letter . . .

*Dearest Klara. I am so sorry that I could not write to you before. You see, I ran
away—*

Ilse scratched out the letters. Wrong. Everything wrong. It was too soon
to write about what happened. Too soon to think about it. She shredded the
paper and burned the pieces in her fireplace. Then she returned to her desk
and took out a fresh sheet of paper. Make a list, he had said. She could do
that much.

She had filled one side of paper when Kathe appeared at her door. "You
look more at home," she said with a smile.

Ilse carefully blotted the last few lines. "Perhaps. I've had more training
with a pen than a paring knife."

"So I told my mother when Lord Kosenmark informed us of recent
events."

"Oh dear. I forgot all about your mother. What did she say?"

Kathe's eyes brightened. "Those are words I should not repeat in gentle
company. Let us just say that Mistress Denk and my mother were in rare
temper last night—both of them grumbling how Lord Kosenmark must
think he was still in court, where the king has more servants than the stars.
They were busy past midnight, setting up new rooms for you. Come, would
you like to see your new quarters?"

Ilse's new quarters were in the west wing, on the opposite side of the
house from her old dormitory. Like Kathe, she had a small sitting room,
with stools and a fireplace and a table for eating or writing. The bedroom
was larger than the sitting room, with a clothespress and an oversized bed
with quilted covers. One wall had a hanging that depicted a woman's sil-
houette, her hair falling into a cascade to her feet. *Lir Triumphant* said the
lettering. A small square window opened onto the courtyard and garden
below.

She realized belatedly that Kathe had stopped talking.

"You have that faraway look," Kathe said. She fussed with the sitting
room's table, wiping away an invisible smudge with her apron. "No more
chopping or mincing or washing up together. No more chatting. I shall miss
that."

"No more scraping out barrels," Ilse replied. "No more polishing radishes."

Kathe smiled, a bit pensively. "You nearly did polish them, I heard."

"No, even I knew better. Does Rosel play that trick on every new girl?"

"Just the pretty ones." Kathe sent her a brief sidelong glance. "You did well with them, from what I saw."

Ilse shrugged. "Yes and no. Lys . . ."

"Lys thought you would take her place" was Kathe's tart reply.

"How? I knew nothing about kitchen work. I still don't know anything, except scrubbing and scraping."

"Ah, but you were an expert scrubber and scraper by the end. The scullions are in tears, knowing that you won't be there to take the worst of the scut work." The humor faded from her face. "Ilse, do not fret about Lys. You did the right thing with the other girls, and none of them were sulking about your good fortune this morning. As for Lys . . . give her some time and she'll settle down."

"What if she doesn't?"

"Then my mother will have a word to say. Speaking of my mother, I must get back to the kitchen before she frightens off the new pastry cook. I'll send up Janna or Steffi with coffee and meat pies for a midday nibble. You'll need to eat well to keep up with Maester Hax and Lord Kosenmark." She tucked a loose strand of hair behind one ear and glanced around. "And we might not have time for mincing and washing, but we will have more time for private talks. It's easier, now that you aren't working for me and my mother. That is, if you like."

Ilse smiled. "Yes, I would like that."

Kathe pretended an interest in the carpet. "I'm glad." Then she shook her head. "Listen to me, babbling nonsense when we both have work to do. Where would you like your tray delivered—here or in your office?"

"In my office," Ilse said, thinking of her lists.

Kathe laughed. "Now you do sound like Maester Hax."

Ilse returned to her new office and her list-making. Before she had finished, Hax sent a note with a new assignment. She spent the rest of the morning making an inventory of the supplies in her office and in Maester Hax's. When she delivered the list to him, he gave her letters to copy and then critiqued the results. After a short noonday meal, they reviewed Lord Kosenmark's schedule.

He rose early, Hax told her, and spent two hours with the weapons master, Maester Benedikt Ault. After breakfast, he generally spent an hour or more with Maester Hax discussing business. He ate his midday meal alone or with visitors. More visitors came by appointment in the late afternoon. Evenings he spent with more intimate friends, or abroad at some of Tiralien's great houses, though at times those friends visited him in the common room.

"We keep a schedule, and he changes it," Hax said. "His company is much sought after."

Her first day ended close to midnight, and she fell into bed exhausted. In the days that followed, she worked longer hours. Earlier ones. Curious ones.

Lord Kosenmark had not created this position out of charity, she soon realized. Letters arrived daily from all parts of Veraene—fine parchment from dukes and counts, marked with elaborate seals, plainer ones from merchants in the interior, anonymous letters from trading posts along the Károvín border. There were even packages from Lord Dedrick, who liked to send gifts when other obligations, or his father, prevented him from visiting. Ilse sorted them all according to Maester Hax's instructions.

"I take one immense pile," she told Kathe, "and from that I make three not-as-huge ones. Then I carry them around for a while, stop, go fetch something for Lord Kosenmark or Maester Hax. Most of the time I wait for them to finish talking in private."

Kathe's cheeks dimpled. "So many *somethings*. No, don't worry. I shan't ask what these somethings are. I know you must be discreet. And I can see you like the work."

Ilse laughed. "Oh yes. I do."

They found they did spend more time together, and not just because their stations had changed. When Kathe visited merchants to order supplies or to arrange for special consignments, Ilse often accompanied her, and they walked to the open-air markets once a week. Those were not the only times Ilse left the pleasure house. She frequently rode in Lord Kosenmark's carriage to the courier or posting establishments with packages or letters bound for distant provinces. Other times she delivered or picked up items from noble households in Tiralien itself, either riding or walking, but always escorted by one of Lord Kosenmark's guards. When she asked why the runners did not make those deliveries, Maester Hax said it was to their benefit if Ilse learned her way about the city.

She came home from one such errand only to meet Lys coming down the side lane with a large basket over her arm. Ilse paused, conscious that she had not seen Lys since their confrontation a month ago. Lys stopped as well and stared. Her face was a blank, but Ilse sensed the anger behind that watchful gaze, which took in Ilse's new clothing, the sheaf of letters she carried, and the guard and carriage behind her. It was as though she absorbed everything, giving nothing back, not even a reflection.

After a moment, Lys shrugged and continued on her way. Ilse let out an unhappy sigh, then hurried to Maester Hax's office, where she knew the secretary waited for these letters. She did not understand why Lady Theysson could not deliver the letters herself—she visited the pleasure house frequently enough with Lord Iani—but Ilse knew that if she asked why, Lord Kosenmark would only deflect the question, or Maester Hax would give her a nonsense answer.

"Thank you," Hax said, taking the sheaf. "Yes. Good. You might not realize it, Mistress Ilse, but Lady Theysson is an accomplished poet. And since these are her latest poems, I shall selfishly dismiss you for your long-delayed dinner. Have you sorted the day's letters?"

"I gave those to Lord Kosenmark this morning."

"Alas, more arrived in the intervening hours. I've locked them in your office, in your letter box. When you are done, bring them to me. Lord Kosenmark is not at home today."

Ilse suppressed a faint sigh. Correspondence was indeed her primary task, and it never seemed to end. Tonight would be another meal eaten at her desk.

She stopped by the kitchen to fetch her own dinner tray, hoping to exchange a word with Kathe before she settled down to another session of work. To her surprise, she found Nadine perched on a stool, eating plums and trading rude stories with the spit boys. Nadine finished off a plum and tossed the pit into the fireplace, then looked around at Ilse's entrance with a flashing smile. "My long-lost love! Come, have a plum with me."

Ilse suppressed a laugh. She could see dozens of plum pits in the fireplace, and she wondered why none of the girls had tried to stop Nadine from making such a mess. Or perhaps that was no more possible than they could stop a crackle of lightning leaping from the sky. "You know that Mistress Raendl will beat you, courtesan or not," she told her.

Nadine eyed her with an expression brimful of mischief. "So I had hoped. Or would you prefer to take her place?"

Impossible. Ilse shook her head and turned to Janna, who tried to smother her laughter without much success. "Do we have anything ready for a quick meal?" she asked.

"Stop her, Janna," Nadine cried. "Don't let her escape. We want a story."

"No stories," Ilse said. "Work. Letters."

"Grim dreary work. Have you been eating prunes again?"

Ignoring Nadine's chatter, Ilse gathered her own supper with Janna's help. If she finished early tonight, perhaps she could spend an hour in the common room. It would not be so bad, not if she stayed in the bright sections, where the visitors played cards or complicated strategy games with boards and markers. Lord Kosenmark had mentioned he had received a new musical instrument, one that operated with strings and hammers set in a box. Eduard had volunteered that he knew how to play it.

She retained that hope until she saw how many letters filled her letter box. Mountains of them, she thought. There were also three letters needing a fair copy, with the notation from Maester Hax that these were urgent and should go into the post this evening with Lord Kosenmark's signature.

Ilse ate her dinner in a hurry and started with the letter copying.

From Lord Raul Kosenmark of Valentain to Count Fredr Andersien. Tiralien. My Lord Count, It is with delight that I read your letter. I remember our conversation last year, when we discussed the increase in taxes and the parallel difficulties of conducting trade across the borders. I admit that while I have not followed the king's policies in that matter, I do have friends with some influence and I can direct you to them . . .

Another one went to Baron Zeltenof, who apparently had asked for advice in governing his newly inherited barony. Lord Kosenmark's letter demurred such knowledge, but Ilse noted that he went on to suggest a list of books, including the memoirs of another young nobleman from the empire days. Strange, she thought. Such advice did not seem urgent.

She picked up the last one, a letter for a king's governor in the northern province of Ournes, which bordered on the kingdom of Immatra.

. . . my lord, I am honored you would send me your thoughts concerning the unrest along the border provinces. Though I am no longer a member of the court or council, I understand that your apprehension is not unusual, nor unreasonable. However, if I did still have influence, I would suggest that we ought not assume aggression without true evidence. As Mandel of Ysterien, wrote three hundred years ago, one generation's prejudice too often becomes the next generation's war. . . .

That letter made her pause. *War?*

She had heard rumors of war since long before she left Melnek. But Kosenmark talked about war as though he had heard more than rumors. Was it possible that the rumors were more than just rumors?

Unsettled, she finished off the outgoing letters, then turned to the stacks of incoming correspondence. Her duties had changed somewhat in the past week. Now she was to open and screen letters from certain addresses.

Absorbed by her thoughts, she cut open the first letter without reading the address:

Dear Raul, Our predictions were correct. The levies for ordinary soldiers have surpassed the increase in taxes, though we are now instructed to use a different accounting . . .

Ilse dropped the letter. This was not an invitation or social letter. Nor was it the typical correspondence between business partners—she knew that from her father's household. She checked the address against her list, feeling faintly queasy. Lord Nicol Joannis, regional governor from Osterling Keep. His was one of the names under "confidential." She had blundered—badly.

I'll have to tell Maester Hax that I opened it by accident. He'll understand.

But her hands were still shaking when she picked up the second letter and compared its name and address to her list. It was another letter for investments, but the address read Duenne's University.

Not my business, she told herself. Lord Kosenmark might receive financial advice from a professor, for all she knew. She put the letter into the proper stack and reached for the next.

Her hand knocked against the edge of her desk. One of the stacks tilted dangerously. Ilse lunged to stop it—too late. The stack tumbled over and the letters spilled across the floor in a glorious cascade. Cursing loudly, Ilse dropped to her knees and hastily started gathering them up. She could just picture Lord Kosenmark's expression if he walked into her office now. At least Maester Hax could not see through two sets of closed doors.

She deposited the letters on her desk then saw she had missed one—a dirty parchment envelope without any address that had skittered underneath her desk. As she retrieved it, the sheet unfolded, and her eyes took in three words, hastily scrawled across the sheet in large blocky print: *Vnejšek. Jewels. Yes.*

Ilse sank back onto her heels and stared at the letter. It read like a game of word links but with strange unaccountable connections. Why was some-one writing such nonsense to Lord Kosenmark?

She reread the three mysterious words, and her skin prickled. Vnejšek was the Károvín word for Anderswar—the magic realm, what the poets called the knot where all magic converged. And *jewels* could only refer to Lir's lost jewels. *Yes.* There her imagination failed. Obviously the sender was answering a question posed by Lord Kosenmark. But why? What did he have to do with Károví's king and Lir's jewels?

She placed the letter in the third pile and returned to her desk. The next letter came from a merchant's guild in the north. The name appeared in the second category. *Keep going,* she told herself. *Stop asking questions and you'll finish sooner.* But the questions refused to subside. Why would this mer-chant write to Lord Kosenmark? She cast her memory over the letters she had copied during the past month. Some were directed to private mer-chants, but many went to the king's advisers in Tiralien, or governors through Veraene's far-flung provinces. Each letter revealed little. It was the larger pattern that left her breathless.

Duenne. The King's Council. Baerne's death. Exile.

Impossible, she thought. *And yet it explained so much.*

He had fashioned his own court, here in Tiralien.

CHAPTER TWELVE

". . . IF YOU PRESSED me for my opinion, I would recommend a barricade of thick posts, bound together with tempered metal. Of course, even metal has disadvantages. If you do not choose the highest quality, the metal rusts or breaks along hidden flaws . . ."

. . . and an alliance often requires careful tending, Ilse thought to herself as she wrote to Lord Kosenmark's dictation.

Ten days had passed since her discovery of Lord Kosenmark's shadow court. What she suspected to be his shadow court, she reminded herself. She had no proof other than three cryptic words from one anonymous writer.

And yet, the more Ilse considered the matter, the stranger she found all of Lord Kosenmark's correspondence. It was like those clever paintings that seemed to depict one scene, but if the beholder closed one eye, or looked through a specially ground glass, the painting showed an entirely different subject. Otherwise innocuous phrases—a request to a duke to remember Lord Kosenmark to their friends, a passage advising another friend to have patience with his errant son—took on new and doubled meanings. A world alongside ours, Tanja Duhr had written about magic's plane. One both surrounded and contained by other worlds. If Ilse was right, she had discovered another such realm here, in Lord Kosenmark's pleasure house.

Ilse only hoped that her face did not betray her. Maester Hax had said nothing when she confessed to opening the letter by accident, but sometimes she caught Lord Kosenmark observing her—as he did now, she realized with a start.

"You write neatly," Lord Kosenmark said. "Your tutors trained you well."

"Thank you, my lord."

He let his gaze linger on her face, as though reading something in her expression, but then shook his head. "How is Berthold today?" he asked. "Tired?"

"Tired but in good spirits, my lord."

She thought Kosenmark looked exhausted as well. There was a languid quality to his speech and faint smudges darkened his eyes. Lord Vieth had invited Lord Kosenmark to a formal banquet next week. Judging from the increase in visitors and correspondence, Ilse guessed there would be more to this affair than just music and delicacies.

Once he finished dictating, Lord Kosenmark reviewed the letter and nodded. "Good. Bring the fair copy to me later for a signature. I'd like all these letters posted today. Speaking of today, did Berthold mention the time for our session with the tailor?"

"This afternoon, my lord. It should be the final fitting, according to Maester Hax."

"The gods grant us mercy, I hope so."

Ilse hid a smile. She had observed one fitting and knew Lord Kosenmark and Maester Hax were to have very fine costumes, but the process proved trying to them both. An artistic man, the tailor had been most particular, saying that the cloth had to fall just right, both standing and in dance.

"You are laughing at me," Kosenmark observed. "Or my tailor."

"Never, my lord."

Kosenmark eyed her suspiciously, but confined himself to waving her away.

Ilse dispatched the letters and reported back to Maester Hax. "Am I wanted now?" he asked.

"Not yet," Ilse said, temporizing. "He signed the letters you asked about earlier, and I've sent them off. And I let him know when the tailor comes today."

"Good. And the thank-you letters?"

"Done. Gone. Sir."

"You've left me nothing to do," Hax said, smiling faintly.

I wish I could do that, Ilse thought. Hax had subsided into his chair and was resting his head on his hands. He and Lord Kosenmark had met until late the previous evening, and she expected they would do the same tonight. "You promised Mistress Hedda that you would work fewer hours."

Hax made a noise in his throat. "Save me from inquisitive women. Did you spy on us?"

"I listened, sir."

"Did Hedda ask you to?"

"No, but—"

"But you are worse than Lord Kosenmark. What happened to that shy girl from three months ago?"

Ilse smiled. "She is here, listening to a stubborn man who is trying to distract her."

He lifted his head and eyed her narrowly. "You are too clever sometimes. And since you insist, would you please fetch Mistress Denk's quarterly report for me? I promised Mistress Hedda that I would not climb the stairs so often."

"What about Mistress Raendl's accounts? Would you like those, too?"

"Yes. Those, too. Take your time coming back."

By the time Ilse completed her tasks, Hax had gone from his office, leaving behind a note that he was in his rooms, and would she meet with him after noon. A new batch of letters had arrived as well, among them a letter and package from Lord Dedrick Maszuryn. Ilse took those at once to Lord Kosenmark, who received them with an especially warm smile.

"Stay," he told Ilse. "The letter might require a reply."

The package proved to be a collection of antique maps. Lord Kosenmark scanned them with obvious pleasure, then broke the letter's seal and scanned its contents quickly.

Ilse could almost tell what it said by the rapid changes in his expression—from pleased to concerned and then to none at all. Kosenmark's fingers tightened around the paper. *Not good,* she thought.

Kosenmark glanced up from the letter. "There will be no answer," he said softly, and crumpled the letter in his fist. "Go. Find something to do. So will I."

Ilse did not wait for him to repeat the order. At the door, she dared a backward glance. Kosenmark was staring out the windows, his fingers tapping a restless pattern on his desk.

LORD KOSENMARK CANCELED all his appointments that afternoon, including the tailor's. Ilse and Maester Hax were together in Maester Hax's office, reviewing the week's schedule, when a runner brought them the news. Hax read the message in silence then released an audible sigh. "Not good," he muttered, and folded the note in quarters.

His words made an uncanny echo of Ilse's earlier reaction. She must have made an involuntary movement, because Hax looked up with a frown. "Curious, Mistress Ilse?"

"No, sir. Just concerned."

"Don't be. I say that for your own peace of mind." He closed the schedule book with a firm thump. "I'll talk to Lord Kosenmark when he's calmer. Tomorrow, most likely. In the meantime . . . read a book, play chess with Nadine or Josef, go for a walk into town. *I* shall take a nap, since nothing else can be done today."

He stood with a groan. Ilse bit her lips against any offer of help. That would only make him more prickly. She would have to send another message to Mistress Hedda and hope that Hax did not find out. He disliked any interference.

Sighing to herself, she returned to her own office and tried reviewing her accounts—they needed no review. She started a new inventory, but that, too, was unnecessary make-work. She had no desire to listen to Nadine's teasing, no matter how charming, nor to Josef's ever-changing stories about his past. She was not in the mood to be entertained.

When the library, too, proved unsatisfactory, Ilse retreated to the kitchens. At this hour, only Janna and Rosel were at their workstations, and none of the scullions were about. Even so, there was a sense of soothing purpose about the place—the sharp scents of freshly ground pepper, the yeasty smell of baking bread, the clatter of spoons and knives and other implements.

More soothing than when I worked here, she realized with an inward laugh.

Kathe sat at the makeshift desk, writing out lists of supplies for the coming week. "You look out of sorts," she observed.

"Maester Hax has given me a holiday."

"Oh, what torment for you. What's wrong?"

Ilse glanced around the kitchen. Janna and Rosel both pretended to be absorbed in their work, but she could tell they had overheard Kathe's greeting. Kathe followed the direction of her gaze. "I have some errands to run," she said mildly. "A few items that I should attend to myself. Would you like to come with me? Just wait a moment while I fetch a few things."

A few things turned out to be a purse of coins and a market basket. She and Ilse left the house by the back door, and continued through the gardens into the neighborhood beyond the pleasure house. It was a bright sunny day. A cool breeze blew in from the harbor's direction. *A good day for a walk,* Ilse thought, then wondered how many of her errands were simply a means to get her away from the pleasure house, while Maester Hax and Lord Kosenmark met about Lord Kosenmark's private activities.

"So tell me," Kathe said. "What is wrong?"

Ilse shrugged. "It's not me."

"Then it must be Maester Hax. Or Lord Kosenmark. Or both."

Ilse gave another shrug, thinking she had said too much already.

"I saw Lord Kosenmark earlier," Kathe said cautiously. "Anyone could see he was in a foul mood. And I heard from Mistress Denk that he canceled his appointment with the tailor this afternoon. Then you come to me, all glum and distracted. If I were guessing, I would say that Lord Kosenmark received unpleasant news from Lord Dedrick. Am I right?"

Ilse nodded. "Though I don't know what the news is."

"Hmmmm." Kathe glanced around, but they were alone in the lane. "Most likely, Lord Dedrick wrote to say he cannot attend Lord Vieth's banquet—possibly more—and that Lord Kosenmark is severely disappointed." She sighed. "It's not the first time. Either Lord Dedrick quarrels with Lord Kosenmark, or Lord Dedrick's father forbids him to visit. The effect is the same."

"It seems an unhappy kind of love," Ilse said, thoughtfully.

"They do make amends, eventually, but you're right. If I were to love someone, he would have to be a great deal more restful than Lord Dedrick. What about you?"

"I don't know. A friend once told me I should marry a scholar."

"A scholar? No, too quiet."

"I like quiet."

"You do, and you don't. You like quiet for reading, but I think you would want a lover who also makes you laugh and think. Someone with a spice of danger, even."

Shadows and light. The image of Theodr Galt appeared in her mind, and she shivered.

"What about Lord Kosenmark?" she asked hurriedly. "When did he first meet with Lord Dedrick? Was it in Duenne?"

"Ah, no. They met here, in Tiralien, at a dinner party given by Lord Dedrick's father. Baron Maszuryn sometimes curses that invitation, but I don't." Kathe fell silent for a few moments, her gaze on the paved street, apparently absorbed in memories. When she spoke again, her voice was subdued. "I was nine when Lord Kosenmark came to court. I remember what a wild reputation he had that first year. A disappointment with his cousin, they all said. Well, it was the same here in Tiralien. He refused all his father's letters. He stayed at home. Eventually Maester Hax persuaded him to accept a few invitations. But then Lord Kosenmark met Lord Dedrick and things improved. So for all their quarrels, I thank Lir and Toc for Lord Dedrick."

"A love to fill in the gaps and insufficiencies of life," Ilse murmured. She had once hoped to find such a love during her yearlong visit in Duenne. Someone to laugh with, as Kathe put it. Someone . . . like a friend, as Baron Eckard once said. Lord Kosenmark, at least, had found such a love, in spite of his own peculiar situation. She wondered what kind of place Lord Dedrick held in Kosenmark's shadow court.

"You should see your face," Kathe said. "I would give a dozen silver denier to hear what you were thinking just now."

"Nothing," Ilse said quickly. "Just considering whether we should take
the long path to market, or the short one."

"Oh, the short one," Kathe said. "I dare not leave Janna and Lys alone
for long. Talk about quarrels!"

The conversation turned easily to gossip about the kitchen girls and then
the courtesans and then what Kathe's mother had said when she found the
fireplace littered with plum pits after Nadine's visit. Once they reached
the market, Ilse helped Kathe with choosing spices, then they continued
to the wharves, where Kathe picked out fresh fish for Lord Kosenmark's
supper that evening. "I shall have to make a special effort," she said. "It's all I
can do for the poor man."

The bells were ringing quarter past four as they returned to the pleasure
house. Kathe left Ilse for the kitchens. Ilse was heading for the stairwell
when she met Lord Kosenmark, who was striding through the back halls.
His hair was matted with sweat, more sweat streaked his face and shirt. He
must have just come from an extra session with the weapons master.

Kosenmark paused in mid-stride. For an uncomfortable moment, he
stared at her with flat golden eyes, reminding Ilse of a hunting cat as it considered its prey. Ilse stepped back, startled. Kosenmark blinked as though he
had just recognized her. He nodded stiffly and continued past.

Ilse let out a shaky breath. If he were this unhappy in love, what must it
have been like when he had no one at all?

The next morning Maester Hax summoned Ilse to a private conference.
"Consider what I say to be a warning for the coming weeks. It has to do
with Lord Kosenmark's private affairs, but since it affects our dealings with
him, I would rather you knew than blundered, or worse, spent your days
speculating."

He paused and rubbed his eyes. Wordlessly, Ilse refilled his cup with
more tea, adding a spoonful of honey, the way he liked it. Hax took the cup
from her hands, but he gave the tea a wary look, as though he suspected Ilse
of secretly adding medicine to it.

"Lord Dedrick wrote Lord Kosenmark to announce his departure from
Tiralien," he said. "At his father's command, he will be absent the entire season, assisting his brother with managing the family estates. This, we are given
to believe, will instill a sense of responsibility and duty in Lord Dedrick."

"And keeping him from Lord Kosenmark. Why doesn't he refuse?"

"Money. Family feeling. The chance his father might disown him. I do not know. Perhaps Lord Dedrick is weary of battling his father. Whatever the cause, I advise that we not discuss the matter further, especially not in Lord Kosenmark's hearing."

"He will notice."

Hax sighed heavily. "Yes, he will. However we cannot help that."

"Will Lord Kosenmark still attend Lord Vieth's banquet?"

"Yes. He has obligations that override personal preferences and moods. Happily, he seems to recognize those obligations. After some discussion, that is." He sighed again and tapped his ink-stained fingers together, as though contemplating the subject. "And speaking of obligations, let us return to business," he said after a moment. "Tell me of Mistress Denk's request for renovations."

That night, Ilse lay in bed, listening to the faint metallic notes from Lord Kosenmark's new instrument—the one with velvet-covered hammers and metal strings. The instrument had proved popular, and now composers all over Tiralien were competing to write pieces for its unique tone. Whoever played it tonight was a skilled musician, playing swiftly and with a marked expression that brought out the loveliness of a very complex passage.

She closed her eyes and tried to focus only on the music, hoping it would lull her to sleep, but her thoughts skipped from one subject to another. Hax ill. Kosenmark troubled on several fronts. Her own secrets weighed upon her like a second piece of music winding through the background—her memories of home and family, of Klara and her grandmother. Her heart still ached to remember them, but she could bear it more easily now. Her grandmother— No, better to think about Klara. It was almost spring. Only a few months remained until her friend made the long journey to Duenne. She would be writing lists, ordering gowns and stockings and shoes and jewelry—all the accoutrements expected for a young woman's season in the capital.

I will never make that journey, Ilse thought. *Or if I do, it will be a very different one.*

A loud knocking yanked her back from the edge of sleep. Ilse pulled on a long robe and ran into the parlor just as Kosenmark's senior runner came through the outer door. "Lord Kosenmark wants you," he said. "Come at once."

But it was to Maester Hax's suite that he took her. Mistress Hedda was just coming out, her dark face grim. "I told him," she was saying. "I told him and told him but no, the stubborn old—" She broke off when she saw Ilse. "Go inside. Maester Hax and Lord Kosenmark wish to see you."

Berthold Hax lay in bed, eyes closed and head sunk deep into his pillows. Kosenmark sat at his bedside, hands clasped together. The air smelled strongly of recent magic, and Ilse's skin prickled as the current streamed over her skin.

Ei rûf ane gôtter. Komen mir de strôm unde kreft.

Mistress Hedda's magical signature was clear and strong. Only when Ilse approached the bed, however, did she recognize Lord Kosenmark's subtler magic, like the impression of his fingers upon the air.

Kosenmark glanced up and nodded at Ilse. Though he masked it well, she could see his distress in the set of his jaw. Then Hax tried to speak and broke into a loud groaning.

"Hush," Kosenmark said. "Save your strength."

"You just want me quiet, my lord." Hax's voice was breathy and faint.

"I want you well."

"I am well. Or I will be soon enough."

"Nevertheless, you cannot attend. You must not."

"I know that, my lord, but neither should the girl."

"She's here. Let us ask her."

Kosenmark motioned for Ilse to approach. "Our friend is quite ill and must keep to his bed. I would like you to fill his place at the governor's banquet."

"And I disagree," Hax said, somewhat louder than before.

"She must learn of it sometime."

"Why? Because I'm dying?"

Kosenmark jerked his face away. "Berthold—"

"I already know about Lord Kosenmark's business," Ilse said.

Both men went still. Kosenmark slowly turned his head and stared at Ilse, his expression unreadable. "Go on," he said softly.

Again she was reminded of a hunting cat. Wetting her lips, she said, "I saw—by accident—a letter with the words *Vnejšek. Jewels. Yes.* It came from your spies in Károví. I don't know the question, but I know it has to do with Lir's jewels. You've had other letters from Károví—I could tell by the handwriting. You are also in contact with nobles in Armand's Court. They ask you advice, and you give it. At least, I suppose you do, since you often send letters to Duenne. You do this secretly, however, and the addresses you send letters to do not always match the ones for letters you receive. I believe . . . I believe you are running a secret court, here in Tiralien. A shadow court, my lord."

A thick silence followed her announcement. Ilse's pulse beat hard against her throat. Surely this time she had dared too much.

"Clever girl," Hax whispered. "Too clever at times."

"How long have you known?" Kosenmark asked.

"Ten days, my lord."

"And yet you said nothing. Not to me. Not to anyone." He turned to Hax. "You see, Berthold. We must let her attend."

"No, my lord. You know my reasons."

"I do. And I disagree with them. But to please you, I promise to take precautions. We both shall."

He touched Hax's hand and murmured a spell. Hax muttered a protest, but already his eyelids drooped. Within moments he was deeply asleep.

Kosenmark studied Hax's face a moment longer. Whatever he saw did not reassure him, because he frowned as he turned away. "Come with me," he whispered to Ilse.

They left Hax's quarters for a nearby room, comfortably fitted with couches and padded chairs. Servants had built a fire; carafes of tea and wine waited on the low table by the fireplace. Rosel was just arranging napkins and silverware. She glanced at Ilse, plainly curious. At Kosenmark's command, she poured out two cups of tea and withdrew, shutting the door behind her.

Kosenmark gestured for Ilse to sit. "So," he said, "you've guessed what I do here. I'd like to know how. Was I careless? Was Berthold?"

Ilse took a moment to choose her words, knowing she had to tread with care. "You were not careless, my lord, and Maester Hax was more than discreet. It was more . . . a series of accidental discoveries."

"Which you connected into a solution. I see." He took up his cup of tea and began to pace the room. "I told Berthold that we had to decide how much to trust you," he said. "I would like to make a trial with you and see how much more responsibility you could assume. Berthold disagreed for several reasons, but mostly because he thinks the burden too great. However, since you already know . . . Would you agree to attend the banquet in Berthold's place?"

He was offering a great deal of trust, she thought. Even as it pleased her to make such a good impression, another part of her wondered why. Lord Raul Kosenmark had constructed an entirely new life in secret. She could not imagine him yielding those secrets to anyone other than an old and trusted adviser. And his oldest adviser, Berthold Hax, had not liked to include her, she could tell.

She met his gaze steadily. "My lord, may I speak plainly?"

"Yes. Please."

She paused to give herself another moment. There was a tautness in his face, around his mouth, and the way he held himself. Perhaps he didn't trust her entirely. The thought helped to dispel her suspicions . . . a little.

"My lord," she said slowly, "I only guessed a part of your business. So I understand only a part of what you expect from me. I need to know more. I would like to know more," she corrected herself.

Kosenmark smiled briefly. "You were right the first time. You need to know much more, I should say. Ask whatever you like."

Anything. She drew a long breath. "Will you tell me why Maester Hax does not want me to attend Lord Vieth's banquet?"

His lips puffed in silent laughter. "You are too clever. You've picked the one question I would not answer."

"Only one, my lord?"

More silent laughter. "You are right. There are many more questions I would prefer not to answer. However this one I will."

He took the seat opposite her, the cup with his untouched tea cradled in his hands. "You have guessed correctly. When Armand dismissed me from court, I did not give up my interest in Veraene's politics. A reasonable person might call it arrogance. Berthold calls it my duty. But like anything to do with court, it's complicated. I shall have to start a few years earlier—with Baerne of Angersee and his son."

Armand's father, who died twenty years ago. Even Ilse had heard stories about his death. A fall from one of the towers, which some called suicide, and some called an accident brought on by drink. The kingdom had mourned for weeks and months, according to her parents.

"Baerne was a good king," Kosenmark said. "A strong one. But like other strong kings, he cast a long shadow over history. Armand's father drank himself to death because he could not live inside that shadow. Armand might have done the same except that Baerne died first. Armand's first act was to dismiss all his grandfather's councillors. Very well. A new reign brings new ways. The difficulty lies with Markus Khandarr."

Lord Markus Khandarr, the King's Mage. Ilse had heard his name in connection with Armand's often enough.

"Lord Khandarr had attached himself to the heir," Kosenmark continued. "We all did, naturally. It's part of the everyday intrigue you find at court. But Lord Khandarr—" He broke off and, with uncharacteristic hesitation, chafed his hands together. "I tell you my opinions, so you understand the work Berthold and I do. But you must not speak of it to Greta or Kathe. To anyone."

Ilse nodded, her throat tight with anticipation.

"I have no proof," Kosenmark said. "But I believe Lord Khandarr has encouraged the worst of Armand's ambitions. Some say . . ." Another pause. "Some say Lord Khandarr has used magic to influence the king. I disagree. I believe Khandarr uses the king's own fears and obsessions to forward his own position in court. I believe—and I have no proof, only intuition—that Lord Khandarr would use up our king and our kingdom as a fire would consume wood, so that he could eventually take Armand's place."

"He would rebel against the king?" Ilse said.

Kosenmark shook his head. "Not rebel. He would make himself indispensable, to king and court and army. At some point, the balance of authority would shift from Armand to Lord Khandarr."

He made a gesture, one hand tilting to the side. Ilse could almost see one figure sliding into oblivion. "That's treason."

"Perhaps. Perhaps not, if the kingdom wills it. But let me tell you the rest. Once Armand became king, he called us one by one into his chamber. He announced that he had no need of our advice. He offered each of us a princely sum to retire in silence." He considered his hands and flexed them, then raised his eyes to Ilse's. "I refused the sum. And I left, of course. I had no choice."

And came here, a city far away from Duenne's Court.

Ilse was acutely aware of Kosenmark's gaze, and how he must be gauging her reactions.

"By continuing to stir the affairs of Veraene, I make enemies," he said. "Hence Berthold's worries. Hence, Lord Dedrick's absence. Does that answer your question?"

"Yes, my lord."

"So I ask again. Would you consider taking Berthold's place at the banquet? I've arranged a meeting with some friends. We take no notes, nor will I bring papers, but I would prefer to have a second pair of eyes and ears for this discussion. Afterward I will ask you your impressions."

"My lord, I have no experience with politics."

"No, but you have eyes and ears and opinions. I would find them all useful."

Throughout the centuries, poets and scholars had argued whether lives were shaped by destiny or choice. The scholars wrote learned treatises about the matter, saying history itself proved their point, that souls were drawn again and again to like circumstances, until those same circumstances were resolved, while poets said our lives were our choices, that Lir and Toc—whatever the gods called themselves—gave us the freedom to choose our own future.

It is much the same thing, Ilse thought. *I have been a scholar. Perhaps I was once a poet. I have lived as Veraenen and Károvín and more. But I have always dreamed of the jewels.*

Destiny and choice together, then. She drew a deep breath. "My answer is yes, my lord. I would like to help you, however I can."

"Good. Thank you." He stood and took hold of her hands in his, pressed them briefly. There was a strange quality to his gaze, of the kind and intensity Ilse had always associated with a king taking an oath from his liegemen. Briefly, she wondered what other lives Kosenmark had inhabited throughout history. Had they, possibly, known each other before?

The thought made her cheeks turn warm. She stirred, and Kosenmark released her hands with a smile. "Until tomorrow then," he said. "It shall prove a new beginning for us both, I imagine."

Later, as she lay in her bed, chasing after sleep, she thought it must be another of his gifts, to inspire his people so effortlessly. The way mages called up magic, the way princes called up loyalty.

CHAPTER THIRTEEN

FOR THE NEXT eight days, Ilse divided her time between Lord Kosenmark and the seamstress. Both were exacting, and more than once she thought fondly about her pots and pans. At least the pots did not drill her in political factions, or scold when she did not hold her pose through an hour-long fitting. Whenever she complained to Kathe, saying she wanted her old position back, Kathe disabused her of the idea.

"You like it," she said.

"Why would I like being scolded and working from dawn until midnight?"

Kathe laughed. "Don't ask me. But I could tell ever since you asked to scrub the garbage barrels that you had strange tastes."

Ilse studied her hands, no longer cracked from hot water and soap. Ink stained her fingers, and she had developed calluses from holding the pen. "I do have strange tastes," she murmured. "And you are right. I do like it, in spite of the lectures."

Lord Kosenmark had opened up many of his secret files. Not all of them. Not even half. And he continued to hold private meetings with Berthold Hax, in spite of Mistress Hedda's lectures about allowing her patient to rest. Hax's only concessions to Mistress Hedda's demands were that he kept to his bedchamber and limited his work to a few hours each day, with frequent breaks in between.

"You are thinking again," Kathe said with an amused smile.

"Always. That is why Lord Kosenmark pays me a salary."

The quarter bells chimed, followed by three peals for the hour. With a sigh, Ilse put down her cup and stood. "Speaking of my salary . . ."

"Already? You hardly took a break."

"I know. I'm sorry. But if I don't finish my reading this afternoon, I'll be spending the night in the library."

"What are you reading these days?" Kathe said curiously. "Not poetry, I can tell."

"Economics," Ilse said. "Treatises comparing the economics in Baerne's latter days to Armand's reign. Lord Kosenmark thinks it would be useful for me."

Kathe shuddered. "You do have strange tastes. Go, then. We can talk more tomorrow—if you have time."

As it turned out, Ilse did not have time, which gave her mixed emotions. She missed having so many chats with Kathe, and she disliked having to conceal the greater part of her activities from her friend. She had told Kathe that Lord Kosenmark was considering another promotion for her. In a way that was true. He had set her a trial and was helping her to pass it by giving her books and papers, then questioning her about the essential points to ensure that she understood them. He was teaching her to think, to dissect information and put it back together in new shapes. It was like a grand game of word links, but instead of words, the game involved ideas and people and kingdoms and history. *And there's more*, she thought. *Much more.* So far, she had glimpsed only the rim of this vast new plateau.

THE DAY OF Lord Vieth's banquet, Ilse teetered between anticipation and dread. The seamstress had completed the last stitches that morning, and Lord Kosenmark had dismissed Ilse for the afternoon, telling her to nap. She took a walk in the gardens instead, though the air was cool and the buds still tight against spring's true arrival. When she returned, she found her door open and Kathe and Nadine waiting inside.

"I have a surprise for you," Kathe said.

"We both do," Nadine added.

Ilse regarded them warily. "What kind of surprise?"

"A happy one," Nadine said. "Come with us."

They took her by the hands and led her into her bedroom, where someone—Kathe, no doubt—had laid out Ilse's new costume. Black silk stockings. A matching shift edged with delicate lace. New black slippers. The gown itself a gleaming waterfall of fabric, dark red silk patterned with teardrops of darker red.

"Bath time," Nadine declared with a wicked grin. "And then we shall take over as your maids."

"I don't need help," Ilse said faintly. "Certainly not for bathing."

Nadine muttered something that sounded like prunes. Kathe shook a finger at her. "Do not tease. Ilse, we are not going to bathe you, but we would like to help you with dressing and such. That is, if you like."

She was caught halfway between laughter and exasperation, but Kathe's smiles and Nadine's mischievous charm were too hard to resist. "I like. I think I do."

She bathed quickly, but alone, as she wished. Returning to her rooms, she found that Kathe had laid out ribbons for Ilse's hair, while Nadine had picked out pins and clasps and jewels from her own jewelry box for Ilse's inspection. Feeling self-conscious, Ilse let them help her into her clothing. Nadine surveyed her with a professional eye, then touched Ilse's hair. "Too damp. However, I know a cure."

She hummed a few words. Warmth brushed against Ilse's face. She touched her hair, which was now dry. "You know magic," she said softly, wondering why she had not realized this before.

"Just a few tricks," Nadine said. "Very few."

She brushed out Ilse's long dark hair, then tied it with hair ribbons into a cascade of loops, which she declared was the latest style. Necklace and earrings followed. Next her new slippers. *Pearls in my hair, Asta winding ribbons, and Baron Mann taking my hand for the next dance . . .*

Ilse's throat constricted. She pushed away all memories of that night and what followed. Tonight was entirely different. She was no gift tied up and wrapped. She was Lord Kosenmark's assistant secretary.

"One more detail," Kathe said. She drew a small vial from her pocket and opened it. "Scent. Do you like it?"

Ilse sniffed a blend of cinnamon and musk, a warm fragrance that recalled the pots of southern spices in Mistress Raendl's kitchen. "I like it very much."

"Thank you. It was a gift from a friend."

"A lover?" Nadine asked with glee. "I thought you were immune to lovers."

"I was to him," Kathe said archly. "We were friends, not lovers. At least that's what I thought. Poor boy." She did not go into more details, but sprinkled the scent over Ilse's hair. "Now just a touch to your wrists and throat. Perfect."

The hour bell rang, sending Ilse into a panic. "I'm late."

"Tell us everything later," Kathe said.

"Remember to laugh," Nadine called after her. "You look prettier that way."

She ran to the entry hall. Kosenmark had already arrived and was prowling from one side of the room to the other. He turned at her entrance, lamplight flashing from the red ruby in his ear. Dressed in shades of dark upon dark, he looked like a shadow at night.

"You needn't run," he said mildly.

"I didn't want to be late, my lord."

He tilted his hand outward. "You are overanxious. No matter, so am I. Come. Let us try to enjoy the evening in all its various parts."

A liveried boy opened the carriage doors. Kosenmark handed Ilse inside, then swung up lightly to sit opposite her. He did seem anxious, she thought, because once settled, he leaned back into the cushions and stared out the window with a preoccupied expression.

As they wound slowly uphill toward the governor's palace, Lord Kosenmark continued to stare out the carriage in silence. Once he frowned and let his glance fall to his hands. He wore a ruby ring on his left hand—one Ilse had previously observed on Lord Dedrick's finger. He studied the ring a while, then sighed. Knowing there was nothing safe to say, Ilse kept silent, too, contenting herself with looking out the opposite window, and counting the landmarks she knew.

When the carriage turned into the courtyard of Lord Vieth's palace, Kosenmark recalled himself. "My apologies for inflicting my moods upon you, Mistress Ilse. Happily, you will spend a few hours among more sociable creatures. Remember what I said before: you are as much a guest as I. Enjoy the banquet and the dancing." He leaned forward and added softly, "I shall come to you when we are to meet."

They emerged from the carriage into a confusion of lackeys and torch holders; runners, guests, and courtiers; carriages and their horses. Around the crowded courtyard, a circle of brick walls rose up against the night sky, bright gold in the blazing lamplight. Kosenmark guided Ilse through the chaos to the wide front doors. They passed into a domed entryway, where a herald announced their names to a tall gaunt man, dressed in a costume of rich green silks, with a fortune of gems upon his fingers.

Lord Vieth, Ilse thought, dropping into a curtsy.

Lord Vieth greeted Lord Kosenmark with evident pleasure and spoke politely with Ilse. Kosenmark answered his inquiries after family and friends, then led Ilse through a passageway decorated with murals of Erythandra's emperors and lined with statues of Lord Vieth's ancestors, and into the gathering hall.

If Duenne's palace were larger or grander, she could not imagine it. A dozen houses as large as her father's could fit inside this one hall, with its polished marble dance floor, its carved columns rising toward the lofty ceiling, its balconies and alcoves. Tables occupied both the central square and the enormous dais at one end. Many of the guests were already seated and servants were moving among them with serving trays.

Lord Kosenmark leaned down and whispered. "You may breathe now."

He was smiling. Laughing almost.

"It's lovely," she whispered back.

He shook his head. "Clearly, you've spent too long in my house. Come, let us cross to our tables. Vieth has an excellent cook. You will enjoy the meal."

They parted at the hall's center, he to sit at the main table, she to take her place among the attendants and lesser courtiers. As Lord Kosenmark predicted, she did enjoy an exquisite meal. Roasted trout followed the spiced soups, then came plates of seasoned rice and pastries stuffed with flaked salmon. What if Mistress Raendl had the resources of Lord Vieth's household? she wondered. What if Kathe came here to serve nobles at their grand feasts instead of the pleasure house? Would it give them greater satisfaction or greater anxiety? Then a singer's voice echoed through the hall, high and clear and pure, and she forgot these questions in her enjoyment.

The song ended. A few guests applauded; others concentrated on their meals.

"How long have you been with Lord Kosenmark's household?" asked the woman to Ilse's left.

"Nearly five months," Ilse answered.

"Ah." Her companion smiled. "We were expecting Maester Hax. But of course we are delighted that Lord Kosenmark found an assistant for his secretary. Is Berthold so very ill then?"

"Not at all. He unwisely ate too well this past week."

"So Lord Kosenmark chose you in his stead. Are you enjoying your first evening at the palace?"

Ilse hesitated, thinking she read more than ordinary politeness in that question. "Lord Vieth is a gracious and generous host. I'm delighted he permitted me to come in Maester Hax's place."

Her companion glanced at her sideways and smiled, as though she guessed Ilse's thoughts. "Indeed," she murmured. "And his cook is the best in Tiralien, even counting Lord Kosenmark's. And yet, if you do not mind the advice, I would caution you to choose your dishes carefully. One wrong mouthful, eaten in haste, can be . . . risky."

She had spoken softly, leaning slightly toward Ilse as though to share a secret. Now she drew back and laughed. They might have been two intimates sharing a joke. Before Ilse could think how to answer, or if she should, the woman turned to a different dinner companion, and begged his opinion of the new fashion in Tiralien, that of blending music with magical illusions.

"Would you call that music or theater?" she asked.

"I would call it a travesty."

His opinion provoked a lively discussion, and from there, the conversation turned to the latest plays from Duenne. Ilse surreptitiously watched the woman throughout the discussion. She had a narrow face and dark complexion; her hair was black and thick, looped into intricate braids and studded with tiny diamonds. One might have thought her plain except for her eyes—lined in kohl with an expert hand, they were dark and brilliant and keen.

Dangerous eyes, she thought. Eyes to remember.

The banquet drew to a close. Soon the guests rose from their seats, servants moved the tables from the hall, and musicians took their places in the corners. As the guests paired off, Ilse withdrew into one of the many alcoves, wanting to watch this first dance. Lord Vieth led a young woman wearing a circlet onto the dance floor. Lady Vieth took her place opposite a heavily built man dressed in the uniform of the king's army. Across the hall, Ilse glimpsed Lord Kosenmark paired with an elderly lady.

More couples took their places and after a few more moments, the music began. Three soft silvery notes from the water flute were answered by a rill of notes from the hammered strings. Old instruments and new, another of the latest fashions. And yet the dance they signaled was one of the traditional dances from the turn of the century. Was the contrast a subtle signal from Lord Vieth to his guests?

Certain of the guests did not dance. They remained by the walls, talking softly with one another, or they made the rounds along the edge of the dance floor. None of them intruded on Ilse's privacy, however, and gradually she lost herself in the pleasure of listening to the music. So she was taken completely unawares when Baron Rudolfus Eckard emerged from the crowds, a few feet away.

Ilse froze. Eckard checked himself in mid-stride. They were both staring, Ilse too startled to even think. It was Eckard who recovered first. "Mistress Therez," he said awkwardly.

Her heart beat fast and hard against her ribs. It took all her effort not to run away into the crowd. She licked her lips, managed to speak. "Baron Eckard."

Eckard glanced around, then came into the alcove to stand beside her. "I must apologize for my clumsiness, Mistress Therez," he said in a low voice. "I had no intention of addressing you so abruptly. I was . . . surprised to meet you here. Surprised but certainly pleased."

His tone was concerned, not accusing. "My lord," she said, "there is no need to apologize. I appreciate your concern."

The first dance was just drawing to a close. The hammered strings had fallen silent, leaving just the water flutes, their clear bright notes like the pattering of rain. Already new couples were taking their places. Eckard gestured toward the floor. "As a great favor, would you dance with me?"

She hesitated, but at his kindly smile, she took his hand and followed him onto the floor.

To her relief, the Baron remained silent through the dance's first movement, leaving Ilse to concentrate on minding her steps and keeping her own face under control.

"You are well?" he asked at last.

His tone was gentle. He was only concerned, she reminded herself.

"I am, my lord."

"Older," he said, in a musing tone. "I see other differences, but I cannot put them into words." He paused. "You must know that I saw your father last month. He is still searching for you. Would you—"

"No," she said suddenly. "Don't. Please."

"Hush. You will attract too much attention. Come with me." Deftly he guided their steps toward the edge of the dance floor, where the crowds thinned to just a few couples. "We can dance more easily here," he said in a conversational tone. And then in a lower voice, he added, "I understand your distress. At least, I believe I do. But would you not want me to tell your family that you are alive, well?"

She shook her head. "Not even that, my lord. I'm sorry, but I—" She drew a long unsteady breath. "I cannot risk it, my lord. Please."

He looked unconvinced. "Are you well? Are you with a good household?"

A pleasure house. A shadow court. The house of an exiled lord.

"Very good," she said. "As far as I can judge."

"You must be," he murmured, "to receive an invitation here. And yet I must not pry. I can see that from your eyes and mouth, Mistress Therez."

"My name is Mistress Ilse," she said, just as softly.

His eyes widened slightly. "Interesting. I should have guessed that you were a resourceful young woman."

They danced in silence through two more movements. Lord Vieth and his stewards had evidently heard of the fashion for music and magic, because illusory stars appeared overhead, their lights winking and rippling in time with the music.

"Are you here for the season?" Baron Eckard said at last.

She shook her head. "For as long as possible, my lord. What about you?"

He smiled. "I'm here for a different kind of season. My daughter and her family have their estates outside the city, and so I've come for a protracted visit. I am to be a grandfather, they tell me."

She congratulated him. "And then you return to Melnek?"

"It depends on the weather."

He spoke in a dry tone that recalled Lord Kosenmark at his most oblique. Lord Kosenmark. Baron Eckard. My dear Rudolfus, he had called him. Yes. Of all the information that Lord Kosenmark had dumped upon her in the past week, he had not disclosed who would participate in the night's meeting, but now she knew at least one.

You've come for more than your grandchild, she thought.

"Hmmmm." Baron Eckard was observing her with curiosity. "You look strangely satisfied, Mistress Ilse. May I ask why?"

She colored, thinking she would have to guard her expression more closely. "Nothing more than the pleasure of a good partner, my lord."

Eckard lifted an eyebrow, but said nothing. They finished out the dance in silence, and when the music drew to its close, he swept into a deep bow.

"I wish you good fortune, Mistress Ilse."

"And to you," she replied.

He bowed again, once more the bland courtier, and withdrew into the crowds.

She danced twice after that with two different young men who introduced themselves as friends of friends of Lord Vieth's grandsons. When the second dance ended, she retreated to one of the alcoves where she had a cushioned bench to herself.

The music paused for an interlude. While the musicians set out new instruments, a chorus of singers sang in rising counterpoint one of the old ballads from the empire days. The song—about war and war's heroes— sounded strange to Ilse in this rich setting, so far from any battlefield.

The song ended. The musicians eased into the next piece—another partnered dance. Just then, she saw Lord Kosenmark, threading his way between the couples, like a splash of midnight among so many brilliant colors. The meeting, she thought, her heart beating faster.

Kosenmark stopped in front of Ilse and held out his hand. "Will you dance with me?"

Startled, she took a moment to answer. "Of course, my lord."

He smiled, but his manner seemed distracted. He led her onto the floor just as an alto horn sounded three resonant notes. The water flutes responded with a second theme, and the pattern was established. This was a very formal dance, one generally reserved for court, for weddings, for other grand affairs. Ilse had just learned it the year before she left home. She hoped she remembered the steps.

Kosenmark touched his palms against Ilse's. "We begin with an introduction," he said softly. "As strangers must."

So he had noticed her hesitation. "Thank you."

He nodded but said nothing more as they moved through the figures for introduction, which were slow and measured, then on to those of a new acquaintanceship, with a faster and lighter pace. Ilse expected him to tell her when the meeting would take place. After a third set passed without him speaking, she began to wonder if something had changed his plans. Though his expression remained pleasant, he was scanning the crowds with quick intense looks.

Be careful of the dishes you choose, the woman had said.

Ilse stepped closer as the next figure required. "My lord, I had a warning."

Kosenmark immediately looked down at her, attentive. "What kind of warning? From whom?"

"A woman. We sat together at the banquet." She repeated what she heard, trying to use the same intonation.

"What did she look like?"

"Dark complexioned—darker than mine. A deep blue gown with the sides cut away to show the undergown. She wore diamonds in her hair." She wanted to add her impression that this woman looked dangerous, but that was too quick, too simplistic a conclusion. "She said nothing wrong, my lord, but her manner was quite strange."

"I see." Kosenmark glanced around the room. "That was Lord Dedrick's sister, Lady Alia. She has her own concerns, which sometimes intersect those of Lord Dedrick's. She wishes to join the Queen's Court and fears that Lord Dedrick's association with me would harm her chances."

"So her warning meant nothing?"

"Not exactly. The king's displeasure should never be taken lightly."

Throughout this exchange, he had held her closer than the figure required. Now he slid a hand along her back, looking down at her with an expression that bordered on warm. Ilse started to draw back when Kosenmark whispered, "I'm sorry. There are those who watch us, and this seems the best pretense. Can you bear that?"

His breath tickled her cheek, but she forced herself to relax, at least outwardly. "I'll try."

"Good. Now, we have a choice. We could end this act with a show of outrage from you. In that case, you would remain here among the ordinary guests, while I attend to certain private concerns. That would spare you any more indignities."

Leaving her outside the meeting. "What is the other choice?"

His golden eyes, so close to her face, took on a speculative look. "You might come with me and attend to those same concerns. It would involve a further ruse, and some damage to your character."

"A dalliance?" she asked.

He nodded.

"Would they believe it? What about—"

"Dedrick? He left me. I'm a disappointed man. That makes it more believable."

Ilse hesitated. She hardly liked to bring up the matter of preferences, but apparently her thoughts were clear from the look on her face. Kosenmark laughed softly. "That, too, would be believable. However, I would understand if you refused. We should have to make a scene then. I would stalk off, leaving you angry but untouched on the ballroom floor. The choice is yours."

Ilse took a deep gulping breath. "I will go with you."

"Very well. Please excuse the familiarity."

His cheek grazed hers, then Kosenmark straightened up with a throaty laugh. His eyes were brighter, his gaze more intense. It took all her control not to bolt.

"Try to look as though you enjoy it," he murmured.

She nodded and leaned against him briefly, her heart pounding. His lips brushed the top of her head. His breath feathered her hair. The dance had taken them to one side of the crowded ballroom, where several arched passageways led to the interior of Lord Vieth's palace. They ducked through one into a servant's corridor. Kosenmark drew back from their embrace. With a light touch, he indicated they should turn left.

As she expected, Kosenmark knew Lord Vieth's palace quite well. He led Ilse through several passageways, then down a flight of steps and along an elegant gallery, decorated with brilliant frescoes showing all the legends about Lir and Toc, from their birth to their season of love, from Toc's blindness to his death and rebirth. At last they came to a doorway set deep into the marble walls. Kosenmark opened the door without knocking and ushered Ilse inside.

She entered a parlor, small and elegant, whose walls were covered in painted scenes of the empire days. Opposite the inner entrance, glass doors opened onto a courtyard, half-lit by lamplight streaming from the windows above and opposite their room.

Ilse took in the opulent furnishings, the polished floors, and rare paintings in one glance. Then her attention was upon the four richly dressed men and women who sat around the fireplace. Baron Eckard. Luise Ehrenalt. Lady Emma Theysson. One stranger she didn't recognize.

Ilse felt a ping of satisfaction at seeing Lady Theysson, she who had such skill with words. Baron Eckard, she had expected. Luise Ehrenalt was also no surprise, considering how often Ehrenalt visited the pleasure house. Still, from all the weeks of preparations, she had expected that far more people would attend.

Baron Eckard started when he saw Ilse. He sent a questioning glance toward Kosenmark, who slid around Ilse and into the last remaining chair. "My lord—"

Kosenmark forestalled him with a curt gesture. "To business. We must be quick before others miss our presence. I've asked you here to discuss our suspicions."

"Suspicions?" said Luise Ehrenalt. "Call them proof. The signs are plain enough. King Leos is obviously preparing for war."

"The signs are not as plain as you would have them, Luise. Yes, we know that Károví has begun naval maneuvers off the Kranjĕ islands. And I received confirmation this week that the king has recalled certain high-ranking officers from Taboresk, Duszranjo, and Strážny. Both clues point to an invasion, yes, but we cannot know where yet, or why."

"Veraene, of course," said Ehrenalt.

"There is no of course," the unknown man said.

"How can you say that, Benno?"

Kosenmark made a quick gesture that brought immediate quiet. "My lord Iani. Mistress Ehrenalt. Please. I have more news to report."

He took a parchment sheet from inside his shirt. Ilse recognized it at once—it was the same she had accidentally read a few weeks before, when she discovered Kosenmark's secret activities. *Vnejšek. Jewels. Yes.* The paper's edges looked more frayed than before, as though Kosenmark had folded and unfolded the letter often.

Ehrenalt's mouth thinned as Lord Kosenmark read the words in his high fluting voice. Lord Iani appeared lost in thought, but then sent a questioning glance toward Ilse. "Lir's jewels," he said softly. "Do you think he's rediscovered them?"

"I doubt it. That is something he would not conceal."

"Why the troops, then?" said Baron Eckard. "Does he think the jewels are here, in Veraene?"

"I'm not certain what Leos thinks. This message answers questions I posed six months ago to my agents in Rastov: Has the king renewed his search for Lir's jewels? Where is he searching?"

"So he's looking in Anderswar," Iani murmured. "That would explain so much."

"But it does not explain the troops," Eckard said. His voice shook with uncharacteristic passion. "Remember three hundred years ago. Remember how Leos Dzavek scoured the borders with magic and plagues. He left a string of ghost cities behind. We must warn the king."

He meant the second wars, Ilse thought—a hundred years after the first ones, when a thief had stolen Lir's jewels from Leos Dzavek. Those were the wars that had redrawn the borders with blood and fire. The ones that had driven the island province of Morennioù to raise a fiery shield to protect itself. Soon after, other provinces had broken away from Duenne's control. To some, those wars were the true end of the empire.

"Armand already knows," Raul said. "As much as he wishes to know, which is not enough to reassure me. If I had one wish, it would be an hour with Armand of Angersee and him listening to my concerns about his kingdom."

"Two desperate men." It was the first Lady Theysson had spoken. She sounded thoughtful. "With the force of kingdoms behind each. Armand has wanted an excuse to attack Károví ever since he took the throne."

"Annexation," Ehrenalt said. It was not a question.

"Probably," Kosenmark said. "We are not at that point yet. There are a few councillors who would require more proof of Dzavek's intentions before they support a war."

"And what constitutes proof?"

Ilse started. Lord Kosenmark's back was toward her, but she saw how his shoulders stiffened, and his head jerked up. That strong, clear voice had not come from anyone inside this room. It had sounded from the air, as though a ghost stood in their midst to address them. Ehrenalt's face went blank. Iani and Theysson made as though to stand, but when light flared at the glass windows, they subsided into their chairs.

The courtyard door swung open and a man entered the room. He was tall and thin, almost as gaunt as Lord Vieth, but without the same quantity of gems and fine robes. His hair was long and brown, streaked with silver. His eyes were the color of yellowed parchment.

He looked at each face in turn. A brief look of disappointment appeared and was gone, almost before Ilse registered it. Then he shook his head. "You have no answer for my question, none of you. How long must we wait before we defend ourselves? Until the gutters in Duenne are choked with blood?"

He's a mage, Ilse thought. Powerful enough to send his voice through walls and doors, to stand among us like a presence. She had seen tricks before, magic workers who could produce the illusion of throwing their voices, but this was no trick. She had heard the voice emanate from air. She had heard it *breathe.*

Kosenmark bent his head, very slowly, as though it pained him. "Lord Khandarr. Greetings."

Ilse stilled a tremor at the name. Lord Markus Khandarr, the King's Mage. How had he found them?

Khandarr stared at Kosenmark without blinking. "You have no answer for my question, I see."

Kosenmark shrugged. "As usual, I have only more questions. Why don't you join us? We were having an interesting discussion."

"I know about your discussion. And I see you are still courting power, Lord Kosenmark."

"No more than you, Markus."

Khandarr's lips parted in a smile. He raised a hand, and Ilse felt the air ripple across her skin. Beeswax and expensive scents gave way to magic's fresh green tang. Khandarr said nothing more, but the air grew thicker until it was hard to draw a breath, and her skin pulled tight across her forehead. A deep painful pinch in her gut made her gasp. Her throat clamped shut, and her vision went dark.

Dimly she heard Khandarr speaking. "Here is my power. It is enough to make you whole."

He flicked his fingers. All at once, the painful hold upon her throat vanished and Ilse could breathe. She gripped the chair in front of her to stop herself from sinking to her knees. Khandarr would like that, she thought. She would not give him the satisfaction.

Kosenmark licked his lips. Sweat gleamed from his face, and his lips had turned pale from effort, but he did not look away from Khandarr. "Thank you, but no," he said. "I shall have to make do with myself as I am."

Khandarr crumpled his hand into a fist. The current vanished. Someone cried out in surprise, and Kosenmark lurched backward. He recovered himself with an effort and faced Khandarr. "Leave us," he said softly, and there was a cold and unforgiving note in his voice that Ilse had never heard before.

"Why should I?" Khandarr said.

"Because you are not yet ready to declare yourself king."

"Neither are you," Khandarr snapped. With that, he whirled around and stalked through the courtyard door, into the darkness, and was gone.

Ilse stumbled away to lean against a wall. All around the others were talking in quick low tones. Iani was reassuring the others that Khandarr had truly left them. Kosenmark murmured a series of instructions to his colleagues. Something about continuing to watch both sides of the border. Iani was to investigate Anderswar. Eckard was to listen for news from the border. Ehrenalt was to keep a watch on the shipping news. Theysson would continue to mingle in Vieth's circles, and to listen.

"Unless you feel the danger too great," Kosenmark said. "Tell me now."

Eckard shrugged. "He knew my opinions before."

"And mine," said Iani. "We have done nothing wrong except talk. Even Armand, with all his suspicions, cannot find fault with us."

Kosenmark bowed his head. Agreement? Acquiescence? Ilse could not tell which. "So," he said. "As we planned, let us return to Lord Vieth's festivities."

They left the room one by one. Kosenmark stayed behind, with Ilse at his side. Nothing had been decided, she thought with faint disappointment. Even the jewels had not provoked the surprise Ilse had felt when she first read those words and realized their meaning. And who had betrayed their meeting? Kosenmark was turning over the same question, she thought, because he watched each person as they departed.

When they were alone, he turned back to Ilse. "Come. Our play is not yet over."

They took a more direct route back, to a different corridor outside the ballroom. Ilse could hear the sound of plucked strings—the musicians were playing a slow-moving wheel dance. A few lamps illuminated the corridor. By their light she could see a doorway leading out to another small courtyard, and another opening into a small sitting room. To her dismay, Lord Kosenmark was eyeing her closely.

"What is wrong?" she asked.

"Your face and mouth are all wrong," he said. "You don't look as though you just had a dalliance. Kiss your hand."

Confused, she did so.

He shook his head. "No good. Kiss hard. Harder. Let me see."

She lowered her hand.

Kosenmark frowned. "It's not working. But I have an idea. Excuse me."

He took her face between his hands. Ilse had just enough time to brace her hands against his chest before he kissed her on the lips. It was a long hard kiss, with all the force of passion, and yet strangely impersonal. Ilse held herself rigid throughout, but he did not draw her closer. He touched only her cheeks, which he held firmly as he tilted her head one way and then the other, pressing his mouth against hers. Just when she thought she might suffocate, he drew back an inch.

"Almost," he whispered in a hoarse voice.

Before she could react, he kissed her again. Softly. A series of tender kisses that sent her heart racing with greater panic. *Pretend, pretend,* she told herself. *He's pretending, too.*

A skilled and expert pretense. Gradually, for he did not seem to be in any hurry, her muscles relaxed, her hands no longer pushed quite so hard against his chest, and her mouth opened to his, and when he paused she kissed him back.

Shocked, Ilse pulled away just as Kosenmark did the same. Through her palms, she could feel his heart beating, and she was all too aware of his warm hands cupped around her shoulders.

He studied her face for a long moment, his expression strangely intent. Not a lover's expression. A searching curious expression that unsettled her more than the kisses had. But all he said was, "Much better. Now you look as though you've been made love to."

"Nothing else?" she asked, her voice unsteady. "We had time for ... other things."

"Not with me. Not nearly enough time."

She smothered a laugh. Kosenmark smiled, though he still looked strained. "Even better. You should appear pleased, delighted, entranced when you leave me—I have a reputation to maintain. Now," he indicated the door to the sitting room, "to complete the illusion, I want you to wait here another half hour. You can hear the bells from here, I know. Then go back to the ballroom and sit in an alcove. If someone asks you to dance, tell them you are weary."

"Where are you going, my lord?"

"To have brief conversation with a friend. Don't worry. I shan't lose my way."

Without waiting for her reply, Kosenmark vanished down the hallway. Ilse retired to the sitting room he had indicated. Like everything else in

Lord Vieth's palace, it was exquisitely furnished, a tiny jewel in a larger treasure cask. Rich hangings covered one wall; a few cushioned chairs circled a table where a line of jade panthers marched across the polished surface; there was even a carafe of fresh water from which Ilse refreshed herself. She was glad for this time alone. Her cheeks burned. Her mouth felt swollen. Part of the evidence, she told herself, though she wished she could wash away the sensation.

After the second quarter bell rang, she reentered the ballroom. No one remarked on her appearance, though one woman glanced in her direction. Ilse found the nearest alcove and took her seat. Not far away, Lord Iani danced with Lady Theysson. Mistress Ehrenalt was drinking wine with another woman. There was no sign of Baron Eckard or Lord Kosenmark.

Then she saw him across the hall, scanning the room with narrowed eyes. His gaze stopped at Ilse and he came directly toward her. Now a dozen people watched his progress across the floor. Others stared at her, and she was conscious how she must look.

"Tired?" Kosenmark said, taking a seat beside her.

She nodded, aware of the heat from his body.

He leaned closer. "We might go."

"To further the picture of our dalliance?" she asked.

"That would be one reason. But I also have more business awaiting me at home."

He offered his arm. She took it, suddenly weary of intrigue and the relentless glitter of Lord Vieth's palace. It was later than she had thought—the midnight bells rang as they made their way between the couples still dancing. Kosenmark appeared untouched by weariness. Only the tension in his arm told her that he was not as relaxed as he appeared.

Unexpectedly, he stopped. Ilse looked up to see Lady Alia Maszuryn blocking their path.

"Lord Kosenmark."

Kosenmark nodded stiffly. "Lady Alia. I had not had the pleasure of speaking with you this evening."

"You were occupied with other pleasures, it appears."

Ilse tried to withdraw, but Kosenmark covered her hand with his. "Please stay," he said. Then to Lady Alia, he said, "Whatever pleasure I derived from this ball is my business, not yours."

"And not Dedrick's?"

"Dedrick knows my intentions. Nevertheless, if he wants to complain, he should do so to my face, and not send a messenger."

"He would if he were here."

"Exactly," Kosenmark said coolly. "If he were here."

Lady Alia stared hard at him. Then she made an angry gesture and stalked away, leaving behind a trail of whispers and muffled exclamations. Kosenmark paid her no more attention. He leaned toward Ilse and whispered, "Do not worry about her."

The crowds gave way before them. With a last effort, Ilse recovered herself enough to pay her respects to Lord and Lady Vieth, but she was relieved when the doors closed behind them.

Outside, the night was fine; the skies were dotted with brilliant stars. Kosenmark handed Ilse into the carriage and climbed in after her. He was silent now. As they passed from the torch-lit courtyard into the streets, shadows swallowed up the carriage's interior, and she could see nothing except the dim outline of his figure. He was leaning back into the cushions, his face turned toward the windows.

"What did you think of tonight?" he asked after a few moments.

His voice sounded rough. Tired.

"It was strange, my lord."

"Very strange," he said, but he was obviously speaking more to himself. A momentary gleam of lamplight illuminated his face. He looked preoccupied, and he was turning Lord Dedrick's ring around his finger. "An evening with success in all the wrong quarters."

The meeting, he meant. Inconclusive even before Lord Khandarr's appearance. She wanted to ask Kosenmark who might have given away his plans, but his gaze had gone remote. She settled back into the cushions, pretending to gaze out the carriage window, while opposite her, Lord Kosenmark continued to turn the ring upon his finger.

Who are you really? she wondered. *What book are you? Has anyone, even Lord Dedrick, read you to the end?*

CHAPTER FOURTEEN

THAT NIGHT IN her dreams Ilse wandered through a brightly lit maze, while faraway bells ceaselessly marked the quarter hour. The echo from those bells was still in her ears when she woke to the bells striking from the nearby tower. A fragment of her dreams lingered, reminding her of the intersecting plots and schemes of the previous evening. Was it possible that Lady Alia's confrontation was another invention? And what about Lord Vieth, who hid any trace of emotion behind that forbidding hawk face. Did he know about Lord Kosenmark's activities that night? Was he a peripheral member of the shadow court, or did he stand to one side?

A flicker of unease passed through her, remembering Baron Eckard. He might not give her secrets away, but what if someone else recognized her? She was not as safe here as she had assumed.

Then I shall have to take care.

Her attention consumed by all the strange events of the previous night, she hurried through her toiletries and dressed. Lord Kosenmark would surely want to discuss those same events. He might even have answers to her questions about Lady Alia and Lord Vieth.

A guard stood outside her door. Ilse checked herself in mid-step. Slowly, almost as though she were still dreaming, she took in the man's tense bearing, the weapons at his belt, and how his expression changed subtly at her appearance.

"Mistress Ilse, Lord Kosenmark would like to see you at once. Maester Hax's quarters."

"What's wrong?" she asked.

"I don't know. Please hurry."

He motioned for her to precede him. Anxious now, Ilse took the corridors at a run. Was Hax ill again? Was there news from court or Valentain? She glanced over her shoulder once or twice, but the man urged her forward.

Two more guards stood outside Hax's suite. Ilse's escort continued inside with her. "They are waiting for you in there," he said, motioning toward the bedchamber. He took up a stand outside the door, while Ilse, her heart beating fast, went inside.

Hax was sitting up in bed and speaking in an undertone with Lord Kosenmark. Ilse let her breath trickle out. So it was not a relapse. *It has to be news about Lord Khandarr.*

At her appearance, Hax broke off talking, and Kosenmark turned around. She caught a flicker of tension in his mouth before his expression turned blank.

"My lord? Maester Hax? You wanted to see me?"

Kosenmark pointed to a spot in the middle of the room. "Yes. Stand over there."

Puzzled, Ilse obeyed. Kosenmark looked as though he had not slept at all. Faint lines etched his face, and bruises marred the fine golden skin beneath his eyes. News must have arrived during the night, but what kind of news would make both men stare at her so?

"Begin," Hax whispered to Kosenmark. "You shall not be easy until you know the truth."

"Not even then," Kosenmark murmured. "Very well. You are right. Mistress Ilse, I would like you to tell me about the day you left Melnek. And why you did so."

Ilse flinched at his soft even tone. "Why, my lord? You asked me these questions before."

"I did, but Maester Hax was not present. He would like to hear your account in your voice, with your words, not mine. Besides, I need to hear the answers again. So. Tell me why you left your father's house."

She needed another moment to collect herself. Start at the beginning, she told herself. Go forward.

She began with the dinner party. But the dinner party didn't explain enough about why, so she backtracked to her hopes about spending a year with her cousins in Duenne, then leapt forward to Theodr Galt's arrival at her father's house. Already the account sounded muddled. It didn't help that Hax was studying her face with a strange intense expression. Kosenmark's face remained a blank.

She took a deep breath to steady herself. She described the dinner, including Baron Eckard's talk about Duenne and its opportunities, but skipped the rest of the details about dances and music and conversation, and went directly to her father's abrupt declaration that she would marry. She finished with the final moments in her room, when she decided to run away.

"It was foolish," she said. "I know it now. But I'm not sure I could do anything different."

Kosenmark and Hax exchanged glances. Had she said something wrong? Before she could say anything more, Kosenmark launched into a series of pointed questions about the dinner party itself. He wanted more details about her conversation with Baron Eckard. What had she asked him? Why had she listened to a stranger's vague account of a distant city? From there, he jumped forward in her story to the caravan: why she stayed and then why she left; why she chose Tiralien when she had endured so much to reach Duenne. Ilse answered everything as completely as she could, adding more and more details to cover the silences between. All the while, Hax studied her with a remote expression that was the twin of Lord Kosenmark's.

"You met no one after you left the caravan in Donuth. How did you pass the sentries at the city gate? They don't often allow vagrants inside."

"Farmers." At Kosenmark's prompting, she gave their names. Nela and Gregor and Maxi and Uwe. "They fed me and gave me a ride in their wagon."

"But you left them after you passed the gates. Why?"

Ilse closed her eyes, feeling dizzy and sick. Why and why and why. She heard Kosenmark repeat the question, a touch of impatience in his voice. "They didn't have much room or money for themselves," she said. "But they did give me names and places where I might find work. I . . . I had hoped to find a position that same day. It was stupid, I know."

She got no response except a request for more details about the places where she tried to find work. It was like reliving those first days, and her face went hot as she went over her encounters at Becker's tavern, the nearby inn, the house with the sympathetic cook. At one point, Hax made a sign to Lord Kosenmark, who leaned close while they conferred in undertones.

"We can trace the farmers through that tavern," Kosenmark said. "From there we should be able to locate these other people."

"If they aren't inventions, my lord. We have no dates. Very few details and just a few names . . ."

"Why would I lie?" Ilse broke in.

Another whispered exchange.

"I disagree, my lord. We should not—"

"We should, I say. Let her hear the accusations."

Cold washed over Ilse, but she kept her voice under control. "Yes. Tell me what crime I supposedly committed."

She spoke to Kosenmark, but it was Hax who answered her. "Your appearance here coincides with certain unhappy events," he said. "That coincidence troubled me before, and after last night, it troubles Lord Kosenmark."

Ilse swallowed against the sudden tightness in her throat. So she was the suspect behind last night's events. "Do you think I'm a spy, my lord?"

He met her gaze directly. "You must admit that the coincidence is strong."

"Very strong," Hax said. "The night you came, two guards failed to make their usual patrol, which allowed you entry onto the grounds. You arrived in a pitiful condition, one well-calculated to overcome any mistrust. You accepted a position far below your abilities, and at the same time, you quickly gained not only Kathe's trust, but also Lord Kosenmark's."

"And yet . . ." Kosenmark paused a moment, his gaze flickered from Ilse back to Hax. "And yet I have confirmed her background with Rudolfus. He did attend a dinner party at Maester Zhalina's house. And the story about her disappearance from Melnek is well known. She is who she claims to be."

"That does not disprove my point, my lord. Whatever we know about her life in Melnek, we know nothing about her actions since. Men can change in three months. So can young women."

"You never trusted me," Ilse said softly. "You never stopped watching me, not since Lord Kosenmark made me your assistant."

"Of course not," Hax said calmly. "Suspicion is one of my duties."

"And you, my lord. Have you always doubted me?"

Kosenmark stirred, as though uncomfortable for the first time. "Not at first, but we know about the letter you opened—"

"That was an accident—"

He cut her off with a sharp gesture. "We know you were curious and strangely discreet at the same time. I would like to believe you, but then came the evidence of last night."

Last night. The room had become so silent, Ilse thought she could hear her blood pulsing in her temples, and the whisper of her breath through the air. Now it became clear to her. Kosenmark had never trusted her. He and Hax had only pretended to.

Kosenmark's next words, delivered in his soft high voice, confirmed her fears. "Khandarr could not have known when and where we were to meet except that someone told him," he said. "All of those who attended are trusted friends. You are not. And after the meeting . . . To say it bluntly, I wonder how someone treated so brutally could respond, even superficially, to my attentions."

The pulsing in her temples grew louder. "You think I would try to seduce you?"

"We thought that possible."

He continued to speak, but she could not hear him. Then the doors opened. Two guards appeared and took her by the arm. She came to herself with a jolt. "Where are you taking me?"

"To your rooms, while we continue to investigate your story."

She had a brief flash of memory: Ropes binding her to the wagon. Brandt saying, *She gets dinner if she behaves.* "At least Alarik Brandt liked it when I pretended for him," she said in a low furious voice.

Kosenmark flinched. "Take her away," he said to the guards.

LORD KOSENMARK PICKED his guards for their strength and loyalty. One yanked her arm behind her back and propelled her from Hax's bedroom, while the other strode ahead, opening doors. Ilse grabbed for the doorframe. Her guard twisted her arm harder. She let go with a gasp. She had one last glimpse of Kosenmark, both hands over his face, then she was through the outer parlor and into the corridor.

The two men pushed her fast enough that she had trouble keeping her balance. They spoke over her head in short phrases. Check that door. Hold the girl back a moment. Careful about the carpet. When she stumbled, the guard holding Ilse pulled her upright, his handling rough but impersonal. When she tried to scream, he covered her mouth with one huge hand.

"Be quiet," he hissed. "It'll go easier for you."

If only someone were about, but Hax and Lord Kosenmark had picked the time well. The courtesans would be sleeping. The chambermaids and runners were occupied elsewhere. By now they were approaching her quarters. She dropped into a heap, refusing to move, but the taller guard simply picked her up and slung her over his shoulder.

He carried her into her bedroom and dropped her onto the bed. Immediately she stood. He pushed her back down and leaned over her. "Stay there, or I will have to get nasty. Lord Kosenmark's orders. Do you understand?"

She nodded silently. From the look in his eyes, she didn't want to test those orders.

"Good." He left, closing the door behind him. A moment later the outer door slammed shut.

Ilse ran and tried the latch. Locked, of course. She rattled the door and felt a stinging sensation. She jerked her hand back and rubbed it. Magic.

There had been no magic in her rooms before Lord Kosenmark's summons. None. She was sure of it. They must have prepared the locks during her interview with Hax and Kosenmark. They expected to arrest her.

But I did not do it. I did not.

Fury took hold of her. She pounded on the door. Someone shouted at her to leave off. Her answer was a shower of kicks and blows, until a burst of magic sent her flying across the room and into a bedpost.

She lay on the floor, bruised and breathless and her skin on fire.

"I didn't do it," she whispered. Then louder, "I'm not his spy. Not his. Not yours."

She broke off, remembering the peculiar nature of this house. Not all the rooms had listening vents installed—Lord Kosenmark's office was inviolate, and surely Hax's rooms and office. But hers . . .

Ilse got to her feet, still unsteady from the magic, and made a careful examination of her room. Nothing hidden behind the tapestry of Lir. Nothing behind her wardrobe. She pulled up a corner of the carpet. The floor beneath was solid. Feeling foolish, she ran her fingers over the walls themselves, even the ones leading into her parlor. No chinks. No hollow sound when she knocked.

She leaned against the door, now quiescent, and released a long sigh. Doors, floors, walls . . .

Ceiling.

She looked up. There it was above the foot of her bed. A narrow recessed slot, covered with a metal grate. How had she missed it before? She climbed onto her bed, trying to get a better look, but the ceiling was too high, and the vent was a few feet beyond the end of the bed. She could see nothing but a dark hole behind its grate.

"Are you listening now?" she said to the vent.

Silence answered her. *I'm a fool to think anyone could hear me.*

She climbed down from her bed and paced the room, trying to think rationally about her situation. Lord Kosenmark had talked about further investigations. Did that mean he had not yet decided her guilt? But what could they investigate? She had spent a few weeks starving on the streets, then found rescue at Lord Kosenmark's pleasure house.

In frustration, Ilse rattled the door's latch. Again, magic burned her fingers and palm. The doors, then, were impassable. Rubbing her hand, she went next to the windows. Gingerly, she tested the fastenings. Nothing bit or burned. Still cautious, she lifted the metal latch and pushed the windows open.

Fresh cold air blew against her hot face. In the distance, she heard Tiralien's bells striking eight o'clock. A haze lay over the city, and the air smelled heavily of salt and mud and fish. More important, she discovered a drainpipe running along her window. Ilse looked down again to judge the distance and felt her stomach lurch. The courtyard's paving stones, three stories below, suddenly looked very far away.

You said you would not run away again, whispered a voice inside her.

I said that when I believed that innocence was proof enough. Apparently it is not.

The next moment, a guard came into view. He glanced up. Ilse jumped back and shut the window. Lord Kosenmark had thought of everything. She'd have to wait until dark if she wanted to climb down the pipe. But at the thought of climbing down that narrow slippery pipe in the dark, she shuddered. It was no good. Even if she dared, the guards probably patrolled at night, too. Or someone else might see her, and report her escape.

Of course. She was not alone in this house. Runners sometimes came through the courtyard. With the coming of spring, the gardeners were out weeding and pruning and clearing away the winter's dead leaves. It might even be Kathe, who sometimes walked through these gardens during her breaks. She would write a note, wait for someone to pass, and fire off her message.

One chance. Kosenmark would not give her another. She had to make it count.

She made another search of her rooms, this time with an eye for writing materials. At first, she was dismayed to find nothing. Then, behind her bed, she found a scrap of paper wedged between the bedpost and the wall. Evidently the chambermaid had missed it.

By jiggling and rocking the bed, Ilse worked the paper loose. She set the paper aside and went in search of ink or lead or anything that she could use for writing.

She found nothing. She had dozens of lead sticks in a jar in her sitting room, but nothing in her bedroom. Nadine's cosmetics would have worked, but Nadine had taken them away after she and Kathe helped Ilse to dress.

She made another circuit of the room. What else could she write with? Her own blood? The thought made her queasy. She paused by the windows, shivering in the cool air. The early spring mornings were cool still, and her fire had burned down. Would they leave her in the cold as well? Or would they give her wood to build a fire?

Wood. Fire. Cold. Coal. Idly her mind skipped over the links, then stopped. Coal. Yes.

Ilse hurried to the fireplace. The chambermaid had been more thorough here, but Ilse found a heap of ashes in the back. Sifting through them, she dug out a thick piece of bark, scorched along one side. "You are my friend," she whispered. "You are my voice to the world."

It occurred to her that Raul Kosenmark would view any message as proof of her guilt. *Let him,* she thought. *I know I am innocent.*

She dusted off her hands and carried the bark back to her bed. She had no desk in her bedroom, but the floor made a good writing surface. She smoothed out the paper. It was smaller than she first thought—hardly as big as her palm. She would have to choose her words carefully and write them strong enough to withstand smudging. Very carefully, she shaped the bark into a point and began to write.

My name is Ilse Zhalina. I am falsely held a prisoner here. Please help me—

The doors slammed open and one of the guards stalked into the room. Ilse scrabbled to hide her note, but the man shoved her away. He caught up the paper and charcoal and was out the door before she caught her breath. She lunged for the door. It slammed shut in her face.

"Please, let me go," she cried out. "I did nothing wrong. Nothing!"

Her answer was a boom as the outer door slammed shut.

Ilse leaned against her bedroom door, shaking. "I did nothing wrong," she repeated in a softer voice. "Nothing. I did not spy for Lord Khandarr. I told no one about your meeting or what you do here. I only opened that one letter by accident. And then I dropped all the letters onto the floor, and when I picked those up, I read the other one. I wish I hadn't. I wish I knew nothing about you or your secret plans. I wish I were free and far away."

Tears leaked from her eyes. Angry with herself for crying, she swiped them away. She didn't want the guards to hear her crying. Kosenmark must have set them to listen at the vents, like dogs waiting outside a rabbit's run. That meant he trusted them with his secrets. Them but not her. Or maybe he was listening himself.

"Are you?" she said out loud. "Are you spying on me? What makes you different from Lord Khandarr? Nothing. You both want power. You both like secrets. All those letters." She spat out the word. "Stupid letters with secret marks and code words and talk about errant sons when you really mean Armand of Angersee. You make it into a game and call it politics. If you cared about the king, you'd be honest with him. You'd see that he did the right thing, instead of running away from court. But you won't hear me, will you? Can you? Can you hear me, Lord Raul Kosenmark of Valentain? Why don't you listen?"

Her voice broke and she slumped to the floor, breathing hard. What if he did listen? What if he sent more guards to silence her?

Let him. Let him do whatever he likes. But I'll fight. I won't pretend the way I did with Alarik Brandt.

The bells rang ten, followed by the fainter quarter bells. Soon Kathe would be awake and in the kitchen. She might try to visit Ilse, to ask about Lord Vieth's banquet. What would she think when she saw the guards? Or would Lord Kosenmark use his famous discretion and give out excuses for Ilse's absence until he verified her story? And if he was unable to do so . . .

Exhaustion flooded her without warning. She stumbled to her bed and lay atop the covers, but images from the past day flickered past in memory. Lady Alia leaning close to warn her. Baron Eckard's shock upon seeing her. Kosenmark's eyes, close to hers, when he studied her after their kiss. *He was testing me. He wanted to see how I felt.*

How had she felt? She no longer knew. It had been so strange. Panic at first, when he took her face between his hands and pressed his lips hard against hers. But those second kisses, not so terrible as the first, those had dissolved her panic and called up warmth.

"And why not?" she burst out. "Why must I be a stone forever? Why can't I feel love or passion or even lust? You aren't made like that. You cut off your own flesh for king and court. And then you lost everything. Why are you allowed to go on? Why doesn't someone tell you, oh, *you* cannot be a lover, you cannot be a man?"

Nothing. No response. He had locked her in and forgotten her. She let her head sink onto her hands. She could hear the thrum of her pulse at her temples. Her eyes felt dry and hot from crying. Dimly, she was aware the quarter bells were ringing again.

A loud click startled her, and the door swung open. Ilse lifted her head and sucked in her breath.

Kosenmark stood on the threshold, a tall dark statue outlined in sunlight.

"They did," he said heavily. "They did tell me that."

Before she could speak, he shut the door, leaving only the echo of his voice behind.

AT NOON, SHE heard noises in the next room. Ilse pressed her ear to the door. One person walking about, she decided. She heard a clinking sound.

More footsteps. Soon after there was a muffled knocking from the outer door. Curious, Ilse tried the latch and found it unlocked. Still unsure of what they expected, she pushed the door open.

Silence greeted her. Silence and an empty room.

Not quite empty, she thought. A large tray with several covered dishes and a sizable carafe waited for her on the table. A clean chamber pot stood by the door. So they did not mean to starve her. Nor would they make her live in filth, but the implications were clear. They did not mean to release her soon.

She tried the outer door next, but she wasn't surprised to find it locked.

The smell of hot food enticed her back to the table. Lifting one lid after the other, she found a bowl of spicy stew and a dish of honeyed apples. There was also half a loaf of fresh white bread, and the carafe contained enough water to last her through the afternoon if she were careful. Better fare than she had expected.

"You can lock me away," she said aloud. "But you cannot make me like it."

A note was tucked underneath one of the plates. *Eat as you wish then go back into your bedroom. We will know when you are done.*

She wanted to throw the dishes against the wall, but they had judged her hunger nicely. The savory clouds of steam reminded her that she had not eaten since the banquet. Hating her weakness, Ilse ate everything quickly and washed down the meal with a large mug of cold water. Then she moved the carafe and chamber pot into her bedroom. The moment she did so, she heard rapid footsteps outside the room and the lock clicked shut.

WHEN THE BELLS rang the evening hour, the same routine took place. She ate less than before, but slowly, wanting to extend the time spent outside her bedroom. Eventually, however, she had to finish. She could guess what would happen if she did not willingly return to her bedroom.

Four times the next day, they allowed her to emerge from her bedchamber. The pattern varied only slightly. Mornings brought her hot coffee and a washbasin in addition to her breakfast. Noon meant a substantial meal. By afternoon, she was grateful when the guards brought her tea and biscuits and cheese. Supper came later than before. She had plentiful water and a clean empty chamber pot every time.

In between those visits, she paced her bedchamber. She had no books to read. She had no writing materials. Whoever had brought that first tray of food had also removed all her pens and paper and ink from the parlor. Besides, what could she write? Another note begging for her freedom?

"I begged you once," she said out loud. "Not again. You'll get no pleasure from my distress."

She had taken to addressing the vent as though it were Lord Kosenmark. It *was* Lord Kosenmark, she was sure of it. These vents led up to his secret rooms on the fourth floor, where no one ventured except by his permission. And that he would not give. He had too many secrets to trust a mere guard to listen to Ilse's ranting.

And so she talked, knowing that talking changed nothing, but it was such a relief to speak openly, she didn't care what the consequences might be. She quoted every poem she knew by Tanja Duhr and the other poets she loved. She talked about the books she liked and the ones she thought pretentious or tedious or overwrought. She spoke of her brother and his flute. But speaking of home brought her close to tears. She broke off and paced for a while, until she recovered her composure. All the while, the silence drifted and settled about her.

"So I left home," she went on. "You wanted to know why. I told you, but I doubt you understand. I hated home. It was like death. All wrapped in silk and scented with herbs, but dead. Dead and silent and locked in the dark. When I left, I said I would never go back. Never. No matter what happened. And so much did. So much."

Her voice caught. She took a quick breath and went on. "Scared. Stupid, scared, and running away. And that was only the first quarter hour."

It was too painful to talk about the caravan, so she didn't. She talked instead about her time in the wilderness—of eating raspberries warmed by the sun, and drinking water so cold it made her bones ache. She talked of how a mouthful of smoked beef tasted like the finest dish served in the governor's palace, and how magic's fresh green scent was more intoxicating than wine.

"I had leaves for my featherbed," she said softly. "I had the sky for my companion and stars for my poetry. And no one could harm me or lock me away. But then I came here."

She paused and took a long drink of water. Three cups left. She would have to ration her water, just as she had rationed her food in the wilderness.

"Here," she repeated, searching for the thread of her speech. "I was free here. For a while. Free to do my work and learn new things. And Kathe was kind to me. Kind and patient even with someone as clumsy and untaught as I was. That must be why Lys hated me so, though I did nothing to her. Janna said she was afraid. Maybe you are, too, and that's why you have all these spy holes—because you're afraid."

Being afraid explained so much, she thought, and she continued on that theme well into the evening, not stopping even when the shadows deepened into night. The guards had left her firewood and new candles, but she left them untouched, preferring the darkness, which made talking easier.

She talked about secrets, speculating that secrets were a kind of contagion in Lord Kosenmark's household. The most obvious were the secrets the courtesans learned from their clients, those details let slip during moments of passion, and those of the courtesans themselves, who came from such varied backgrounds. Just as plain to her were the spy holes set about the house, those she knew about and those she guessed at. She wondered aloud if Duenne's Court was the same. If it was, such an atmosphere surely lay behind Armand of Angersee's character. Most definitely behind Lord Kosenmark's.

Her voice grew hoarse and low, but still she talked. About truth. About speaking out honestly, no matter how difficult.

She stopped, thinking she had heard something. She tilted back her head and listened hard. Yes, and it came from above, very faint but she was sure of it—a sound like the wind sighing through the trees. Then silence.

CHAPTER FIFTEEN

A THIRD DAY passed. A fourth. By the fifth day, she stopped talking altogether and spent her time staring out the window. She had sunk deep into waiting, and when the knock sounded at her bedchamber door, she did not react at first.

A voice called out to her as if from a great distance. She ignored it. But whoever spoke proved as stubborn as she. They called and called again until eventually she roused herself and opened the door.

Raul Kosenmark stood at the opposite end of her small parlor, his back pressed against the wall. He looked so different, she nearly didn't recognize him. Dark rumpled clothes. Hair pulled back in an untidy queue. His face slack with weariness. It was more than just his outward appearance, however. He seemed strangely diminished to her eyes.

He cleared his throat. "We found the farmers."

Farmers? she thought hazily. Oh yes. Nela and Gregor. Kosenmark had wanted to confirm her story. A part of her wanted to ask how they did. The urge faded. Opening her mouth and producing words in a row felt like too much trouble right now.

"They spoke very well of you," Kosenmark went on. "You need not worry about what they might think. The person I sent to make inquiries told them you were seeking a recommendation for a better posting."

Ilse continued to stare at him silently. What kind of reaction did he want from her?

Kosenmark stirred uneasily. "I heard everything you said. And you are right. I am afraid. And arrogant. Or maybe they are two sides of the same page. My brother used to say the same thing, but it's been years upon years since anyone else dared to. Thank you for being honest with me."

Another pause. His gaze flickered to one side, then came back to hers. "And I wanted to say you were right about other things. About this house. And how I listen. It reminded me that someone else might have overheard my talks with Maester Hax."

It took her several moments to comprehend what he was telling her.

"Who?" she said at last. Her voice sounded rusty from disuse. She cleared her throat and tried again. "Who was it?"

"I don't know yet. But I think I know how to find out."

She waited for him to explain. Kosenmark smoothed his hands along his trousers. He looked unnaturally nervous, but she had had a great deal of practice with waiting.

"I'd like your help," he said at last.

"With catching your spy?"

He nodded. "Berthold and I discussed the matter. We think the person belongs to this household. And they must have duties that take them throughout the house, but also they must have errands in the city, so they can pass along the information to their associates."

Someone invisible, she thought. One of the runners? A guard? It couldn't possibly be one of the courtesans. And yet they, too, left the house, either to visit special clients or on their twice-weekly rest day. Slowly her thoughts woke as she pieced the clues together.

"But why now?" she whispered. "Why not ask these questions before?"

Kosenmark made a hasty wave of acknowledgment. "I'm sorry. I was too quick to blame you. We both were. We should have listened to your explanations before we locked you away."

But you did listen after all. The thought brought a faint smile to her lips. All too soon it faded as she realized why he had come. "You want me to help catch this spy."

"Yes." Some of the tension leaked from his face. "I've arranged with Berthold—"

"I never said I would help you."

Kosenmark jerked up his chin, and color ridged his cheeks. Very slowly the color faded. "I'm sorry. More proof of my arrogance. I should not expect you to involve yourself with my plot and maneuvers and petty machinations that are so damaging to king and kingdom."

"I would not go that far," she murmured.

There was a flicker of amusement in his expression. "You were very clear on that point, I thought. However, I would like you at least to speak with Maester Hax. Tell him what you told me. Let us try to convince you that our intentions are better than before."

She considered his request. She had no reason to love his cause, not after five days imprisoned in her room. On the other hand, it would do no harm to speak one last time with Maester Hax before she left this household. Because she would have to leave; she could not remain in Lord Kosenmark's service after what she had said to him. She had no idea where she might go. Not Duenne. But there were other kingdoms with cities and universities and large merchant houses that needed secretaries and scribes, and she knew Kosenmark well enough to know he had a kind of honor, even with enemies. He would give her a recommendation in exchange for her promise to keep his secrets. That much *she* could promise with honor.

"I'll come," she said reluctantly. "Does he want to see me right away?"

Kosenmark shook his head. "Take your time. Wash and fix your hair. I'll have Kathe send up refreshments to Berthold's rooms. You've not eaten today, I know. And if you would, please bring your writing case."

He nodded, his manner businesslike, and left.

Ilse thought the gesture appropriate. *We are conducting business,* she thought as she changed into fresh clothes and made herself presentable. *And now we are finished with it. Tying off the last frayed strings and snipping them clean.*

It felt odd to open the door and walk through. Even outside, in the corridor, the strange sensation persisted as she walked to her office for her writing case, then back through the residential wing to Maester Hax's quarters. Twice she encountered runners on their errands. They both paused and asked about her health, which told her that Kosenmark had kept her confinement a secret.

I'll be gone soon, she thought, giving a noncommittal reply. *The truth about last week won't matter.*

She felt a pang, thinking about Kathe and Nadine and the others here. Then she remembered how impossible it would be to continue as Maester Hax's assistant, and she braced herself against regret.

Lord Kosenmark and Maester Hax were conversing in quiet tones as she entered the room. Maester Hax was sitting up and leafing through a stack of papers while they talked, occasionally referring to one. His manner was so reassuringly normal, she could almost believe the past five days had not occurred.

Kosenmark looked up at her entrance. "Welcome, Mistress Ilse. I'm glad to see that you've recovered enough to join us."

"You requested my presence," she said warily. Kosenmark's tone sounded forced, though the situation might account for that.

"So I did. Have you brought the letters from Baron Eckard?"

Ilse glanced from Hax to Kosenmark. "The letters?"

"Yes, the letters that arrived this morning. He told me at Lord Vieth's that he often found it difficult to post his letters because of all the chaos about his daughter's household. I'm glad to see nothing prevented him this last time."

Ilse stared from one man to the other. Kosenmark had lied to her. They never meant to explain things to her. They only wanted her to help flush out the spy, who might be listening right now through one of the pipes or vents.

Before she could say anything, the doors opened and Lys came into the room with a heavily loaded tray. Kosenmark turned to Hax, as though nothing had happened, and said something about the latest afternoon party given by a Lady Issnôlt. The two exchanged desultory comments about the affair, seemingly unaware of Lys or Ilse. Lys went about her work silently. Only once did she glance toward Ilse, a brief look that was impossible to read.

Ilse waited until Lys had left the room. "My lord was not entirely truthful with me," she said quietly.

Hax rattled his papers noisily. Masking her words, perhaps? Kosenmark's next move confirmed it. He rose swiftly and silently to stand by her side. "We were as truthful as we dared to be," he whispered. "Hush. I will answer your questions, but speak softly. Please."

She met his gaze, tight-lipped. But when she spoke, she, too, whispered. "You do not trust me. Very well. But tell me this: Will you talk to the king? Will you tell him everything you've learned?"

"We have," Kosenmark said, still speaking in low tones. "Many times over. I think war—this war—is wrong. Wrong because it is unprovoked. Wrong because it serves no purpose other than to forward one man's ambitions and another man's obsession. But I recognize that we must remain prepared. I would not wish Veraene to sleep while Leos Dzavek launched an invasion."

Ilse paused. "You told the king?"

He nodded. "Dozens of times. We sent our reports. I offered . . . not my advice, exactly, but my concerns. The king never replied, and after the third time, he sent our runners away from court."

She let out her breath, not certain how to reply. When Kosenmark gestured to one of the chairs, she sat and accepted the cup of coffee he poured with his own hands. She sipped and let the heat sink into her bones, gradually feeling more a part of the outside world.

Kosenmark refilled her cup without her asking. "I do listen," he said softly. "Not always well. Not always with my full attention. I can be over-hasty, as you know, and good intentions are no excuse for any injustice. But I am willing to learn."

She glanced at Hax, whose pale eyes watched her steadily. "We will talk," he said. "After we resolve a few matters. You understand the risks, I believe, Mistress Ilse. Grant us a few moments of your trust, and we shall grant you hours or days of ours, if necessary."

They used none of the constraint she had noticed in the past few weeks. Was it because they trusted her at last? Or were these words for whoever listened?

"Is there no other way?" she said. "Short of intrigue?"

"None that we have discovered," Kosenmark said.

"Unless you count a direct challenge," Hax said.

"And that I will not—"

A knocking interrupted him. Kosenmark broke off and stood. "Come in."

The door opened onto one of the guards. "Captured, my lord. Just as you said."

Ilse started up. The spy.

Kosenmark and the guard had already vanished through the doors. Ilse spared a glance for Maester Hax, who sank back into his pillows. He looked exhausted, but he waved her on. "Go. See who it is."

A knot of guards told her where to look—the servants' corridor between Maester Hax's quarters and another set of rooms. A girl was crying and babbling loudly, all mixed together, but in all the noise, Ilse could not make out who it was.

Kosenmark had made his way into the center of the commotion. "Let her go," he said. "She won't get away this time."

A scuffle broke out. Then the girl broke through the guards and fell to her knees in front of Ilse.

Rosel. But I thought—

She'd thought the spy would be Lys. Lys who hated Ilse. It was far easier to believe she also harbored ill-will toward Ilse's master, not Rosel, who only wanted to please her best friend.

Or perhaps she wanted to please someone else.

With a scowl, Rosel jumped to her feet and tried to push past Ilse, but Kosenmark caught her by one arm. Rosel squawked and tried to twist free, but he held her easily.

"I didn't do it!" she cried out. "I didn't do anything. I swear. It was her!"

She jabbed her finger at Ilse. Kosenmark dragged her back from Ilse. "No lies," he said. "We can tell the difference. Especially now that we know where to look. Benno. Come here, please."

Lord Iani squeezed between the guards. "This closet?" he asked Kosenmark, pointing to a wide door set in the wall.

"That one, yes."

Iani ran his hands over the doorframe, his expression turned inward. "Ei rûf ane gôtter," he murmured. "Komen mir de strôm. Widerkêren mir de zeît. Ougen mir."

The air went taut and thick, and a sharp green scent filled the corridor. Ilse heard a noise off to the side—the guards were subduing their prisoner—but though her stomach turned at the sounds, she could not take her gaze from the closet. Its outline had turned indistinct, as though a mist rose from the floor, but there was no mist.

Iani continued with a stream of Erythandran, and the green scent intensified. Now Ilse could make out figures moving through the mist. Lys. Janna. One of the runners. Two of the chambermaids. Ilse even saw herself, walking slowly along the corridor, then pausing, as though uncertain where she was. One chambermaid opened the door and took out several blankets and a stack of clean sheets.

Next came Rosel, hurrying down the corridor with a tray filled with dirty dishes. The girl paused and looked around, clearly nervous. She set the tray on the floor and drew a thin metal rod from a cord around her neck. Ilse strained to see what Rosel did with the rod but the girl's shadowy form had disappeared into the closet.

Time flickered past and Rosel emerged with a stunned expression on her face. She snatched up her tray and ran down the hall, her image growing fainter with every step.

"More," Kosenmark said. "I want to see more."

Iani gave a sharp nod. Now he spoke so quickly that his words became a hum, as blurred as the images he conjured up from the past. Time flickered and spun and jumped. Impressions from the weeks and days past overlaid each other. Runners. Guards. Maids. An errant cat. Ilse saw Rosel enter the closet more than a dozen times, always with that thin rod in her hand.

"Enough," Kosenmark said abruptly.

With one last phrase, Iani scattered the magic into nothing. Ilse drew a long breath, aware now of an ache in her chest. Rosel was sobbing and pleading to everyone and no one. She had not meant any harm. She had only wanted to help her friend. It was for Lys. Lys who was treated so unfairly after that bitch—

Kosenmark slapped her across the face. "Shut up. You spied on me. You knew the consequences. You cannot tell me you did not."

Rosel gasped once and went silent. Her cheek flamed red where he'd struck her. Without any apology, Kosenmark fished out the cord from beneath her collar. The metal rod dangled and spun from its clasp. "A thief's finger," he commented, handing his findings to Iani.

Iani examined the device a moment. "Treated with magic to draw the tumblers into position. An expensive tool. Whoever suborned the girl has money."

"That much we already guessed. Take her upstairs," Kosenmark said to the guards. "And keep her under control until Lord Iani and I arrive."

Rosel wailed once, then went limp. Undeterred, the guards hooked their hands under her arms and dragged her away. It was all too much like her own ordeal, Ilse thought. She leaned against the wall, faint with disgust at herself and everyone else.

Garbled voices sounded on all sides. Kosenmark speaking with Iani. Kosenmark giving more orders to the remaining guards. Runners who arrived, only to be sent speeding away on errands. Ilse kept her eyes closed, wishing them all away. She sensed a presence close behind her. A hand gently touched her arm, and Kosenmark's voice spoke into her ear. "You may go if you wish."

She turned her face away. She knew what came next. Iani and Kosenmark would question Rosel. They might lock her away, or hand her directly to the watch. Or perhaps they would mete out their own punishment. After all, Lord Kosenmark's was a shadow court. It might have its own shadow judges.

Kosenmark had gone. So had the others, thankfully.

Curiosity pricked at her. She hesitated. Curiosity was a dangerous thing in this household.

Ilse swung the door open. It was just an ordinary linen closet, lined with shelves that extended from floor to ceiling, all stacked with pillowcases, handkerchiefs, and baskets of clean rags. Ordinary, except for the magic permeating the air. Old faint magic from Rosel's several visits with her lock pick. Fresh strong magic from Lord Iani.

Someone had pushed the baskets to either side on one shelf. Ilse saw a square panel measuring about a foot in either direction—a listening portal. A small lock, made of dark metal, was set into the panel's left side.

She placed her palm over the lock. Even with all the magic buzzing around her, or perhaps because of it, she could tell the lock was metal and nothing more.

Careless, she thought. *Or perhaps he had assumed he would never hold sensitive discussions in Maester Hax's bedroom.* A dozen other explanations and counterexplanations presented themselves, spilling through her mind like glittering beads.

I don't care. I don't care anymore what he does. What or why or when.

Another wave of faintness came over her. Suddenly she wanted nothing more than to sleep. She wandered through the wing, going from sitting room to parlor and once into a room obviously used by the courtesans. None were right. She needed to be private, secure from any chance visitor.

At last, she returned, unwillingly, to her rooms.

Someone (Kathe? Lord Kosenmark?) had thoughtfully left a tray of food for her on the table. Ilse ate mechanically. She rejected the coffee, and drank down mugfuls of water instead, trying to clear the sour residue from her mouth. She tried to think about her situation, but she was too tired and too distracted. Her thoughts flitted from Rosel's pleas, to the crack of Kosenmark's palm against the girl's face, to the strong scent of magic inside the linen closet.

A quarter bell sounded. Another one. Finally a cascade of bells marked noon, and with it a soft knock sounded. A moment later the door opened and Kosenmark came inside. He surveyed the room briefly, then took the chair opposite her. "My apologies for intruding, but we have some unfinished business to discuss."

Ilse shrugged, too tired to show any anger. "What else do we need to discuss? You caught your spy."

Kosenmark folded his hands together and rested his elbows on his knees. "I came to apologize for lying. And to say I would lie again, if that meant I could prove you innocent."

"My word wasn't enough."

He hesitated. "For me, yes. Berthold is harder to convince. He said I ought to watch your face when we caught Khandarr's spy."

Ah. Yes. And she thought it was for her benefit that Hax ordered her to observe the capture. She might have been angry, if she had not been so worn out by her own ordeal. As it was, she only felt a great weariness.

"Do you believe me now?"

"We do. Both of us."

She shook her head. "What about Rosel? What are you doing to her?"

He dropped his gaze, distinctly uncomfortable with the question. "Lord Iani is with her still, to put our safeguards in place, before she leaves this house."

Safeguards. A chill passed through Ilse. "What kind of safeguards?"

Another uncomfortable pause. "Lord Iani has operated upon her with magic," he said slowly. "Rosel is sleeping now. She feels no pain, but when she wakes up, she will be in a sick house, fevered and unable to remember anything that happened in the past two months."

Ilse's stomach turned over. Briefly she wondered what Lys would say about her best friend's sudden departure. From there, it was an obvious leap to her own situation. "Is that what you planned for me?"

"Yes."

Wrong. That was so very wrong. "Why that?" she whispered. "Why not dismiss her from the household? Send her to another city where she cannot do you any harm."

"That city does not exist. We have allies and colleagues everywhere in Veraene, even in Károví. Besides, I was trying to protect her."

"How? By destroying her wits?"

"We have not—" With an obvious effort, Kosenmark lowered his voice. "We have not damaged her. We simply removed the dangerous memories— the ones that are as dangerous to her as they are to me. Ilse, look at me."

He reached toward her, but she recoiled. Kosenmark vented a sigh. "I am telling you the truth. If we did nothing but dismiss Rosel, the men and women who hired her would kill her, for no other reason than to make certain she could not tell anyone about them. Now they must realize she cannot betray them. It was the best I could do."

And he would have done the same with her. He would have obliterated her memories and tossed her into Tiralien's streets without any regret. Once, she had admired him. Now . . .

"You don't believe me."

"I do," she whispered. "That is what frightens me."

Kosenmark opened and closed his mouth. "I wish I could convince you that I'm not a monster. But that might be another lie." A pause, while he appeared to struggle for what to say next. "Can you possibly understand how it was, in Baerne's Court? Yes, we practiced intrigue. We had to so we could survive. Politically survive, I mean. Then came Armand as the king, with Markus as his adviser, and the survival became literal. Fara—"

He broke off and rubbed a hand over his eyes. That name was like a cry, and for a moment, a much younger Raul Kosenmark sat opposite her.

When he did continue, he kept his hand shading his face. "Fara was the Countess Hanau. You wouldn't know her. She took me as her student when I was a boy. She taught me about political factions and alliances and how they shifted from one quarter hour to the next. She told me, bluntly, that my personal disappointments were nothing compared to my duties to king and kingdom. Then she taught me how to fulfill those duties. How to think. To listen. Yes, in that way, too. And when they said to me, Oh you cannot be a lover, you cannot be a man, she said, Oh yes, you can. Then Armand killed her."

She had not thought the silence could deepen, but it had. It was like a tangible thing, heavy and dark.

Kosenmark eventually lowered his hand. He kept his face averted, but Ilse could see a silvery gleam in his eyes. "She trusted," he said. "So did I. We hoped that Armand would prove another Baerne—Baerne in his younger days. It was a foolish hope, given what we knew about Armand's character, but not completely unreasonable. We had not reckoned with Markus Khandarr. He saw Fara as a rival. He convinced Armand that she was dangerous to his authority. Then, one day, she complained of a headache and dizziness. Twelve hours later, she lay unconscious in a wasting fever. But she didn't die. Not right away. Not for three months."

His voice wavered. He clenched his fist and went on in a harsher tone. "The mage-physicians who attended her, one after the other, could do nothing. They couldn't even help her to an easier death. She lay there, burning and burning and yet never able to die. Not until Khandarr decided she had suffered enough. No, I have no proof, other than the man's character. He might have assassinated her. He might have struck her down suddenly. But it is a sign of his character that he did not want to simply eliminate a perceived adversary. He wanted to punish her. Of that I am certain."

She had heard scraps of this tale from Mistress Raendl and others, but nothing so harrowing as the complete story. "I'm sorry about what happened. Very sorry. It does ... explain things."

Kosenmark flexed his hand and studied it dispassionately. "Perhaps. But it does not entirely justify how I treated you. You had it right. I am both arrogant and afraid. To that I can add ashamed and sorry. More than sorry." He laughed a dry pained laugh. "Khandarr hardly needs to plot against me. I do well enough myself. You see, we can always arrange another meeting, but I cannot replace someone who cares as deeply as you do for truth and honor."

Ilse shook her head, uncomfortable with his praise.

"It's true," he said. "Whether you accept it or not." Now he drew a deep breath. "We've made a false beginning. I would like to make amends, but though such grievous misunderstandings can be mended ..."

"They cannot be forgotten," Ilse said, finishing the quote from Mandel of Ysterien's essays on alliances. She smiled faintly. "You gave me those essays to read last week." And then she saw where the conversation was heading. "Do you want me here still?"

"I do. Do you wish to stay?"

She meant to say no. But what came out was "I don't know."

He nodded, his manner subdued. "Please take another day—as many as you need—to decide. If you decide to leave, I can recommend several good households in Tiralien. Or even Duenne, if that still appeals to you. You might go anywhere you like."

"What about . . ."

"My shadow court?" He smiled briefly. "A good name for it. Shadows are dark things. We need more light. Let me just say that I trust you. I would not make you a prisoner for my own shortcomings. Meanwhile, you've had a difficult week. Stay in your rooms and rest before you make any decisions."

"I'd rather not rest here," she murmured.

To her surprise, Kosenmark flushed. "No, of course not."

He did not linger, but took his leave with just a few words. Ilse closed the door behind him and leaned against it. Only then did she see a small wrapped package on Kosenmark's chair.

She took it up and unwrapped it. A book. An old book—centuries old judging by the faded ink and delicate parchment.

Carefully, she opened the cover and drew a sharp breath. It was a rare volume of Tanja Duhr's poetry—a priceless object. Hardly believing what she held, Ilse carefully turned the pages, breathing in the scent of old paper and leather. This was the same volume she had hoped to find in Duenne's book markets, the volume of Duhr's poetry from after the first wars. There, there was the poem she had written for her lover.

> *When you are gone, I feel more than absence.*
> *The moon dims. The summer warmth recedes.*
> *The air itself grows thin . . .*

A thin strip of paper fluttered from between the pages. Cradling the book in one hand, Ilse retrieved the paper.

To Ilse Zhalina. A gift in return for your gift of conscience and truth. Thank you.

SHE SPENT THE afternoon outside on Lord Kosenmark's extensive grounds, wandering the intricate paths of the several formal gardens. When she tired of them, she took refuge in the tiny patch of wilderness, hidden in a grassy ravine between the paths. There, amid the luxurious tangle of old dried raspberry brambles, she found a bench carved to the likeness of a gnarled trunk. A few hardy wildflowers had spouted beneath it.

She made herself comfortable and leaned back, eyes closed, listening to the birds twittering. Off in the distance, Tiralien's bells rang, but she did not count the hours or the quarter hours. She sat. She soaked in the warm sunlight, which told her about time's passage by the change in shadows as they drifted across the clearing.

After a time, she heard leaves crackle along the path above her. Ilse said nothing, and soon the footsteps retreated. Another quiet interlude passed. She heard one of the kitchen cats hunting mice. She heard the birds twittering in the trees and the first frog chorus of the season. The sun was sinking, she could tell by the cooling of the air. More footsteps approached—louder and swifter—then a crashing sound as someone scrambled down the slope, ignoring the path.

Ilse did not open her eyes. If it was Lord Kosenmark, she did not wish to speak with him. Not yet.

"Ilse."

The sense of floating within a timeless empty bubble vanished, and Ilse reluctantly opened her eyes.

Nadine stood over her. Nadine dressed like a boy in loose cotton trousers, and looking not at all like an expensive courtesan.

Nadine folded her arms and glared at Ilse, plainly annoyed. "Idiot. Kathe searched the entire grounds looking for you. She came by here—I know it. But you hid."

"I didn't hide. I just . . . didn't want to talk."

"I call that hiding. Don't you care how much you worried her? She was frantic. I told her I would dig you out of your hiding place and drag you back inside." She tilted her head. "You do look ill. Lord Kosenmark told us you were, but I didn't believe him."

"Now you do?"

"Maybe." She dropped gracefully into the second seat. "Why did you come out here?"

"Because I hated staying in my rooms."

"Ah." Nadine plucked one of the wildflowers and murmured a spell. Slowly, the petals unfolded into a velvety pincushion. "For you," she said, handing the flower to Ilse.

Ilse accepted it with a smile. "Thank you. And I'm sorry I worried Kathe. I just needed time to myself."

"Thinking time?"

Ilse nodded. "What about you? Aren't you on duty?"

"I have permission," Nadine said cryptically.

An unpleasant thought occurred to Ilse. "Did Lord Kosenmark send you out here?"

At that, Nadine laughed, a long wondrous peal of laughter that seemed to make the sun shine brighter. "Oh dear, no. I do nothing for Lord Kosenmark, nothing but pleasure his clients, which is why he values my services. I came out here for me. And you."

Ilse's skin prickled with dismay. She took refuge in smelling the flower.

"Did you quarrel with him?" Nadine asked.

Ilse smothered a laugh. "Is nothing secret?"

"Nothing," Nadine said cheerfully. "Now tell me. No, I shall tell you. You quarreled with Lord Kosenmark. A good thing, I say. He's far too arrogant and handsome and powerful and rich. He needs a tiny sharp goad. And you are tiny," she said with a glance at Ilse. "Am I right my friend?"

"Right enough." Ilse sighed, thinking of how she disliked quarrels.

"Are you leaving us?" Nadine said more quietly.

"I don't know."

Nadine hesitated. "I hope you stay." Then she flicked her chin away, in a nervous gesture. "Rosel is gone. To the city hospital, they tell me. And Mistress Raendl looked a perfect thundercloud, as though she had eaten an entire wagonload of prunes."

Ilse said nothing. Any thought of Rosel made her queasy. Her own role in that matter was not entirely without blame.

"He was worried about you, too."

No need to ask who Nadine meant.

"I heard from Kathe that he insisted on attending you himself. He even fetched your meals and would not let the chambermaids do their duty. He chased them away, saying you needed quiet."

"Perhaps he felt guilty," Ilse said drily, "about working me so hard the week before."

Nadine smirked. "You lie badly. What happened at the banquet? I've heard interesting stories about you and Lord Kosenmark."

Her pointed look made clear what kind of stories she'd heard, and Ilse's cheeks warmed. "He was avoiding someone, and he asked me to help. Nothing more."

"He should pay you extra for such favors. Ah, I didn't mean to make you unhappy. I'll be quiet, if you let me sit here a while longer. Eduard is teaching Mikka and Tatiana how to play the new hammer strings, and I cannot bear the noise."

Ilse made a gesture of acquiescence. They sat in silence, a thing so rare with Nadine that Ilse wondered if another courtesan had disguised herself as Nadine. Or was this young woman the true Nadine, and the other a performance, given to everyone and not just those she pleasured?

She was a lovely young woman, Ilse thought. Like a dark brown cat, draped over her seat as though she reclined upon silken cushions. Her lean face could be in turn sensuous or asexual, and her expression flickered from merry to serious and back. Where had she come from? How had she come into Lord Kosenmark's service? As the setting sun glanced through the bare trees, its light reflected from a thin silvery scar along Nadine's throat.

Ilse reached out and traced its length. "Who did that?"

Nadine shivered and closed her eyes, her long lashes brushing her cheeks. "A friend."

"Are you sure about that?"

"Oh yes. Sometimes friends make mistakes. Grievous ones that cry out for us to stay and prove we are true friends."

"Does that mean we never disown our friends, no matter what?"

She heard a whispering sigh, as though Nadine recalled a difficult choice in her past. "It depends."

"On what?"

Nadine tilted her head and smiled, her teeth flashing white in the sun. "It depends on the friend. And you. And what you find in your heart."

She flowed to her feet and ran back along the path toward the pleasure house, branches swishing behind her.

Ilse remained outside another hour, thinking of what Nadine said, of what her own feelings were. (And what were those feelings? Strange and confused. Did it really matter what she felt or believed? Apparently Lord Kosenmark believed it mattered, or else he would not have lowered himself so, spoken so honestly. That is, if she could trust him to be honest and not playing yet another role.)

She made a disgusted noise. Stop it. Either believe him or not.

Twilight had fallen before she finally came inside. There, she found that the maids had swept, dusted, and aired her rooms. Lamps were burning in both her bedroom and her sitting room. A carafe of good wine and a meal waited on the usual table. She took the tray into the nearest parlor and ate there, listening to the faint sounds of music rising up from the common rooms.

Stay or go. Help Lord Kosenmark or choose a different path. The questions pursued her back to her rooms. The lamps had guttered, so she relit one and took it with her into her bedchamber. The room felt more silent than usual. She could barely hear the music from below, and she wondered if Lord Kosenmark sat above, or wherever the listening vent opened, and listened to her footsteps over tile and carpet, the hiss of the brush through her hair, the minute sounds as she changed into her nightgown. That he listened no longer bothered her as much, and she wondered what that said about her.

Sometimes friends make mistakes. Grievous ones.

Did that make Lord Kosenmark her friend? And could she make a difference if she stayed?

Destiny or free will? She had a choice, she decided. Which meant she ought to choose wisely.

And if I cannot choose wisely, I must choose the best I know how.

She glanced up at the vent. He would be listening, she was sure of it.

"I'll stay," she whispered.

CHAPTER SIXTEEN

THE NEXT MORNING, however, she was at a loss how to act. She had expected Lord Kosenmark to hear her declaration to the air and to send a runner with a summons, but the hours trickled away, bell by bell, until those of high noon sounded. No one came to her during the hour she spent in the library. She walked through the lower gardens one more time and noted how all the wildflowers had bloomed. But no one came to her with a message, though she frequently left word of her whereabouts.

She returned to her rooms but immediately left them. She could not bring herself to visit Lord Kosenmark's office, or even hers, without a formal invitation. And going to Maester Hax was impossible until she spoke with Lord Kosenmark. The common rooms would still be empty at this hour, and she decided to spend an hour there.

She met Kathe on the stairs. Kathe looked tired and somewhat distracted, and she was carrying a tray of covered dishes. "Ah, there you are," Kathe said with some relief. "I've come with your dinner."

"When did you start carrying trays?" Ilse asked.

"When I was seven," Kathe said. "And whenever we are shorthanded. Come. I imagine you are sick of your rooms. You can take your lunch on the balcony, and we can have a small chat."

She led Ilse down a gallery on the second floor to the balcony where they had chatted when Ilse first came to the pleasure house. Against Ilse's protests, she laid out the dishes, just as though Kathe were the serving girl, and Ilse her mistress. "You could be," she said. "If I had come to your house up north."

"But you didn't. And I didn't stay there," Ilse said.

"No, we both came here. And I'm glad for that. I hate the cold."

"It's not so terrible . . ."

"Frost and ice and snow showers, from what I've heard." Kathe shuddered. "Ugh. And speaking of chills and cold, you should eat while your soup is hot. Here's a nice spot, with plenty of sun but not too much."

Ilse applied herself to eating while Kathe chatted to her about all the house trivia. How Janna had tried to befriend Hanne. How Steffi and Dana had come to shouts and scratches over one of the stable boys, then made up the next hour when they discovered he had bedded the newest chambermaid. Her voice lost some of its humor as she told Ilse how Rosel suddenly took ill the day before, and how Lord Iani himself, who was visiting the house, tried to cure her fever, but things took a bad turn. Ilse listened and compared the scraps of truth amid all the lies and distortions. She wondered what Lord Kosenmark had told the guards to make sure of their silence.

"And we lost Lys," Kathe added, with a self-conscious glance at Ilse.

Ilse paused, her soup spoon halfway to her mouth. "Lys is gone?"

"She gave notice yesterday," Kathe said. "She told us how Rosel had no one else in the city to look after her. But when my mother could not tell her which sick house, she demanded the answer from Lord Kosenmark, and he refused. She said some words to him. I thought he would throw her from the house himself, but he did not. He . . . He was very odd. Anyway, my mother had offered Lys a letter of recommendation and Lys refused it. That made my mother so angry she couldn't speak." She smiled ruefully. "Yesterday was not the best of days."

No, it was not, Ilse thought. Her stomach felt queasy, thinking of Rosel, then Lys who followed her friend into a kind of exile. She had not expected Lys to prove so loyal.

"I'm sorry that you've lost two girls so quickly," she said.

"Not your doing," Kathe said. "Besides, though they were our best girls, I think we shall do better with them gone. Janna told me about her cousin's friend, who is looking for a better posting, and I thought I might ask Hanne if she had a sister or brother who would like to come south. That would give her some company from home."

Their conversation was curtailed by a runner from Mistress Raendl, saying that the new pastry cook had arrived and would Mistress Kathe please attend the first interview.

"Ah, the pastry cook," Ilse said.

"We've taken to calling them by number and week," Kathe grumbled. "Though not to their faces."

She hurried off, leaving Ilse to ponder what might happen if Kathe took over as chief cook and left her mother to do the pastries herself. That was as likely as her taking over Lord Kosenmark's business.

Lord Kosenmark. He would not send for her, she realized. And he would relay no orders. He was waiting for her decision. Should she seek him out? But the thought of traversing the pleasure house made her stomach flutter.

A hint first, she thought. *One for him, and one for me.*

Someone had returned her writing case to her rooms during the morning. Ilse wrote a quick note, apologizing for her delay, and asking Lord Kosenmark what her next assignment should be. "Take this message to Lord Kosenmark," she told the first runner she met. "But do not disturb him if he's occupied."

Within the quarter hour, the runner had returned with a fresh note in Lord Kosenmark's script: *Come to me upstairs, please.*

She came with writing case in hand. The alcove outside his office was empty, and the door stood open. Kosenmark stood by the doors leading to his rooftop garden, but his desk was covered with stacks of letters, maps, and scrolls, while another table held the remains of his breakfast. Dinner, too, she thought, taking in the quantities of dirty dishes.

"Mistress Ilse." He looked at her expectantly.

She found it strangely hard to speak. "My lord. I've come to ask about my day's work. If you have any for me, that is."

"Ah." His mouth relaxed into a pensive smile. "Work. Yes. We have much to do."

He gestured toward the chairs by the fireplace. "I wanted to talk with you about the meeting at Lord Vieth's—the one Lord Khandarr interrupted so easily."

"Was there more than one?" Ilse said, half to herself. She caught the briefest of changes to Kosenmark's expression. "I'm right . . . there was more than one meeting. Wasn't there?"

Kosenmark tilted his head and regarded her with a half smile. "What do you think?"

"There were two meetings," she said slowly, watching his expression for clues. "More than two. One was the public meeting where you expected an interruption. Now I remember how disappointed Lord Khandarr looked. He expected to discover more of the people in your shadow court, but you brought only the ones he knew about. When you left me to wait outside the ballroom, you met secretly with the others one by one. Or perhaps in pairs."

He was shaking his head. "You are too clever, Mistress Ilse. I'm glad you never *did* spy upon me. Yes, it happened just as you just described. However, because we could not meet all together, we were unable to reach any conclusion about the news from Károví. Since then, we've suspended any further meetings."

To resolve other matters, she thought. Yes. How much had he told the other members of his shadow court about his suspicions?

"They know," Kosenmark said softly. "Both the beginning and the end of that affair. You should know that Mistress Ehrenalt disagreed with my methods—with very loud and plain words. But enough of that. You asked about your day's work. I have only one task for you right now. Or rather, a question."

He motioned again for her to sit. She did, but he remained standing, pacing around the chairs as he talked. "It's about King Leos. And the news about his search for the jewels. We have watchers and listeners in both courts—Lady Theysson calls that keeping a vigilant guard." He paused in his flow of speech. "You spoke very strongly against intrigue and spies. I cannot say you are wrong or naïve, but I cannot agree. Not entirely. If we close our eyes, we walk in blindness."

"If we stop our ears, we live as the deaf, our senses muffled by a willful ignorance," Ilse said, completing the quote.

He smiled. "So you did read all those texts I gave you. Yes. We must watch and listen and gather our clues. But as you warned me, we cannot watch only for clues we expect. Lady Theysson and Lord Joannis expect war. Lord Iani expects a search for the jewels. Baron Eckard admits he does not know what to expect, and that troubles him more than anything. So I ask you: What do you expect?"

Ilse thought for several long moments before she answered. This was a test of sorts, whether Lord Kosenmark intended it for one or not. "Not war," she said at last. "Not unless Veraene begins one."

"Interesting. Why?"

"Because it's not like his nature. You gave me books to read about his earlier years, and I've heard stories from my grandmother, who lived under his rule for thirty years. He's known as a good king. A strong and careful king. He would not launch a war unless provoked. And . . . he's old."

"Why should that prevent him?"

That was harder to answer. She tried to put into words the vague impression she felt whenever she heard Leos Dzavek discussed. "Because he is old," she said. "Because for all his magic, he *will* die someday. He would not launch a war if he could not live to see its end."

Kosenmark paused by the fireplace and stared into it. Except for the shadows, the tiredness had vanished from his face, and behind that shuttered face, Ilse sensed great concentration. Finally his gaze cleared and he looked around at her.

"What if he thought the jewels were in Veraene?" he said.

"That would be a provocation, I think. But what makes me curious ..." She paused.

"Go on," Kosenmark said. "What makes you curious?"

"Not what but why," she said. "Why did he start searching for the jewels again? They were lost over three hundred years ago."

"Perhaps the key to that lies within our borders, with our king," Kosenmark's voice turned thoughtful. "Armand of Angersee spent a childhood immersed in tales of the old empire, and more tales about his grandfather's victories over the Károvín. It was like growing up in the dark shadow of a mountain, with no chance to escape into the light."

"He wants to prove himself as good as his grandfather?"

"Better," Kosenmark said. "He wants to revive the old empire. But for all that he is king, he needs the support of his nobles. If Leos Dzavek does not provide him with sufficient reason, Armand might manufacture one."

"So Leos Dzavek's motives do not matter?"

"They do. Like you, I'm curious why he's renewed the search for the jewels."

"Because he found a clue?" Ilse said. "Or because ... because he knows of Armand's character, and he wants to prepare his kingdom." It was like piecing together a puzzle. One answer begat another and another. "He's old," she went on. "Old and possibly dying. He wants to ensure Károví's safety, even after he's dead."

"Ah, yes," Kosenmark spoke in a wondering tone. "It is strange to think of a world without Leos Dzavek. It would be like seeing the sky without the sun, I think. And yet it must happen someday. He is a man, and however powerful his magic, he must someday cross the void. But that uncovers a new problem, one I think the priests had considered when they refused to let old kings prolong their lives with magic and the jewels. Any other kingdom expects their king to die. Any other king has appointed an heir. At least the sensible ones do. But Leos Dzavek has no queen or consort. His last heir died fifty years ago. There is no one to succeed him on the throne."

"Civil war," Ilse said, breathless.

Kosenmark nodded. "And more. Bloodshed and chaos within, and Veraene's armies pressing across the borders. In that case, Armand would gain his victories, but the cost would be bitterly high. As you said, the people of Károví are loyal to their king and kingdom."

"But with Lir's jewels, whoever succeeds Dzavek can defend Károví against anyone, including those within the kingdom."

Kosenmark did not look convinced. "Perhaps. Magic is well enough, but when you balance it against treachery and deceit, I wonder if treachery would win by a wide bloody margin. However, I imagine Leos Dzavek knows more about the factions in his court than I. His plan is a good one, as far as Károví's welfare goes. Let us hope—"

He broke off, frowning.

Ilse waited a moment. "What do you hope, my lord?"

He shrugged. "Merely a worry. Leos Dzavek has a reputation for strength and honor. Let us hope that in his quest for the jewels, he does not mislay those virtues."

Like the story of the woman who lost her beloved children while she bargained for a silver necklace. Ilse saw that Kosenmark, too, was lost in recollection. "I saw him once," he said softly. "It was at Baerne's Court, during negotiations over the Kranjě Islands. And once more, let us say, when he was not aware of my identity. His eyes are what you notice first—old and tired and clouded with age. But if we can believe the poets, his eyes were very different when he was young—a blue so dark, they appeared black."

"The darkest violet, like summer storm clouds," Ilse quoted, "like the oceans at night."

She glanced up, straight into Kosenmark's golden eyes. Unsettled, she looked away. Kosenmark stirred restlessly. "So. You know my thoughts now, and I've heard yours. Thank you. I only have one more request of you today, Mistress Ilse. That is to visit with Maester Hax."

She could not prevent herself from wincing at Hax's name.

"Do you object?" Kosenmark said.

"No, my lord." He was right—she had to speak with Hax before things could return to normal. "I do not object at all, but I confess I'm not looking forward to it."

"Ah." He smiled faintly. "I sympathize."

She blew a breath and smiled. "Thank you. I will go to him now."

She collected her writing case and stood. Kosenmark had already turned toward his overflowing desk. Undoubtedly his own work had accumulated during the past five days while he kept watch over her.

"My lord?"

He looked up. "Yes, Mistress Ilse. You remembered something else?"

She shook her head. "No. Not about that. But I wondered . . . Is it possible you might visit with Baron Eckard during his stay in town?"

"Most likely," he said, his tone cautious. "We were friends in Duenne. Friends make visits. Why?"

This favor, asked face to face, was harder than all her speeches delivered to an anonymous air vent. "I had a question. Or rather a favor to ask him. If he could, when he returns home to Melnek, tell Mistress Klara Thaenner that he saw me safe and well. And if he could, tell her I found the books I was looking for, though not at the bookseller I expected."

It was a risk, letting Klara know anything, but she thought it one worth taking. Baron Eckard had proven himself discreet. Klara would do likewise.

Kosenmark studied her a moment. No pity. No amusement. It was an expression she had not seen upon his face before. Then he smiled gently. "Of course. I'll send him a note today."

HER VISIT WITH Maester Hax turned out to be short, but less difficult than she feared.

"So," Hax said, when the servants admitted her into his bedroom. "We are to be colleagues again."

She heard no sarcasm in his tone, but she couldn't be certain. "A chief secretary and his assistant are hardly colleagues."

"Ordinarily no," Hax agreed. "But ours is not the ordinary household. You brought your writing case? Good. Unlike Lord Kosenmark, I do have a few tasks for you, and for these you will need to get the details exact. Write this down please . . ."

And off he launched into a series of complicated tasks, so much like that first day that Ilse nearly expected him to hand her another list of names. He looked stronger, she thought, writing as fast as she could to keep up. She could see how his color had improved, even since yesterday. His voice, too, had more strength, and his gestures were once more airy and quick.

"You're smiling," Hax observed. "Do you find our topic amusing?"

He had been expounding on better accounting methods for the pleasure house expenses. Ilse shook her head but continued to smile. She would get no apology from Maester Hax, but she found she didn't care. He was better, and she was glad. When he mentioned that she would see a greater quantity of correspondence than before, she nearly laughed.

"All the letters this time?" she said, under her breath.

"All of them," Hax said drily.

He turned a very bland expression toward her. That alone confirmed her suspicions that he had withheld most of the letters before.

She spent the rest of that day immersed in work. By evening, it seemed

as though the past week had not occurred. There were a few reminders—
the book of Tanja Duhr's poetry in her rooms, the new keys Lord Kosenmark sent to her, giving her access to his office, and a slight but noticeable
difference in how Mistress Denk and Mistress Raendl addressed her.

The changes rippled through her days. While Hax slowly recovered
from his illness, Ilse took on more of his duties. Hax ordered new copies of
keys for his office so that she might refer to his files. Lord Kosenmark re-
worked the spells for his own office so that she might have full access to all
his correspondence.

Hax had not lied about giving her all the letters. She read all Lord Kosenmark's letters before Hax himself and, once Lord Kosenmark determined
the answer, handled all the replies. Doing so, she learned to associate these
names with faces she'd seen at Lord Vieth's. Emma Theysson sent letters by
private courier, in which she enumerated changes in the royal shipping patrols. Lord Iani wrote more obliquely, using excerpts from ballads and epic
sagas, whose lines contained names for known points in Anderswar's ever-
changing realms. At times, his letters made no sense, speaking of color sig-
natures and voice memories.

"He is hunting Leos Dzavek," Lord Kosenmark explained. "A soul
leaves imprints in Anderswar. The imprints fade over time, but never completely disappear, so Benno has the difficult task of sorting through three
hundred years of Leos Dzavek's journeys."

"Is Lord Iani the only hunter?" Ilse asked.

"No," Kosenmark said softly. "We must expect that Lord Khandarr is
searching there as well. That is the danger."

Hax supervised Ilse's work from his rooms. She would visit him each
morning to have him review what she wrote and how she sorted the letters.
Lord Kosenmark was present for several of those sessions, and then they
discussed not just the letters but also their implications.

"You think Armand will be sensible, my lord?" Hax said.

"Baerne was sensible," Kosenmark said. "So was Armand's father before
he sank into drink and madness. Armand has the seeds to make a good
strong king."

"You talk as though to convince yourself," Hax observed.

"I am convinced."

"For now."

Kosenmark glanced at his secretary. "For now," he agreed, but he sounded
uncertain.

A month after Lord Vieth's banquet, Hax resumed his duties, but with a less rigorous schedule than before. He spent his mornings with Lord Kosenmark. Most afternoons, he slept, waking in time to spend an hour or two with Ilse, reviewing her work and giving her new assignments for the next day. After a light dinner, he read, often falling asleep before the bells struck eight. The routine suited him, he said, and Ilse had adjusted her day to fit his.

"Has Lord Khandarr left Tiralien?" she asked him one afternoon when Hax had declared that he felt too wakeful to nap. None of the letters implied that Khandarr had departed the city, but Ilse knew that Lord Kosenmark sometimes received news by visitors to the pleasure house.

Hax shrugged. "Not yet. We've sent inquires to friends in Duenne, but we use roundabout messengers, as you can guess. Word should come back by next week, if the roads are good."

The roads were not good. Spring rains had washed out several highways, mudslides had made other points impassible for the caravans, and the Gallenz River had risen several feet, overflowing its banks at points. News traveled slowly, even by private courier, and though Lord Kosenmark hid his moods well, she knew he was fretful. He would be, until he had word that Lord Khandarr had appeared in court.

"And if he hasn't?" she said, half to herself.

"Then we must inquire again. Lord Khandarr is a mage. As you observed to Lord Kosenmark, he might be investigating the same clues we do."

"Is that good or bad?"

Hax laughed drily. "Both. The king must know the state of his borders. Besides . . ."

Without warning, the vitality drained from his face. Hax let his head sink onto his hands. "I hate it," he whispered. "I hate that I have two good hours before my body wants sleep. Very well. We shall finish these letters, then I will nap."

Ilse watched him anxiously. His voice sounded fainter than usual, even knowing he was ill. She'd heard from Kathe that, tired and yet unable to sleep, Hax had finally relented and used Mistress Hedda's sleeping potion.

Hax lifted his head. "What?"

She looked away, embarrassed that he had caught her staring. "Nothing, sir."

"You," he rasped, "are too much like Mistress Hedda. Fetch me those papers from Lord Kosenmark's office and we shall review the next week's schedule. Now where is that ink pot? Ah, there."

He stood and reached across his desk for the ink pot. Unexpectedly, he stopped, and his eyes went blank with surprise. "Ilse?"

Ilse looked up in time to see Hax's face go stiff and gray. He collapsed, spilling papers and ink over the desk and onto the floor. *No. No, no, no.* Then she was running from the office and shouting for a runner. Within moments, a liveried girl clattered down the steps from Lord Kosenmark's office.

"Fetch Mistress Hedda," Ilse said. "Now! Run!"

She darted back into Hax's office. Hax remained crumpled over his desk, motionless. Her heart thumping hard, she rounded the desk and saw that his lips moved. He was breathing, a frightening bubbling sound that made her go cold. She bent close and laid a hand on his shoulder. "Maester Hax, I've sent for Mistress Hedda. She will be here soon."

Hax's fingers spasmed into a fist. "Soon. Get him. Please."

"Who? Lord Kosenmark?"

He made a strangled sound, wet and harsh. Ilse dashed out the door again, and ran into Kathe, who carried a flask in her hand. "Ilse!" Kathe was gasping for breath. "Freda said that Maester Hax—"

"He's had a fit," Ilse said. "Stay with him. I'm going to find Lord Kosenmark."

"In the training yard," Kathe called after her.

She hardly knew how she could run so fast without stumbling. Down the stairs. Out the closest side door. Down the lane and through the gates to the rear courtyard where Lord Kosenmark had his sessions with his weapons master.

He was there, wooden sword beating a fierce attack against Benedikt Ault's rapid defense. "My lord," she cried, running to him. "Maester Hax needs you."

Kosenmark stopped in mid-swing. Not waiting for him to speak, Ilse seized his free hand. "Now, my lord!"

She didn't know what he did with his sword. She only knew that he had taken her hand and they were both running through the pleasure house and up the stairs to Hax's office.

Mistress Hedda had not arrived yet, but Kathe had been feeding Hax the concoction left for such a crisis. Kathe herself looked shaken, though she continued to speak calmly to Hax. She had made him as comfortable as she could in that short time—clearing away the papers, giving him sips of wine between those of medicine.

"Come," Hax whispered. "Raul. Please."

Kosenmark crossed the room. Kathe withdrew. Ilse started to follow, but Kosenmark motioned for her to stay. He dropped to his knees beside Hax and bent close. "Berthold," he said, and his soft high voice went higher.

"Closer," Hax wheezed.

Ilse heard nothing of their whispered conversation, but she heard how Kosenmark's voice flattened out, and how Hax paused between each word. *He's dying. He knows it,* she thought. How did a man bid a friend good-bye forever?

"Promise," Hax said. His voice had gained strength. "Remember."

"I remember, Berthold. Hush. Rest."

"Promise," Hax repeated. "In case . . ."

"In case, yes. Berthold, I promise."

A spasm rippled through Hax's body. His head jerked to one side, and he went limp.

Ilse pressed a hand over her mouth. *He's dead.*

She knew it from the dreadful stillness of his body, from the tears on Kosenmark's face. From a deeper quiet in the room.

Kosenmark took Hax's hand and pressed it between his. "Good-bye, my friend."

Footsteps echoed from the entryway, and Mistress Hedda appeared. "My lord."

She had a small box clutched to her chest. She was panting, and her hair had fallen from its coil. When Kosenmark did not acknowledge her, Mistress Hedda stepped forward and touched Hax's wrist, then his temple and his neck. She nodded silently. "My lord, I'm so sorry. I was not quick enough."

Kosenmark let out a long trembling breath. "You . . . You could not have stopped it, Mistress Hedda. He was old and sick and—" He broke off and wiped his hand over his face. Ilse saw the sheen of tears upon his face; she heard more in his thick voice.

He stood, a bit unsteadily. "See to his body. I must make arrangements for the death rites. Come with me, Mistress Ilse."

Ilse hurried after him, catching up to him in the stairwell. He headed upward, feet dragging over the tiled stairs. Once he stumbled, then caught himself. Today there was no grace in his step, no image of a hunting leopard. Every movement had turned heavy and slow.

*   *   *

ILSE WORKED THE entire afternoon under Lord Kosenmark's direction, but she remembered only certain pieces, and those by the physical clues left behind. Ink stains on her fingers meant she had written letters at Lord Kosenmark's direction. The ache in her throat and chest were reminders of grief. Receipts stacked on her desk came from public couriers hired to dispatch letters throughout Veraene.

The first went to Hax's scattered family—a much younger brother who worked a farm in the kingdom of Ysterien, a sister employed in Duenne's largest counting house, an estranged wife and two sons. Ilse had come to think of Hax as someone born to serve the Kosenmark family, and so the news about this unfamiliar, unexpected past gave her a strange unbalanced feeling. She felt as though she had been walking upon a solid floor, only to have the wood and marble turn transparent and reveal the catacombs beneath.

By evening the letters were dispatched, the body prepared, and the pleasure house was ready to receive those in Tiralien who gathered for the death rites. Lord Kosenmark had met with Mistress Denk and Mistress Raendl, then retired briefly to his private rooms. Ilse spent the last hour picking over her gowns, helpless to decide what was proper. When Kathe found her, she was still dressed in only a shift, weeping over an old scrap of paper with Hax's handwriting.

"Come," Kathe said. "The others are below."

She helped Ilse into her best gown and led her to the pleasant sunlit hall, where they had laid out Maester Hax's body. Lord Kosenmark stood by the outer doors, greeting the mourners as they arrived in twos and threes from all over Tiralien.

He looked asleep, Ilse thought as she stood a moment by the silk-draped bier. She noticed that someone had brushed out his fine white hair, which for once did not threaten to slip its band and float freely. His hands, now resting still, so still, looked paler than usual. There were still ink stains, as though he had recently been writing, and she could imagine them lifting up to sketch a point in the air.

She had liked him, respected him. For a brief while she had even hated him for mistrusting her so. But then, as mistrust had warmed back into friendship, she had come to love him as a teacher, a friend. *Even as the father I wished for.*

Tears blurred her vision. She wiped her cheeks with the back of her hand, thinking that she could never laugh again. At her side, Kathe wept openly. So did Mistress Denk, Mistress Ehrenalt, and all the courtesans.

Lord Kosenmark moved to the bier. His eyes were red, she saw, and his face was masklike. Grief lay just behind it, in the gleam of tears upon his lashes and the way he glanced at Hax and immediately away. With a hint of his old grace, he signaled to Lord Iani.

Lord Iani approached the bier and laid his hands over Hax's. His face went tense with concentration, and his gaze turned inward. "Ei rûf ane götter," he said. "Komen uns Lir unde Toc. Komen uns de kreft unde angesiht."

A thick green scent overwhelmed that of the flowers, and a silver light burned at Iani's fingertips. Iani closed his eyes and continued, "Komen uns de lieht. Komen uns de zauberei. Nemen unsre brouder sîn vleisch unde âten unde sêle."

The light spread over Hax's body, turning the flesh transparent and transforming the bones into incandescent lines within. Lord Iani continued his litany until a burning nimbus surrounded both him and the body, turning the sunlit hall dark by comparison.

Lord Iani stepped back. Lord Kosenmark lifted his hands. "Vân leben ane tôt," he said. "Vân tôt ane niuwen leben. En namens Lir unde Toc. Iezuo!"

Light blazed to a painful brilliance, so bright that Ilse saw only pinpoint stars wheeling before her eyes. A fresh summery scent filled the room, like that of roses and lavender and the sharp green scent of crushed grass. When at last her vision cleared. Ilse saw a handful of white ashes where Hax's body had laid.

Magic, the strongest she had ever witnessed. Her mother would have cringed away, unnerved by such power; her father would have closed his eyes, indifferent. Her grandmother ... Once Ilse had believed her grandmother disliked magic—so many in Duszranjo did, even if they did not follow the old laws—but after that brief twinning of souls, and seeing Naděžda Zhalina's life dream, Ilse thought her grandmother would have observed it as dispassionately as any cat did. *It is nothing more than a weapon, to be wielded for good or evil.*

"From life to dust, from this one death to the next life," Iani said softly.

All the mourners stood in silent meditation while the magic drifted and swirled around them. The gods have given us no prayers, Ilse thought. No rituals of cloth and candle and mystic symbols. Only this moment, this silence, as the soul makes its leap into the void.

A sigh went out from all those present. Kosenmark stepped forward and scooped the ashes into a small golden casket. He held the casket a moment, eyes closed, as though bidding Hax a second good-bye, then gave it to a waiting servant. Ilse knew the instructions Hax had left for his death. He wanted the ashes sent east, to his brother in Ysterien, there to be disposed as his brother wished. How would that man feel, receiving the small package next month, possibly a few days after the letter itself? Would he keep the casket in a remembrance chamber, as the old Morenniouens did? Would he bury the ashes as they did in Duszranjo? Would he watch over the ashes and remember his brother from long ago?

Servants were passing among the mourners, handing out cups of wine. More servants laid out platters of food on the side table. The company would pass the evening telling stories about Hax and spend their grief in talk. Ilse remained apart from the others, and when Kathe offered her a wine cup, she shook her head. Too soon, she thought. Too soon for talk or drink or even food. She drifted toward the windows and, leaning over the sill, breathed in the scent of roses. A trace of magic's green lingered here. Iani and Kosenmark had not entirely erased their magic, and she could discern both Lord Iani's fair signature and Lord Kosenmark's darker one.

She felt a warm brush of air. Someone touched her sleeve. Ilse looked up to see Lord Kosenmark, a wine cup in his hand. "Please come with me," he murmured.

He headed toward the door, catching up a wine carafe as he went. Ilse hurried after him, and she saw how a few glanced up at their passing.

Kosenmark paused briefly outside the hall, then indicated the nearest stairs. When they reached his office, he dismissed the waiting runner and motioned for Ilse to precede him into the room. She went inside and paused, uncertain, but Kosenmark walked past her to the garden doors, so she hurried after him.

It had been weeks since she last visited Lord Kosenmark's rooftop garden. The sparse gray and brown branches were now draped in luxuriant greens. Flowering vines curled around the tree trunks, and she saw flashes of dark blue and ruby and gold between the silver brown trees.

Kosenmark continued along the looping path until they came to the low stone wall that marked the garden's edge. Below, she could see the various sections of the pleasure house grounds—the rolling lawn, several formal gardens divided by walls and hedges, the wilderness patch where she and Nadine had talked. Beyond lay more buildings and stables, but these were invisible behind the trees of the lower gardens.

Kosenmark dropped onto a stone bench and poured wine into his cup. Ilse remained standing, watching his face for clues.

"I brought only one cup," he said. "My apologies."

On impulse, Ilse reached toward him. "My lord, may I share your cup?"

Kosenmark regarded her with a strangely intent look. "If you like."

He tilted his hand toward the bench. She sat beside him and accepted the cup.

When she had drunk, he took back the cup and refilled it. Instead of drinking, he cradled the cup between his hands. Some of his distress had leaked away, and he smiled pensively. "You startled me just then," he said. "I thought you had found a way to listen to my thoughts. You see, I wanted to ask you a very great favor. To share my cup, if you will."

Her pulse leapt in surprise. "How so, my lord?"

"It involves a promise I made Berthold. Three years ago. The one he reminded me of just this morning."

He drank, then handed the cup back to Ilse. She accepted it, observing how his hands rested uneasily in his lap. They were long and lean hands—as expressive as Berthold Hax's had been, but stronger. Able to wield swords and pens and influence and wealth.

Kosenmark turned his face upward toward the sky. "My friend is gone," he said softly. "I cannot change that, no matter how I wish otherwise. What I can do is to continue the work that he and I first planned two, nearly three years ago. But for that I need someone I can trust, someone with a mind and heart to match Berthold's. Will you do me this favor? Will you take his place?"

Surprise stopped her from speaking for a moment. "My lord, I don't know enough to help you."

"You know more than you admit. For the rest . . . I'll teach you. What's important is that you are intelligent and honest. You will tell me when I am wrong. When I'm arrogant. When my so-called concern for the kingdom falls into petty intrigue. I value that. Will you help me, Ilse Zhalina?"

She suddenly had the same sensation as when Alarik Brandt had offered his trade. Danger lay in that direction. Danger and misery and possibly death.

Ah, but if she chose to refuse Lord Kosenmark, that would leave him without a friend and councillor. He trusted so rarely.

There was a ritual in Duszranjo, when two men declared blood friendship—her grandmother had described it. Lord Kosenmark was no brother, but the intent was the same. Ilse poured new wine into their cup. She dipped a finger into the wine and ran it along the cup's rim. *Water from my body, wine from a single cup,* the ritual said. *Mingle yours with mine, and thus we are bound together.*

Ilse intended to perform only half the ritual, to declare her loyalty, but before she could drink, Kosenmark stopped her. "My turn."

He dipped his finger as she had and circled the cup's rim. "Now drink."
He offered her the cup.

"But my lord—"

"I know the ritual. I also know the vow must be mutual."

So it was, she thought, but she had not expected that from him.

Heart beating fast, she took the cup and drank. Kosenmark did the
same.

CHAPTER SEVENTEEN

FOR A MONTH following Berthold Hax's death, Lord Kosenmark closed his pleasure house to business. Visitors instead of patrons filled its many rooms, and they spent the hours talking about Berthold Hax—stories from his past, longer stories about how his life intersected theirs. Ilse listened at times, surprised more than once by the unexpected details these stories revealed.

Most of her time, however, she spent with Lord Kosenmark in Berthold Hax's old office, now hers, discussing Károví's plans and how they involved Lir's jewels.

"We have a drought," Kosenmark said, studying the map he had spread over Ilse's desk. "A drought of information."

He traced his finger along the border between Károví and Veraene. Using his reports from the past few months, Kosenmark had laid out markers to show troop numbers and locations for both kingdoms. Green for tens, blue for hundreds, red for thousands. The number had shifted several times over the past six months, according to what Ilse had read. Károví had concentrated its troops along the northern east plains, where several well-known passes led through the mountains into Immatra and Veraene. Veraenen troops were thickest at the kingdom's border near Melnek, but lately Armand had increased the troops in Ournes, on the opposite side of the mountains from those same Károvín troops.

Kosenmark's restless tracing had dislodged several of the markers. Ilse replaced them carefully. The sight of so many markers near her old home gave her pause. "You knew that he was raising the levies," she said, more for herself than to remind Kosenmark.

He released an unhappy sigh. "Yes, I knew that. But the picture brings home what words and numbers cannot. Armand has managed to erect a barrier nearly as impenetrable as the one out there."

He indicated a wavering line drawn through the oceans east of the continent. Toc's Judgment. Lir's Veil. The name varied with the speaker, but they all referred to the burning wall of magic that had appeared three hundred years before, during the second and bloodiest of the wars between Veraene and Károví.

The analogy was apt. Three couriers had gone missing in the border mountains in the past month. Ilse knew the passage to be a difficult one—rockslides, sudden storms, an accidental fall—all these could kill even the most experienced tracker. But three in a single month . . .

Kosenmark tapped the markers, causing them to skitter over the maps. "Never mind," he said, when Ilse tried to put them right. "We don't need to know where Armand and Leos have put their troops. The only thing that matters is that the borders are closed to us."

And to everyone else, Ilse added silently. No tolerance for smugglers. No trade except with special permits, issued by the regional governors and confirmed by auxiliary representatives from the capital. The many new troops stationed at passes and border towns were there to enforce and assist. Kosenmark had sent out orders to his agents to stop sending back reports, but he could not tell if they had received those orders.

"What if you sent your messengers through Immatra?" she said, indicating the northern plains. "Armand doesn't keep many troops along that border. Or would that still prove too dangerous?"

"Too far," Kosenmark said shortly. "By the time we get a report, the situation has changed five times over. We need wings," he said softly. "If we had the wings of birds, we might fly across the mountains."

Ilse studied the map. The border was the difficulty. High mountains guarded those borders even better than all of Armand's troops. Leos Dzavek had used that border to his advantage in both wars. If only they could erase those mountains, or even carve a new unknown pass through them.

"Ships," she said, at the same time as Kosenmark.

He grinned at her. "It must be a good idea, since we both thought of it. Tell me more, Mistress Ilse."

She hesitated, then shook her head. "I was thinking merchant ships, but that seems too simple."

"True. Armand will require all the merchant ships to carry special permits. Ah, but the fishing fleets—they go out to sea for weeks or months."

Meaning that hardly anyone would notice if they took a few weeks longer for their catch. Ilse traced the curve of the Károvíen coastline. Islands dotted the waters there and there. To the north, a few larger islands made a barrier against the winter storms. A lone fishing boat could land undetected either place.

Kosenmark rested his head on his arms and studied the map through slitted eyes. "It still won't be easy. We'll need bribes for whoever carries the message or messenger to the islands. And careful planning to deal with the coastal patrols. Unless"—he glanced at Ilse—"you think I'm pursuing more of those useless games."

She knew the question was genuine, but the answers that came to her were suspect. Was it because Lord Kosenmark's activities had changed, or was it because her perspective had changed, from prisoner to trusted subordinate? The latter, she suspected.

"You are thinking hard," he observed.

Ilse colored. "Not as hard as I did a few weeks ago."

Kosenmark laughed, albeit hesitantly. "Perhaps you are being too harsh."

"Upon myself? Or upon you?" she murmured. "But I do wonder . . . I saw nothing wrong at first, only after you locked me up."

"And so you do not trust your judgment. But before you condemn yourself for inconstancy, ask yourself if there is a difference between what we did last month and today. Or rather, can you see one now?"

Ilse felt her way slowly through the answer. "No and yes," she said at last. "Both involved intrigue and deception. One does concern the future. But I don't know . . ."

Her glance met Kosenmark's. He was watching her closely with those bright golden eyes. Unsettled by his gaze, she made a show of rearranging the markers into neater rows. The markers represented living soldiers now, but if Armand had his way, they might soon represent dead ones.

"Armand would be wrong to start a war without provocation," she said at last. "Leos would be right to defend himself, but not at any cost. That much seems clear, but the rest . . . I lose the rest in shades of gray and brown. Even good intentions are not always enough."

"Sometimes they are all we have. We must guard them carefully and not—"

A knock interrupted them. Kosenmark frowned and glanced over his shoulder. Ilse thought he might ignore the knock—he sometimes did—but when a second rapid knock followed, a peculiar expression came over his face. "I wonder . . ." he said under his breath.

Before he could complete that sentence, the door swung open. Lord Dedrick stood in the foyer, one hand resting on the doorframe. His hair was wind-blown, and he still wore his dust-covered riding clothes, as though he had just dismounted from a long journey.

Dedrick came into the office and knelt at Kosenmark's feet. "I came as soon as I heard. How are you?"

Kosenmark opened and closed his mouth, so plainly astonished that it took him a moment to answer. "I— Never mind how I am. How did you get back here? Did your father—"

"He doesn't know." Dedrick took Kosenmark's hands in his and kissed them. "I left home as soon as I heard about Berthold, my love. I even have a gift for you—one of those old books you like so much. I found it on a trip into town, in between drudging about on the estates with my brother. The bookseller tells me it's quite rare."

"The baron will not be pleased," Kosenmark murmured.

Dedrick exhaled sharply and let his gaze drop to their hands. "No. He will not. I shall have to persuade him with soft words and clever arguments. At least this time I have my sister's support in the matter. That should count for something."

Kosenmark closed his eyes. He seemed not to hear Dedrick's flow of words, explaining how he first heard the news in a letter from his sister, Lady Alia, who had it from someone else among the Queen's Companions, and that several days before Raul's own letter had arrived. Ilse had once thought Kosenmark's face unreadable. Today she could read his emotions far too easily. He looked, she thought, like a starved man come upon an unexpected feast.

"Come upstairs," he said in a hoarse voice. "We must talk. Now."

Without saying more, he led Dedrick from the room and the two were soon running up the stairs. As the door swung shut, Ilse could hear their voices echoing from the stairwell. She let out a long breath. So. The beloved had returned. Hardly surprising, given their long attachment. Why then did her head hurt so?

I'm an idiot. A selfish blind idiot.

With greater force than necessary, she rolled up the map, scattering markers over the floor. Ilse cursed fluently and gathered them up from the corners of her office. She stowed everything away and cleared off her desk. *Letters,* she thought. *I can always sort letters.*

She used up a half hour, but when she found herself rereading each letter six times without comprehending its contents, she stopped. No use working today. As Lord Kosenmark had said, they had a drought of news from all quarters. And Lord Kosenmark would not conduct any more business today, except that of the most personal kind.

Her stomach twinged. Enough, she told herself. She washed her face, and drank deeply of the water in her room. Tepid and stale, it nevertheless washed away the bitter taste in her mouth.

Downstairs, the common room was relatively quiet. Lord Iani was asleep on the couch, his head on Lady Theysson's lap. Adelaide and Johanna sat apart, involved in some private conversation, but Eduard and Josef were talking with Lady Theysson and Lothar Faulk, one of Lord Kosenmark's senior agents who oversaw the network of couriers and runners. Nadine perched on the corner of a nearby chair, weaving intricate patterns with a length of string.

"Have they vanished for the day?" Lady Theysson said.

"I believe so," Ilse said. She settled herself on one of the chairs.

Nadine paused in her weaving and glanced at Ilse, a brief searching look. Ilse smiled faintly and shrugged. Nadine's eyebrows lifted into an arch, but she resumed her weaving without comment.

"It was his wife who didn't understand," Eduard said.

They were talking about Hax again, obviously.

"Perhaps they both misunderstood each other," Lady Theysson said. "Think, Eduard. He left her with three small children so he might study military history. You must admit that Berthold should have discussed the matter with her first."

"He did. She refused to listen."

"So he said."

"Perhaps she loved him too much," Josef said musingly.

"Hardly," Nadine said. "She wanted to possess him. When he refused, she broke off the marriage."

"A very strange way of possessing him," Lady Theysson said.

"A very strange love," Nadine said. "But consider, she never remarried, nor did he." With a grand gesture, she unraveled her string. "But I say we've talked enough for the day. Eduard, go fetch us something to drink. And ask Mistress Raendl for those tasty sugar biscuits. The kind without the raisins."

"I like the raisins."

"They remind me of ants," Nadine said tartly. "Go." She waved her string at him.

Laughing, he went off to the kitchens and soon returned with a heavily laden tray. Nadine picked up one of the powdered biscuits and made a face. "Ants," she murmured. She glared at Eduard, who grinned back. "Your punishment is to serve all these lovely people," she declared. "All except Mistress Ilse, whose devoted servant I am."

Lady Theysson tweaked Lord Iani's ear. He woke with a snort. "Dinner?" he asked sleepily.

"Tea and biscuits," Theysson said. "Get up, Benno. You've slept away the afternoon."

Eduard served out wine and tea and biscuits, while Nadine supervised his work, her voice and gestures a perfect imitation of Mistress Raendl. "I can act the daughter as well as the mother," she said. "But I know Mistress Kathe would set the girls upon me. Fierce creatures, they are." She turned to Ilse. "Come, you've not told me what you'd like to drink."

"Tea," Ilse said mildly. "Just tea."

"What about a biscuit with ants?" Nadine said, her eyes bright and challenging. "And after, you could tell us one of your famous stories."

"Ah no." Ilse shook her head. "No stories. Not tonight."

"Why not? It helps us to pass the time. It takes our mind off troubling thoughts."

She spoke lightly enough, but Ilse thought she heard an edge to Nadine's voice. "Which story did you want to hear?"

"The one about Lir cutting her hair."

"A story of grief," Lady Theysson said. "Yes. That would be good."

Grief and death and love. Ilse felt a pinch in her stomach. Not that story, not now, with her mood so strangely unsettled. She shook her head again. "I'm sorry. I'm not— I wouldn't tell it properly. Not tonight."

Nadine let her glance settle on Ilse's face for a moment. "Perhaps not," she said. "You do look tired. Let me play storyteller instead. You can tell me which parts I did well, and which I should practice more."

She wrapped up her string into a ball and drew herself up straight, hands resting one within the other in her lap. Quiet dropped over the common room as the others settled to listen.

Like many legends about Lir and Toc, the story began with Toc's gift of his eyes.

"When Nil pressed upon Darkness," Nadine said softly, "he divided Day from Night. And yet that division was a subtle thing, a mere changing from pitchy blackness to a dim possibility of light. We are gods of mists and shadows, Lir said to Toc, and it was clear to him that though she loved their mother Darkness, Lir yearned for something brighter than this constant gloom."

Nadine's voice was soft but clear, evoking the whispers of dawn, Ilse thought. Closing her eyes, she leaned back into the couch, giving herself up to the story.

"You think her a shallow creature, perhaps," Nadine went on. "But think. We are her children, born during that season of love at the Mantharah. In the midst of winter's drear, or when our souls are wrapped in the shadows of inward gloom, we grieve. We grieve, and if we cannot find the sun within ourselves, we die.

"Toc saw that it was so with Lir. And because he loved his sister, he plucked out his eyes—one for the burning sun, one for the cold bright moon—and set them in the skies. Lir found her brother, sitting blind to the glory he had created, his face wet with blood. She wept. She wept and her tears spangled the night sky with stars. And when she had done with weeping, she forged a sword from sunfire and starlight and oiled it with their mingled blood. With that sword, she cut off her hair, her night-black hair, and from its length she wove a sheath for it."

Ilse listened as Nadine recounted how Lir sang for a century and a day about Toc's deed, and how, when she had done, she and Toc made love upon the Mantharah, from which flowed all the life in this world. Would she end the story there? Ilse wondered. No, her tale continued seamlessly into the next fable, when the season of delight ended with Death, another of Nil's children, who came slouching from the edges of chaos. Love. Death. Grief. Rebirth. The gods serving as the mirror and pattern of our lives.

Nadine ended the tale with Lir brushing open Toc's empty eyelids and seeing two bright points of light. "And so," she said, "and so and so and so . . . he lived."

A hush followed her last words. Benno Iani looked pensive. Eduard reached a hand toward Faulk, then withdrew it. Emma Theysson touched her fingertips to her eyes, lips, and heart. *Respect,* said the gesture. Respect and gratitude for the performer. Just at the point when the silence weighed upon them, Nadine stirred. "Eduard," she whispered. "Music, please."

Eduard rose without any banter this time and seated himself by the hammered strings. He touched the keys gently and soundlessly. Another pass, and Ilse heard the whisper of velvet upon the metal strings. Smiling, Eduard rolled his fingers lightly across the keyboard, and a shiver of sound broke the room's hush. Within a measure, Ilse recognized the piece as a new composition by one of Tiralien's well-known musicians, celebrating spring's arrival. The first movement began slow and brooding, but soon brighter notes overtook the minor ones.

After Eduard played two more pieces, Mikka joined him at the keyboard, and they played a series of happier melodies. The others began to converse in low tones. Nadine resumed her string patterns, though her face had taken on a pensive air. One by one, the party broke up. Faulk beckoned to Mikka and Eduard, who broke off their playing to follow him into another room. Soon after, Emma Theysson whispered in Benno Iani's ear, and they, too, disappeared to other regions of the house.

"Young lovers," Nadine said in her most indulgent tone.

"And the not so young," Josef said, grinning at her.

"Hah! I'm but a child, even more than Mistress Ilse here."

She sent a sidelong glance at Ilse. Unsettled by the directness of her gaze, Ilse picked up the tea carafe but found that it was empty.

"Would you like more?" Nadine said.

Ilse glanced up and away. "No. Thank you."

Nadine sighed and exchanged a look with Josef. "I told you," he said. "She likes me better."

"She likes prunes better," Nadine said tartly.

They began to bicker, in the way old friends do. When Ilse stood to leave, they broke off only long enough to say good-bye.

With some relief, she came to the quiet upper regions of the pleasure house. No lamps burned here, leaving the halls in a pleasant half-light from the windows, their corners and alcoves brushed with faint shadows. By habit, she stopped by her office. Kathe had sent up a carafe of tea. Ilse poured herself a cup and sifted through a few invitations that had arrived in the past hour. A boating party with Lady Ulik and her family. A visit to the theater with Lord Rossim. An announcement of someone's marriage. All of them went into her letter box, for Lord Kosenmark's attention the next day. Or the day after, she thought. She had no idea how long he and Lord Dedrick would seclude themselves. She rubbed her head, which ached fiercely.

"Mistress Ilse?"

Ilse looked up. A runner stood in the door, an apologetic look on his face. "I did knock," he said hastily. "Three times. It's just that there's a gentleman below. He says he's to meet with you today, and that it cannot wait."

One of Lord Kosenmark's agents? she thought, her pulse beating faster. So far, she had met only Faulk. Then she recalled Mistress Denk mentioning that she had recently contracted with an architect for a pavilion in the upper gardens. "Did you send word to Mistress Denk or Lord Kosenmark?" she asked.

"No, Mistress. The gentleman said most definitely that he wished to speak with you."

Very strange. "Send him up, then. And let Kathe know I'd like tea and fruit for our visitor."

She searched through her cabinets for any papers concerning the pavilion. Mistress Denk had given her a copy of the plans and the initial estimate. Perhaps the architect had new drawings, or he wanted to confirm when to start work. If so, she would have to speak with Lord Kosenmark . . .

"Therez."

Ilse froze. It was a man's voice, soft as a whisper and low, with an accent she had not heard in over six months. Very slowly, she turned around.

Her father stood in the doorway. Tall and lean, just as before, but with a stoop to his frame. He was dressed in plain traveling clothes, gray layered upon gray, which gave him the air of having materialized from the shadows. In a way, he had.

"Therez?" he said, his voice uncertain now.

"How did you find me?" she choked out.

Petr Zhalina blinked and glanced around the office, taking in the books and writing supplies and locked chests. There was a new hesitation in his manner, as though he did not quite believe that he was looking at his daughter. "Never mind how. You are well?"

Ilse made a quick gesture. "Dobru. At least—well enough."

Another pause while he stared at her. Then he cleared his throat. "Why didn't you write to us?"

She said nothing. What could she say that she had not made clear by running away?

When she didn't answer, Petr Zhalina frowned. "I looked everywhere for you. Everywhere. I sent Gersi out with messages to all the cities and towns within three days' ride. I wrote your cousins in Duenne, asking if you'd found your way there. I even wrote to my uncles in Duszranjo."

"Duszranjo?" she said, at last startled into speech. "Why there?"

He shrugged. "Because you always talked about it. Remember how you begged your grandmother for stories?"

That was years ago, when I was a child. Or have you forgotten?

"I wouldn't go there," she said. "I would have gone to Duenne—"

She broke off at the sudden quiet appearance of Hanne in the foyer, carrying a tray laden with dishes and carafes and cups. Ah yes, the refreshments. From the look on Hanne's face, the girl had overheard enough to wonder and worry.

"Thank you, Hanne," Ilse said quickly. "Just leave the tray on the table. We can serve ourselves."

Hanne slipped past Petr Zhalina into Ilse's office. As she set the tray on the table, she lifted her gaze to Ilse's. Ilse gave a tiny shake of her head.

Hanne sank into a brief curtsy and hurried from the room and down the stairs. But in making way for Hanne, Petr Zhalina had come inside the office. Now he stood just a few feet away, with only the desk between them.

He's just a visitor. He cannot do anything more to me.

Kathe had included a carafe of wine and a plate of sugar biscuits, as well as the tea and fruit. Ilse gestured toward the tray. "Would you like tea or wine? Something to eat?"

"Tea. If you please."

He spoke stiffly, clearly uneasy. Eyeing him with discreet glances, Ilse poured tea for him. He looked older, far older than half a year would make. His hair had gone entirely silver, and there was a new pinched look to his face. She could almost see the bones through his skin.

Unwilling to approach him, she set the cup on her desk. Her father picked it up with a nod and drank. "Thank you. This is very good tea, Therez."

The name was like a tiny lash, flicking against her sensibilities. Willing her voice to remain calm, she said, "My name is Ilse, not Therez."

Another blink. Now she could see that his hands trembled, causing the tea to spill over the cup's rim. She ought to offer him a chair, but she could not bring herself to continue these pretend civilities. In a fit of contrariness, she poured wine for herself and drank, still watching him. He was drinking in fast deep gulps, as though desperate for it. When he set his cup down, she refilled it. His color had improved within the last few moments. He no longer looked so ill, though he did look weary. How long and fast had he ridden that day?

He refused a third cup. She gestured to the fruit, but he shook his head. "Therez . . . I don't know what to say. We thought you died. Your mother hasn't slept a whole night since you ran away, and your brother—"

"Who told you?" she said abruptly. "You never said."

"A man," her father said slowly. "His name was Alarik Brandt. He wrote me last month."

Cold washed over her skin at the sound of Brandt's name. "But how did he know?"

Her father stared at her with an odd expression on his face. "How? He heard about you in one of the taverns here. A serving girl told him stories about a rich girl she knew. A runaway from Melnek. When Brandt asked for particulars, she described you exactly. Even the name matched—Ilse. The same one you told Brandt."

Lys. It must have been Lys. Or maybe Rosel. They left her memories enough to recall Ilse and how she arrived at Lord Kosenmark's house. But it didn't matter which one. What mattered was that Brandt knew where she lived. Now she remembered Volker and Brenn telling her they came every spring to Tiralien. Brandt might have seen her when she went to market with Kathe—

"You do know this man, don't you, Therez?"

A bitter taste filled her mouth. "Oh yes," she said thickly. "I know Alarik Brandt. I took passage with him from Melnek. Didn't he tell you that part?"

Her father frowned. "Not exactly. He told me you took passage in Mundlau."

Something was wrong, more wrong than Alarik Brandt finding out where she lived and writing the news to her father. Her father's voice sounded oddly strained, and his mouth puckered as though he tasted something disagreeable.

"I took passage with him in Melnek," she repeated. "I was there, hiding in Brandt's caravan, when Váná Gersi came to our camp. Brandt knew that. He charged me double—"

Petr Zhalina gestured sharply. "Therez, I checked the man's reputation. All the agents say he's strict and reliable. And I didn't want to mention it. Not yet. But the man said he had trouble with you. Some money went missing just about the time you ran away from him . . ."

She wanted to scream that her name wasn't Therez and that Brandt was a liar, but she could see that her father wouldn't believe her account. Hands shaking, she finished off her wine and poured a second cup. Her father was staring at her now, as though he could not recognize her.

"Therez, did you hear me? Did you steal from him?"

"I heard you," she said in a low voice. "No, I stole nothing. And I'm alive. Are you satisfied? Will you leave now?"

"Not without you."

Ilse took a quick step backward. "No."

"What do you mean no? You are my daughter—"

"Am I? I thought I was an entry in your ledger books. Something you could trade to Theodr Galt. He won't make that trade now, I imagine."

Petr Zhalina's face darkened. "How dare you say that?" he whispered. "You who came to this kind of house." He jerked out the words one by one. "Know this, Therez Zhalina. You may come willingly with me, or I can notify the watch that you belong to me."

He circled the desk and grabbed for her. Ilse darted around the other side, but her father moved faster than she thought possible. He intercepted her before she reached the door and seized her by the wrist. Ilse tried to

Ilse closed her eyes. *Stone, I am rock and stone.*

Kosenmark took hold of her elbow, laid another hand on her shoulder, and led her to her chair. He pressed her shoulder gently until she collapsed into it. Then he withdrew, but only to shut the door, for she could sense his presence as clearly as ever.

Moments later a wine cup was held to her lips. "Drink. Drink all of it."

"Is he gone?" she asked.

"Yes. He is not here. He cannot harm you. Drink, please."

Under his coaxing, she finished the cupful. He withdrew then. More sounds—of a fire lighting—then he was back and chafing her hands. She was cold, though the day was warm. Her stomach had squeezed into a knot. She thought she might be sick.

"No more wine," he said. "Else that would send you to bed with a headache. And you looked quite ill when I saw you downstairs. I want a good return for my new secretary's wages."

He spoke lightly, teasingly. Ilse tried to laugh. A sob came out instead. She pressed a hand over her mouth to smother the next. "I'm sorry. I'm sorry," she whispered.

"Sorry for what?"

"For showing you that, my lord."

"Ah. That." His voice was gentle. "I think I've shown you that, too. And you might call me Raul. We've earned our friendship, I think. Or if you can't think of me as a friend, what about a sister? I sound more like one, I know."

She gave a strangled laugh, which turned into crying, as she finally gave herself over to an outpouring of grief. Raul stayed by her side, waiting in patient silence until her weeping quieted to sobs and then exhausted silence.

"I wish I had not told him," she said.

"So does he." Raul paused. "Would you like me to talk with him—privately?"

She shook her head. "No. It won't take away what I said."

"As you wish." He paused again. "But there is another matter. I heard what your father said about Brandt. If he does travel here regularly, you will have to take extra care when you go abroad in the city."

A shudder went through her at the thought of Alarik Brandt. She wasn't safe anywhere, not even in Tiralien. Brandt might decide to do more than spy on her. Or her father might petition the watch, just as he threatened. Lord Kosenmark surely would not care for the notoriety from that.

"I'll have to leave," she said out loud.

"Leave?" Raul said, surprised. "Why should you leave?"

twist free, but her father caught her other arm and pushed her a͓ the wall.

"Bind my arms, why don't you?" she cried out. "Alarik Brandt did that

"He should have whipped you." Her father was breathing hard fro͏ effort of holding her still.

"Maybe he did. Maybe he wanted to sell me. Just like you, selling ͏ Theodr Galt."

"You—" Her father's voice broke with anger. "You ruined that con You and your thoughtless—"

"I was not thoughtless. I asked for a say in choosing my husband denied me that. You wanted to sell me to the highest bidder. It's to͏ now. I sold myself instead."

His fingers tightened, making her wince. "What are you saying whispered.

Ilse jerked her chin up, met his eyes. His face looked gray in th͏ light, or was that her imagination? *Tell him. Lie. No. No more pretendi͏* made a trade," she said. "Just like you did. I begged Alarik Brandt to ͏ me his whore. I said I would do anything to hide from you."

She closed her eyes a moment, remembering that exchange. Alarik's glittering in the firelight. How she had deliberately shucked off her clot͏ The sensation of his callused hand on her breast. Her father was le͏ against the wall, shaking his head in disbelief. "No. That can't be true."

Stop it. You've done enough.

But she couldn't stop, not until she had told him every ugly detail.

"It is true," she said. "I lay with every man in that caravan. Six a n Four in the mornings. Five weeks of that until I was sick and with child it kept me away from you. Now do you understand?"

He covered his face with both hands. "Oh, Therez. Oh, child."

Ilse said nothing. There was nothing left to say.

Only then did she notice a shadow falling into the room. Lord Ko mark appeared in the doorway. His glance swiftly took in Ilse and ther father. He came inside and laid a hand on Petr Zhalina's shoulder. "C͏ Maester Zhalina. You look ill. Let me escort you downstairs."

Petr Zhalina slowly lifted his gaze to Kosenmark's face. Only grad͏ did he seem to recognize who this tall, high-voiced man might be. jerked away from Kosenmark's touch and stumbled out the door. Whe͏ reached the edge of the foyer, however, he paused. "Your grandmother ͏ last month," he said without looking back. "We buried her ashes in mountains." Then he rushed down the stairs and was gone.

"To . . . to save you the trouble, my lord. My father said he would summon the watch."

"That is no trouble. You are my responsibility."

"But my lord—"

"Raul. Call me Raul. Would you like water now? Tea?"

She shook her head. "No, my lord."

His eyes narrowed with the briefest hint of humor. "You are a stubborn young woman."

Ilse tried to summon up a smile, but it was too soon. She rubbed her head with one hand. When Lord Kosenmark handed her a cup of water, she accepted it gratefully. Weeping had left her with a dry mouth and sore throat, and she felt shaky, as though she had run fast and far.

I have. I still am.

Kosenmark touched her arm. "You look worried. Is it about Brandt still?"

She nodded reluctantly.

"I have an idea about that," he said. "It won't make the precautions unnecessary, but it might make them easier to bear. Or rather, it might help you with being less afraid."

Less afraid. That was something she wanted to hear. "I'd like that, but how?"

"Lessons. Ones without paper or pens or dusty old books. We could start now, if you like."

There was nothing but kindness in his expression. So strange, so different from how he had looked just a few hours before when Lord Dedrick had arrived. Lord Dedrick. She gave a jump. "My lord, what about—"

"Lord Dedrick?" Kosenmark's expression went opaque, making Ilse wish she had not asked. But the look vanished, to be replaced by a wry smile. "Lord Dedrick went home to plead his case with his father. Do not worry about him. Come, we have at least a few hours before dark—long enough for you to decide if you like this new venture. But you best change into clothes you don't mind getting dirty—trousers and a jersey. Oh, and boots. Meet me back here when you're ready."

He urged her out the door. Still wondering what kind of lessons he meant, she hurried to her rooms and changed into a set of old clothes from her kitchen days. Her momentary energy deserted her suddenly. She sank onto her bed, thinking, *What have I said to my own father?*

Nothing more than what she'd thought these past six months.

A trembling overtook her. One, two quarter bells rang while she rocked to and fro. Stupid, weak, silly creature. No, not that. A stubborn creature, just like her father. But that was just as terrible a thought. Panic bubbled up into a high-pitched laugh. Ilse clamped her lips shut. Went rigid. Then forced out a breath, then another and another, until she thought she had recovered her self-control.

Never that. I shall never do that.

But it was enough to stand, to drink a long draught of water from the pitcher in her rooms. To think of what Lord Kosenmark had offered her. Lessons to defend herself. It was ... not enough to erase what had happened before. But it was enough to give her strength for tomorrow.

Still unsteady, she finished dressing. When she returned to her office she found Raul wearing the clothes he used for his weapons practice. "I've notified your new tutor," he said. "He's waiting for us below."

He led her down by the back stairs and out a side passage into the courtyard where Benedikt Ault waited, arms folded and smiling. He was a lean spare man, his dark hair brushed with gray, clipped so severely she could see his scalp. Though he stood a head shorter than Kosenmark, he had an air of strength and speed. He smiled faintly at them both. "Another session, my lord? Or was I too easy on you this morning?"

"Both and neither, Benedikt. Here is your newest student."

Ault nodded, but he was studying Ilse with narrowed eyes—assessing her, she thought. She glanced from one man to the other. "Swords?"

"Knives, then swords," Kosenmark said. "But first, the hand-to-hand techniques—if you agree. And if Maester Ault agrees. Benedikt, can you teach her enough to do battle with me?"

"Certainly, my lord. Stand to one side and watch," he told Ilse. "I want to demonstrate first on Lord Kosenmark. Then you shall try the technique on me. Lord Kosenmark, if you please ..."

Kosenmark took a stand opposite his teacher, feet planted apart. "See," Ault said to Ilse. "Square, like his. Now watch. My lord?"

Ault held out his right hand and made a fist. Kosenmark gripped Ault's wrist. "Open the hand like so," Ault said, demonstrating as he spoke. "Now step left, outside the attacker's foot. Roll the wrist toward you, lifting your elbow. So."

Ault broke free of Kosenmark's grip, whipping his elbow past Kosenmark's throat. One, two strikes toward Kosenmark's face and his groin, stopping short each time. Then he swiveled around, swinging his other hand in an arc toward Kosenmark's temple.

"Again."

He repeated the movements slowly, explaining as he went. Then he dismissed Kosenmark to one side and told Ilse to take his place.

Kosenmark sat by the wall, while Ilse took his place. Ault studied her stance a moment. "Almost, Mistress Ilse. More like this." His hands pushed and pulled her arms, shoulders, and feet until he was satisfied. "Now, hold out your left hand and make a fist."

She did so. He grasped her wrist.

"Think of someone you hate," Ault said under his breath. "Imagine they have just captured you."

Her father. Alarik Brandt. Theodr Galt.

"Which one?" she whispered.

"The one you wish most to break free of."

Ilse looked into his face and tried to picture Theodr Galt. No, she had escaped him thoroughly. Brandt, then. For a moment, she panicked. She fought down the panic. Concentrating on doing exactly what Ault showed her, she stepped left and pulled hard. Ault gripped tighter. Ilse jerked her hand back. When she felt him loosen his grip, she twisted free. What came next? A strike. And another. She tried copying Ault's fluid movements, but she could guess how clumsy she looked.

"Make the fist before I grab you," he said as she rubbed her sore wrists. "Then relax your hand and move fast. We'll do it slowly until you learn the motions, however."

They practiced that move a dozen times. Ault showed her two more techniques, both starting from the same position. Once she had them memorized, he made her repeat each one slowly at first, while he critiqued her every move. The next round he exhorted her to move as quickly as she could. By the time he announced the lesson was over, her arms and wrists ached.

"Good enough for one day," he said, nodding. "We'll repeat these techniques tomorrow and the next day and the day after that. Now sit over there and watch. You might learn something from Lord Kosenmark's lesson." He turned toward Kosenmark, who was already standing. "Shall we show her steel, my lord? Or do you prefer the wooden practice blades?"

Kosenmark's teeth flashed in the bright sunlight. "Steel, Benedikt. It fits my mood today."

Ault and Kosenmark selected their swords from the rack. "First position," said Ault, raising his sword.

"Ready."

Ault's blade swung toward Kosenmark's. A quick series of strikes and blocks followed, the swords moving so fast they changed into bright blurs as metal caught sunlight. Ilse held her breath. There was a pattern, she could almost see it from how one blade turned and twisted and met the other in a crash, and then the same happened but in reverse as Kosenmark and Ault each took turns advancing or retreating across the yard. Ault, of course, was the master, and every movement showed it, but Kosenmark was far faster and more agile than she had expected. He was strong, too; more than once he caught Ault's sword and nearly wrenched it from his grip.

It made Ilse think how strength and skill were not enough. So many other factors could change a man's life within a heartbeat.

I believed I was safe, too, she thought. Safe from Brandt. Safe from her father.

She began to see why Kosenmark had offered her the gift of these lessons. There were no guarantees, but with the right instruction, she could learn how to keep away from dangerous choices such as those that led her into servitude with men like Alarik Brandt.

Or if she could not avoid them entirely, how to break a hold, turn a weapon, run toward freedom.

Kosenmark sent her a glancing smile as he dodged a thrust from Ault. He was still smiling, grinning as he parried the next stroke.

That is what I want, Ilse thought. *I want to be fast. Strong. Like him.*

CHAPTER EIGHTEEN

ILSE REPORTED TO the practice courtyard early the next morning, expecting to find Kosenmark and Ault at their drills. To her surprise, the place was empty except for one long lean cat, which had stretched itself along the crown of the wall in the sunniest spot. It opened one eye lazily, yawned, then shifted to an infinitesimally more comfortable position.

"I wish I were still sleeping," Ilse said.

The cat's only response was to twitch one ear.

Benedikt Ault came through the gate. He glanced to where the cat had just moments before lain. He gave a wry smile, as though amused. "I see you are prompt," he said to Ilse. "Good. Are you also ready?"

"As ready as I can be. Where is Lord Kosenmark?"

Ault opened up the weapons rack, shook his head, closed it. "He went on an errand in the city. We are to start without him."

He had her work through the same techniques from the day before. More than once, Ilse allowed herself to be distracted by birds flitting past, or the cat, which eventually returned to its post on the wall. Her distraction earned her more than a few bruises and some sharp words from Ault. Trying to concentrate on his instructions, Ilse wondered briefly why she had agreed to these lessons. Because Lord Kosenmark suggested them. Because she wanted to please him. She frowned. No. Because she wanted that same grace and strength she saw in Kosenmark when he fought with Benedikt Ault.

"Better," Ault said after the twelfth repetition. "Especially considering that you are a beginner. Remember what I told you about imagining your enemy. If you were to face a genuine attacker, you would not need that spur, but then you would also need to know the movements without thinking. Think. Memorize. Think again. Act. Ah, my lord, I'm glad to see you."

Kosenmark came into the courtyard. He was barefoot and dressed in old cotton trousers cut very loose. He nodded politely to Ilse, but she could see the tension in his mouth and the faint line between his eyes. "How goes the lesson?" he asked.

"Well enough," Ault said. "Perhaps you would like a bout while Mistress Ilse rests."

Kosenmark hesitated, then nodded. Ault gestured toward the wooden practice swords. Both men picked out blades and took their positions.

It was like and unlike their bout from the previous day. After a salute, the two exchanged a flurry of blows, their wooden blades rattling loud in the morning. Kosenmark pressed hard, but as she watched, Ilse gradually realized that Ault did not press back. Though his blade moved in a blur, he used it only to guide Kosenmark, not to attack him.

Abruptly Kosenmark stopped. His face had a sheen of sweat, but he was not breathing hard. "Tired, Benedikt?" There was an edge to his voice, and he had not lowered his weapon.

Ault smiled grimly. "If you think so."

"Benedikt . . ."

"My lord, I suit the lesson to the student and his condition. You know that."

Kosenmark lowered his weapon. The tightness around his mouth had gone, and his eyes no longer had the unnerving blankness. "Yes, I do know that," he said. "My apologies."

"None required, my lord. Will you practice your next pattern, while I attend to Mistress Ilse's lessons? Use the heavier blade, I suggest."

Kosenmark exchanged blades and went to the far corner of the courtyard to practice a complicated series of moves. Ilse resumed her old position. She didn't know Ault well—until yesterday, they had only spoken in passing—but she thought his smile was a shade warmer than before, as though he were satisfied about something. However, he only said, "Show me the second sequence, Mistress Ilse. The one that begins so . . ."

He guided her through the sequence, making comments and suggestions and corrections after every move. Off to the side, she could hear the soft thump, thump, pause, thump of Kosenmark's feet on the dirt as he practiced.

"Good enough," Ault said. "We should end for today. You will be sore," he added. "That, too, will pass."

She nodded, absently rubbing her wrists, which ached. So did the bottom of her feet. And her legs. She was surprised her scalp didn't hurt.

Glancing up, she caught Ault's amused smile. He probably knew exactly how she felt. "Take a warm bath for your muscles, and I shall have Mistress Hedda prepare a salve for your wrists. Do not stint on the warm water," he said. Then to Lord Kosenmark, "Your turn, my lord. Would you prefer unarmed combat today, or another bout with the sword?"

"Sword," Kosenmark said shortly. "Steel this time. I believe my control is better. Mistress Ilse, when you are done with your bath, please report to my office. We have some business to discuss."

Her pulse jumped. "New business, my lord?" she asked. "Or old?"

"Both and neither," he said. "And ask Mistress Raendl to send up refreshments for five guests as well."

He turned back to Ault before she could ask what or if he had discovered something.

Ilse hurriedly washed and changed her clothes, her thoughts running through all the possibilities for this meeting. *We've received nothing in the past week. No letters. No special courier today. Even yesterday, the post contained nothing. Nothing, except . . .*

Except Lord Dedrick, who had just returned from his father's district.

She paused in tying the ribbon around her braid. Lord Dedrick must have heard new rumors. Yes, that had to be the reason. With renewed speed, she finished her toilette and caught up her writing case. A brief stop by her office for her notes on the Károví situation, and then she was running up the stairs.

When she came into Lord Kosenmark's office, the vast sand glass was just turning over in its cage; the last sands of the old hours and minutes were still falling through the smaller glasses. A soft chime sounded, marking the new hour. Six months since she first walked into this room. How quickly she had accustomed herself to its rare beauty. These days, she noticed the books and papers and maps, less frequently the new paintings or statues that Lord Kosenmark sometimes acquired. Most days, her focus was on the man himself and what he said, not his belongings.

Voices sounded from the landing. Kosenmark came into the office with Luise Ehrenalt at his side, both absorbed in conversation. ". . . better to describe the situation just once, Luise," Kosenmark was saying. "That way everyone can hear your concerns—and you will have some. Mistress Ilse." He paused and his eyes narrowed briefly. "You will regret ignoring Maester Ault's advice about the bath, but I am glad to have you so punctual. Please, both of you, go directly into the gardens. The others should arrive soon."

"Including Lord Dedrick?" Ehrenalt said.

She and Lord Kosenmark exchanged pointed looks. "Someday you must share your network with me, Luise," Kosenmark murmured.

"When you share yours with me," Luise said. "But in this case, the news came from Adelaide. She saw no reason to keep that from me."

"True. Yes, Lord Dedrick will be present. Now, if you will excuse me, I will take a few moments and make myself look less like a street ruffian."

Ehrenalt appeared caught between amusement and irritation. When Kosenmark made a shooing gesture toward the door, she went, shaking her head.

With the coming of summer, all the foliage had turned lush and thick. To Ilse, Lord Kosenmark's gardens were like the pattern of his mind—lovely and intricate and deceptive. Even so small a garden had its secret nooks, and the paths were laid out so that just a few steps had taken them out of sight of the doors. So she wasn't surprised when Luise said to her, "Lord Kosenmark loves a good mystery. I sometimes think he ought to be a street juggler."

"Or a trickster prince, sent to teach us truth with lies." Ilse caught Luise's curious look, and added, "Just a poem I once heard."

"I know the poem," Luise said drily. "And it fits. More than you might realize."

They had reached the garden's center, where benches circled a tiled section. Ilse busied herself with arranging her case and writing materials, aware that Luise Ehrenalt was studying her with that same curious expression. She was saved from any further comments, however, when Emma Theysson and Benno Iani made their appearance. While Luise greeted them, Ilse skimmed through her notes on the Károví situation.

Faulk arrived soon after and seated himself with an air of weariness. "My lords are coming in the next moment," he said, waving a hand toward the doors. "Most likely they are arranging what and how they wish to tell us whatever they mean to tell us."

"Lothar, you are being elaborate again," Emma said, but she was smiling.

"You mean convoluted," Faulk replied. "It fits my mood, and besides, that is my chief qualification for being here. Ah, here they come."

Lord Kosenmark came into view, alone. He stopped at the edge of the clearing and scanned everyone's faces, as though gauging their mood. Jittery, Ilse thought, supplying the answer she would give. Jittery and curious and hopeful all at once. *His* mood was harder to read.

"Where is Lord Dedrick?" Faulk asked.

"Home," Kosenmark said. "It seems he made a promise to his father."

"A promise or a compromise? And were the terms advantageous?"

Kosenmark sent him a warning glance, but merely said, "Our business does not depend on his presence, but on the news he carried from Duenne."

Ilse let out a soundless exhalation. So it was news from Duenne—disturbing news judging by his expression. She expected him to lay out the details now, the way he spread out his maps and scrolls, but Kosenmark appeared strangely hesitant.

"What is it?" Faulk said. "A crisis? A scandal? Did Lord Dedrick discover a treasonous plot?"

"You might say that," Kosenmark said. "First the part we expected— Armand has begun inviting certain nobles into private interviews, mostly the older and more conservative members of court. I'm interpreting these interviews as a means to forge alliances on smaller issues. Stepping-stones for the larger issue of war."

"Is he having any success?" Theysson asked.

"Some. Baron Quint, among others, are persuaded by Lord Khandarr's arguments that we would conquer the invaders before they cross our borders."

"Quint." Ehrenalt looked as though she had tasted something sour.

"What about your father?" Theysson said. "Where does he stand?"

Kosenmark shrugged, clearly uneasy. "He's made no public declaration, but everyone knows his opinion. Which means he finds himself at the center of the opposition despite his efforts. Or rather, his studied avoidance of any effort." In a softer voice, he added, "We cannot sustain a war without cause. My father should know it. He should take a stand."

"Perhaps," said Iani, "he waits for his son to take action."

"I cannot. Not when the king himself dismissed me from Duenne."

"He dismissed you from his Council," Theysson argued. "But you could go back to court and lead the opposition yourself. Berthold once thought you might—"

"Berthold is dead," Kosenmark said flatly. "Besides, we are caretakers, not rebels."

The leader of the opposition is not a rebel, Ilse thought, but she could see that both speakers had left a great deal unsaid. Theysson and Kosenmark stared at each other a moment longer. It was Kosenmark who dropped his gaze to the tiled pathway. Theysson shook her head and sighed.

Faulk stared at Kosenmark, his eyes flat and bright. Kosenmark met his gaze steadily. "Lothar, you appear displeased."

"Not displeased, my lord. Simply puzzled. You see, I have a dozen agents in Duenne—five in the court itself, one of them in the king's bed. For all that, I have no genuine news from Duenne. Nor do you, except for insignificant rumors brought to us by the usual means. And yet Lord Dedrick has uncovered a raft of plots and alliances and schemes, all within a single month. And so I'm curious if Lord Dedrick mentioned the name of his excellent source."

"He did. His sister."

"Interesting. The queen recently appointed Lady Alia as one of her companions, am I right?"

"She did."

Ilse held her breath. She could feel Kosenmark's anger, running just beneath that still blank face. Faulk had to realize it, too, because his thin smile carried a hint of nervousness, as though he sensed the danger of his games.

"We all know Lord Dedrick," Iani said quietly. "We can trust him."

"But can we trust his sister? Her concerns are not the same as Lord Dedrick's. Or ours."

"Enough, Faulk." Theysson flicked her fingers to one side. "Your suspicions are valid, I admit. However, I'd like to hear the rest of what Lord Kosenmark has to say."

"Yes," Ehrenalt said. "I can see by his face that he's told us only half."

"Less than half," Kosenmark said in a breathy voice. "When Dedrick brought me his news, he also brought me a gift. A gift of great significance, though he didn't realize it himself."

As he spoke, he took a small square packet from his shirt, wrapped in oilskin. He untied the strings and unwrapped the oilskin with meticulous care, and then the layer of silk underneath. No one spoke for a moment, then Ehrenalt leaned forward. "A book?" she said doubtfully.

"An old book," Ilse said.

Kosenmark favored her with a smile. "Very old. The antiquarian provided Dedrick with a certificate of its authenticity, stating that the book was produced three hundred years ago. Dedrick bought it for me because he knows I love such things. I put his gift away without examining it until late last night. And when I did . . . Let us say that sleep became a difficult matter."

Ilse half stood to get a better view of the book. Clearly an antique, just as Kosenmark said, its covers were two thick squares of dark red leather, stiffened by wood, Ilse guessed, and fastened with leather ties along its spine. The ties had almost disintegrated with age, and the covers were scored and cracked so that the wood showed through. Kosenmark had not opened the book, but she could see how the pages had turned dark, and though he handled it carefully, bits of parchment crumbled away and floated toward the ground.

"This book contains the memoirs of Karel Simkov," Kosenmark said. "He served two decades in the Károví army. Just before Dzavek invaded, Simkov deserted to Veraene at first, then settled in the Kingdom of

Ysterien, away from the front. There he took a position as a prison administrator, having had such experience in Rastov."

Ilse glanced from the book to Kosenmark's troubled face. The others
seemed impatient for an explanation. Except for Benno Iani. He was smiling,
lips parted and gaze bright, as though he guessed the book's significance.

"A prison administrator," he said softly. "Was he there when—"

"Yes," Kosenmark said shortly. "He was."

"Explain," Ehrenalt said. "What is the connection?"

"Prisons," Kosenmark replied. "Simkov held a trusted position in Rastov's military prisons. He assisted with interrogations, and oversaw the prisoners' welfare, both good and bad. It seems that one day, the king himself
delivered a prisoner to Simkov—a man named Benacka."

"Ah," Theysson breathed. "Now I understand."

So did Ilse. Benacka. Dzavek's most trusted lieutenant. The man who
stole Lir's jewels from Leos Dzavek and hid them from all Erythandra.
Dzavek had recaptured the man but not the jewels. The night before he intended to question Benacka, the man killed himself. Furious, Dzavek had
launched a war against Veraene, believing the jewels to be somewhere in
that kingdom. And here was the missing link between all those mysterious
clues from Károví.

"Does Leos Dzavek know this book exists?" she asked.

"I doubt it," Kosenmark said. "Simkov published them under his new
name, Barend Happ. He paid to have a dozen copies printed. This might be
the only one left."

"How do they help us? Do they help us?" Theysson said. "What do they
say?"

"I don't know the how yet. What I can tell you is that Simkov spent five
evenings alone with the prisoner. His task was to extract information—to
interrogate the man—but, according to his memoirs, they spent most of the
time just talking. Or perhaps that was Simkov's usual method to gain his
subject's trust. Whatever the reason, that final evening Benacka rambled on
for hours about the jewels."

"What did he say?" Iani said urgently, reaching for the book.

Kosenmark stepped back and lifted the book high. "No. I'm sorry, Benno,
but no. I would prefer you did not read this book. Not until we've decided
certain things. According to Simkov, Benacka made no sense. He complained how the man hinted and teased but said nothing outright. However,
I think if the right person read these memoirs, they would find a treasure of
clues here."

"The right person being Leos Dzavek?" Theysson asked.

"I haven't decided."

"You wouldn't give the book to Armand, would you?" Iani asked.

"No. At least, I think not."

"So what are your plans?" Faulk said.

Kosenmark vented a breath. "To be honest, I don't know. Dzavek might use the jewels for defense alone, but as Mistress Ilse observed to me, the king is old. Who will inherit the throne when he dies? Who will inherit this book or the jewels? How will they use them?"

"Count Risov?" Ehrenalt said. "He's the senior member in Council."

"But not the most powerful," Theysson said. "That would be Duke Markov."

"Markov or Karasek," Faulk said. "Karasek shares responsibility for the armies and he's more popular. He's also a mage in his own right."

"But Markov has more years in Council. He also has an ally in Duke Černosek, and if his reputation is genuine, Černosek is second in magic only to Dzavek himself."

Ilse listened as the others rambled on about Károví politics. She recognized all the names from reading Hax's notes and her discussions with Lord Kosenmark, but she could not pluck out the facts as fast as the members of Kosenmark's shadow court. So she listened and concentrated on memorizing more details about Károví's Council and the mutable factions therein.

"So you see it's not a simple choice," Kosenmark was saying. "Even if I trusted Dzavek himself—and I'm not certain I do—I cannot trust Markov or Černosek or Risov. Possibly Karasek, but what if his ambitions include taking the crown and using the jewels to extend Károví's borders?"

"War," Theysson said softly. "It would mean Armand gets his war. And we pay the cost."

"Yes," Raul said heavily. "We do. So do those in Károví."

"Every choice is a risk," Ehrenalt said. "We must act."

"Yes, we must act. But how?"

He cradled the book in one hand and rubbed his forehead with the other. He was missing Berthold Hax, Ilse thought. Hax's experience. Hax's knowledge about history and politics and economics. Hax's ability to take the tangled skein of facts and rumors and possibilities and lay them out in clear patterns.

"What do you want from us?" Theysson said after a moment.

"I want you to think about our choices," Kosenmark said.

"And these are?" Ehrenalt said.

"Give the book to Dzavek and hope that he finds the jewels. That Armand will drop his war plans. Or . . ." He started to rub his forehead, realized he was doing that, and sighed. "Or we do something else, and I have no ideas for that."

He began to wrap the book again into its layers of patterned silk and dull oilskin. So that was it, Ilse thought, surprised. It was so unlike his usual way of conducting a meeting that she half expected him to keep talking, to give out orders or recommendations, once he had finished with the book's protective covering, but Kosenmark said nothing.

"What do you want from us?" she said, repeating Theysson's words. "To think?"

"To think. To consider," he said. "To search your hearts and minds and past lives for any reason we ought to give aid and comfort to our king's enemy."

"I see." Theysson studied her hands a moment. "How long are we to consider this matter?"

"Until we know how to act."

Theysson exchanged a glance with Iani, who shook his head. They both stood and murmured a farewell to Kosenmark, who was still studying the book. Faulk left by another route. Ehrenalt waited a few more moments, as though, like Ilse, she expected Kosenmark to say more, do more. When it was obvious that he would not, she stood, her disappointment clear, and left by yet another path.

Ilse busied herself with putting away the pens and paper she had not used. When she looked up again, Kosenmark still had that same troubled expression on his face. "So what should I do, Mistress Ilse?" he said. "Should I play the traitor for the sake of peace? Or should I try to preserve the outward honor of my name and my house? Either way, I break my oath to preserve the kingdom."

"I'm . . . I'm not your conscience," she said.

"It would be unfair to lay that burden upon you. However, I do value your opinion."

Still she hesitated.

He saw it and smiled. "Then answer me this: What would you do?"

That question was equally difficult, she thought, *but perhaps he only needed to listen for a change.* That much she could give him.

"I'd write to the king," she said. "Yes, I know you've done so before, but I would do it again. I would argue that we cannot buy glory with the blood of others, that glory seen from a distance might be an illusion, that war is neither evil nor good, except in how we conduct it and the reasons we choose for embarking on one."

His smile grew pensive. "Excellent suggestions. But let us say you did send the king this letter and he answered with silence. Say further that you did send respected ambassadors and he turned them away. What if you persuaded others to speak your words and act out your deeds, in their names and not yours, so that the king would be influenced by the idea and not the person? What if you did that and his only response was coldness?"

Here, then, was the crux.

"Lady Theysson wants you to take the crown, doesn't she?" she asked.

"She has suggested it."

"And so did Maester Hax. And others, too. Am I right?"

He nodded.

Puzzles within puzzles, and schemes within schemes. Even those in the shadow court had their intrigues and their factions.

"But you don't agree," she said, more to herself than to him.

Kosenmark regarded her for several long moments. "Because I see a king who needs direction, not opposition. Besides, there are other players, and other ambitions at work. Remember, it is far harder to rebuild a kingdom than to fracture one."

"But what if that kingdom were like a ship about to founder because its captain cannot or will not see the rocks?"

"For that . . ." He drew a deep breath. "For that I would have to be certain beyond doubt of those rocks."

They had come back to his original question: how to act when neither choice was entirely good, and yet act they must. Perhaps that was a part of the difficulty, she thought. Lord Kosenmark had trained all his efforts to influence, and not to action.

Kosenmark fell to studying the book again, as though he could read its contents through the wrappings. Such a small object, hardly wider than his hands, the pages so fragile she could see a dusting from the paper all over the ground by Kosenmark's feet. What if? she thought. What if Simkov had never written those memoirs? What if Dedrick had not visited that particular antiquarian? As well to say what if Armand of Angersee were born with a different nature.

"If only the king had had a different father, and a different grandfather," she said softly.

"So I often thought," Kosenmark said. "He was different, as a young child. He needs more courtiers like you, who see the man and not the king."

She shook her head. "I see the king, too. And only from a distance."

"But your observation is the key, I think. Perhaps you should be Veraene's ruler instead of Mad Armand or Khandarr the Merciless . . ."

"Or Lord Kosenmark, the Meddler Prince."

Ilse froze, hand over her mouth, aghast at what she'd said. Kosenmark had a peculiar expression on his face—she couldn't tell if he was furious or simply astonished.

Finally he released a long audible breath. "I would make a very bad king, I think."

"Not so very bad," she managed to say.

There was another brief pause. Then Kosenmark tilted back his head and laughed, long peals of real laughter. He was still laughing when he wiped his eyes with the back of one hand. "I did ask you to be honest, didn't I?"

Ilse's cheeks burned with embarrassment. "Once or twice," she muttered.

He was grinning at her now, a look of pure delight that she had not seen for at least a month. Her own heart lifted and she found herself grinning back. Just as quickly she glanced away and covered her mouth with a hand.

Kosenmark took hold of her hand. "You must not take back those words," he said. "I need your honesty as much as I need your fine sense of honor or even your cleverness, all of which you've gifted me with today."

Ilse shook her head. Her pulse beat far too quickly for comfort, and she did not trust herself to speak. Her companion merely smiled. "Come," he said. "I meant what I said. Bring your case inside. We have letters to write and plans to make and books to read."

CHAPTER NINETEEN

WHEN LORD KOSENMARK said books, he meant one particular book—
Simkov's memoirs.

"Read to the bookmark," he said. "So you can accustom yourself to his
style."

"Why do you want me to read this book?" she asked. They sat side by
side, at Kosenmark's desk, with the book carefully opened to its front page.
Even though she itched to turn the page and read, she mistrusted this apparently sudden change in Kosenmark's thinking.

"To be honest, I am hoping that if you read the book, it might give you
ideas on what we ought to do with it. If we do anything with it."

"Why not give the book to Lord Iani?"

His gaze met hers briefly, just long enough to unsettle her. "Lord Iani is
a good friend and much-valued adviser in matters of magic. But he cannot
keep anything from Lady Theysson, who might find this information too
interesting to leave untouched. As you noted, she wishes me to be more
forthright with the king."

"She wants you to challenge him outright," Ilse said. "And you think she
might use this information to further that cause."

"Exactly. Whereas you find me merely adequate."

Ilse swiftly dropped her gaze to the book, conscious that her cheeks were
burning. A light touch on her arm made her jump. "I'm laughing at you,"
Kosenmark said. "You're supposed to laugh back."

"I did," she said somewhat tartly. "You didn't like it, my lord."

"Hah. If that was laughter, I would fear to see you— Never mind. You
can stop staring at the title page, Mistress Ilse. I promise not to tease you
anymore."

"Liar," she murmured, and saw from the corner of her eye that his mouth
twitched.

"Read the first section," he said again. "Then I will show you the important passages."

Kosenmark was right. The antiquated style and script took some time to decipher at first, and though the memoirs were better written than many others she had read, Ilse found them dull and uninspired at first. Simkov had led an ordinary childhood. Third child in a large family. Father in Rastov's local militia. Mother a clerk at the university. She had died giving birth to Simkov's younger brother.

"He was a bureaucrat," she said to herself.

"One with an excellent memory. Keep reading."

She forged on through the account of his schooling, the discovery that he could memorize complete passages of the older poets and historians without any effort. It was this talent that brought him to the garrison commander's attention. They had thought to make him an agent for the crown, sending him across the border to evaluate conditions in Veraene and the northern kingdoms—Dzavek never fully trusted the old empire to remain quiescent—but though an excellent observer, he proved an indifferent spy. More than once he had given himself away because he could not project himself into the many roles required by his profession.

". . . And so, after several years of shifting from post to post, I came back to my home in Rastov. My father had retired with a good pension. My sisters had all established their own families, some in the city, and others in Ždor-by-the-Sea. My two brothers had gone west into Duszranjo. It was then that I received my appointment to the Imperial prison."

To become an interrogator, using his memory to absorb every detail of word and voice and gesture while he questioned prisoners. For the most part, it was not a demanding role. The king was not a vindictive man, and the prison was often empty, but there came to Simkov the usual assortment of Veraenen agents, rabble-rousers, or disaffected nobles whose plots crossed a certain line.

Unaware, Ilse had read far beyond the bookmark, and had reached the halfway point. Dull his life might be, but she had a clear picture of life in Rastov three centuries ago. A kingdom on the brink of war, though no one knew it.

And it was a day in spring when I had an unexpected visitor to my office, a man in the king's livery, bearing the king's seal, as though one proof were insufficient to prove the authenticity of his message. *I have a new prisoner for you,* the letter read, *but first I would like to meet with you and discuss his treatment.*

Behind her, Kosenmark ordered food, and when it came, he set out the plates and served Ilse while she continued to read. A gap marked the interview between Simkov and Dzavek. Apparently Simkov chose discretion for the historic moment, even though he lived in a different kingdom, under a different name.

Three days passed with Simkov visiting Benacka's cell every few hours. They tried the usual tricks where they shortened or lengthened the time between meals. They banged pots outside his cell at midnight. All unnecessary tactics, Ilse thought. Benacka must have been half mad with fear already, the same fear that drove him to suicide. He talked, according to Simkov, obsessively about Dzavek, rambled on as to how it was his destiny and his doom to chase after Dzavek, just as Dzavek had chased after him through Anderswar and then Veraene, when Benacka had leaped across the void in the flesh to escape. He had not succeeded. Dzavek had cornered him on a lonely island.

> . . . He spoke of an endless sea, the indigo waves rolling toward eternity. Leaping from Anderswar back to human realms, one might suspect that he had leaped too far, to a world beyond ours, for such is possible when magic involves itself, but the man swore he had landed in Erythandra, saying he recognized the stars and their patterns.

Could he mean Morennioù? But wouldn't the stars look different, there on the far side of Lir's Veil?

Ilse shook her head. The island didn't matter. What did matter was that now she could see why Dzavek had attacked Veraene three hundred years before. With Benacka dead before Dzavek could question him, Dzavek must have scoured every step of that final chase—not finding them in Anderswar, he must have decided they lay hidden in Veraene. If he suffered from an obsession, it was a carefully reasoned one, she thought.

She ate in Kosenmark's office, wholly absorbed in the puzzle he had given her. Kosenmark said nothing. He refilled her water cup when she emptied it, and set more food in front of her, until he saw that she truly could eat no more. "Go and forget about the problem for today," he said at last. "We'll talk more tomorrow, after drill."

She tried to forget, as he suggested, but Ilse spent the remainder of that day pondering the question, even while she went about her ordinary duties. Every task—from reviewing accounts, to checking over the various household budgets, to sending out letters of business—recalled Simkov's mundane life, and from there it was a quick and obvious leap to Simkov's prisoner. When at last she finished her work, she went to her rooms and read the books on magic that Mistress Hedda had lent her. Those told her much about magic but nothing about how to wield this new and burdensome secret. So, though the bells were striking ten, she ensconced herself in Lord Kosenmark's library to read books on diplomacy and warfare. In between, she played word links with herself, hoping for that leap in associations that might provide her with a solution to Lord Kosenmark's dilemma.

The next morning, she came to drill tired and muddled.

"You should not wear yourself to tatters like that, Mistress Ilse," Kosenmark said.

She thought he looked as weary as she felt, but she said nothing.

"It will do her good," Ault said. "Practice under adverse conditions. That would be my next step. Perhaps I should thank you, my lord, for assisting with her lessons."

Kosenmark made a noncommittal noise and picked up a wooden knife. "Speaking of assisting, when did you intend to start Mistress Ilse with knife techniques?"

"When she was ready. Today would not be best, I think."

"What about adverse conditions, Benedikt?"

"Perhaps you would like to take over as her teacher, my lord."

Kosenmark glanced at Ilse. "No, Benedikt. This is your province. My apologies."

"None required, my lord."

Ault took Ilse through her first and second patterns, then set her to practice alone while he and Lord Kosenmark went through a long complicated pattern for swords. From what she glimpsed, it appeared to be a pattern that Lord Kosenmark had studied but not yet mastered. At Ault's command, Kosenmark would perform one or two moves, then stop while Ault expounded on the proper stance or some other seemingly trivial detail.

"Now for the practical application," Ault said, taking up a wooden blade.

Ilse paused in between repetitions of her drill. Ault glanced at her but said nothing. He and Lord Kosenmark touched blades.

"Begin with the first set, my lord."

Their motions were slow, as Benedikt Ault countered and blocked with his blade, each stroke and parry meeting those Lord Kosenmark made while he executed the pattern. It was like a dance, Ilse thought. A graceful endless dance. Yet something about it bothered her. No matter how hard she stared, she could not discern any pattern in their movements.

Gradually Ault increased the speed of his blocks and parries. Kosenmark responded. Faster and faster, yet not the blurred speed of their sword bouts, and so Ilse could follow the action and reaction far more easily than she expected. Now she began to see what Ault had lectured Kosenmark about—the necessity for that particular lunge, followed by that particular block, followed by a curious sidestep that led directly to the next attack.

Strike. Parry. Feint. Strike. Disarm.

Just as she thought that, Kosenmark made another sidestep, then brought his blade up and, with a twist, wrenched Ault's blade to one side. The next moment, he set the point of his sword to Ault's chest. The final movement of the pattern.

Yes, she thought. *That is how we must do it.*

The two men bowed. Kosenmark turned around. He hardly looked winded, though the pattern had lasted more than two quarter bells. He must have seen something in her face, because his own expression changed at once. "Benedikt," he said in a high light voice. "Would you indulge us for today? Mistress Ilse and I need to discuss a certain matter."

Ault glanced from Ilse back to Kosenmark. "As you wish, my lord. We can make up the time tomorrow, if that meets your schedule." He saluted Lord Kosenmark with his blade and bowed to Ilse, who thought she detected a glimmer of curiosity in his carefully bland expression. However, Kosenmark was urging her out of the drill yard.

"You have an idea," he said, once they were alone in his office.

"A very vague one, my lord." By now her first satisfied thrill had faded, speeded by doubt and the realization that she did not have an answer to his dilemma, only the barest insight into how she might approach it.

Kosenmark was tapping his fingers with obvious impatience. He stopped himself with a self-conscious grimace and let out a sigh. "I am not testing you," he said. "I asked you for ideas, not a guarantee of success."

Well then. She took a moment to collect her thoughts. "It was during drill," she began. "When I watched your pattern with Maester Ault. I thought . . ." It sounded worse and worse to her now, and in spite of Kosenmark's encouraging expression, she found it difficult to say out loud her glimmering of an idea. She dropped her gaze to her hands, thinking that if she continued to drill, she would have new calluses from knife and sword, just like Lord Kosenmark's.

"Go on," Kosenmark said. "I promise not to laugh."

Liar, she thought. But that reminder helped her to speak. "I thought of drills, my lord. Your drill, and how each move led to the next. And then I thought, what if . . . what if you used the book as a feint?"

Kosenmark quirked his eyebrows but said nothing.

"You cannot give the book away," Ilse went on. "If you give it to Armand, Lord Khandarr would use it to recover the jewels, and once he did, Armand would declare war against Károví. It seems illogical, but I can imagine him saying that such a war was just and necessary to prevent future wars."

"Yes," Kosenmark said. "It is his favorite saying. Which proves you do listen closely." He leaned back in his chair and touched his fingers together one by one, as though working through the implications of what she said. "But why not give the book to King Leos?"

"Because you cannot," Ilse said softly. "Treason is not your nature."

Kosenmark's gaze flicked up to meet hers. "Very true."

"So you must keep the book," Ilse said. "Use it like a sword, and drive these two kings in the direction you wish."

"A feint," Kosenmark said slowly. "Yes, I believe I see what you mean. A dangerous course, Mistress Ilse. If we act too openly, the king could argue treason, no matter what our motives. Or if we act too subtly, the feint might go unrecognized and we achieve nothing."

"Lord Khandarr is a subtle man."

"Which adds to the danger. He has an army, and I do not."

"But you do have an army," Ilse said. "An army of ordinary people who do not wish to go to war unless war is truly necessary. Merchants. Farmers. Scholars. Weavers."

Kosenmark shook his head. "It would take an entire kingdom in revolt, and then we have war within, which is no better than war with Károví. Ah, but—" His gaze went inward, and his fingers tapped a rapid beat. Ilse wished she could read his fleeting thoughts, but she kept silent, waiting for him to speak again.

"An army," Kosenmark breathed. "The soldiers themselves, and their officers, would dislike going to war against an invincible enemy."

"But he's not—"

"They do not know that. A feint, Mistress Ilse. You said it yourself. However, it will take careful planning. We must use hints instead of petitions, suggestions rather than open action."

And so they began with rumors. Kosenmark laid out the initial plans. Lady Theysson and Lord Iani offered improvements. Ilse spent her time writing letters in different scripts, addressed to strange names in faraway cities. With these letters, which traveled circuitous routes, Kosenmark spread rumors among the border garrisons that Károví was rebuilding its defenses, inspired by the weaponry and tactics from the empire days.

"Will he understand?" Ilse murmured.

"He will. He already knows Dzavek has renewed his search for the jewels."

Using Faulk and his agents, Kosenmark planted more rumors deep within Veraene's borders. Rumors about dire increases in taxes, disguised as new fees laid upon guilds and independent merchants. And there would be more fees and taxes in the years to come, and more levies of troops. From there, rumors became genuine news of unrest in the border provinces. Within three months, reports about riots came back to the pleasure house.

"Have we gone too far?" Ilse said.

"I don't know," Kosenmark said. "My hope is that we demonstrate the consequences of war to Armand. Let him see what it means to him, and to Veraene, if he embarks on a long troublesome bloody war, with only uncertain support among the populace."

"He is a stubborn man," Ilse said. "Lord Khandarr, I mean."

"Much like me," Kosenmark said.

She wanted to disagree, but stopped. Though she could supply a dozen arguments against the comparison, there were similarities between these two men. Both were stubborn. Both were ruthless. Intent, she told herself. That is the difference between them.

But would intent matter to those who died?

She took up a much-folded square of paper from the stack of reports they had received from Ournes, where a garrison had mutinied. Ordered by the king to quash the rebellion, Khandarr himself rode to Ournes to resolve the matter.

... he arrived while the soldiers were still fortifying their position. The king had assigned him a company of guards for protection, but of course he needed them no more than the sun needs the candle. I saw it all from the nearby hills. The mass of soldiers advancing toward the garrison walls. The glitter of spears and swords atop the walls as the mutineers watched. Then a single man approached the gate alone. He shouted. I thought at first he demanded entrance. Fool. Then he proved me wrong. Whatever he shouted made the air turn bright and heavy. So heavy, I found it difficult to draw my breath, even so far away. Then came a wind. Then came a burst of fire within the walls. Then ... And you must credit with what I say next. I saw the soldiers along the perimeter wall burning, burning, and yet they did not die. Even when their bodies fell into ash, I saw the shimmering outline of their souls twist in agony.

Shivering, Ilse folded the paper again and set it aside. No matter how many times she read the account, the horror never faded.

"That bothers you," Kosenmark said. "What Khandarr did to those soldiers."

She met his unblinking gaze. "It does, my lord. Those who died in Ournes. Or in the riots last month. They are not markers on a map. They are not numbers in a game. How many have died to serve our secret plans?"

Kosenmark did not flinch away. "Too many. I agree. But those numbers will be as a few faint embers in comparison to the inferno of war." He sighed. "If I could speak a single spell to visit wisdom upon the king, I would. I cannot. So, in my stead, I send portents and signs. And today I send a petition."

Ilse started. "But you said—"

"That was before. I believe Armand is ready to hear us. I sent him a letter this morning, while you were busy with your other work. You see, I came here four years ago because the king dismissed me. I told myself that I could not act without his sanction, I could only influence. But I had made an oath to Baerne to serve Veraene with heart and mind and blood. That oath did not vanish on his death. The time has come for me to act."

"What did you say?" Ilse whispered, going cold with apprehension.

"A warning. Anonymous for now." He shrugged. "Call it habit, or call it ordinary caution. I am too close to the matter to tell the difference."

It was a short note, he told her. *Short and blunt, delivered like a thrust with the sword,* Ilse thought as she listened. The note read:

We have secured word of Lir's jewels, Our demand is this—break off your preparations for war, or we shall ensure that Leos Dzavek has the weapons he needs to defend himself.

Cold washed over her. *He has made his choice,* Ilse thought. *And the kingdom's.*

She only hoped it was the right one.

CHAPTER TWENTY

THE DAY AFTER his message started toward Duenne, Kosenmark made numerous changes to his household. He hired more guards to patrol the grounds and built a separate dormitory for them by the stables. He brought Lord Iani to the house and had him add layers of new spells to every gate and wall and window. He also gave out that he had removed certain valuables to an unnamed location. When asked, he hinted that there were rumors of armed bandits who had lately made Tiralien their headquarters. The result was that other nobles increased their guards, and the city watch began a new recruitment campaign to handle all the new requests for more patrols.

Even with all these precautions, Ilse felt uneasy. It was the waiting—waiting and silence and a strange inactivity in the pleasure house. It had been three months since the whisper campaign began, nine months since she first arrived at Lord Kosenmark's house. To Ilse, it felt as though she had lived a half dozen lifetimes, and none of them the same. At Kosenmark's suggestion, she drilled longer with Maester Ault. Her first awkwardness had passed, and she could execute the most basic techniques for defense. Just as Lord Kosenmark had suggested, Ault started teaching her knife defense and the first moves for an attack.

Today they had added a late-afternoon session with the weapons master. Raul Kosenmark stood opposite Ilse with a wooden knife in one hand, its "blade" angled upward. Benedikt Ault stood to one side, arms folded, eyes narrowed to slits, as he watched.

"Begin!"

Raul lunged forward and swung the wooden knife around toward her neck. Ilse sidestepped the knife and blocked Raul's arm with a chop to his wrist. Before he could recover his balance, she seized his wrist with one hand and his elbow with the other. One twist, and his knife flew from his grasp. Another twist bent Raul over. Ilse flung one leg over his shoulder, throwing him to the ground.

Raul's face was red from effort, and he looked winded from the fall, but he was grinning. "You're getting dangerous."

Ilse released her hold and stepped back. "You let me."

"A little." He stood up, rubbing his shoulder. "Not as much as I did last week."

"She learns quickly, my lord," said Ault. He was smiling, that thin tooth-tipped smile Ilse had learned to recognize as approval. "Next month she won't need your help. We'll start the next level—blade attacks, first against unarmed fighters and then against those with knives. More unarmed blocks as well. But you made a few mistakes here. First the blade. Where was it?"

She had not stopped to consider that. Then she saw the blade, half-covered by dirt, within Raul's reach. "I forgot to look."

"And forgetting means death," Ault said. "You dropped Lord Kosenmark next to his weapon. If he were a genuine assassin, he would have slashed you across the throat."

Ilse flushed. "I forgot."

"It's a common fault." Ault's tone was neutral, which took away any sting of embarrassment. "And my lord, you must endeavor not to predict her moves. That is a common fault with beginners, and one without an excuse."

Raul looked as though he were trying not to laugh. "True, Benedikt. I wanted—"

"You wanted to let her throw you. Very good, my lord. It does help to let her at first, but she needs a challenge, or else these lessons mean nothing. Now Mistress Ilse, come here and try to move on me. We shall take it step by step. Ah, you thought you'd mastered the throw? Think again. You've mastered the first step, but remember: every turn, every gesture, every breath counts. Stand ready."

Raul took his position by the wall, while Ilse dropped into a waiting stance.

Ault picked up the knife and hefted it. She tensed, watching his face and not his hands, as he had taught her. The moment she blinked, however, Ault flashed into motion, arm sweeping up and around toward her chest. But the weeks of drill did their job. Ilse darted left and blocked, gripped his arm, and threw him to the ground. Ault coughed once, then grinned. "Very good."

"I thought you were reviewing the technique slowly," Raul said.

"I will. I just wanted to test her readiness, my lord."

"Hmmmmm."

They went over the moves by inches, though all the while Raul's presence nipped at her awareness, as it always did. Blade ready. Here came the arc. Step to one side. Keep clear of the blade. Remember to breathe. Grab the wrist. Other hand exactly here, where the finger bones meet. Twist and press. Change hands. Thumb here. Keep the attacker off balance.

"Now push, push!" Ault cried. "Keep me away from the knife. Yes, keep going. Ah. Better. Much better."

Ilse twisted harder, forcing Ault to his knees before she released her hold.

Ault picked himself up lightly and dusted off the dirt. "Better. Do that six more times and I shall believe that you understand. When you do, I will show you two ways to break a man's arm, and one way to strangle him, once you have him down."

He took her through the sequence again. And again. Her muscles ached and sweat made her shirt stick to her skin, but she hardly noticed. *Almost there. I almost have it perfect.*

A movement at the edge of the courtyard caught her eye. In that moment, Ault slid past her defense and flipped her over his shoulder. She tried to roll onto her feet, but Ault had the wooden blade pressed against her throat. "Dead," he commented. "Be aware of your surroundings, yes. But do not forget the enemy right in front of you."

Her ribs ached from the fall, her trousers had a new rip at the knees, and her hair had come undone from its braid. She tied back her hair into a loose knot and wiped the dust from her eyes. Only then did she see what had distracted her—one of Raul's private couriers had entered the gates. Raul stood near the man, a fan-shaped piece of paper in one hand. He was frowning.

He beckoned to Ilse and handed her the sheet. "An invitation from Lady Theysson. Read it, please, and tell me if you think the affair worthwhile."

Ilse took the letter and carefully unfolded it. Following the latest fashion, which called for unusual shapes and textures for invitations, this one was written on delicate translucent paper, which had a pebbled texture. The ink was a violet so dark, it appeared almost black.

Lilien House, Tiralien. To Lord Raul Anton Maximiliam Kosenmark. My dear Lord Kosenmark, I fear I must call off the picnic that I had planned for tomorrow. Other obligations have intruded, among them a host of unexpected visitors to my household. However, Benno insists that we do not give up the excursion entirely, especially since he would like to present his cousin to you, newly arrived from Duenne. Write to me as soon as you might, and let me know the best time and place for such an introduction.

After another paragraph of flourishes and polite nothings, the letter ended with all of Lady Theysson's titles and names.

"Very . . . polite, my lord."

"So I thought. Did you notice anything odd?"

She scanned the letter again. "Unexpected visitors" could only mean agents watching her house. Ah, Lord Iani had no cousins in Duenne. Perhaps that phrase translated to news from the capital. But that would not account for Raul's unease. "I don't understand. Or rather, I think I understand what she means, but not why it bothers you."

"Look again," he said. "Notice how Emma spelled my name."

There was nothing wrong with the spelling. Ilse stared at the invitation, trying to see what Lord Kosenmark meant. Oh. A soft exclamation escaped her. "It's not her script. Almost, but not quite. Lady Theysson slants her *X*s more, and the loops for these *L*s are too wide."

Raul nodded. "The marks are all correct, however."

Kosenmark and his closest associates used a series of unobtrusive marks on their letters—an underlined word, a tiny dot in the margin. The number and placement changed with every message according to a pattern Kosenmark had worked out. A wrong mark might indicate a letter gone astray. What did it mean when the letter had all the right marks, all the usual code phrases, but the script did not quite match?

"Would she dictate the message?" Ilse asked.

"I doubt it."

He took the letter and folded it carefully into its fan-shape, still frowning. Behind them, Ault was watching surreptitiously, even while he busied himself with checking over the weapons in their rack. How much did he know about Lord Kosenmark's other activities?

"What do you mean to do?" she asked. "Could you send another letter to Lady Theysson?"

"The straightforward method. No. If someone has infiltrated my courier network, my letter will not reach Emma but her substitute. So . . . I believe I shall accept this invitation to meet Benno's newly discovered cousin."

"But my lord—"

He cut her off with a gesture. "No arguments. Send a runner to fetch pen and ink."

Reluctantly, she did as he ordered. Once the courier had left with his letter, Raul turned back to Ilse. "I should return before dark. If I do not, send out two squads from the guards. Have them search the district around Hansenau Square. That is where I suggested that we have our introductions."

She nodded, still uneasy with his decision.

"One more favor." Kosenmark hesitated a moment. "If Lord Dedrick visits, tell him I've gone to investigate a curious matter. But do not tell him where I'm going. He comes here on his father's sufferance. I doubt the baron would thank me for leading his son into danger."

"What if Lady Theysson comes here?"

He smiled briefly, without humor. "Then the matter becomes more dangerous than curious."

"Why not send Lothar Faulk, my lord?"

"Because I sense we do not have the time or the privacy for arranging that." He looked at her again, searchingly. "Are you worried, Mistress Ilse?"

She blew out a breath. "Yes."

Kosenmark grinned. "Thank you. Will it relieve you to know I'm bringing an escort of guards?"

She flushed. Of course he would bring someone to guard his perimeter. She ought to have remembered. "I'm sorry," she murmured.

"Don't be sorry. I'm glad you care enough to argue with me."

He drilled every day, Ilse reminded herself, as she and Ault helped Kosenmark arm himself. He knew knife and sword and unarmed combat, and he was taking a squad of guards. Whatever danger he faced, he was not going unprepared. Still she had a sick feeling as Kosenmark gave her a cheerful wave and departed.

As though he guessed her thoughts, Ault set Ilse to learning a new and complicated sequence of knife strikes and blocks. It took them another hour before she could go through the pattern without reminders, and another hour before she felt comfortable with the moves. "You have it," Ault told her. "Now practice it slowly."

She was tired and hungry and far sweatier before Benedikt Ault dismissed her. "You're quick but you think too much."

"How can I remember the patterns unless I think?"

"Practice, Mistress Ilse. Practice until your body remembers for you."

They agreed to meet again in two hours, after supper. By then, the sun would have set and the air would be cooler. Torches would give them enough light, Ault claimed, and if not, well, it was good practice for her.

She was halfway to the baths when a runner intercepted her. "Mistress Ilse."

Lord Kosenmark was her first thought. "What happened?"

The runner shook his head. "Nothing. That is, Lord Dedrick came for Lord Kosenmark. They told me you would know where to find him."

"He's not here. He had an important visit to make."

But at her answer, the runner glanced around nervously. "Could you speak with him? He seemed rather anxious."

He should be anxious, Ilse thought as she followed the runner up to the second-floor parlor, where Lord Dedrick waited. She had no idea what she might tell him, other than Lord Kosenmark had gone on an errand. Saying "a curious matter" would provoke him.

Dedrick stood with his back to the door, hands clasped behind him, while he examined a painting on the wall. Ilse paused and knocked softly. The moment she did, Dedrick spun around. "Where is Raul?" he demanded.

She took a deep breath. "Lord Dedrick, I'm sorry, but Lord Kosenmark is not at home."

"Did he say where he'd gone?"

Ilse glanced at the door. The next room appeared empty, but a vent by the fireplace doubled as a listening pipe, and there were peepholes as well. "To investigate a curious matter, my lord. He should be back by dinner. Will you wait for him, or would you prefer to leave a message?"

Dedrick turned pale. "What curious matter? And where did he go? I have important news."

"I'm sorry, Lord Dedrick, but Lord Kosenmark didn't tell me."

"He did. I can see by your face."

Ilse bit back the angry retort that came to her lips. Dedrick was clever and stubborn. Soothe the man and he might go away. Provoke him and he would probably lash himself to the doorpost until Raul returned. "Can you tell me the news?" she said in a soft voice.

Now it was Dedrick who peered into the next room. Ilse closed the door and led him away from the fireplace. He bent close and in a soft voice said, "The watch found one of Lord Kosenmark's couriers dead in the harbor. His throat was cut."

Her stomach lurched at the news. "Who?" she whispered. "When?"

"I don't know his name. Faulk wouldn't tell me. All I know is that the watch discovered the man's body this morning. Faulk heard of it . . . however Faulk hears these things."

Khandarr's agents, she thought. Or someone in alliance with Khandarr.

They must have intercepted one of Lady Theysson's messages and used it to create their own false message. He suspected that. He's not going into the trap unaware.

"I have more news," Dedrick said.

"More?"

"Armand has summoned Lord Iani to court. Benno left Tiralien yesterday. He and Emma didn't want to be so obvious as to come directly here, so they sent word through the usual channels." He paused and ran his hands through his hair. "Raul didn't answer. And he always answers. That's another one of his tests. Send word, wait for a reasonable reply. Benno couldn't wait. He left for Tiralien by sundown, but Emma set Faulk to investigate. That's when he discovered what happened to the courier. Now will you tell me where he's gone?"

Ilse hesitated. Dedrick had the look of someone who would not leave unless dragged out by six of Lord Kosenmark's strongest guards. She spun around and marched out the door, Dedrick followed close behind. "You cannot walk faster than me," he told her.

Ilse ignored him. She skimmed down the corridor to the nearest runner. "Fetch the guard captain," she said. "Have him bring a squad. Hurry!"

The guard captain and his squad arrived within moments. Ilse spoke at once. "Captain, Lord Dedrick is not feeling well. He needs to return home at once."

"You cannot do that to me," Dedrick hissed.

"I can and I must. Captain, you have my word that these are Lord Kosenmark's wishes. He left explicit instructions—"

"And I say you are lying," Dedrick shouted, his face dark and furious. "Listen to me, Captain. You must send two squads after Lord Kosenmark. He's in danger. And I have news that he must hear."

"Mistress Ilse?" The captain turned to her.

"Send an escort with Lord Dedrick back to his father's household," Ilse said. She turned to Lord Dedrick. "You must go home. Lord Kosenmark wishes it. So does your father."

Dedrick shuddered at the mention of his father. Yet with an obvious effort, he seemed to bring himself under control. He glanced from Ilse to the captain. "Very well. But I do not need an escort. My own groom can do well enough."

"You should have a few men accompany you," Ilse said firmly. "To ensure that you reach home safely."

Dedrick jerked up his chin. All the guards went alert, but then Dedrick released a long breath. "So," he said. "Yes. I see that you are right, Mistress Ilse. Thank you for your consideration."

He gave Ilse a stiff nod. At the captain's signal, three of the guards detached themselves from the group. Dedrick regarded them with distaste, but he made no further protests and allowed the guards to usher him from the house.

Ilse waited until she was alone with the guard captain, then relayed Lord Kosenmark's instructions about Hansenau Square. "That's on the other side of the harbor," he said. "We'd need an hour if we go on foot. Maybe longer."

"What about horses?"

"We don't have enough for two squads."

"Send one squad mounted, then, and the second on foot."

He nodded. "Well enough, Mistress."

Only when he had gone did her body react to the news. A shudder went through her. She nearly did not make it to the nearest bench before her legs turned watery and she sat with a thump that jarred her teeth.

Murder. Betrayal. Simkov's memoirs. The feint turned against Lord Kosenmark. It didn't matter if Lord Khandarr acted from panic or cold deliberation, if his agents reached Lord Kosenmark before the guards did, they would murder him and blame Tiralien's street thugs. One squad of guards was not enough to protect him. Even if these two reached Hansenau Square in time, there would be an outright battle.

She turned from the gallery and threaded her way toward her rooms. Her stomach growled. Dinner, she thought faintly. Then a bath. Or perhaps she could eat while she bathed. No, evening was coming on, and Maester Ault expected her soon.

Worn out with anxiety and the long drill, she fell into a doze while eating in her room.

"Mistress Ilse . . ."

Someone was shaking her by the shoulder. Ilse started up, forgetting where she was for a moment. In the background, the quarter bells were ringing. Her vision came into focus. It was the guard captain's second hovering over her, his face taut and worried. "What's wrong?" she said.

"Lord Dedrick. We sent an escort with him just as you ordered . . ."

A sick feeling came over her. "I can guess. Lord Dedrick lost his escort, didn't he?"

The man nodded. "The guard squad came into the stables just as we were leaving with Lord Dedrick. He must have overheard something, because he had a strange look on his face. I didn't think much about it at the time. But half a mile from here, we had stopped because a mule train was blocking the streets. Lord Dedrick started cursing, saying that his horse had gone lame. He pretended to look at its off back hoof. Before we knew it, he'd disappeared into an alleyway and was gone."

"You sent the guards after him?"

"Yes, but they could not find any trace of him. Should we send out another squad?"

Ilse thought fast. Kosenmark had hired extra guards, but with three squads already dispatched, they had barely enough to patrol the grounds, and she wondered if Khandarr's agents would also attack here. She could alert the city watch, or report the business to Lord Vieth in his palace.

No. We cannot start to confess our secrets now.

Besides, none of them could reach Lord Dedrick quickly enough. Meanwhile, Markus Khandarr's secret army was hunting down Raul Kosenmark. She had to warn them both.

The thought made her go weak. This was no practice drill.

And if I do not, he will die.

That decided her. "I'll go," she said. Her voice came out thick and uncertain. She swallowed hard and tried again. "I'll go after Lord Dedrick. If nothing else, I can delay him until Lord Kosenmark's guards fetch him to safety."

She ran to the practice courtyard. Ault took in her urgent manner with a single intent glance. "Trouble?" he asked. "I heard you sent out the guards."

"More than trouble," she said, pulling out a knife at random.

Ault laid a hand over her wrist. "Not that one. Not for what you're doing."

She stared at him. "You know?"

"No. And I don't want to know. But I can guess any number of reasons why you sent out the guards. And why Lord Dedrick was shouting. And why both Ferenz and Gerrit were cursing him roundly. Here, let me help you."

Under his swift attendance, Ilse soon found herself wearing wrist guards and a mail vest. He strapped one knife sheath around her arm. A second sheath slid into her boots. The knives were longer than she used for practice, and their blades were steel, not wood. Ault nodded when she had done. "Remember your drills," he said softly.

Ilse took off at a fast run. After all her errands this past winter and spring, she knew the fastest route to Hansenau Square. She hoped she didn't have to run that far. Just far enough to overtake Lord Dedrick. Just fast enough that she could delay him long enough for the guards to reach Lord Kosenmark first.

Six routes to any room in the pleasure house. With the city, you multiplied that number by a thousand. Her one hope was that only two main streets opened into Hansenau Square. One came from the city's southeast quadrant. One avenue led directly from the bridge that connected the north and south halves. There might be dozens of alleys, but most ended in courtyards or the back walls of another building.

She sped through the market square, where vendors were closing their stalls. Past the Little University, called that because so many failed scholars lived in the neighborhood. Down a shadowy alleyway and its smelly taverns and wine shops. Someone hailed her, but Ilse did not stop. She slowed only when she came into view of the city patrols at the next square. They might question why she was running, why she had so many weapons about her person.

She ducked down to the footpath beside the river and ran as fast as she could. A stitch burned in her side before she reached the bridge. There ahead, she saw Lord Dedrick, just crossing over. She pounded after him, ignoring the stitch in her side.

He saw her then and took off at a run. Cursing, Ilse chased after him. They led a game through the next mile, he dodging and hiding, she trying to circle around him. But Lord Dedrick was not nearly as winded as she, and he kept ahead of her. The light was failing by this time. If she didn't overtake him soon, she might lose him in the twilight.

They had come into the counting house district, a few neighborhoods away from Hansenau Square. Tall faceless buildings lined both sides of the empty streets. Ilse slowed, wary and nervous in the silence. Where had Dedrick disappeared?

Then she heard a noise that sent a chill through her.

Metal crashing against metal. A loud voice—the guard captain's—calling out orders.

The next moment, Dedrick came stumbling around the corner. He sighted Ilse and dragged her back until they were pressed into a narrow alcove beside one doorway. "How many guards did Raul take with him?"

"A squad," she said.

His face went ashen. "Not enough."

"Why? Did you see how many Khandarr sent?"

"Twenty. Thirty. It was hard to count."

"What about the two squads we sent?" That would make twenty guards.

But Dedrick was shaking his head. "I only saw one, and they were on foot."

Dear gods. It would be a slaughter. "Come with me," she said. "We have to find the watch."

"There's no time," Dedrick said. "I have a better idea."

He darted across the street to the next building, where an open stairway climbed its walls to the roof. Ilse hesitated, then climbed after him, wondering what he meant to do. When she reached the roof, she saw that he had sprinted ahead to the building's edge. There, a walkway led over the streets to the next building.

Dedrick crossed over, with Ilse a few steps behind him. She gave one glance to the skirmish directly below—a seething noisy mass of people that seemed more of a mob than two sets of fighters—then ran to catch up with Dedrick. "That was the main group," he said in a low voice. "There have to be more. Khandarr wouldn't leave things to chance."

It was then she realized that none of the fighters were mounted. "I sent two squads, one mounted. What happened to them?"

"Don't know. But I have an idea. Quick. Come with me."

They crossed six more streets. Ahead lay an open area—Hansenau Square. Dedrick swung over the edge and started down a ladder.

"Where are you going now?" she whispered.

"We passed another group. I'm going to lead them away. You go ahead and warn Raul."

"But you don't know—"

Ignoring her, Dedrick scrambled down the ladder and landed with a soft thud on the packed dirt of the alley. Twilight made it difficult to see, but Ilse could just make out a dozen figures moving along the street. Dedrick straightened up, as though he had just spotted them. A pause, then he darted down the nearest alley. The shadows swarmed after him.

He might do it, Ilse thought. He was nearly as tall as Lord Kosenmark, nearly the same build. If only he could run fast enough.

She waited until the lane was empty, then crawled down the ladder, hugging the rails as close as she could. The ladder ended a few feet from the street. Ilse dropped down lightly. The moment she did, someone came up behind her and efficiently captured her. "Who are you?" said a man's voice.

It was Herrick, one of the senior guards. "I'm Mistress Ilse," she said. "I've come to warn Lord Kosenmark."

Herrick muttered a curse. "I thought so. Come with me."

He took her at a run down the lane and into Hansenau Square. At once, several other guards appeared. Herrick gave a password, and one guard pointed to an arched doorway across the square, where a tall figure was pacing back and forth. Even from this distance, Ilse could recognize Raul Kosenmark.

Raul came forward to meet them. "What is it? Why are you here?"

"My lord, we expect trouble," Herrick said.

"More trouble, you mean," Raul said. "But I take your point. Come with me, Mistress Ilse. Out of the middle of things."

They left the middle of the square and squeezed into a recessed entryway, while Herrick and another guard took positions outside. "Now tell me, quickly, what has happened," Raul said.

Ilse told him about Lord Dedrick and the murdered courier. "Khandarr, or whoever it is, sent at least three groups, maybe more. I sent two squads, just as you said, but one has disappeared. I don't know where. The second squad engaged with one group a few streets away. Lord Dedrick led another group away."

Raul swore under his breath. "You could not stop him?"

"I tried, but I—"

"My lord," said Herrick. "We have more visitors."

Raul drew his knife from his belt sheath. "Then we make ready. Ilse, stay behind me, please."

A half dozen guards appeared from various points around the square. Six, Ilse thought with rising panic. That was not even half a squad. She jerked her gaze to Raul. "Why only six?"

Raul grimaced. "I did not wish to attract too much attention. Yes, I was wrong."

He drew a second knife from his boot. Herrick and a guard named Klaus took positions to either side of Raul. They made an effective wall, but Ilse knew that one man down meant the wall would be breached. She took the knife from her boot and hefted it once. The hilt settled into her palm, but did not settle her nerves. She bit her lip and tried to remember her drills.

Fluid shadows swarmed from all three entries into the square. Within moments, the fight was joined, everyone moving too swiftly for Ilse to keep track of. Two of Raul's guards went down within moments, but managed to take out three of their opponents before they fell. Herrick faced three at once. Raul and Klaus fought shoulder to shoulder against five heavily armed men, dressed in rough patched clothing. They looked like brigands; they moved like warriors.

Herrick went down, bleeding and jerking. One man he'd faced was on his knees, bleeding. Another was dead, but the third one went for Raul's undefended side. Ilse threw herself at the man, slashing wildly with her knife.

The man spun around, parried her next stroke, and aimed at her face. Without thinking, Ilse flung up her arm. The leather guard split. Fire burned the length of her arm. Dodging another blow, she realized she was no longer by Raul's side. She had no time to worry about that. The man lunged at her. She spun away and nearly skidded on something slippery. Blood. Her blood.

There was no time for her to be sick. The man was circling her, grinning. Her heart was banging against her ribs. Ilse forced down her terror. She gripped her knife, angling it upward as Maester Ault had taught her, and edged around to keep facing him. *If I must die, I will die with a fight.*

The man feinted left. But Ilse saw his weight shift in the other direction. When he hefted the knife to his other hand and brought it down, she sidestepped the blow and ducked under his arm. Her hand closed around his wrist, just long enough to deflect the blow and steady herself. She kicked out hard. He grunted and twisted around, but by then she had moved behind his attack. Using all the force she could muster, Ilse thrust her knife under his arm. The man dropped with a gurgling cry.

Ilse stared, sick and shocked. *I did it. I stabbed him. I killed him.*

She had no time to think more. A heavy arm flung itself around her throat. Ilse tried to twist free, but her attacker's grip was too strong. She threw herself backwards. The man staggered. Ilse choked down a breath, kicked and hammered at the man's shins. The man went down, with Ilse on top, and they rolled over and over, kicking and punching. One hard blow stunned Ilse. She fell back against the paving stones, cracking her head. Before she could recover, the man gripped her throat with both hands. Fighting for breath, she scrabbled at the hands with her nails, but her vision was already going dark.

Abruptly the hands fell away. A heavy thud sounded next to her. A dreadful gurgling sound. Then someone lifted her head from the hard stones. "Ilse? Ilse, can you breathe?"

She tried to talk. Sharp pain lanced through her throat. She retched and then choked on her vomit. Raul turned her onto her side and held her while she heaved blood and bile onto the stones. Gently he laid her head on his lap and ran fingers over her throat. Through the roaring in her head, she heard his fluting voice murmuring in Old Erythandran. A kiss of air upon her face. The sharp scent of green. She drew a long breath, less painful than before. Swallowing still hurt.

"Who? What?"

"Hush. Do not speak. You are badly hurt."

She heard a ripping sound. He was doing something with her arm now. It occurred to her that she heard nothing else. No fighting. No other voices. "Herrick?"

"Dead. So are Klaus and all the others. So nearly were you. Come. We must try to walk away from here."

Raul helped her to stand. Vaguely, she realized that he was injured, too, but how much she could not tell, nor could she think clearly enough to worry about it. He urged her to walk, holding her upright though he was grunting in pain. What followed was an agonizing stumbling journey through dark streets and back alleys. The water salt scent receded. Ilse was aware of climbing uphill a distance, then back down toward a dimly lit row of shops and taverns. Raul guided her along a cramped and muddy lane, to a low door sunk into the stone wall.

He knocked once and fell against the doorframe, still holding on to Ilse with his one arm. "Call me Stefan," he whispered in her ear. "And I shall call you Anike."

She didn't have time to wonder why. The door flung open and a stocky man in a dirty apron demanded what they wanted. In a gruff voice, Raul demanded a room.

"You look a mess," the man said. "I won't have any brawlers here."

"Don't want to fight," Raul grunted. "Did that. Want wine. Lots of wine. And sleep."

"And whatever else you can get, eh?" The man leered at Ilse. "She looks too bloody to fuck."

"Like 'em that way."

"So I see. Well, come with me, rough boy. I wants two silver denier for the room. Two more for the wine, and that's cheap. Sheets are extra."

Raul shoved coins into the man's waiting hand. "Lots of sheets. Lots of wine."

The man peered at him curiously. "What's wrong with your voice?"

Ilse roused herself. "Nothing's wrong with his voice. Not to me."

"Oh I see. You're both strange. Well, go inside. I'll send a girl with the wine and the sheets."

He gave Raul a candle and warned them against setting fire to the place.

Raul helped Ilse into the room and lowered her onto the bed. A mattress, really. Moldy straw. A dirty cover. She tried to take in her surroundings, but the candle cast only a little light, and her vision had gone blurry again.

"Let me see what they've done to you," Raul said.

She started in shock at the sight of his face, just a few inches from hers. One eye was swollen shut. Blood caked his hair and streaked his face, which had a pinched gray look under the blood and dirt.

"You look terrible," she whispered.

He started to laugh, then winced. "So do you, Anike."

When the wine and sheets arrived, he tore the sheets into rags and soaked them in the wine. With a deft hand, he washed the many scrapes and bruises that Ilse had not noticed before. She tried to take up a rag, to do the same for him, but he pushed away her hand. "Let me take care of us both. Besides, I know more about wounds than you."

He worked quickly and gently; still, she had to grit her teeth against the pain. Every part of her body registered an injury. Lips swollen and bleeding. A cut over one eye. Scrapes and bruises on her knuckles. More bruises on her shins. Her knee twinged when she bent it, but Kosenmark told her that nothing had broken.

He left her arm for last. Unwinding the blood-soaked bandage was more painful than all the rest put together. The cloth stuck to the blood and pulled at her wound. Ilse clenched her teeth but could not help crying out. Raul stopped at once and poured her a cup of the wine. "It's dreadful stuff, I know, but it should help."

She forced down a mouthful. Her stomach heaved at the bitter metallic taste, but nothing came up. Bit by bit, she finished off the cup. Meanwhile Raul had soaked another rag with wine and told her to bite down hard while he worked. Between the wine in her stomach and the rag in her mouth, she managed to endure the rest, though she was sweating heavily and tears streamed from her eyes.

"A bad cut," Raul said as he wound a new bandage around her arm. "Badly bruised as well. Did you know you could fight? I saw you once. Ault would be proud of you. I know I am."

He continued to murmur praise and nonsense alike until he was done. Ilse collapsed against the wall, unable to talk. The wine roiled in her stomach. She closed her eyes and fixed her thoughts on keeping it down. Nearby, she heard more splashing and grunts from Raul. He must be washing his own wounds. She wanted to ask how he did, but talking was too difficult.

"How do you feel?" he asked.

"Better," she whispered.

He gave a wheezing laugh. "You lie badly."

"That is what Lord Dedrick said."

"Ah, yes. Dedrick. You said he and Faulk found out a problem with our letters."

"Courier. Murdered. Knew it because Benno wrote you. No reply."

She heard him draw a sharp breath. "Benno wrote to me? Why?"

"Khandarr. Summons to court. Left yesterday."

There was a brief silence, broken only by Raul's quick breathing. Ilse opened her eyes. Raul's mouth had a hard angry set. His face, still smeared with blood, made her stomach lurch with sudden fear. "So," he said lightly. "Lord Khandarr has given us an answer to our petition, it appears."

He glanced toward the hole that served as a window. Another building blocked any view of the sky, but it was obvious that full night had arrived. Then, from very far away, Ilse heard the bells striking ten. "You should rest," he said. "I'll keep watch."

Against her protests, he covered her with the cleanest blanket and helped her to lie down. her head was spinning from the wine. Or was it because she'd lost so much blood? The fight seemed like a hundred years ago. She opened her mouth to tell Raul that he should rest himself, when she felt a light touch at her forehead, heard his voice whispering in magic, then nothing more.

HOURS LATER, HER sleep broke to the bells ringing. One. Two. Three. Much fainter, like a vibration in the air, came the quarter hour chimes. The echo persisted long past the bells, and then she realized she heard a voice, murmuring words in a strange language.

Ei rûf ane gôtter. Komen mir de strôm. Komen mir . . .

"Stefan?"

"What is it, Anike?"

Raul's voice sounded fuzzy. She shook her head to clear it and levered herself to a sitting position. One candle sputtered on the floor and by its light, she saw Raul Kosenmark sitting across the room, his back braced against the wall. Sweat coated his face. He'd taken off his shirt and was twisting around. With a muffled exclamation, he fell back against the wall. From the next room came an answering thump and a string of curses.

"What are you doing?" she asked.

"Ribs," he panted. "Bruised. Cracked."

The candle flickered and died. Cursing softly, Raul lit a new candle, which smoked badly but remained alight. Five more lumps of wax, the remains of other candles, littered the floor. He must have remained awake the entire time, she thought.

"Can you use your magic?" she asked. "You know healing."

"Know some." He was twisting again, and now she saw he was trying to reach underneath his right arm. "Can't quite reach—ah, that hurts." He tilted his head back and closed his eyes, breathing hard. "I need to . . . touch. Otherwise no good."

He made another attempt to reach his ribs, his lips moving rapidly all the while. A rich green scent filled the air, and Ilse herself felt a wave of relief wash over her, but apparently the magic did Raul no good, because he broke off swearing loudly.

"I'll fetch a surgeon," she said.

"No!" Then more softly. "No, we're safe enough, but only if we don't attract attention. More attention, I should say. Right now the landlord thinks we are two drunks who got into a fight."

"Wine, then."

He shook his head. "I need my mind clear."

His color looked worse than before, and his skin was slick with sweat. When he glanced in her direction, his eyes were glassy with fever. "What about sending a message home?" she said, trying to keep the panic out of her voice.

"No message," he said. "Besides, I don't trust anyone to deliver it."

A loud thumping sounded at the wall behind Raul. He shook his head. "Last hour they were fighting. The hour before that, they were making love, or something close to it. Ah—"

He broke off with a hissing and closed his eyes. His lips moved again, but there was no change in the air. Was he going delirious?

"Ilse . . ."

"Yes, Raul."

"I . . . Ah . . . I need a very great favor."

"What is it?"

"A way . . . with magic. Something Benno showed me. Might bother you."

"That doesn't matter."

Raul wheezed out a laugh. "Good to know. Especially after I— Ah, damn it that hurts. Come here, then. Be careful of your arm. Closer. Put your hand right . . . there."

Ilse settled herself next to Raul, her injured arm draped over her lap.

This close, she could see the dark ugly bruises mottling his chest and side. She had to lean into the crook of his arm and reach around to the injured ribs. Placing her hand over the bruises, she felt the bones slide beneath her fingers. Raul hissed, but when she started to draw back, he shook his head fiercely. "Keep your hand there. Please."

He shifted his weight. Ilse tried to relax against him. She almost jumped when he put his free arm around her shoulders.

"You see why I asked?" he murmured.

She nodded. "I see." But they would need to be close if he was to guide the magic current from the air, into her, and then back into himself. Bracing herself, she rested her head against his chest. His breath stirred her hair as he whispered the summons for magic. He smelled of sweat and blood, with traces of wood smoke and cedar. His skin was softer than she had expected—smooth like a woman's—but no one could mistake him for anything but male.

Ei rûf ane gôtter. Komen mir de strôm. Komen mir de maht. Komen mir de viur . . .

Warmth fluttered inside her—warmth and the glimmering of desire. Just as she became aware of it, a flood of magic subsumed everything else. Her blood was alive, buzzing with magic. She could sense it flowing through the air, through Raul's hands and into her body then back into him. His magic. Her magic. Theirs. Without thinking, she leaned her face against his chest. A warm soft touch against her hair. Raul had stopped speaking, but she heard the echo of his words inside her mind.

Komen mir. Komen mir.

Gradually the voice changed. She no longer felt Raul's hand on her shoulder, nor his chest against her cheek. She was walking through a dark void filled with magic's current. Bells rang out, high and clear, and overhead a hundred thousand voices sang a strange ethereal music. Here Toc had once walked, as he passed from life into death and back into life. Here, she could reach back into past lives. A lover's face flickered past, dark and lean. She cupped her hands, seeing within her palms three bright spots of colors. Magic, stronger than she had ever imagined. She lifted her hands high and the points of color became flames . . .

Ilse. Ilse, can you hear me?

With a blink, her vision shifted from eternity. Her head spun from the sudden change. Sparks and specks of darkness whirled before her eyes, and she still heard the echo of music from the void. Gradually, these remnants of the magic faded, and she became aware of her surroundings. Raul still had his arm around her, and her cheek was against his bare chest, as though just a few moments had passed, but the candle had burned out, and a faint gray light streamed through the window.

"Thank you," he said.

With his help, Ilse sat up. "Did it help?" she said, carefully avoiding his gaze.

"Very much."

She glanced at his chest and away. His eye had swollen shut, but his color was much better, and he moved without obvious pain. "We should go," he said. "It's just past dawn, and we've mended enough to travel faster. Dedrick . . ."

Belatedly she remembered Dedrick, his impulsive flight through the streets to lure Khandarr's men away. *I forgot him entirely.* Guilt brought her a fresh wave of queasiness.

"He will have escaped or not," Raul said. She noticed he carefully kept his gaze averted. "But once we are home I want to send a messenger to his father's house."

Ilse closed her eyes. *He might be dead,* she thought. *Wounded or taken prisoner. All because he loves this man.*

Both of them moving stiffly, they gathered up their belongings. Outside, the streets were empty. Wisps of fog blurred the corners and gutters and potholes. Closer to the river, it rolled over the banks, making it nearly impossible to see their footing. When Ilse stumbled and wrenched her sore knee, Raul supported her with an arm around her waist. "I'm sorry. We cannot stop to rest."

His arms were strong, and in spite of his words, he did not set a cruel pace, but before long, she was stumbling from weariness. Her arm throbbed, her head ached, and her knee buckled with every third step. She no longer could tell which direction to take and had to trust Raul to guide her. By the time they reached the pleasure house gates, the sun was up and the first delivery carts were making their rounds.

Just as they came into view of the gates, two figures appeared behind the bars, their weapons ready. "Who is it?" one called out.

"Lord Kosenmark and Mistress Ilse Zhalina."

The gates swung open, and the first guard ran out. "My lord. Let me help you."

Raul held up a hand. "Don't leave your post. I'll take care of Mistress Ilse myself. Send a runner to Captain Gerrit and tell him to double the guards right away."

Ilse vaguely heard shouts as the guards summoned a runner. Her head was swimming from pain and weariness. She could do little more than hang on to Raul with her good arm. He bent down, as though to lift her into his arms, then grunted and swore softly. "Just a few steps farther. I'm sorry I cannot carry you."

"It doesn't matter." Her voice came out as a hoarse whisper. "We are home."

"Home, yes." She felt his chest shake with strange laughter. "Home for us both."

Holding her close, Raul brought her through the grounds and to the nearest door, which stood by the practice courtyard. The sun had risen above the house; the warm sweet scent of lilies drifted through the yard, and the dust of their passage hung in the air. It was as though they had stepped into a small quiet bubble, while far off she could hear the noise and shouts sparked by their arrival. There would be more noise and fussing inside, once Kathe and Mistress Hedda saw their condition.

To her surprise, Raul Kosenmark did not open the door. "One moment," he said softly. "And then we shall give ourselves over to the nurses and the surgeons. Can you stand, or do you need me to hold you?"

She thought she would be numb to anything, after all the shocks and terrors of the previous night, but she found she was mistaken. Raul Kosenmark stood very close to her, and for a moment she could see nothing else in the world but his bruised face, his one eye swollen shut, the other like a great golden sun. "I can stand," she said, not quite trusting her voice.

"Liar," he said, and leaned her against the wall. He took both her hands in his. "You saved my honor once before. Tonight you saved my life. Thank you, Anike."

His hands were warm, and she thought she could still catch a whiff of the magic he had worked hours ago. It made her giddy, or was that because of the blood she lost?

"You do not need to thank me," she said. Then she added, "Stefan."

At that he laughed. It was a raspy smothered laugh, but she heard his wonder and delight plain enough. "Oh, Anike, if only—"

A clamor swept from the house, breaking the quiet. Ault and a crowd of guards appeared, followed by Kathe and Mistress Denk and more runners bearing a litter. Kathe took charge of Ilse at once, shooing away Raul. "We've sent for Mistress Hedda," Kathe told her. "What happened?"

Ilse shook her head. Above the din, she heard Raul giving an explanation to the rush of questions. Something about Ilse delivering a critical message. The appearance of brigands. All of it true, and yet not all the truth. Stefan and Anike were gone. Lord Kosenmark and Mistress Ilse had taken their place.

And what if you were king? What would we call each other then?

CHAPTER TWENTY-ONE

THE NEXT FEW hours passed in a confused jumble of faces and voices. At Mistress Hedda's orders, Kathe took charge of Ilse. She soon had Ilse lying in her own bed, dressed in clean clothes and with most of the blood washed away. Within the hour, Mistress Hedda came to her side, and with Kathe assisting, she cleaned out Ilse's many scrapes and cuts, muttering words like stupid and arrogant and reckless all the while.

We were both stupid. Stupid and careless, Ilse thought hazily. Raul should have gone directly to Lady Theysson's house instead of trying to lure out Khandarr's agents himself. And she, she ought to have notified the watch the moment Lord Dedrick came with his news. But the watch patrols were stretched thin these past few weeks, with everyone clamoring for more patrols, and more guards, in every quarter of the city.

Warm water splashed over the gash in her arm. A shock of pain went through her, and she cried out. Dimly she heard a commotion outside the door, but then Mistress Hedda's face appeared above hers. Someone placed a knotted cloth between Ilse's teeth. "Bite down."

Ilse bit down while more warm water flowed over her arm. A pause. Then the pungent scent of garlic filled the air. Mistress Hedda dabbed at the wound with a gentle touch, commenting, "Wine is well enough, I guess, if there's nothing else, but for today, you'll stink a bit so we can clean out the infection. Tomorrow we try rose tea. At least he knew better than to close the wound. Otherwise, I'd have to cut it open to pick out all the dirt and threads."

"How is he?" Ilse whispered.

"Well enough," Mistress Hedda said drily. "Better than he deserves. There's a lovely long gash across his scalp. He's been kicked and scratched and slashed and even bitten. I did work enough magic to open that eye, but he's not so pretty right now." She paused in winding a fresh bandage around Ilse's arm. "He told me one of those thugs made a mess of his ribs, but that you helped him use magic to mend them enough so he could walk."

"A little."

"Interesting. Is that why Lord Kosenmark asked me to teach you magic?"

Her pulse jumped in surprise. "When did he say that?"

"Last hour. In between cursing me for scrubbing his tender scalp too hard." Hedda set aside the roll of bandages, then carefully soaked a sponge in the garlic mixture. "Come. We must clean out these scratches and scrapes. Even the tiny ones can be death."

She worked with a gentle and sure touch. Still Ilse was trembling before she had done. "It didn't hurt so much last night."

"You were too busy to notice," Hedda said with a sympathetic smile. "And what with you and Lord Kosenmark working magic, that held off the worst of the aches. Which was lucky for both of you. Otherwise I doubt you or he would have lasted so long. You never told me that you knew magic."

"I don't. Just a few words."

"Perhaps you had a talent in a previous life. That happens, you know." Hedda patted Ilse's skin dry with a fresh cloth. The garlic mixture stung, marking all her scrapes with pinpricks. Knuckles. Mouth. Knees. Palms. Her throat still hurt when she swallowed. Tentatively she ran her fingers over it. The flesh felt swollen, and she could almost feel the imprint of fingers around her throat.

She glanced up to see Mistress Hedda shaking her head. "What's wrong?"

"Wrong? Nothing more than you almost died." Hedda took up a packet of herbs and fussed with it a moment, picking at the threads sewed along its top edge. In a softer voice, she said, "The first night you came to us, I said you had trusted someone too easily. Do not make that same mistake again. Lord Kosenmark . . ." She glanced up toward the ceiling to the vent over Ilse's bed. "He asks a great deal of everyone," she said distinctly. "Too much, in my opinion."

"He does the same with himself," Ilse said.

Hedda sighed and shook her head, but did not argue the point. "Well, you've had enough of nursing for now. Sleep. You won't have much choice, I imagine. I'll come back this afternoon to change these bandages. If we keep these wounds clear, you shouldn't need more than a week in bed."

She gave Ilse a tonic, which sent her into a deep and dreamless sleep. It was late afternoon, the bells striking six, before she woke again. Someone had drawn the curtains, leaving only a thin gap where the setting sun streamed through. The air smelled of crushed herbs, and for a moment, she imagined herself back in Melnek. She turned her head toward the window, saw her tapestry of Lir, and remembered in a rush where she was.

"Ilse?"

A tall sinuous figure rose from the nearby bench and came to her bedside.

Nadine, dressed for the evening in a costume of pale rose silks that flowed around her like a strangely colored waterfall, lit by the evening sun. She laid her hand over Ilse's forehead. "How do you feel?"

"Nadine." Ilse coughed to clear her throat—it hurt less than before—and tried again. "Nadine, what are you doing here?"

"Watching over you, oh foolish one. And a thankless chore it is, listening to you snore the afternoon away. Or rather a part of the afternoon. Kathe had the hour before me. Hanne watched before her. Mistress Hedda told us that we were not to leave you alone."

"Why?"

"Why what? Why did we volunteer? Or why did you try to get yourself murdered?"

It was too difficult to work through Nadine's intricate nonsense. Why indeed? She opened and shut her mouth, suddenly overcome by a great apathy. Speaking was too much trouble. So was thinking. Her nose itched. She tried to scratch it, but her hands had turned heavy. Nadine delicately rubbed it for her, then fell to stroking Ilse's hair. Soothing. Yes. That was all she wanted, to lie here with her eyes closed and let her thoughts drift without care.

"You scared us all," Nadine said softly. "Running off alone through the streets. Idiot. You might have killed someone."

I did kill someone, Ilse thought.

She must have spoken out loud, because Nadine's hand paused, then resumed its gentle caress. "With a knife? Is that what Lord Kosenmark has been teaching you, down there so early in the morning? Ah, never mind. I can guess. Kathe nearly chased after you last night, when the first guards came back alone. She was sensible, however, and sent out the watch. They found Herrick and the other guards, but no sign of you or Lord Kosenmark. What happened?"

"A fight."

"So I gathered. What kind of fight?"

"Attacked. By brigands."

"Ah, yes. Those brigands. I've heard a multitude of fascinating rumors about these mysterious robber bands who descended upon Tiralien in the past month. Strange that they have never before attacked someone outright. But never mind. I understand you cannot tell me anything more." She smiled unhappily. "So, my warrior maid. Are you strong enough for a visit from him?"

Her voice was low and sad. Her expression strangely compassionate.

"You mean Lord Kosenmark?" Ilse asked.

"Who else?"

Without waiting for Ilse to answer, Nadine touched her cheek and withdrew. Voices sounded outside the door. A moment later, Raul Kosenmark entered her bedroom. In the dim light, he looked no different from any other day, but when he happened to cross through the band of sunlight, she could see that bruises mottled his face, and a pink scar showed at the edge of his scalp. One eye still appeared puffy and dark.

He sat by her bedside and gave her a crooked smile. "So. We lived."

In spite of her cracked and swollen lips, she smiled in return. "We did, my lord."

"Mistress Hedda tells me that you need a few days to rest. You lost a great deal of blood."

Ilse's smile dropped away with the memory of Herrick jerking and twitching as he died. She turned her head away and stared out the gap between the curtains. She let out a long sigh, which did nothing for the tightness in her chest. Raul gathered her hands in his. "Think of it this way, Ilse. We must live well, so that we honor their memory."

"How many died?" she whispered.

"Everyone who came with me—Herrick, Klaus, Varin, Azzo, and Bekka. In the second squad, we lost no one, but Captain Gerrit was badly wounded. Mistress Hedda saw to him last night long before we returned. The first squad never met the enemy, it seems. Before they reached the bridge, the city watch intercepted and detained them, saying someone had accused them of public brawling. They would have brawled," he added under his breath, "if they had reached their goal, so perhaps it's fitting. I shall have to see to their release tonight."

"Who sent them? Khandarr?"

"I believe so. I collected a few items—a knife and a ring. Those might tell us something."

Ilse nodded. She tried to think out the implications of last night—the runners intercepted, the broken code—but her thoughts scattered and whirled in useless confusion. All she could think was that her advice had wrecked everything. Tears leaked from her eyes. She tried to swipe them away, but her hand flopped to one side.

Raul took a handkerchief and did it for her. "What's wrong? Other than murder and betrayal?"

"I was stupid," she whispered. "Stupid and reckless."

He tucked the handkerchief in his pocket and resumed possession of her hands. "You are second-guessing yourself. Yes, we made a mistake—one with terrible consequences, which I see you have thought of."

"I did everything wrong."

"Not everything. You lived. I lived. We won't make the same mistakes again."

"Just different ones," she whispered.

"That, Anike, is called life. And you must not brood. I've taken measures to guard the house. And by the way, Lord Dedrick returned home safely, if not directly. The watch took him up with the brigands at his heels, and returned him to his father." His voice turned dry. "Baron Maszuryn wrote to me himself. He has suggested that Dedrick remain within the household until he recovers his senses. I agreed. The streets are not safe."

The news about Dedrick made it all clear to her. He wanted to encourage her, the way a general or prince would a valued soldier.

What about his words to you outside? whispered her treacherous memory.

It means nothing, nothing, nothing.

That Raul smiled at her again, a strange twisted smile that made his bruises and scars ripple, did not help. "Stubborn woman," he said. "I was going to make a suggestion, but I see you are in the mood to oppose everything, sensible or not."

Ilse opened and closed her mouth. Something in his tone pricked at her memory. Then she recalled Mistress Hedda's warning. "Is it about magic?"

Raul made an exasperated noise. "Ah, that woman. She told you, didn't she?"

"Of course she told me."

"She should not meddle so."

Ilse wanted to observe that he meddled, all the time, but she could not bring herself to make a joke. Not yet. He seemed to read her mood, because this time he leaned forward, so that she could not avoid his gaze. "I am serious about everything I said. You must not blame yourself for last night. And you do have a talent for magic. How much I cannot say, but I do know that I could not have walked home without your help. So I ask you, would you like to learn more? Mistress Hedda is willing to teach you."

She looked away, then back, unnerved by his proximity. However discolored and distorted his features, this man knew how to use voice and presence and warmth to persuade, and even though she was aware of the ploy, she found herself responding. She frowned, irritated with him and with herself.

"You look suspicious," Raul observed. "Or have I sprouted wings and scales?"

"Just the scales," she said weakly. "Green ones."

He grinned. "Shall I take that as a yes? You could start tomorrow."

"No. No and no." Mistress Hedda appeared in the doorway, glowering at him. "My lord, I told you this morning, you cannot rush these things. Mistress Ilse lost a great deal of blood, not to mention her bruised and mangled arm. And the knee, which traipsing about the streets all night did not help. She cannot think of starting magic lessons before ten days."

"Four days," Raul countered. "I could hire a mage-surgeon to cure the arm and knee."

They were arguing over her like cooks in the marketplace, Ilse thought. She also noticed he had not let go of her hands. "Ten days," she said, extracting them from his. She had the satisfaction of seeing Raul look self-conscious. "When may I start my work?" she asked Mistress Hedda. "My real work, for Lord Kosenmark."

Mistress Hedda shooed Lord Kosenmark to one side. She touched her warm dry fingers to Ilse's throat and then her wrists. "Bend the knee."

Ilse drew her knee up slowly. It twinged, but not as badly as she expected. Hedda nodded, then gently probed the flesh around Ilse's bandages. "No fever. No sign of infection. Good, good." She studied Ilse's face closely, lips pursed, as she considered her patient's health. "You do sound stronger. Let us revisit the question in four days. By then, the worst bruising will be over, and you'll have more strength. You were lucky not to injure your writing hand. Lord Kosenmark?"

Kosenmark had taken a seat on the bench. He glanced from Hedda to Ilse and back. "Very well. I would not have it said I bullied her. Have I bullied you?" he said to Ilse. "You must tell me when I press my arguments too hard."

"That," Mistress Hedda said, "would be a daily recital."

Raul rubbed his hand over his mouth. He was frowning, but Ilse could see that his eyes were bright with amusement. "I did not ask you," he said. "But my secretary."

Ah, yes. His secretary. Ilse dropped her gaze to the covers, where her hands made two small humps underneath. She had nearly forgotten.

You must never forget again, she told herself. *He is your master, not your friend. Nothing has changed.*

TO HER RELIEF, she did not receive another visit from Lord Kosenmark for nearly three days. Others came to visit, but for the most part, she drowsed and slept and drowsed again. Judging from Mistress Hedda's muttered comments, her arm was healing well. She would always have a twisting scar from her forearm to her elbow, but the wound had closed, the muscles and flesh were no longer so bruised, and there was no sign of infection.

Her strength came back rapidly, and by the fourth day she grew bored. Another good sign, according to Kathe. With Mistress Hedda's permission, Lord Kosenmark had Ilse's locked letter box moved into her bedroom, where she sorted through his dwindling correspondence. Most of the letters she could forward directly to Lord Kosenmark—they came from his father, the duke, and concerned the family estates, or from Lord Kosenmark's younger brother, who had recently married. Nothing came from Duenne or Károví, or even from agents located within Tiralien.

"I sent word out about the recent . . . incident," Kosenmark told her, when she commented on this. "Faulk and I need to devise a new set of codes. And Faulk does not trust all our couriers these days. Until things are more secure, we can only work through slower channels."

He made it sound as though they had suffered only a temporary setback to their plans. But Ilse had other visitors from within the pleasure house, and from those conversations, she pieced together a different picture.

"Poor Lord Dedrick," Kathe said. "Lord Kosenmark paid him a visit yesterday, which did not go well. Or rather, he paid Baron Maszuryn a visit. A very short one. I doubt Lord Kosenmark will repeat it."

She said nothing more, but Mistress Denk added later that Baron Maszuryn had ordered his son to remain at home for the next month. "They had a rare argument, Lord Dedrick and his father. In the end, Lord Dedrick won another six months at home, but eventually he must return to Duenne or forfeit half his inheritance."

That, Ilse thought, *might account for Lord Kosenmark's distracted manner. Strange that he had not mentioned the episode to her. It's his private affair,* she reminded herself. He might have discussed such a matter with Berthold Hax, who had served Lord Kosenmark and his family for decades, but not her.

Still, she found it unsettling when it was Hanne, and not Lord Kosenmark, who told her about the many new guards patrolling the grounds, and how all deliveries to the kitchen were inspected before Mistress Raendl allowed them inside. "Janna says it's because someone is making war on Lord Kosenmark. That is why they attacked him in the streets, and you, too, when you tried to warn him."

"Are you afraid?" Ilse asked her.

"Oh, no. Well, sometimes. Janna tells me not to be foolish. They won't attack here, not with six guards at every window, and the city watch making extra patrols in our neighborhood."

Ilse watched Hanne's face as the girl chattered on, telling her more about the guards, and how some were women, and she had never imagined that women could fight, too, though she ought to have guessed, since Ilse took lessons from Maester Ault.

"Is it true you killed a man?" Hanne said in a breathless voice.

"I don't know. I tried. Is it true that you're happier?"

Hanne flushed and dropped her gaze. "Yes. I still miss my mother. And my older sister. Not my brothers," she added with a shy smile. "But Kathe says I might make a trip north this summer. Just for a visit."

Eventually the ten days came to an end. It was a bright hot day. The sun was little more than a white smudge overhead as Lord Kosenmark helped Ilse into the carriage that would take her to Mistress Hedda's rooms. He seemed more preoccupied than usual, she thought.

"I wish you success," he said.

"And you, my lord," she replied.

He started. "In what matter?"

She glanced pointedly at the three guards just mounting the carriage, then toward the driver with his club and the two other guards on their horses. Kosenmark's gaze followed hers, and his mouth quirked into a wry smile. "Oh that. Yes, we can talk more about those matters tomorrow."

"Today," she said. "If your schedule permits. And I know it does."

Kosenmark muttered something under his breath, but he was smiling.

Mistress Hedda lived just a few streets away, where she rented a set of rooms above a prosperous inn. As Ilse came into the common room, escorted by her guards, Hedda took in the scene with a grimace, but said nothing. "Come with me. They"—she indicated the guards—"can wait down here. I won't have your concentration broken by their fidgeting."

Her rooms occupied one corner of the second floor. The main room was large and sunny, cluttered with tables and benches in a brightly colored chaos of jars and vials and books and artifacts. Herbs hung from the ceiling and more herbs grew in pots by the window. Ilse sniffed. She smelled magic, mixed with the scents of rosemary and thyme and damp earth.

"I would think you didn't need the herbs," she said. "Though they do smell nice."

"And that's good enough for me," Hedda said as she puttered about the room, collecting candles and boxes as she went. "Besides, magic costs more than a few herbs do. It costs me and it costs my patients, and I'm not just talking about money. It changes us. Like poison, some say. Sit over there," she said, pointing to the table and its benches.

Ilse took a seat while Hedda set a candle on the table, then scattered dried herbs around. A light green scent filled the air around them. Hedda touched her fingers to the candle and spoke a few words in Erythandran. A light sparked at her fingertips, then a flame caught at the candle's wick. "We start slowly. We start with you, your thoughts, and your concentration. Nothing more. Did you ever work magic before Lord Kosenmark showed you?"

"A few times. Nothing much."

"Are you thinking of turning mage?"

The older woman's tone was dry. Ilse could not tell exactly what Hedda thought of the matter. Oh, yes, she had agreed to teach Ilse, but only after a few crisp exchanges with Lord Kosenmark, which Raul had reported to Ilse, laughing as though he found her arguments amusing. Ilse herself wasn't sure what to make of these lessons. Try them, Raul had insisted. Think of them as one more weapon at your command.

Except that magic isn't a weapon, Ilse thought. *It is only mankind that changes its nature.*

But Raul Kosenmark had read her wishes very well. She *did* want to learn. She wanted to know what the old mages of Erythandra knew, when they first summoned the magic current. To ride upon the song and storm, to other worlds and other planes, as Tanja Duhr had written.

"It's too soon for me to know," she said. "I only know that I would like to learn more."

Hedda shrugged. "We start with the same lesson, no matter what. Make yourself comfortable first. Now I want you to look at the candle. Don't let your gaze wander. Just look at the candle and nothing else. Concentrate on the color, how it smells, the shape of the flame. Good. Now draw the circle tighter. Shut out everything but the wick and the flame. See the flame's heart. Look for how it changes color. You can, you know. With magic, you can see the specks of time as it passes through the air."

Her voice dropped into a singsong. Ilse barely heard it as she tried to concentrate on the flame and nothing but the flame. *Breathe,* she heard, half aloud, half in memory. *Watch. Touch with your mind. Hold fast and let go. Remember and forget.*

She heard laughter, felt the shift of balance. For a moment, she remained poised on the brink. She thought of the scholar painting her veins with fire. She thought of Raul Kosenmark. Then her balance tipped toward magic and she forgot all about the world.

A clawed hand touched her cheek. Ilse my love, my love, my love. She turned toward the voice but saw only the surrounding darkness. A rank scent brushed against her senses. Stiff feathers, like countless minute spines, tickled her bare skin. Ilse, Ilse, Ilse.

Words melted from one language into the next, from Veraenen into Károví into Immatris into ones she had never heard before except in dreams. The air stank with smoke though no fires broke the darkness. Her awareness was but another stream of her magical reverie, upon which she floated as though a bird upon the wind while darkness cradled her and the clawed hand teased and stroked her, calling up desire.

It might have been an hour, or a century later when she woke to a gray twilight, and the sight of Mistress Hedda's square dark face opposite her. The candle, now a misshapen heap of wax, had burned out. The air felt warm and close, in spite of the open windows. From the nearby tower, the bells were just striking late afternoon.

Ilse blinked. Her head felt light, as though she were not quite entirely connected to her body. "What happened?"

"You summoned the current," Hedda said. Her face was still, her eyes watchful.

"Was that wrong?"

"No, just . . . unexpected." Hedda glanced toward the door. "The guards came up last hour. I sent them away. You didn't hear?"

"No." She wet her lips and felt tiny cracks. "I was looking at the flame."

"What else?"

A claw tracing patterns on her bare skin. A voice saying, Ilse my love, my love, my love.

"What is it?" Hedda demanded. "What are you remembering?"

"A voice," Ilse said weakly. "A voice that knew me from before. I can't remember all the words, but I remember a hand touching me. Not a human hand. It said I've been to Vnejšek—to Anderswar, I mean."

Without a word, Mistress Hedda rose and busied herself by the fireplace. Moments later she returned with a cup of tea, which Ilse gratefully accepted.

"You went beyond what I intended today," Hedda said, her voice thoughtful. "It means you have a talent, and memory of past talent in magic."

"Is that good?"

Hedda smiled faintly. "Yes and no. The memories will help in studying magic, but all magic is dangerous. That much your people had right."

"They are not my people," Ilse said softly. "And even though my father and grandparents came from Duszranjo, they didn't believe those old laws."

"Not in this life, perhaps," Hedda said, undaunted.

She came with Ilse down the stairs where the guards waited. "Go home and rest," she said. "Think if you want to go on. If you do, send me word. We can work out a schedule with Lord Kosenmark."

A message waited for her in her rooms when she returned.

Come to my office. A matter of some importance has come up within the last day, and I need your advice.

Khandarr. So Kosenmark would meet with her today. She was afraid he would put her off. She read the note again, taking in its impersonal wording, the fact that this message carried no signature, and that he had not sealed it with magic or wax, as was his habit. Uneasy, her hand went to her arm, where the healing scar itched.

When she arrived at the landing, Kosenmark opened the door at once and ushered her inside. There had been no runner outside the door, which told her that he wanted no chance listener, even though the door was thick and spelled with magic.

"Did a letter come?" she asked.

"Yes. But not the kind you think."

He was studying her intently. Only now did Ilse notice that he wore a plain brown shirt and trousers, as though he had come directly from drill. He even wore a knife at his belt and one in his left boot. A letter, but nothing to do with the king's business. What then?

"I made a discovery," he said bluntly. "One that concerns you."

Her pulse jumped. "What kind of discovery?"

"About your recent past. I nearly dealt with the matter alone, but since it does concern you, I reconsidered. Are you strong enough for a short expedition across town?"

Her father had returned. Or Klara had arrived in town.

Kosenmark tilted his head. "Your father is not here. Nor anyone from Melnek."

"Are you reading my mind, my lord?" she said in a shaky voice.

"Just watching the pictures on your face. No, the matter does not concern your father, though that might be easier. Perhaps you should stay here . . ."

"I want to come," she said quickly. "Please."

He nodded slowly. "Very well. But you look too conspicuous in those clothes. Change into your drill uniform, or something like it, and meet me by the stables."

When she arrived at their meeting place, she found Kosenmark and several guards standing by a covered wagon. Stable boys were guiding horses between the wagon's shafts, while Kosenmark's chief groom supervised the saddling of more horses. All the guards were heavily armed, some with crossbows, some with knives and swords. Even the driver carried a spiked club, which he set into a socket by the dashboard.

"Get in back," Kosenmark told Ilse. "We have a distance to cover."

He helped her into the wagon, which had low benches along each side. One of the guards climbed up beside the driver, and she could hear the others mounting their horses. In the shadowy light inside the wagon, Kosenmark's face looked grim and drawn, as though he had not fully recovered from his injuries. She wanted to ask more details about this expedition, but when she opened her mouth to speak, he immediately shook his head. "You will understand soon enough."

Out the stables. Along the packed dirt lanes behind the pleasure house. Gates squeaked on their hinges, but no one challenged them as they left the grounds. Soon Ilse lost track of where they might be. The ride took them over smooth pavements, onto uneven stones, over more dirt that squelched beneath the wheels, and then onto a wooden roadway that creaked with their passage. She smelled saltwater and heard the thin cries of gulls overhead. A gulping sound reminded her of waves against pilings. Were they by the wharves?

At last the driver reined the horses to a stop. The guard came round and opened the flap. "All clear, my lord."

Kosenmark dismounted and helped Ilse down from the wagon. They had come to one of the many warehouse districts by Tiralien's northern docks. The closest slips were empty, but farther on, Ilse saw crowds of sailors and dockhands swarming from ship to shore. No one looked in their direction. She glanced at Kosenmark, who was inspecting their immediate surroundings. His left hand rested casually on his hip, near the knife.

"Come with me," he said.

With their mounted guards as escorts, Raul and Ilse followed the docks until they reached a narrow lane heading north. When they came to an old warehouse, Raul knocked softly. The door opened to reveal more guards, who stood aside to let them enter. Raul went inside at once. Ilse hesitated a moment, thinking she did not like where he was leading her. Inside, she could just see Raul's figure. He had halted, his back toward her. So. He would not persuade or refuse. She followed.

They threaded their way through a maze of rooms to a staircase, which brought them down to an underground storage room, lit by torches. Two more guards, armed with swords and dressed in leather armor, came to attention. Behind them, Ilse saw a low wooden door, with bars across it. The smell of salt and mud was strong here, as well as other smells she could not identify.

Raul gestured to the guards, who unbarred and opened the door. The chamber beyond was pitch-dark. Something inside grunted and Ilse heard a scuffling. Raul took one of the torches and passed within. Ilse took a moment to collect herself before she came after.

The room was dank and close, its floor a composite of mud and rotting planks. Above the ever-present salt tang, Ilse smelled sweat and urine and dung. The grunting had stopped, but something or someone was breathing loudly.

Kosenmark held up his torch. By its light, Ilse saw that a naked man lay on the ground. Ropes bound his hands behind his back. Chains shackled him to the wall, and a knotted rag pulled his mouth into an unnatural grin. When Raul thrust the torch at the man's face, the man recoiled. Ilse recognized him at once.

Alarik Brandt.

She pressed a hand to her mouth. A glance toward Kosenmark did nothing to reassure her. He was staring at Brandt, his face strange and masklike in the torchlight. "How?" she whispered. "When?"

"He was delivered into my hands last night. Why and by whom you need not know."

Brandt had stiffened at Raul's voice. Now he moaned, trying to speak through the gag. Even in the sputtering torchlight, she could see the fresh blood on the man's swollen face, the livid bruises around his throat, arms, and groin.

"What will you do with him?"

"Whatever you like. We are here to render judgment."

Raul shoved the torch into a bracket and hauled Brandt to his feet, one arm hooked around his arms. He took out one knife and held it pressed against Brandt's throat. Brandt struggled briefly, then went limp. Ilse moved until she was in his sight. She wanted to shut her eyes, turn away, but could not bring herself to do either. Fascinated and repelled, she ran her gaze over his body, seeing where his captors had beaten him, wondering if he, too, had screamed and struggled and railed against them.

Brandt's eyes focused gradually on her face. His mouth worked at the gag—he was trying to say something. Possibly her name.

"Do you remember cheating me?" she asked softly.

Brandt shook his head. She took that for denial.

You lied to me, she thought. *You lied to my father. You are lying to yourself. Is that how you manage to go on?*

"Four a night," she said in a low voice. "Six when I got used to the work. You wanted me to last. And I did."

With a muffled cry, Brandt lunged at her. Ilse started back, but Raul had already yanked Brandt off his feet and twisted his arms backward until the man collapsed. With a glance toward Ilse, Raul drew his knife and bent over him. "Wait for me upstairs," he said to Ilse.

Her stomach lurched. "That's murder."

"No more than he murdered the boy Volker."

Ilse went cold. "Volker? Dead? Are you certain?"

"Yes. I have the word of his brother. He beat the boy to death, the day after you escaped. Now go. Or you will see things you should not."

"His blood is already on my hands," Ilse said. "By my word he stands accused."

"By yours and others'," Raul said thickly. "Now go and leave me to my work."

He indicated the door. Brandt had begun moaning, a high-pitched keening that made Ilse's skin crawl. *I'm a coward,* she thought, turning around. *A weak and treacherous coward.*

Her blood pounding in her temples, she climbed the stairs to the next floor. Her legs gave out then and she sank to the floor. None of the guards spoke or approached her. Perhaps they guessed what was happening in that room below. Finally Raul appeared and held out his hand. Silently she shook her head and stood without his help.

Outside, they climbed into the wagon, and the guards took their places. She remembered little of the ride back. Her thoughts kept going back to that underground room. Flickering images of Brandt's face. The stink of blood and human waste. How strange Raul's face looked in the torchlight.

Only once did she speak. "He is guilty. Yes. But so are we."

After that, she sank back into reverie. When the wagon stopped with a jerk, she cried out. The guards dispersed. Raul escorted Ilse into the pleasure house by one of the side doors. The corridors here were empty. Perhaps he had given orders to keep these halls clear. She didn't know. She found it hard to collect her thoughts. When he touched her arm, she jumped.

"Come upstairs," he said softly. "Please."

Still numb, she mounted the stairs behind him. Once they reached his office, however, she hurried past him to the garden door. She went outside, still walking as though in a dream, until she came to the stone wall by the garden's edge, where her strength finally deserted her. She sank onto the nearest bench and closed her eyes. Evening had fallen during their expedition. A cool breeze spun around her, carrying the rich scent of blooming roses.

She heard footsteps. A whiff of musk as Raul sat beside her. She detected another scent, too, a rich and coppery one that she thought must be Alarik Brandt's blood.

"You killed him."

"Yes."

A shudder went through her. "How?"

"A knife across his throat."

Ilse's hand went to her own throat. "So I thought."

"I gave him a warning before I did," he said. "I told him that Lir and Toc did not suffer cruelty. Nor would I tolerate human predators in this kingdom. I killed him, but first I castrated him."

"Was that necessary?"

"Yes. I killed him quickly—he did not suffer long—but I wanted to make sure that Alarik Brandt remembers this deed and this judgment in his next life. It's a fair trade. His nightmares in reparation for yours."

Against her will, Ilse's gaze went to Kosenmark's hands. They were clean of blood, as were his clothes. He must have taken care not to bloody himself. She looked into his face then, but his expression was blank of any emotion.

"Tell me why you did this," she said. "Was it for Veraene?"

"In part." His voice was as unreadable as his face.

"Meaning . . ."

"Meaning whatever you like." He drew a long breath. "Meaning that you are free to travel anywhere without fear of Alarik Brandt. I dislike cages. If you wish to leave this house, you will find none to prevent you."

On impulse, she reached out and took his hand. Raul started but did not draw back.

His skin was warm and smooth. His pulse, underneath her touch, was soothingly regular. *Lord Raul Kosenmark,* she thought. Prince of shadows. Secret guardian of Veraene's honor. Perhaps that was the difference between him and Markus Khandarr.

I love him, she thought. *We all do.*

A part of her wanted to flinch away from that thought. A part accepted it. After all, Hax had loved this man. So did Lord Dedrick and all the rest of Raul Kosenmark's shadow court. They were all like flowers turning to follow the sun.

And sometimes, the sun turns its face to follow us.

And like a flower in the sun, she had no reason to question why he had acted for her. It was enough to sit beside him, hand in hand. She closed her eyes, thinking she could remain there indefinitely, breathing in the cool sweet scent of roses. The next hour bell sounded from the nearby tower, sweet chimes that rang softly through the twilight. In rooms far below, clients were choosing their partners, and pairs of lovers had retreated into private chambers. Raul withdrew his hand from hers and held out his arm. "Come," he said. "The kingdom's further business awaits us."

CHAPTER TWENTY-TWO

THE KINGDOM'S FURTHER business appeared to consist of waiting.

"No letters," Ilse said, after a few days had passed without any correspondence.

"I expected none. At least, none written with paper and ink."

Raul had taken to reading old epic poetry and teaching himself to play the newest game imported from Duenne. He *would* like it, she thought, viewing the multileveled board with its game pieces carved to resemble gods and characters from those same epic poems. He carefully moved one ivory prince toward another, paused, and scowled. A deadlock, Ilse observed.

Raul moved the piece back and tried a more oblique set of moves. He seemed entirely unconcerned with her presence or anything else, as though capturing Alarik Brandt had been his last act in the outside world. There was not much they could do, Ilse admitted to herself as she went on her rounds for the day. A few last reports had trickled in from their fishing fleets in Károví, but until he and Faulk had reorganized their courier system, Raul had stopped the flow of messages to and from the pleasure house. And without Benno Iani, they could not track Leos Dzavek's investigations into Anderswar. Ilse proposed once that she make the journey, but Mistress Hedda bluntly told her that she was not ready. For once, Lord Kosenmark agreed.

At least she had her sessions with Maester Ault, who added sword work to her drills with knives and hand-to-hand combat. And two afternoons a week, she rode with her guards to Mistress Hedda's sweet-smelling rooms, where she worked through a series of exercises that would give her better control over her magic. In many ways, those lessons resembled the exercises Maester Ault assigned, and Ilse came to view them—magic and swordplay—as two sides of a single coin.

She also spent hours in Raul Kosenmark's company. Talking. Arguing. Discussing matters as large as the kingdom, and as small as the weather. There were times she thought he liked her company for its own sake. Other times, he seemed moody or reserved. Some of that she blamed on the peculiar lack of news from abroad. Some, she reminded herself, came from Lord

Dedrick's absence. But it grew harder each day to keep Lord Dedrick in mind. It was as though she had spent a lifetime warming her hands over dead coals, only now to discover fire.

Fires warmed, she told herself. Fires also burned.

A month after Alarik Brandt's death, she returned from Mistress Hedda's to find Lord Dedrick in the entry hall, talking with Mistress Denk. She had one moment to see him—truly see him—before he noticed her presence. A handsome man. Long full hair drawn back in a jeweled band, a half dozen strands in narrow braids—the latest fashion among the young rich nobles. Today he wore an exceptionally rich costume of wine red silks that set off his dark complexion.

Dedrick smiled at something Mistress Denk said. Then he glanced toward Ilse; his smile faded and his expression changed from pleasantly bland to one she could not decipher.

"Mistress Ilse."

"Good afternoon, Lord Dedrick."

"I see that you recovered from your injuries."

She nodded, smiling politely. Of course he came here as soon as his father allowed it.

"Does Lord Kosenmark know you've arrived?" she said. "Shall I send a runner?"

"He knows. He asked me here for dinner."

Oh yes. She could have predicted that as well, if she were thinking clearly.

She made a polite excuse and hurried up the stairs. Just as she reached the balcony, a door opened below, and she heard Lord Kosenmark greet his lover.

His lover, she repeated firmly. Remember that. It didn't matter how often Lord Kosenmark dined with her. It didn't matter about Alarik Brandt. Or that night in the inn. Or any other memory she had used to feed these new feelings she had. (And if she was honest, not just abstract feelings but desire.) Lord Dedrick was his chosen lover, and nothing she wished or dreamed could change that.

With a start, she realized the voices were louder and more distinct. They were coming upstairs. Ilse fled through the doors to the far stairs and ran up them, not stopping until she had reached her rooms. Only when she had closed and locked the doors could she stop to catch her breath.

I know the word links now. Start with fool. Fool and idiot and thick wit—

Gradually she brought herself under control. She lit the lamps and poured herself a cup of wine with trembling hands. A headache nibbled at the edge of her awareness.

"Ei rûf ane gôtter," she whispered.

Air brushed against her cheeks—thick and scented green, like the pine forests above the Gallenz River. Ilse breathed in the scent, feeling new energy course through her body. She stared at her own hand, clenched in a fist, as her focal point. Her vision narrowed to a vein along one knuckle, then to a single point where flesh and blood and bone coincided. The headache faded, her pulse slowed. She was poised between the here of Tiralien and the faraway of magic's other planes.

Feathers and spines prickled her arm. Her focus broke, and with a sickening rush, she fell back into herself.

She lay facedown on the hard floor, her head spinning from hunger and magic. The lamp had burned down, and a twilight darkness filled the room. Ilse stumbled to her feet. She made it to the sideboard and drained three cups of water. Only then could she relight the lamp.

I must look terrible.

It doesn't matter what you look like. You need to eat.

She washed her face and smoothed her hair. Outside her rooms, the wing was quiet, but she could hear sounds from the rooms below, signaling the start of business for the evening. She headed for the back stairs, where she knew she could avoid any of the guests. Midway to the next landing, however, she heard voices from above. Loud, angry voices.

"Bastard!" Lord Dedrick's shout echoed down the stairwell. "You damned fucking bastard."

"Dedrick, come back. I swear it's not what you think—"

"And what should I think?"

Ilse strained to hear Raul's answer. She heard nothing but the blood pulsing in her ears.

Dedrick laughed. "That's what I thought. You can't tell me any different than what the whole city is saying. Damn you for a liar and a coward." Then louder, "Damn you, Raul. Damn you for every fucking hour I spent on you. I wish I'd never—"

He broke off and came hurtling down the stairs. Ilse tried to outrun him, but before she reached the next landing, Dedrick overtook her. He stopped at the sight of her, and his lips pulled back from his teeth. "You," he breathed.

He pushed past her at a run, his boots ringing over the steps. Ilse closed her eyes and pressed both hands over her mouth, too shaken to move or think. A door banged open and closed below. Muffled shouts penetrated the walls—Dedrick shouting for his horse and groom.

She glanced up the stairwell. Silence up there.

It's not my business.

He is my friend, at least.

She wavered a moment, then went up the stairs. The door stood closed. Ilse pressed her ear against it and listened. She heard nothing. No footsteps. No muttered soliloquies. Only a thick and unsettling silence. Her heart thudding faster, she knocked.

No answer.

Ilse retraced her steps to the kitchen. There she poured a jug of Raul's best wine, and fetched a wine cup, napkins, and water carafe. The kitchen girls ignored her. Mistress Raendl accorded her a brief friendly nod; Kathe paused and glanced in her direction, obviously curious, but Ilse hurried away before she could say anything.

As she expected, no one answered her knock the second time either. Ilse balanced the tray on one hip and tried the latch. Raul had locked it. She hesitated only a moment before she laid her palm over the lock and spoke the words he had taught her.

Ei rûf ane gôtter. Lâzen mir drînnen Ilse Zhalina.

Magic prickled at her fingertips—she felt a brush of his signature as the magic recognized her voice and words—and the door swung open.

Raul had doused all the lamps, leaving the room in a dim gray darkness. Coming inside, Ilse could make out only shadows and the vague silhouettes of the desk and chairs. Farther on, tall gray squares marked the windows. These stood open to the evening sky, now obscured by heavy clouds. Rain was in the air, and the salt tang smelled heavier than ever.

"Lord Kosenmark?"

Silence answered her. He might be in the garden, she decided. Steadying the tray, she picked her way across the room. She had just reached the far doors when Raul's voice broke the stillness.

"Go away."

Ilse stopped. He was somewhere to her left—there among the thickest shadows. She turned, and a movement caught her eye—Raul, lifting a hand to his face.

"I brought you wine," she said.

"I don't need it."

His voice was high and whisper thin.

Ilse set her tray on the nearest table and lit a lamp. Raul sat propped against the wall, knees drawn to his chest, one hand covering his face. She filled the wine cup halfway in case his hands were not steady. She thought they would not be. When she turned back, she saw that Raul was watching her through slitted eyes.

"Go away," he repeated.

"No."

His mouth rippled, but he said nothing. Ilse knelt in front of him and offered the cup. Raul stared at it, then at her. "Have you come for pity or curiosity?"

"Neither. I came for friendship."

He made an inarticulate sound, deep in his throat, like an animal in pain. Then with an abrupt movement, he took the cup. His sleeve fell back, and she saw marks upon his wrists that looked like bruises. A faint scent of magic hung in the air, but she couldn't tell if the magic came from him or her.

Raul drank. Blinked and peered at her, as though seeing her for the first time. "You look tired," he said, his voice no longer so strained.

"A little."

He nodded. "You brought only one cup?"

She shrugged.

"Here, share mine."

His fingers were hot, hers cold. She sipped the wine, thinking she tasted salt tears on the rim.

"I'm sorry," Raul said. "I was rude."

She poured more wine and gave him the cup again. He drained the wine, then cradled the cup between his hands. This close, she could see tears upon his face. More gleamed on his lashes.

"Did you love him so much then?" she asked softly.

Raul's fingers tightened around the cup. "Once. Very much. But he— I'm a difficult man, as you know."

Ilse watched him, uncertain what to say.

Raul laughed faintly. "You don't say anything. You must agree."

"No. That's not it—" She stopped and tried again. "You are not perfect. But you have been kind and generous to me."

Color edged Raul's cheeks. "I think you should go," he whispered. "Please. I can't— I ought to be alone. Thank you for your concern. But please go."

Ilse nodded. She set the wine jug within his reach and the water jug beside it. Raul had closed his eyes, shutting her out. His face was stone-still, and his breath came deep and regular, as though he were exercising profound control.

A last glance from the door showed her Raul with his head tipped back against the wall, his throat exposed, as though offering it to an unseen knife.

RAIN BEGAN SHORTLY after midnight. Ilse heard it thrumming against the windows and upon the roof in her dreams. In the morning, sunlight broke through the clouds, but by afternoon the downpour had resumed.

Raul did not appear that morning for drill. Ilse practiced knife blocks for an hour, jumping every time she heard footsteps outside the courtyard. Eventually Maester Ault dismissed her. "You're not thinking. Besides, it's too muddy and wet, and you don't know enough about fighting in muck."

If the schedule held, she would spend her next few hours with Raul. On coming to her office, however, she found a short message from him. *We have no business today.*

No signature. No magic to seal its contents.

She let out a long breath. That, too, was predictable.

Throughout the day, she heard a dozen stories about what happened. Lord Kosenmark had tired of Lord Dedrick. No, it was Lord Dedrick who had broken with Lord Kosenmark. It was Baron Maszuryn who had forced the break. No, the break was Lord Kosenmark's fault, because he had not pressed harder to see Lord Dedrick the past month. Whatever the cause, Lord Kosenmark had taken the matter badly.

Ilse smothered a pained laugh when she heard that last comment, spoken in whispers among the chambermaids. *Badly* seemed such an inadequate word for what she had witnessed last night. However, she said nothing, only shook her head and went about her work.

For three days Lord Kosenmark kept to his rooms. When he did finally emerge, he made no pronouncement nor gave any explicit orders, but he made it clear that he wished to be left alone. Ilse met with him but once a day, for less than an hour, while he reviewed his schedule with her. A schedule of nothing, she thought. He drilled alone these days. He spoke little to Ilse or anyone else, she learned from Kathe, though he was unfailingly polite. He spent his mornings writing letters to his family and sending them by runner to Ilse, who posted them. He spent long hours in his rooftop gardens.

In this way late summer passed away into autumn. Hanne made her visit to her family up north, and returned with breathless stories and laughter and a fervent wish never to repeat such a long journey again. The hills above Tiralien faded from green into yellow, the skies deepened in color, and the seas became an indigo expanse brushed with gray. Unusual storms were driving in from the oceans, some making their way into the bay. That same night, the temperature had inexplicably dropped and snow was falling, a bizarre autumn snow that melted as soon as the flakes touched the ground.

Even though her office had no windows, Ilse had the impression she could hear and feel the snow brushing against its walls. Cold and soft and relentless, like her father's whisper. One of the lamps flickered, sending shadows over her desk. She paused in her work, a sheaf of papers in her hand. She had come to this house on the verge of winter.

Just one year ago, she thought. It seemed longer.

She doubted anyone remembered, however. Nor that she had turned seventeen the previous month. Certainly not Lord Kosenmark. She sighed and went back to reading her notes about Duke Feltzen. Feltzen and his son had requested an interview with Lord Kosenmark. They had recently come from Duenne's Court and wished to discuss the current situation. According to her notes, Feltzen was an unambitious man whose family had their duchy from the civil wars, three hundred years ago. Strange that he would choose to visit Lord Kosenmark so openly. Perhaps Lord Kosenmark knew the reason, but he had not shared it with her.

With another sigh, she put away her notes and checked over her writing materials. Paper for taking notes. Blotting paper. Pens and a penknife. Ink and water. All ready, including her self-control. She gathered up her materials and descended to the second-floor parlor where the meeting would take place. Raul had already arrived. He stood, bent over a table spread with papers. He glanced up, his expression the usual one of blank politeness. "Mistress Ilse, you are early."

"Yes, my lord." She took a seat in the corner and opened her writing case.

Raul turned his gaze to the papers, leaving Ilse free to watch him in silence. He looked weary, grieved and weary, as he had ever since Dedrick left him. Faint shadows circled his eyes, and his luminous skin was drawn taut beside his mouth. Oh but he was beautiful in her sight. It was not the gold of his eyes, but their shape when he studied something intently, the light catching the iris just so. Not the full mouth, but the shadow his lip made when he laughed. Not the long lean hands, but the way they gripped a knife or wielded a pen. He was unaware of her, and yet he had made it impossible not to love or desire him.

Love. Once she had thought never to feel love or desire. Alarick Brandt, her time with the caravan, had burned away all such hopes. But then, like the bare trees, when winter gave way to spring, she had felt the warmth of passion. A painful, consuming emotion. A dangerous one.

I wish my heart had remained dead, she thought.

With a start, she realized Raul had stopped reading and was studying her in return.

"You look wan," he said. "Are you ill?"

She shrugged. "Tired, my lord."

Raul went back to reading. Ilse fiddled with her pens, rearranging them in order by size. It had been a mistake to come early. It was all a mistake. No matter how she tried, she could not rout out this exquisite pain. The poets said it was the lover's choice, to follow the knife from tip to hilt.

But I am not a poet, and I do not wish to die of love.

"Lord Kosenmark?"

"Yes, Mistress Ilse?"

"I need to speak with you, my lord. After your meeting with Duke Feltzen, of course. But soon. Please."

"What about?"

She drew a breath to steady herself. "About finding you a new secretary."

Kosenmark straightened up. "You wish to leave?"

She nodded. "I think it best."

"But why—" He stopped. A look of comprehension passed over his face, followed by a careful blankness. "Yes. I see. We must talk, but not here and now." He glanced from her to his papers with a distracted air. "Let me conduct this meeting alone. Come to my office in two hours, and we can discuss everything in private."

She started to protest that she could work, but Raul had already turned his attention back to the papers. With a sigh, she put her writing materials back into her case. It was what she needed, she told herself. A fresh start, with new friends and a different employer. She might even go to Duenne as she first planned.

She was telling herself the same thing two hours later when she arrived at the fourth floor. Lamps were burning in their brackets, but the alcove was empty. She tried the door and found it locked. Of course. He always kept it locked when he was absent. Locked to everyone except her and him.

He shall have to change the spells once I leave, she thought.

She almost turned around. Only the knowledge that it wouldn't be easier tomorrow stopped her.

Reluctantly, she laid her hand over the latch and spoke the words to unlock it. The door swung open and a puff of cool air blew from the dark rooms within.

Ilse lit several lamps and built up the fire. Then she sat by the fireplace to wait. In the corner, the largest sand glass turned over slowly, its contents flashing like silver in the lamplight. A beat of silence, then the chimes rang softly. Once, twice . . . all the way to ten. Already the smaller glass was tilting toward its next revolution. It was impossible to stop time, she thought. Like the wind, like the ocean tides. Like the pull of her emotions. She could not resist it.

Restive, she stood and went to the garden doors. Outside, a light snow was falling again. Clouds blotted out the stars and moon, but lamplight from the office illuminated the nearest paths. Summer's lush foliage had long withered and blown away. Now silvery lines painted the stark branches. One intricate pattern exchanged for another, she thought.

She pushed the doors open and went outside. The air was crisp, and a breeze whirled the snowflakes around her. Hugging her arms around herself, Ilse threaded her way between the rose-marble statues and ornamental trees. Clean cold air, like that of Melnek in late autumn. Memories of childhood chased through her thoughts. More recent memories soon overtook those. She passed the bench where Raul told her about Brandt's death. He wanted to set her free, he'd said. Free to leave Tiralien, and make a life in Duenne if she wished. She'd misread his intentions then. She'd misread them during their long conversations, their lessons with Ault. She'd flirted with dreams and imagined herself Raul's equal, like Stefan and Anike, free of titles and rank.

But she was a merchant's daughter, and he was Raul Kosenmark, heir to House Valentain, and Prince of Veraene.

"Ei rûf ane gôtter," she murmured. "Komen mir de lieht."

Light coalesced at her fingertips, casting a green-gold halo around her. She held the beacon aloft, then on impulse she set it free to drift skyward, catching on the falling snowflakes.

"Ilse?"

Raul stood at the open door.

"Duke Feltzen?" she asked breathlessly, trying to bring her voice under control.

"We completed our business."

His tone was unreadable, like his shadowed face. She wanted to make excuses, thinking that she had chosen a bad time for this interview, but Raul was beckoning her inside. "The night air is treacherous. Come inside, and we can have our talk."

Ilse walked past him swiftly, catching a whiff of cedar and wood smoke and musk from his skin. Desire welled up, that strange new desire, all the more powerful from its previous absence. She suppressed it ruthlessly, but she knew her face was hot. When she reached the chairs, she bent down to fuss with her skirt hem, brushing away bits of leaves and twigs from the garden path. Perhaps he would attribute her ruddiness to the cold.

Raul had ordered wine. He poured for them both and handed her a cup. His favorite pattern, she remembered. Rose petals etched upon dark red crystal, the pattern so faint you only saw it when the light glanced over its surface.

She drank a swallow. Raul cradled his cup in his hands, his gaze somewhat absent.

"So you wish to leave," he said at last.

She nodded.

"I admit I have been difficult to work with this past month."

His voice sounded higher than usual. She had once found that aspect of him unsettling—hearing a woman's contralto tones from the throat of a fully grown man. No longer.

"It was a difficult time," she said. "I understand."

"Then why? Are you tired of your lessons? Have I given you too much work?"

She shook her head. "Nothing. You did nothing wrong, my lord."

"Are you certain of that, Anike?"

Ilse stood up with a start. "My lord . . ."

Raul held up a hand. "Wait. Let me speak."

Her pulse beating fast, she sank back into the chair.

"I once said I would not make a cage," he said. "I meant that. And I think . . . I think I understand why you wish to leave. If you wish my help in finding a new position, I will give you that. It's the least I can do for how I treated you."

"But my lord—"

She broke off at the change in his expression.

"I was wrong," he said. "Wrong in so many ways. The way I acted. It was not fair to you or to Dedrick. But I was being selfish and arrogant. I told myself it was mere friendship. I lied. Or rather, I wanted your friendship and more, so I took more. In the end, I drove Dedrick away. Now I've done the same with you. I cannot ask you to forgive me, but I am deeply sorry."

For a moment, Ilse could do nothing but stare. It was impossible to take in his words at first. And then, like a star winking into existence, came the thought, *That is why Dedrick left. He knew. He knew Raul Kosenmark loved me.*

An impossible word—love—too great for her to comprehend.

But the star burned bright inside the darkness.

She managed to draw a breath against the sudden thickness in her throat. Love. It was not just a creature of her imagination. It was real, this gift of joy. She had but to speak, to choose. Her heart, which had seemed to stop, raced forward.

Raul had not moved since he spoke, did not take his gaze from her face. He looked, she thought, as though he were memorizing her features, one by one. Like a starved man who sees a feast receding from his grasp. Ilse set down her wine cup. Stood and circled the table. She felt weightless, skimming inches above the floor, and only when her fingertips touched his cheek, did she find herself anchored securely. Raul's eyes went wide. Ilse cupped his face in her palm, bent down, and kissed him upon his lips. Once. Twice. His breath puffed against her, an exhalation of surprise and delight.

"Come with me," she whispered, drawing him toward the doors to his private rooms.

They passed quickly through a maze of rooms, where doors and closets and passageways led in all different directions. It was dark in his bedchamber, the room lit only by the shimmer of snow through the windows. With a word of magic, Raul lit the nearest lamp and turned toward Ilse. He unbuttoned his shirt and let it slide onto the floor. Ilse laid a palm over his chest, feeling the rapid beat of his heart.

"Whatever you wish," he whispered. "However you wish. Whenever you wish."

A momentary panic, which faded before desire. "I wish for you."

She unbuttoned her dress and let it slide to the floor, next to his shirt. She stepped from her shoes. Another brief surge of irrational dread, then she lay on the bed. Raul was now dressed only in his trousers. He knelt beside Ilse, his face going taut. Without looking away, he unlaced his trousers and slid them over his hips.

In form, he was nearly like any other man, thick and rising stiff and red with passion. In size, however, he was more like a boy, and underneath the penis was a smooth hairless expanse, as though magic had burned away the flesh and hair.

"He was a master surgeon," Raul said in a thin voice. "He left no scars that I could discover. He helped me as much as he could."

Ilse reached out and took him into her arms. "You are beautiful. Come to me now, please."

He slipped into bed next to her and covered her mouth in a kiss. Terror veered sharply into a desire so strong it overcame everything else. She kissed him back, tasting cedar and wood smoke. Sweat and passion. His warm skin against her shift. Then he tugged off her stockings and shift and was running his hands over her body, kissing her all the while.

"Ei rûf ane gôtter," he murmured. "Ei rûf ane kreft unde strôm. Ane liebe de gôtter."

A sharp green scent enveloped them as he entered her. Magic saturated the air, so intense, that her blood sang and her pulse thrummed. There was no moment like it. No time before, no time after. Only now.

CHAPTER TWENTY-THREE

"**MARRY ME,**" **HE** whispered.

"Marriage?" she said breathlessly. "What would—"

"—my family say?"

A puff of laughter escaped her. "Have you found a way to listen to my thoughts as well?"

They lay close together, she with her cheek against his chest, he stroking her hair. Magic's green scent lingered, mixed with sweat and musk and perfume. The snow had ended, and a pale dawn lit the windows.

Raul paused in stroking her hair. "This is why I love you. You keep me honest. No, I have not found a way to listen into your thoughts. If I had, I would have asked you to marry me long ago." He slid down so that they were face to face. There was just enough light to see that his expression had turned pensive. "It's asking a great deal," he said. "Considering who I am. What I am. But would you anyway?"

Yes. Now. Forever. Ah but he was being too impetuous. She tried again. "What about your family?"

"My mother and brother will be quite pleased. If it matters, so will my sisters."

"You have sisters?"

"Three," he said, laughing. "You look shocked. Dismayed, even. Are you saying no?"

"I'm— What about your father?"

"He will agree. Once he comes to know you." Raul traced the outline of her face with one finger. "You are already more than a lady and a duchess to me. What comes after is just an outward ceremony."

Duchess. The thought left her breathless.

Raul brushed a loose strand of hair from her face and kissed her again. "There is no hurry for you to answer me yes or no. Let me court you properly, as I should have courted you before. Give yourself time to think over what you want. Then decide. Until then . . ."

Until then. Yes.

* * *

ILSE WOKE TO the bells ringing late morning. Her eyes opened to an unfamiliar bedchamber, flooded with sunlight through the tall windows. She took in a few scattered details—cream-colored walls, a few brightly colored paintings in between openwork shelves, the fragrance of cedar mixed with that of sun-dried linens. A warm body pressed against her back.

Raul stirred and nuzzled closer, one arm drifting over her body. "Good morning, love."

It was as though he said that every morning. A strange sense of vertigo overtook her.

"What's the matter?" he said softly.

"I love you."

His laugh tickled her ear. "You mentioned that last night. Once or twice."

She had mentioned a lot of things. Embarrassed at the memory, she buried her face into the pillow. What must he think of her? What would the rest of the house think, once they learned about last night? Because they would learn soon enough.

Raul kissed her shoulder. "You seem unhappy. Are you sorry?"

"No. Not that."

"But you are not yet easy with me. I understand." His weight shifted imperceptibly, so that his body no longer pressed so close. "I think I was babbling last night," he said. "Many things. All of them true."

At that she laughed weakly and hiccupped. "You lied. You *can* read my thoughts."

"You're very sweet when you hiccup. Did you know that? No, I cannot read your thoughts, I can only guess from the pictures your faces makes, or the colors of your voice, or the scent of your gestures. We should take a holiday today, just you and I. Would you like that?"

The sudden change in topic left her dizzy. "A holiday?"

"Yes. Something fun."

She twisted around to face him. "Fun?"

Raul grinned wickedly. "You look confused. Should I get a dictionary?"

He was deliberately provoking her. "What kind of holiday?" she said.

"I don't know. Riding. Or we could visit the theater this evening, if your hiccups have stopped. I've heard that Vieth has engaged musicians for a special performance for the city. It would make up for our last outing. Would you like that?"

Music. It had been so long since she last heard real musicians. Not since Lord Vieth's banquet. Swiftly upon that memory came one of Lord Dedrick's sister, confronting Raul Kosenmark about Dedrick. Ilse had not forgotten the expression on Lady Alia's face, nor how Ilse must have appeared to everyone there.

Raul must have read her thoughts from her face, because he murmured, "I promise no one will bother you. They must see that it's different between us. But if you would rather stay within the grounds, that, too, would be a delight."

Extravagant. Like a brief and gaudy fire. She suppressed that thought. "I'm not afraid. Let us go and hear these famous musicians."

But Raul was not content to leave their schedule to chance. He rambled on about how they might spend their holiday together. Breakfast first. Then they might drill together, though Ault would surely scold them for being so tardy. Afterward, would she like to walk through the gardens? It seemed as though Raul wanted to make up for the month's lost hours. When Ilse protested, he reluctantly admitted that she should leave him long enough to bathe and dress in clean clothes.

Ilse returned to find Steffi and Janna laying out dishes on the table by the windows. Raul immediately came forward and took her by the hand. "What took you so long?" he said with a smile, as he escorted her to her chair. Ilse glanced around in time to catch Janna's surprised look.

Janna leaned and whispered to Steffi. Ilse's cheeks warmed. Raul, apparently oblivious, sat opposite her and poured coffee for them both. Only after the two girls left did he shake his head. "Everyone will know within the day. Do you mind?"

"No." She smiled. "No, I don't."

"Evidently not because you aren't hiccupping. Come, let us discuss our holiday."

"Half a holiday," she countered, thinking that he was too much like Nadine. They were both the children of wind and storm and unquenchable fire. Nadine. Ilse had a moment's qualm. They would have to talk, she and Nadine. But now Raul was eyeing her with curiosity.

"Why half a holiday?" he asked.

"Because if I insist on half, then you will agree to one holiday and not ten. What about Mistress Denk's accounts? And reviewing the tax assessment? What about," she dropped her voice, "our work for the kingdom?"

That had an even stronger effect than she had anticipated. "Our work, yes." He let out a sigh. "We had news from our friend last night. Duke Feltzen. It concerns Armand and our recent diplomatic exchange."

Feint. Parry. Strike. The next move was to disarm, she thought. "Did Armand send him?"

"I cannot tell, though I suspect Lord Khandarr did. The duke himself is just as he claims—a colleague of my father, a loyal subject who is concerned about Veraene's welfare, even above his own. He had heard how I opposed the war talk and came with news that Armand is reconsidering his approach to Károví. If we can believe it, Armand now speaks of diplomats instead of troop levies, and whenever a councillor proposes conflict, he recommends caution and tact and taking the long view."

Ilse studied his face. "But you don't believe him."

"I don't know. We must confirm the news, of course."

"It sounds . . . hopeful."

"It's meant to." He vented a long breath, still obviously troubled. "But that, too, can wait. Let us enjoy the harmony and tranquillity of now and here."

"Even though tomorrow's shadow reaches toward us?" she murmured.

"It reaches and yet cannot touch, for when it does, tomorrow becomes today," he replied. "You are right about tomorrow, my love, but I want and need a day that concerns us alone."

At drill, Maester Ault observed their performance with a face even blanker than usual. Once, Ilse thought she detected a glimmer of amusement in those dark eyes. Before she could decide, Ault barked at her to pay attention. He lectured Raul even harder, driving him through his sword patterns at a speed that turned the blades into gray blurs.

"Dismissed," he said. "My lord, I see you found your point of concentration at last."

Raul shot him a quick look, but Ault's hooded eyes revealed nothing. Ilse turned away at once and busied herself with putting away her weapons. Within the day, Raul had said, but it seemed everyone had discovered it far sooner.

"Come." Raul touched her arm lightly. "We can bathe and return to our plans."

Ilse glanced from him to Ault, who stood with his arms folded across his chest, ostensibly gazing skyward. "Yes, but separately," she murmured. "Not together."

Raul followed the direction of her glance. "Yes. I think you are right. We should be somewhat discreet. For today," he added under his breath.

But during the walk from the courtyard to the baths, Ilse had the impression of many eyes, like a constant light flickering of tiny raindrops over her skin. First there was Ault, who bade them good-bye and a good-day, but when Ilse glanced around as they left, she caught a speculative look on his face. Then there were the bath attendants, whose faces were utterly bland as she and Raul parted into separate bath chambers, but Ilse heard their whispers as the doors closed.

Raul finished before she did, leaving a message for her to join him in his office. The bath attendant's voice was nothing but polite, but Ilse caught the woman's curious glance as she turned away. Then, on her way to the fourth floor, she encountered Hanne, returning with an empty tray. Hanne went wide-eyed, then ducked her head and hurried past. A moment later, Kathe appeared on the stairs. She, too, carried a tray, and she was smiling with undisguised delight.

"Since when do you carry trays?" Ilse asked, somewhat archly.

"You know how long," Kathe said with a laugh. "And you, since when do you sleep until late morning, now that you aren't one of my kitchen girls?"

"Since today."

They studied each other.

"You have changed since you came to us," Kathe said softly. "In good ways, I think."

"But not you," Ilse said. "You've always been my friend. We should—" She stopped, embarrassed. "I mean, if you like, we could take a walk in the gardens, or into the parks, if you have time to spare."

"Oh, I am not the one with the busy schedule. Let us say tomorrow. I daresay if I tried to claim you today, Lord Kosenmark would share a few words with me. Or my mother would. We have a new pastry cook, you see . . ."

She rolled her eyes.

"I see," Ilse said, laughing. "One of these days, you shall have to speak with your mother about the pastry cooks."

Kathe grinned. "Someday. But not today."

She shifted her tray to one side and hurried down to the kitchens, while Ilse continued upward.

AS HE HAD promised, Raul courted Ilse throughout the following months. He took delight in presenting her with gifts of jewels and silks, perfumes and paintings, and rare books that he discovered in the back rooms of Tiralien's finest antiquarians. He even commissioned an artisan to create for her a tiny sand glass, which they used to play word links. When she thought he had run to the end of his inventiveness with gifts, he hired a ship and crew. With two more ships as their escort, they sailed southward along the coast. He showed her Tiralien from afar, as it looked with the sun setting behind it, its towers like a ruddy crown amid golden fire, then ordered the ships to sail down the coastline to Fuldah, Lunendal, and Konstanzien, around the point where Osterling Keep stood, and toward the open southern seas. They spent a night with all the lamps on the boat lit, and Ilse could only think of diamonds sparkling on the black silk waves.

And when they returned to Tiralien, he brought her to Lord and Lady Vieth's next banquet and danced with her alone.

"You are my gift," he told her, when she protested his latest offering, a string of pearls she found upon her pillow.

"I am not a thing," she murmured. She let the pearls slide through her fingers. They felt like silk beads, so fine they were. Fine droplets of white, catching all the colors of the world in the lamplight. He had matched them to her newest gown, another gift she should have refused.

Raul touched her cheek with his hand. "I'm sorry. I only meant that I cannot do enough."

"Gratitude—"

"—is a bitter root, but sweetened with love, it pours strength and joy into the soul."

She smiled, somewhat pensively. That morning she had found a bouquet of flowers in her parlor, with a note reading, *I wish you joy.*

The note had no signature, but the flowers, blooming far out of season, had a faint whiff of magic about them.

Nadine. She had not openly avoided Ilse, but they had not spoken alone since Raul's break with Dedrick. Even when they did speak, Nadine's voice took on a polished brittle quality. Her courtesan's voice, Ilse thought. Used when she entertained a stranger.

I wish you joy. The words carried so many different meanings. *I forgive you for wounding my heart. I'm sorry I tried to wound you back. I would like to be your friend.*

She was still thinking of Nadine that same evening, when she and Raul sat in the upper gardens in the new pavilion, wrapped in fine woolen robes against the evening damp, counting the stars as they appeared. Spring had nearly arrived. Hard buds lined the branches, and the air tasted green, as though magic hovered just beyond their perception.

"You seem troubled," Raul said.

"I was thinking about Nadine."

"Ah." He kissed her cheek. "Is she angry with you?"

"Not anymore."

One of the guards coughed. Ilse drew back from Raul's next kiss.

"What's wrong?" Raul said.

"I never feel entirely alone with you," she murmured. "Except in your rooms."

"Our rooms. It never bothered you before."

Ilse breathed a sigh. How to explain that she understood why the several perimeters of guards, even within the pleasure house grounds, while saying that she disagreed.

"I had hoped this secret war between you and Markus Khandarr was finished," she said in an undertone.

"I hoped the same thing. Secret wars inside a kingdom often turn into wars with its neighbors. And do not think that Károví is the only one of our neighbors who watches us anxiously. Immatra would gladly take over the province of Ournes, if their king thought us preoccupied. Ysterien, too, might decide to expand its borders. If only Benno could write to me, then I would know what Markus is doing."

Benno Iani had disappeared from view, and Emma Theysson reported that she had heard nothing since he left for court. In place of their regular spies, they now depended on news from merchants or clients who visited the pleasure house. Even that required delicate planning, for Lord Kosenmark would not openly involve the courtesans in this business.

"We had no guards on the ships," she said.

A moment's silence. "We did. All the sailors had weapons. And . . ." Another brief pause. "And I hired three more ships to keep watch from a distance. I'm sorry I didn't tell you before. I didn't want you to worry."

Cold prickled her skin. "I wish you had told me."

"I did not wish to argue with you."

Instead he had lied. Or rather, he had not lied outright, but he had concealed things from her. A sick feeling washed over her. "Raul, all the reports say you've won your battle with Markus Khandarr. Let things be now. Or are you just playing more games?"

"I am not playing games, Ilse. I know this man and I know—"

"It's the same old excuses, Raul. If you only—"

They both broke off at the sound of nearby voices. One of the guards was hailing someone. Ilse heard the exchange, then the sound of weapons going back in their sheaths. The next moment, a house runner came toward the pavilion. Another followed, carrying a lantern.

"Mistress Ilse."

The runner bowed and presented a thick packet to Ilse.

Ilse glanced at Raul. He gave a tiny shake of the head. No gift then.

She took the packet, which was heavy and wrapped in oilcloth and tied with leather cords, as though prepared for a long journey. Inside the oilcloth, she found an inner packet wrapped in heavy paper and a card with writing. She motioned for the boy with the lantern to come closer so she could read it.

Mistress Therez Zhalina, Lord Kosenmark's household, Tiralien.

"Who brought this?" she asked in a faint voice.

"A private courier," the first runner said. "He arrived from Melnek, he said, and asked to wait in the house for any answer."

Raul leaned close. "Read it," he said softly. "It's nothing but words."

"Words." She gave a nervous laugh. "Words are sharp and dangerous."

"Indeed. But don't let his words be stronger than you."

He was right, as always. Taking a deep breath, she opened the inner envelope, which contained a thick sheaf of papers, tied with a ribbon. A smaller sheet lay on top. It, too, carried her name, and this time she recognized her brother's handwriting.

The letter was dated from Melnek, three weeks ago.

Dearest Therez, I wish I had written earlier, when Alarik Brandt's letter came to us. I wish I had written after our father came back from seeing you. I wish any number of things to make writing this letter easier. But I did not. So now I must write to say that I have very bad news. Our father has died . . .

She must have made a sound, because Raul leaned close, his arm around her shoulders.

"What is it?"

"He's dead. My father is dead." Her throat closed on the word.

"Oh my love, I'm sorry."

She tried to read on, but could not make sense of the words. She crumpled the letter and closed her eyes. Raul spoke quietly to the runner, who vanished at a run. Very soon the boy returned with a flask. Raul held it to Ilse's lips. "Drink."

She did, the alcohol burning down her throat, making her cough. Anger was gone, so was the first shock. Inside she felt only emptiness, and a small bright flame of grief. She turned her head away. "No more."

"Are you able to read it now?"

She shook her head. Raul sighed and took the letter, motioning for the boy to stand behind him with the lamp. As he scanned the page, Ilse saw him frown, then his face smoothed to a neutral expression. "What is it?"

"He invites you to come home."

She flinched. "No. I cannot. What does he want from me?"

"Nothing. Just the opposite. Your father made a new will this autumn, leaving you a third of his possessions. Ehren has sent you a copy of the will and a list of all your father's possessions. He asks that you choose which items you prefer. You need not visit, however, though they would like to see you."

She hugged herself tightly, saying nothing.

"He also says that your mother is not well."

If she knew Ehren, that meant seriously ill.

"Just like our father," she said. "He gives me a list of goods before he mentions our mother. Does he think I care about money?"

"Ilse. He's your brother, not your father. Do not blame him."

He reached toward her. She shook off his hand. "Do not tell me what to do, Raul. You were not there when Ehren told me to marry Theodr Galt."

"Does that mean I have no right to say what I think?"

Two quarrels in one evening. Both left her shaken. Ilse took a deep breath. "Speak, then," she said in a tight voice.

Raul nodded. "Very well. I know you are angry. I understand. And perhaps your mother and brother might have done more. But Ilse, your brother grieves, however clumsily. Do not cut him off without any reply." In a quieter voice, he added, "It's the right thing to do. And you believe in doing the right thing, I know."

He made no move to embrace her, neither did he turn away. Another turning point—past the first joy, past the first genuine argument. She released a long sigh. "You are right. I should, I will write to Ehren. But no visits. Not yet."

"I say the same myself," Raul said softly. "I mean to visit my father, who is old. I have any number of duties waiting for me. A brother."

"Three sisters," Ilse added.

"Three barbed and dangerous creatures."

He opened his arms. She leaned into them, feeling strangely bereft of desire, but craving his warmth and no longer caring about the presence of guards and runners. Gradually the strangeness fell away, as though an invisible, magical veil concealed the two of them from the world. Perhaps this was how kings and queens managed their lives.

She almost laughed to think of it. Almost.

CHAPTER TWENTY-FOUR

ILSE WROTE A short note to Ehren that same night, knowing delay would only make her task more difficult.

"...I cannot promise when I will visit, but I can promise that I will. Someday. But please understand that I cannot make my home in Melnek. I've made a new life with new companions. I cannot fit myself into old expectations. ..."

The phrases sounded stiff to her ear, and she was painfully aware she had not mentioned their father's death, nor their mother's illness. With a sigh, she added a postscript. "Ehren, I'm sorry for how this letter must sound. It is difficult for me to express everything I think or feel or hope at this moment. I will write again before the month is over, and then I will answer all your questions about the will."

Before she sealed it, Ilse gave the letter to Raul to read.

He read it through in silence, then regarded the last page a moment before he handed it back. "You are honest, not cruel. If your brother is as clear-sighted as you, he will understand."

Ilse folded the sheets together. "I hope so. To be fair, we were both trapped by our father. We just chose different paths."

Raul took her hands in his. "I'm sorry."

She started. "For what?"

"For what I said outside. For not trusting you."

Ilse laughed softly. "That's odd. That's what I wanted to say to you."

SHE SENT HER letter to Ehren the next day. She told herself she would send him a more complete answer within the week, but it was a full three weeks before Ilse attacked the set of papers Ehren had sent her. Finally, late one afternoon, she locked herself in her old office, vowing she would not emerge until she had read and answered everything.

She started with the letter. For all its brevity, it took her an hour to comprehend.

The facts were simple. Their father had returned from Melnek in good health but he had spoken little of Tiralien itself. They had lost their hoped-for contracts with the shipping guild, but had acquired new contacts for the overland routes through Baron Mann, and this new business required all of Petr Zhalina's attention throughout the spring and early summer. *In retrospect, we ought to have foreseen what happened,* Ehren wrote. *Worn by months of anxiety, he tired easily, and needed constant reminders for details he once recalled without effort.*

He grieved, Ilse thought. *In his own way.*

You never acknowledged that before, said her conscience.

She expelled a breath and willed her muscles to relax. Her father had grieved to lose his daughter. He had also tried to barter her life for a contract with Theodr Galt. Both statements were true. She could do nothing about it. She read on.

In late summer Petr Zhalina had taken ill from the fever. By autumn, he gave the business entirely over to Ehren, thereafter growing so weak, so fast, that Isolde Zhalina asked him if they should write to Therez.

Our father told us, "Therez is dead. I spoke with a stranger named Ilse."

Ilse propped her head against both hands. Eyes closed, she thought of Raul. She thought of magic. She thought of anything except her final meeting with Petr Zhalina. After a while, she had collected herself enough to go on.

Little remained. Petr Zhalina refused to summon his daughter, but the next day he gave a new will to Ehren. A week later he died, and soon after their mother took ill from the same fever. Ehren thought she would recover with time and careful nursing.

He had declared her dead. And yet assigned her a third of his possessions.

Ilse slammed her fist against the desk. "Damn you," she whispered. "Damn you twice over."

She set the letter aside and poured herself a cup of plain water, before she took up the inventory of her father's possessions, all written in Ehren's neat script.

. . . One mansion in Melnek, thirty rooms, well-maintained. Attached to item 1, the following . . . Warehouse in Melnek center . . . Kerzstal Street . . . Storage barns, three, on the western docks . . .

The list of properties and possessions covered twenty pages, including several tracts of land outside Melnek, which Petr Zhalina rented to farmers.

He also owned town houses in Duenne, more warehouses in Mundlau and Donuth. Ehren listed each one by number of rooms, the land attached, its condition, and an estimated value. Lists of personal items came next—his clothing, jewelry, the painting and statuary in the house—and Ehren had included a brief description and a valuation for each. Ilse found herself reading each entry with care, half hoping the list might provide her with a new portrait of Petr Zhalina. *Where is your heart? Do the clues lie in the goods you sold, or the gems you acquired?*

In the end, she found only a few more surprises and many disappointments. She reshuffled the pages into a neat square, retied the ribbons, and set the bundle aside. She drank a cup of watered wine, while she considered how to answer her brother's proposal about the will.

He offered her the choice of taking her share in money or lands or even in jewels and other personal items, saying that their mother agreed to abide by whatever Ilse decided. Making amends for the past, Ilse thought. She felt a twinge of anger. The offer came far too late, and yet . . .

Unable to bear it any longer, she sought out Raul, who was gazing out the windows of their bedroom, an unheeded book in his lap. He looked around with a questioning smile.

"I love you," she said.

"Is that how you've spent your afternoon?" he asked. "Considering that subject?"

"No. I already knew the answer." Standing behind his chair, she rested her hands on his shoulders. Raul leaned his cheek briefly against her arm, and she felt a ping, a knot of tension sprung. Was this how love progressed, then? From passion to comfort to mutual sustenance?

"I read Ehren's letter," she said. "And the will. All twenty pages."

"You have a meticulous brother. Have you made any decisions?"

She took a deep breath. Of course he had read enough to know about Ehren's proposal. "Yes. I will accept his offer. How or what, I don't know yet."

"Ah." Raul placed his hands over hers. "Would you like to hear my advice?"

She liked how his hands felt, the palms warm and rough, the sense of strength and gentleness combined. She especially liked how his hands sought her, whether in the night or like now, to offer comfort. "Tell me. Or rather, tell me what you think. I can't promise I'll agree."

Raul nodded. "Fair enough. Consider this, then. You might find it easier to accept your inheritance in money. If your brother needs to, he can sell certain items. Let him choose what to keep and what to sell. I can have my agent contact his for the details of the transfer."

Ilse kept her gaze on their hands, brown against brown, like honey and tea. "Taking the money seems so cold."

"Not entirely. Accepting your inheritance will soothe your brother's sense of guilt, and your mother's. If it troubles you to accept only coins, then pick a few items for mementos—a painting you loved or some jewels that you used to wear."

Sensible advice, which took into account both her needs and her heart. Delicately given, too. Though he did not mention, nor did she, such an inheritance would grant her independence.

"You're right," she said. "I'll write Ehren tomorrow."

Raul tilted his head back to look up at her. "You don't sound convinced."

Ilse shrugged. "It's not that. It's . . . It hurt to hear what my father said about me. It hurt that I can't talk to him again. Or argue with him. Or even tell him I was sorry. And yet, if he were here, I couldn't say any of those things." She swallowed against the ache in her throat. "I am his daughter, whether I like it or not."

He lifted her hands and kissed them. "You are Ilse. You are yourself, and no one else."

THEY DINED TOGETHER in midafternoon then separated once more, Ilse to write her brother, Raul to visit several city councillors. The visits were ostensibly social, but Ilse knew that Raul wanted news about Lord Khandarr's doings in Tiralien. The war, as she called it, had subsided to doubts and suspicions on Raul's part, but not entirely. It was not peace, it was more like an uneasy truce, where both sides ceaselessly watched the other.

For her own task, she carried her papers and writing materials to her old office—the one Berthold Hax had assigned her when she started as his assistant. A whiff of paper and ink lingered in the room, along with a sense of hopefulness that she associated with those early days as Hax's assistant. Her own held too many painful memories—Hax's death, Dedrick's return from the capital, the last and most bitter argument with her father.

I lay with thirty men.

Your grandmother is dead.

She blew out a breath. Enough. She laid out her writing materials and arranged her pens, which helped to settle her thoughts. She selected a sheet of foolscap from the stack, dipped her pen in the ink, and tapped away the excess. *Pretend you are writing a report for Mistress Denk,* she told herself.

Three drafts later, she had a letter she could send to Ehren without regret or shame. She made a fair copy on good parchment, signed it, and set the letter aside to dry. Her task was done. But she paused, the pen still balanced between her fingertips, as though it wanted to form another word or two. The runner would ride back to Melnek tomorrow . . .

Ilse dipped her pen in the ink.

Dear Klara . . .

She crossed out the line and started over.

Dearest Klara. You know I left home suddenly. I don't know what my family said, or what other rumors you heard, but here is the truth—the truth through my eyes, at least.

She wrote without pause, knowing that if she stopped, she might not have the courage to start again. She would not tell Klara everything—that would be too painful—but she would tell her as much of the truth as she could, as though Klara sat across from her, listening to the words Ilse set to paper.

. . . and so I left home, as quickly and secretly as possible. It was a difficult journey. I had intended to vanish into Duenne's streets and find a position, but I had to change my plans suddenly. I will not say more. Imagine what you like. Imagine a difficult painful time. That is all.

She paused. There was no need to talk about her time in the kitchens. Or the business with Rosel's spying. Even talking face to face, Ilse was not certain she could adequately explain things. She went on.

Eventually I found a home in Tiralien. And Klara, I found more than I looked for. He is more than any poet or historian. He is . . . He makes me laugh, Klara. He makes me think. You would like him.

Ilse spent the rest of the afternoon clearing up long-neglected business. Officially she was no longer Lord Kosenmark's secretary, but she continued to handle most of the usual tasks. Before she was aware of it, evening had arrived. A runner brought her word that Raul had returned and was below in the common room.

"Tell Lord Kosenmark I shall come down directly," Ilse said.

She washed away the dust and ink, then hurried down the stairs. The evening had already turned busy. Dozens crowded the common room, their voices rising in a thick hum. Ilse sighted Raul in the far corner, between Lothar Faulk and Emma Theysson. Covered dishes and wine jugs crowded the table in front of them. Raul looked up with a smile and beckoned to her.

"You look virtuous," he said as she took the seat beside him. "You must have spent the day in your office, penning reports."

Ilse laughed, self-consciously. "Kathe told you."

"Hardly. It was your own inky fingertips that betrayed you." He leaned closer. "We'll make up for the time lost between us."

Faulk made a wry comment about new lovers. Emma shushed him, but Ilse could tell she was thinking of Benno. Ilse evaded Raul's embrace, staving him off by tossing a fresh plum at him. He caught it one-handed and bit into it, grinning. She was about to follow with a second plum, when a ripple of movement by the common room's double doors caught her attention.

A glittering, perfectly coiffed and ornamented Dedrick Maszuryn stood at the entrance to the common room. The dark red silks of his sleeveless jacket swirled around, as though he had just that moment arrived. His face, caught in the bright glow from the chandelier, was still and dark and resolute.

Raul followed the direction of her gaze. Ilse heard his sharp intake of breath. Then, in one fluid motion, he stood and advanced toward Dedrick. Ilse held her breath, thinking she ought to call the guards. Surely Dedrick could see he wasn't welcome here.

They met in the center of the room, which fell silent. Both men spoke in low quick voices. Ilse could not hear what they said, but she could see how Dedrick punctuated his words with quick gestures, as though to forestall any arguments. Raul lifted a hand. Dropped it as Dedrick made a placating gesture and spoke urgently.

Raul glanced back toward Ilse. He appeared to hesitate. Then, with a shake of his head, he took Dedrick by the hand. The two men vanished through one of the side doors.

Ilse closed her eyes, trying to quell the sick feeling in her stomach. All around, the conversations bubbled to life. Eduard resumed playing the hammered strings, while Mikka accompanied him on the lap harp. Ilse heard Emma speaking to Faulk, telling him to make way, then the rustle of silks as someone took Raul's empty seat. Warm steady hands placed a wine cup within hers. She caught a whiff of a familiar spicy perfume.

"You must eat," Nadine said. "Then drink some wine. You look ill."

"I'm not hungry."

"Yes, you are." Nadine picked up a roll and broke it into pieces. "Small wonder, with you working all day in a stuffy office. Here." She fed the roll to Ilse in small bites, then followed that up with a few sips of wine. Gradually Ilse felt the tightness in her stomach ease. She accepted a chicken pastry and nibbled on that with more appetite.

"Better," Nadine said. She exchanged a glance with Emma, who looked concerned. "What say you, Lady Theysson? Should we send this child to her rooms?"

"That is best," Emma said. "And I'll send word to Lord Kosenmark. He'll come to you as soon as he finishes whatever business came up. You know that it's business," she added in a softer voice.

They would not let her go, however, until she had eaten a few more pastries and finished off a glass of wine. "Kathe could send up a tray," Nadine said as she walked with Ilse to the stairs. "But knowing you, you will forget to eat that as well. You are turning into Berthold Hax before your time. Shall I come with you? As a friend?"

Ilse smiled at her delicate phrasing, and shook her head. "I'd rather be alone. Thank you, Nadine."

The fourth floor was quiet. Only the faint sounds of night insects came through the open windows of the landing, and within the office itself, the hush was absolute. As Ilse passed into the private rooms, she had the impression of passing into a void.

The private rooms themselves reminded her of the house in miniature—rooms opening into other rooms giving way to a passage that angled between still other rooms—parlors and sitting rooms and even a tiny library the width of two chairs. When she had first come to the pleasure house, Ilse had not thought much about the rooms beyond Lord Kosenmark's office. Her duties brought her there seldom, and when they did, she came only to deliver trays with meals or drinks, or to take away the dirty dishes. The chambermaids who cleaned the private rooms were silent girls, who did their work under Mistress Denk's personal supervision. That first time she had gone to his bed, she had not looked anywhere but to him.

At the center of the suite was a dressing room. Doors led off to a privy and washroom and various enormous closets. Ilse hesitated, then walked into the largest closet. She pressed her hand against a panel in the far wall.

The panel slid open to reveal a long narrow room that ran along the entire side of this complex. Unlike the other rooms, it was bare of furniture. A few high windows let in light during the day. At night, rows of lamps illuminated the entire space, their light glancing over the many square grates set into the floors and walls.

The listening room.

Raul had shown her this room their second evening together. She could still remember his explanation of which pipes and grates led to which rooms. He used it still, she knew. No chambermaids cleaned here, and she could read which grates he visited by the footprints in the thin layer of dust upon the floor. She ticked off the rooms' names as she passed. Kitchen. Common room. Several parlors used by the courtesans for particular clients. Her old bedroom.

Ilse knelt beside one grate that showed no sign of recent use. Here in the middle of the corridor, she heard a soft susurration, the sound of air moving through the vents and pipes, as though the pleasure house were breathing.

She pressed her ear against the grate. At first she heard only the pulse within her ear, then as she became accustomed to it, she heard the faint whisper of voices below. She turned her head slightly. Now the sounds were magnified, and she distinctly heard wine being poured.

"...mistake to come here..."

Dedrick's voice. Ilse pulled away a moment. So she had guessed right.

Her pulse beating faster, she listened again.

"...going to Duenne. And so I thought—"

"Your father is a wise man."

"My father had nothing to do with my going to court." Dedrick drew an audible breath. Laughed softly. "My apologies. No, it was not my father's doing. I decided, at last, to follow your advice and make myself useful to society and my family. I said it was best if I put a very great distance between us, Raul. Then last night, it came to me..."

Ilse pulled away abruptly. Her head swimming, she pressed both hands against her eyes, while all around her the whispers echoed.

THE BELLS WERE striking twelve before Raul came into the bedroom. He carried a shaded lamp, which cast only a dim light at his feet, none on his face. When he saw Ilse, he stopped and drew back a step, as though surprised. "You were waiting for me?"

She nodded.

Raul tilted his head. "It was not what you thought."

"How do you know what I thought?"

"From the way you are sitting here in the dark."

He set the lamp on a table and began to unbutton his shirt. He seemed preoccupied—not guilty or irritated or any of the emotions she would have guessed after such a meeting. Now that Raul was here, with her, she could see that Nadine was right. Whatever they discussed had to be business. Still Ilse could not rid herself of the memory of Dedrick's tone when he first addressed his former lover. She wished she had listened longer, if only to dispel those doubts.

So ask.

I can't.

Why not? Don't you trust him to answer?

I do, but—

Ilse took a deep breath. "Raul. Why did— Why did Dedrick come here tonight?"

Raul glanced around. "To apologize. To say good-bye. Dedrick is going to Duenne next week."

She tried to pretend surprise. "That was a very long good-bye."

"He had a proposal to make. So I listened."

Raul continued to undress, his expression distracted, as though he was still turning over whatever he and Dedrick had discussed. Ilse watched him, taking pleasure in how he moved, in spite of the doubt nipping at her.

"He loves you still, doesn't he?" she asked quietly.

Raul sighed. "I believe so. However, he brought me news I cannot ignore."

"News about Markus Khandarr?"

"Among other things. Lady Alia had leave from the queen for a visit this spring. She mentioned to Dedrick in private that Armand and Khandarr both spend more time in the old wing of the palace. I know which section she means. Baerne had the court mages set layers of spells on those rooms so that no one could spy on them. It's all very vague, of course, which makes me believe the news more than not."

Ilse shifted uneasily. "I . . . I heard something of what he said."

She felt, rather than saw, Raul's glance. "I thought you might," he said in a neutral tone. "But not everything?"

"No. Not everything. I'm sorry."

He waved a hand. "No matter."

Ilse clasped her hands together, relaxed them. "What did Dedrick offer then?"

Raul still had not approached her. Though he had professed not to care, she could see that he did care, deeply, that she had spied on him. Then he shrugged. Some of the stiffness left him, and he sat beside her on the bed. "To use his words, he offered to be my eyes and ears, where others had turned blind and deaf, out of concern for their own affairs. It's risky," he said, half to himself. "Khandarr knows about the connection between us. But he must also know that we are no longer together, which offers Dedrick some protection."

"Is that enough?"

"I don't know. I do know that Dedrick insisted. Said he would spy for me whether I agreed or not. So I agreed, if only to enforce some caution. We had to work out a method and some channels for sending messages between here and there. That's what took so long."

Ilse said nothing. She could only think that Dedrick had made this offer because he loved Raul, and he still had hope. And she hated herself for those thoughts.

"You believe me?" Raul said, after a moment.

"Of course."

"Then trust me. Don't just sit there in angry submissive silence."

Ilse flinched. "Raul . . ."

He rubbed his face and sighed again. "I'm sorry, that was not fair of me."

She reached out and caressed his bare shoulder. "No. Neither was I being fair to you."

I love you. I'm sorry. I forgive you. Please forgive me.

Each anticipating the other, they pulled off their clothes and lay down. He was a skillful lover, she was desperate for physical release, and they both reached passion quickly. When she rolled from atop him, Raul kissed her softly upon her lips and cheeks and neck. But afterward, lying in his arms, Ilse felt the tension underneath his apparent calm, like a reflection of her own.

CHAPTER TWENTY-FIVE

LORD DEDRICK SOON departed for the capital in state, attended by an entourage of servants, retainers, and younger relatives. His journey lasted a leisurely month. When he arrived, he sent letters to all his acquaintances in Tiralien, filled with descriptions of the road and half-humorous complaints about dreary inns, bad food, and the tedious business of establishing his own household in the palace.

That was but a prelude, as Raul explained to Ilse.

Next came a series of what Raul called the public letters, which contained the expected accounts of court life. These came infrequently, because Lord Dedrick, at Baron Maszuryn's direction, spent most of his hours cultivating the more influential nobles at court.

Once, Dedrick alluded to earlier times with Lord Kosenmark.

"He's hopeful," Ilse said, reading Raul's brusque reply.

"He's a foolish idiot," Raul said drily. "But it works in our favor by distracting Markus."

Four months passed before the first of Dedrick's private letters arrived. He wrote them in code on durable parchment, rolled them into narrow waxed tubes, and left the packages at various drop points in Duenne. Faulk collected them and forwarded the letters via his personal couriers to other agents throughout Veraene. Each of them added their own codes to the envelopes—security marks, Raul called them—and by these marks, Ilse could trace their routes through the kingdom.

. . . It is just as Alia told me, in one of her more confiding moments. Armand claims to work toward peace when he speaks in the public assemblies, but in private, he is seeking allies for war. My personal informants have mentioned the old palace wing as their meeting place. Yes, my informants. I have managed to build a small network of agents within the palace. Some are disaffected councillors. Some, you will be surprised to hear, are associates of the queen herself. Yseulte is loyal to her husband, but sometimes, in private, to her

innermost circle of ladies, she has expressed fear that Armand's endeavors will leave behind a tangled legacy for his heir. . . .

. . . We were right to suspect the old wing, but Armand proves himself too clever. (Unless it is Markus Khandarr who provides the cleverness.) Armand meets with one faction in the old wing, another during small intimate hunting parties, while a third or fourth visits his private suite in the evening. No one suspects yet, because each believes they are the only supporters. . . .

. . . a difficult week and the most frustrating yet. The purpose, as you say, is war. But there must be more. For all Armand's schemes and maneuvers, the majority of the Council do not support war without a just cause. . . .

A period of silence followed. They had agreed upon an irregular schedule, Raul said, but Ilse could tell he worried. When at last, at summer's end, a seventh letter appeared, brought by an itinerant knife sharpener, Raul appeared as worn and frayed as the letter itself.

A well-traveled letter, as evidenced by its battered tube, stained by the red mud of the southern deltas, and steeped in the pine tang of northern forests. Once they were alone, Raul uncapped the tube and let the paper slide into his waiting hands. Even from a few feet away, Ilse felt the air tighten, and caught the faintest whiff of green. Dedrick's signature. And keyed to Raul's hand as the recipient.

"He's taking a great risk," she said cautiously.

Raul scanned the letter in silence, his frown deepening.

"What news does Lord Dedrick have?"

Raul handed her the letter without answering. By this time, Ilse could decode Dedrick's letters without referring to the key, and she swiftly read through the pages.

Benno makes very few appearance in court. He looks well enough on the surface, but his face lacks animation, and when we chance to encounter one another on the palace grounds, he excuses himself immediately. My informants can tell me little, except that Benno keeps to his rooms, or Lord Khandarr's. It seems impossible to extract him from Khandarr's hold, but Faulk promises he is working on that situation as well. In happier news, I can report a growing restlessness among the nobility. . . .

"But does restless mean dissatisfied?" she murmured.

"We can hope," Raul said. "Read what he says about the troops."

Armand had recalled a third of the troops from the borders, she read, but he continued to demand higher than usual levies, and he refused to drop the many trade restrictions between Veraene and Károví.

He says these measures keep us secure. He claims that troubling reports have reached him about Leos Dzavek's intentions concerning relations between the kingdoms, ones we cannot ignore given past incursions by the northern prince.

Raul smoothed out Dedrick's letter and studied it, as though searching for clues in its stains and creases. "I don't trust Armand. I especially do not trust Markus Khandarr."

Ilse stirred. "I cannot help thinking that we . . . that I made a very bad suggestion."

"About the book?" Raul smiled ruefully. "A year or more will tell us the answer to that. For now . . . I believe we made the best decision from a very bad lot."

BY LATE SUMMER the flow of correspondence, both public and private, slowed to a trickle, then died off into silence. Raul grew more anxious as the weeks passed, until Ilse thought everyone must perceive it, from Mistress Denk to the newest chambermaid.

This afternoon, as they faced each other at weapons drill, she could see his thoughts were absent—not upon her, or his weapon, not even on Benedickt Ault, who studied them with narrowed eyes. Perhaps it was best that they used wooden swords today.

They touched blades and waited for Ault's command.

"Begin!"

Raul lunged forward in attack. Ilse met his first blow, then side-stepped to avoid the next, using the new sequence Ault had taught her the week before. A rapid give-and-take followed, and to her surprise, Ilse nearly got a touch on him. She circled around, trying to draw his attention with a series of quick thrusts at his knees and then head. *Make him work,* she thought. *Make him think about now, here. About Tiralien and not Duenne.*

She sighted an opening and lunged forward, sliding her blade past his. "Death," she said, gasping.

Raul glanced down at the sword point against his chest. "Death for us both, my love."

Something blunt pressed her side—Raul's blade, angled upward, beneath hers. She had been so intent upon her attack, she had neglected her own defense.

Ault came striding up, his disgust plain. "You cannot rely upon one or two good techniques," he told Ilse. "And your performance, my lord, was inexcusable. I need not say more." He drew a deep breath, regarded them both coldly. "Tomorrow we try a new approach. Separate sessions. Different drill patterns. Give me a month, then I'll set you against each other."

He dismissed them, telling Ilse to report for the first session the next morning. Lord Kosenmark would drill later, in the afternoon.

"I don't like it," Raul said later, as they bathed together. "You might do me an injury at our next drill together. Or worse."

"You will survive," Ilse said. She poured handfuls of water over his back to rinse away the suds. It was so good to see him smiling, relaxed, she didn't care about the separate drills.

"What about you?"

"I will survive."

"Cold unfeeling woman," he said, his voice going husky.

It had been weeks and months since they last made love. Oh yes, they kissed each other and held each other. Ilse even knew that passion had not died. It ran in deep strong currents, even while Dedrick's silence made the air thick with tension. But now and now and now... The old songs ran through her thoughts as she kissed Raul with a fierce desire.

"Now and now and now," he whispered. "My love is now and forever. My love is yesterday and tomorrow."

They held hands as they ran up the stairs to the fourth floor and their private rooms. A runner overtook them on the third landing. "My lord," she called out, breathless. "Visitors. Lady Theysson and Lord Iani."

Ilse gripped Raul's hand. *Lord Iani? Here?*

Raul had gone stone-still. He blinked, then seemed to recover himself. "Where did Mistress Denk put them? The Rose Parlor. Good. Send refreshments, and tell them we come at once."

The runner sped away. Raul paused a moment, his hand over his face. Ilse touched his shoulder, felt the slight tremble as his control wavered. "There can be nothing good," he whispered. "Nothing."

"No," she said. "But we must not shrink away from it."

He dropped his hand and managed a shaky smile. "Indeed. Let us go see what Benno has to say."

In the Rose Parlor, Benno Iani sat on a brocade-covered divan, his head resting in both hands. Emma Theysson sat close beside him, one arm draped around his shoulder. A tray with wines, coffee, and strong spirits stood untouched on the table before them.

Without looking up, Emma said, "Benno came last night. He rode straight from Duenne to here in ten days. I made him sleep until he could not sleep any more. He—" Her voice shook. "He brought you a letter."

At the word *letter*, Iani dropped his hands to his knees. His eyes were bloodshot, his skin blotchy and rough. For a moment, he stared at Raul, his gaze unfocused, then he smiled faintly. "Yes, I brought a letter for you, Raul. From our friend Markus."

Raul inhaled sharply. "Why did Armand release you, Benno?"

Iani shook his head, still smiling. "Armand had nothing to do with it, my friend. It was Markus Khandarr who released me. That's how the court works, you know. Khandarr speaks, the king obeys. I kept disbelieving it, and so does everyone else. Otherwise the entire court would—" He broke off, frowning at his hands.

"Was he like this last night?" Raul asked Emma.

She met his gaze with hard bright eyes. "Oh no. Last night he couldn't speak at all. Khandarr wouldn't let him."

Iani shuddered. "I told him. I told Markus that one man should not have that much power. No one." Again he blinked, as though trying to clear his vision. "Khandarr struck me then. Odd how he likes to use his hands instead of magic, or magic when hands would do. Ah love, I should not have told you that part," he said softly to Emma, who had begun to weep. "I will survive."

"What happened?" Raul said, just as softly as before.

"Treachery," Iani whispered. "Ambition. The ingredients of any court. A heady mixture edged with poison." He paused, chafed his hands. "No, let me tell it properly. From that first day, when I arrived in court. Markus Khandarr summoned me at once to his private chambers. He said that if I practiced magic without his permission, especially if I crossed into Anderswar, that he would have Armand execute me for treason."

"He is a monster," Raul said, his voice close to breaking. "I knew that years ago. Benno, you have not answered my first question. Why did Markus let you come back to Tiralien?"

"To bring you a letter. A very important letter. Here, read it. I know the news—he made me watch—but I will not . . . I cannot not say it. Not yet."

Iani slid an envelope from his shirt and offered it to Raul. Even a few steps away, Ilse could see that it was thick expensive parchment, the color of new cream. Warily, Raul leaned over the table and took the envelope from Iani. Almost at once, he gave a startled exclamation and dropped it.

"What is wrong?" Ilse said.

Raul did not move except to rub his hands together, over and over until Ilse's skin crawled. Emma Theysson was silent. Lord Iani waited with preternatural patience. Finally Ilse bent down and picked up the letter from the carpet.

Magic. Magic so thick and strong it stung her fingers. She recognized the signature, too—Markus Khandarr's.

Silently, she handed the letter to Raul. "Open it," she whispered.

He took it, shuddering. When he broke the seal, light flared along the paper's edge, and Ilse felt a gust of air against her face. Raul gave no sign that the magic had affected him, but she could see the effort it took for him to fold back the flap and open the letter. She caught a glimpse of a few short paragraphs written in a square black script, before Raul turned the letter so that only he could read it.

His jaw tightened. Then, abruptly, his face turned gray.

"What is it?" she asked.

"Lord Dedrick has . . ." Raul spoke with obvious difficulty. "This is a letter to inform me that Lord Dedrick died two weeks ago. He . . . chose to ride a stallion that he could not master and lost control. The stallion pitched him over the side of a cliff onto the rocks below. Lord Khandarr wished me to hear the sad news as quickly as possible."

Ilse reached toward him, but Raul shrugged away from her touch. "There's more."

Of course. There was always more. "Go on."

"When questioned, Lord Dedrick admitted that he and I had been lovers. He also admitted that he loved me still, in spite of how I betrayed him, and would do anything to regain my affections."

"That was hardly a secret—"

"No." Raul smiled thinly. "But Markus likes to hear people confess their secrets. I learned that in court." Then he glanced at the letter, and his face went blanker than before. "Would you like to hear the rest?"

She wanted to wrap him tightly in her arms and shut away the world, but he was beyond any such refuge now. "Tell me," she said as calmly as she could. "What else does the letter say?"

"He said he knew about Dedrick's spying. He knows everything about our couriers and our agents. Faulk is dead, by the way. So are Faulk's brother and Rusza Selig. You might not know her name—"

"I know her." A round-faced woman who had a deep gurgling laugh. Dead now.

"She was a merchant," Raul went on, ignoring the interruption. "She carried letters for us sometimes. The charge for all of them was possession of treasonous documents. Armand had them executed and their bodies thrown into the garbage pits. He even mentions you, my love."

Ilse's throat closed. Of course he would. She and Raul had not hidden their love from the world. Quite the opposite. "What does he say about me?"

"He remembers you from Lord Vieth's banquet last winter. He also questioned Dedrick about everyone in this household, and of course, poor Dedrick could not hide anything. He said . . ." Raul paused and closed his eyes. "He said I loved a woman named Ilse Zhalina, beyond all reason and hope and honor."

CHAPTER TWENTY-SIX

A LENGTHY SILENCE followed, broken only by Benno Iani's labored breathing. Finally Raul crumpled Markus Khandarr's letter into a ball and set it upon the table. "Tell me what happened, Benno. Tell me every detail, even the ones you can't bear to remember. Especially those."

"No," said Emma Theysson, her voice rough with anger. "Benno is too ill to play your games. He ought to be sleeping except—"

"Except he came to give his report," Raul said softly. "And give it he must."

Emma Theysson glared at Raul, who met her gaze steadily. "Don't you see?" he asked. "I'm not the one insisting upon it. Lord Khandarr is the one."

Iani was nodding. "Raul is right, Emma. I must tell him. I must." He picked up his coffee cup with trembling hands and drank deeply. Lady Theysson steadied his arm, glancing toward Raul as though to gauge his reaction, but Raul's face was impassive.

Iani drained his cup, then rinsed his mouth with water. "Officially the king summoned me to court," he said at last. "But you know it was Lord Khandarr who gave the command. He kept me under close watch the entire time, and ordered me to halt any magic studies except those he approved. In short, he made me a hostage."

He drew a deep breath, as though to collect himself. Emma Theysson poured spirits into a wine cup, but Iani waved the cup away. His looks had noticeably improved in just moments—his hands were steady, his eyes clear and alert. Ilse's skin prickled with the realization that Khandarr had bound his magic into Iani's person, like a poison. Speaking was the antidote.

Iani went on. "And so we lived through the autumn and winter. Then Lord Dedrick arrived. Khandarr set spies on him at once. Of course, he knew that you and Dedrick had broken off, and he knew about Mistress Ilse. I had hoped those together would make him careless, but no."

"Markus was never careless," Emma Theysson said bitterly.

Raul made an impatient gesture. "Keep going, Benno. Everything, remember."

Iani nodded. "Everything. Yes. Well, Lord Dedrick was cautious at first. He visited only those whom his father had selected as appropriate colleagues and mentors. He attended only the unexceptional gatherings. And though he acknowledged me in public, he never tried to write me privately, or visit my rooms."

"What gave him away?" Emma said.

Iani spread his hands. "Nothing. Everything. Lord Khandarr intercepted all the public letters. I know because he told me. *Nothing in them,* he railed, *but lies and misdirection.* But he also knew that you like secrets as much as he does, Raul. So he kept a watch. Who knows what happened next? Perhaps Khandarr's spies overheard a careless word between Lord Dedrick and his agents. Perhaps Khandarr had him followed every moment, because suspicion is his nature. I only know that they arrested Lord Dedrick with a letter to Raul in his hands."

Their faces all turned toward him at the same time. "Which letter?" Emma demanded. "Benno, you never told me—"

Iani massaged his throat, looking puzzled. "I could not. Not until I spoke with Lord Kosenmark. But it was because of the letter they arrested him."

"What did Dedrick say in that letter?" Raul said. His voice sounded thick, almost masculine.

"He wrote . . ." Iani struggled to speak, as though he fought against an invisible compulsion. Clearly, this was not part of Markus Khandarr's scripted report. "He wrote about Armand's plans to charge Lord Kosenmark with treason. Armand intended to send Markus himself to Tiralien with a squad of soldiers. They were to arrest you in secret and search your house for the evidence."

For Simkov's book, Ilse thought. *For the key to finding Lir's jewels.*

"Once he found the jewels, he knew Dzavek would attack. Then Armand would need no justification for war, because war would come to him. Lord Dedrick forgot all caution, it seems, and hurried straight with his letter to Faulk's rooms."

For a moment, no one spoke. Ilse felt a cold sickness in her stomach. Emma was hugging herself. Raul sat stiffly, his face gray. "What else?" he said.

"Just the interrogation."

"Go on then."

In short blunt phrases, Iani told how the guards dragged Lord Dedrick to the prison where Markus Khandarr waited. Iani had attended as his witness. The interrogation was brief but painful.

"Khandarr used magic to force the truth from him," he said with a shudder. "Dedrick tried clamping his mouth shut, but it was like fingers forcing his lips open. Invisible magical fingers that did whatever Markus ordered. And then the words. They . . . they crawled out of his mouth like worms. All about you. About your work here."

"Markus knew already," Raul murmured. "He must have."

"He suspected. Now he has proof. But not the proof he wanted."

"What do you mean?" Ilse said.

"Ah, the spell was for truth, you see. And so Dedrick could not invent any treasons. He could only repeat the words you always used whenever Luise or Emma or I urged you to take the crown. *I am the duke's son. I am sworn to loyalty. I cannot and will not act against the king, unless the king himself acts against Veraene. And that he has not done.*"

"Ah." Raul pressed his hands together. "Those words."

"Khandarr was furious," Iani said. "He called up magic so thick that I could hardly breathe. Dedrick fought hard against it. Gods, I thought his throat would burst. And then . . ." His eyes went wide and blank as though recalling that final scene. "And then it did."

Ilse pressed a hand against her mouth. Emma Theysson did the same. Only Raul did not move or change his expression.

"Blood everywhere," Iani whispered. "Over me. Over Khandarr and the stone floor and bars to Dedrick's cell. I even saw blood upon the ceiling. Blood and— Khandarr tried to revive him with magic, but it was far too late."

He dropped his head into his hands. A tremor went through him, then he was still. Emma Theysson stroked his hair. Her hands were shaking, and tears glittered on her cheeks. It was impossible to offer comfort, Ilse thought. There was none. Not after such a report.

Raul stood and walked to the door. Ilse heard him send runners for soup and bread. He sent another to Mistress Denk with orders to prepare a private room for Lady Theysson and Lord Iani's comfort. His gaze, when he turned around, had a strange wild light, but his manner was gentle as he knelt by Iani's side. "Benno, I want you to stay here. Eat and rest. Keep Emma by your side. I . . . I promise I shall do whatever I can for you. Whatever it takes. Even if that means doing nothing at all."

Iani lifted his head, bewildered. "What are you saying?"

"You will see." Then Raul was striding toward the door.

"Where are you going?" Ilse called out.

Raul glanced back with a thin smile. "I am going to think."

His footsteps rang off the tiles as he ran down the stairs. Ilse hesitated only a moment before she hurried after him.

She overtook him at the landing. "Raul, where are you going? Talk to me!"

"Why? You heard what Benno said. Khandarr will murder us all unless I—" He broke off and rubbed his hand over his face, wincing. "There will be no more shadow court. I'll go home to my father. Take up my duties as his heir. It's all that's left to me."

"You must not give up," she said. "Not yet."

"Why not? Dedrick is dead because of my arrogance. And for what? Perhaps there is no difference between Armand and me, except in degree. He would send thousands to die in his wars, and I allowed Dedrick to go alone into danger."

"So you will do nothing?" Ilse asked.

"I cannot do anything else."

His voice, soft and low and barely under control, broke on the last word. By instinct, she reached out to touch his arm. Raul flinched away. The expression on his face reminded her of the day he had released her from her imprisonment. Worse. He had seemed diminished then. Now he looked defeated. *He should be king*, Ilse thought. *He could be, if only he were free to act.*

Free. Of course. With that, all the shock and confusion bled away. She knew what to do.

"If you cannot, then I must," she said.

That caught his attention. "What do you mean?"

"I must leave you," she said. A pang went through her. She nearly recanted before she had finished. Quickly now, she told herself. Say the rest before you lose heart. "I must leave you," she repeated. "For a time. So Markus Khandarr cannot threaten you through me. So you can act. However you deem necessary."

Raul's face drained of color. "No," he whispered. Then louder. "No! It won't do any good, Ilse. Khandarr will murder you. And he would force me to watch. Just as he did with Benno and Dedrick. He will do it because you were once connected with me. That's the only reason he needs—"

"But if you do nothing, we might all die in that bloody senseless war that Armand wants. Or if we survive, we might wish we had not. Is that what you want for this kingdom? Is that what you want for yourself?" Her voice dipped into bitterness. "If you choose cowardice, that is your own affair. But do not make it mine."

His chin jerked up. His face flushed. "If you think me a coward, you do not know me."

"I think I never did," Ilse said, her voice rising higher. "You once said you needed my honesty. You said you wanted me to speak the truth, my lord. Were you lying? Or did you hope I'd always agree, no matter what? That I should *pretend*? Never again, Raul. I will never pretend again. Not even for you. If you think I can, if you think I would, *you* do not know *me*."

They glared at each other.

Raul was the first to let his gaze fall away. "I need to walk," he muttered. "Somewhere. Anywhere."

He spun around, stumbled, and caught himself. Ilse watched him lurch down the stairs. He was clumsy in his despair, as though Khandarr had robbed him of that, too. *Let him go,* she thought. *He needs to grieve alone.*

She leaned her forehead against the cool plaster wall. Far below, she heard Raul call out to one of the guards. She ought to return to the Rose Parlor. Ought to see to Benno and Emma. Or no. Let them have quiet together.

She took refuge in a parlor on the second floor. There was a couch, wide enough for two. She only needed space for one. She stretched out and laid her head on the soft pillow. Sleep, however, was impossible. Images flickered before her mind's eye—Benno's shaking hands, Emma's hard gaze, Raul's stone-faced expression as he listened, the shock in his eyes when she said she would leave. It didn't matter if she closed her eyes. She could not blind herself to memory.

One hour passed. Then more bells rang. Ilse tried to count, but lost track. She heard a tentative knock once, but did not answer. The second time, a voice called out her name—Kathe, chasing after her again. Kathe would be worried. Had she pieced together what happened? Probably. Kathe knew far more than Raul credited her for. Or perhaps he knew and trusted her. That was why he gave Kathe the task of tending Ilse when she first arrived, bloody and near death.

The door opened. She caught a whiff of cedar and wood smoke as Raul knelt by her side.

"I'm sorry," he whispered. "I should not have left."

Ilse blinked. "Where did you go?"

"Everywhere. Up into the hills. By the docks. I had to walk. I could not stand it otherwise."

"Did you take a guard?"

"I don't know. I must have. I didn't notice. Come." He helped her to her feet. "Let us sit in the gardens a while."

They had a supper outside, then walked beneath the green-leafed trees, along graveled paths lined with late-blooming roses and other flowers Ilse could not identify. Russet and orange and deep gold blossoms, arcing from long graceful stems. Rains had come and gone during the afternoon, leaving the air cool and fresh.

At the garden's far edge, they sat close together on the stone bench. Sunset was just settling over Tiralien, gilding the rooftops and towers with its ruddy light. To the east, the skies were turning dark; the seas were the color of a dark blue wine. Raul said nothing, but gazed over the cityscape toward the coast. His mood was quiet—there was no trace of the morning's crisis, except for the faint lines etched between his brows.

"Raul . . ."

"Hush," he whispered. "We can talk later."

Before she could answer or refuse, he had folded her into his arms and was kissing her hard. In between, he was murmuring the words *no* and *never* and then *now, please now.*

MORNING CAME WITH the pale sunlight glancing through the windows. Ilse woke to find Raul studying her with wide golden eyes. Like twin suns, she thought. Like Toc's points of lights, when he opened his eyes to Lir. Her heart contracted at the thought. *We are, both of us, Toc, sacrificing our sight to our beloved.*

Then Raul sighed and closed his eyes, turning away from her.

"You said you would never run away again."

"You said you would never lock me in a cage," she replied.

His only answer was a helpless gesture, hand turned outward.

Raul said nothing more about it for the rest of the day, but Ilse watched the minute changes in his expression throughout the morning and afternoon. She saw how he winced at times, as though catching himself on an invisible wound. Her own eyes were dry. Her grief hidden within, the tears filling her heart until she thought it might burst.

When twilight was falling, she led him outside to the wilderness gardens, where the servants had spread thick carpets over the grass. They leaned against the tree trunks and gazed upward at the star-speckled skies. Ilse knew there were guards about them, but they had withdrawn to a discreet distance. She and Raul would have at least this small circle of privacy outside.

"Even here," he murmured.

"What about here?" She could feel his heartbeat, quick and strong, against his chest. If she left him—once she left him—she would miss this the most.

"Even here we are not really outside. I sometimes wonder what it would be like if we, just the two of us, vanished into the hills for a month."

"Wouldn't we be hungry?"

"I would hunt for you. And you could bring your stone knife."

"My famous stone knife. I lost it my first night in Tiralien."

"And I didn't buy you another? How careless of me."

A leaf whirled through the air, landing at their feet. Another one followed. Autumn was approaching, the warm mild autumn of the southern coast. Though as Josef often reminded them, Tiralien was the north to him. He, like Raul, came from the hot southwest provinces, where winter was a wet and stormy season.

"Winter soon," Raul said, echoing her thoughts. "Two years since you came to me."

"I arrived twice, I think," she said. "Once at your door, and once at your heart."

Raul was silent a moment, but his breath felt shaky against her hair.

"You are right. I did promise never to lock you in a cage."

He spoke in a whisper so soft she could barely make out the words.

"I meant that," he went on, still in that faint whisper. "But what I said before is true. Markus needs no excuse to murder you. He would do it to remind me he can. To remind others. At least if you remain here, I have a *chance* to protect you."

Ilse reached up and touched his cheek. It was wet with tears. "But if I stayed with you, you would be just as much a prisoner then, my love. You would be like Toc without his eyes, only there would be no sun and stars, and that I could not bear."

He buried his face in her hair and held her close. "I would make you my queen if I could."

She had known that from the start. But a wish could not change their lives.

We've had lives before, she thought. *I remember them all now. You were a diplomat, a spy, a pirate in Andelizien. I was a princess, a scholar, a bonded servant, and mage. And once we sailed together to that new world called Morennioù. If the poets and scholars are right, then we shall find each other again, if not with these lives, then in the next. By choice. By fate.*

Forcing herself to speak steadily, she said, "I do not wish to go, but I must. Once I do, you must make new plans."

"No."

"Yes. Promise me. Stop Khandarr. Persuade Armand. Something. Or else we live apart forever." Her voice failed at the last word. "I hate this, Raul. But you see how I'm right. We cannot pretend any longer that we are safe here. We must act. You must act."

He shivered in her embrace. "You . . . you are inexorable."

"Part of my charm."

He shook in silent laughter that poised on the verge of grief. "What about you? How will you spend your days, then? Not hiding in silence. That's not like you."

Ilse suppressed a start. Ah, he knew her too well. *I want to study magic,* she thought. *More magic. I want to learn what Mistress Hedda refused to teach me—how to cross into Anderswar in the flesh. Then I can search for the jewels myself and . . .*

What came after discovery, if discovery, she had not decided yet. But the jewels were the key to ending the wars, the key to forging . . . not a true peace. That would only come with a change of kings on both sides. But finding them was a start. And the task had to be one she carried through alone.

Raul stirred, restless. She kissed his shoulder, his neck. "I don't know yet."

A brief hesitation, as though he detected the lie. Then, "*Will* you come back?"

"Raul, I can't promise anything. Neither can you."

"When?" he said again, his voice going thin and sharp.

She held him tight. Tighter. *Now is the mother of When,* she thought. *And if tomorrow runs toward us, let it run swiftly.*

"I will come back," she said. "When everything is right."

If the gods were kind. If he would have her still.

CHAPTER TWENTY-SEVEN

THEY DISCUSSED HIS future intentions, her departure, just as they had discussed politics or poetry or the interwoven threads of history, magic, and passion.

"Shall we start with your plans or mine?" Raul asked.

"Yours," Ilse said. "Mine are indefinite."

"As indefinite as the ocean mist," Raul said lightly, "or the winter rain clouds drifting up toward the sun. Though Tanja Duhr reminds us that the ephemeral is not necessary intangible. All poetry aside, I have only the vaguest of notions yet. Do you wish to know them?"

She shrugged. "The question isn't whether I want to know—I do—but whether my knowing is safe. Or useful."

He studied her several long moments, and she had the impression of a dormant fire behind those golden eyes—as though he had buried his passion. Barely. She could sense the heat flickering against her skin. If he chose, he might awaken the embers and burn through all her defenses in a moment. But then his lids sank to half-slits, the warmth receded, and she found she could breathe more easily.

"Tell me what might be important," she said.

"Ah, that. Well, I thought I might build a new shadow court. Not here, but in Károví."

Startled, she opened her mouth to ask a dozen questions. She stopped herself.

"No curiosity?" he asked, half-smiling. "Or rather, you don't want to know."

"I do," she confessed. "But I don't know—I won't—"

"Neither do I," Raul said softly. "Call it instinct, or inclination. I think it's time we paid attention to those who serve the kings, instead of the kings themselves. One rock cannot halt the running tide. Just so, a single man cannot contain the flood of history. We must build our bulwark against war using many grains of sand."

Starting with Duke Feliks Markov or Duke Miro Karasek, Ilse thought.

Both were long-standing members of the Imperial Council who shared responsibility for the armies. Karasek was more popular, but Markov was older, he'd advised the king decades longer. Rumor said that if Dzavek were to die, Markov had the larger faction and could take the throne. She wanted to ask how Raul intended to approach them. What assurances he would give them. (Because they would surely demand them.) What he meant to do with Simkov's book, if anything.

But no, if she asked him those questions, he would expect answers to his.

Raul watched her intently, as though he could guess the link and chain of her thoughts. "Your turn," he said.

Uncertain, she said, "What do you wish to know?"

"Very little."

"Liar," she breathed.

That provoked a tentative smile. "True. But let us confine ourselves to where you plan to spend the next months or years away from me. Will you grant me that much interference?"

Her heart gave a ping of grief. She contained it. "Yes. It's only fair."

They had been sitting on opposite sides of the desk, just as they had during her first interview. Raul stood and spread a detailed map of the continent over his desk. Ilse came around the desk and stood by his side. She knew this map well. Raul had commissioned it before leaving Duenne, and the mapmaker, an artist as well as craftsman, had created a work of exquisite precision. Different-color inks marked the political borders and differences in terrain—light brown lettering for the Ysterien kingdom in the far southwest, dark blue for Duenne and its environs in the central plains, and vivid green to represent cities along the east coast. Károví, too, was rendered in perfect detail from the green breadth of Duszranjo Valley set within the Železny Mountains to the silvery-gray that marked the snow-dusted plains stretching north of Rastov. Ilse ran her fingers over the point east and north where, if the legends were true, Lir and Toc created the world in their season of love.

Raul, too, studied the map. Once or twice, he touched a city's name, shook his head, and let his fingers glide past.

"You have an idea?" Ilse asked him.

"Yes. No. My instincts suggest a city on the eastern coast." He glanced at her. "However, I suspect those are not instincts, but selfish desire."

Ilse touched his hand, which hovered close to hers. "Your instincts are not entirely wrong. But I cannot choose a home too close to Tiralien. That might provoke suspicion."

"Markus will be suspicious no matter what."

All their discussions came back to that concern. After some debate, Ilse had proposed that she find work as a secretary or clerk. Her newly acquired fortune made it unnecessary, but she wanted to keep her mind and hands busy, and both agreed that would create a more convincing impression of her building a separate life.

Raul made another circuit of the map with his fingers. North. South. The western provinces. "What about Melnek? It might look more natural if—"

"No."

He breathed a sigh. "It was just a suggestion. You have friends as well as family in Melnek. More important, Baron Eckard resides there. He can provide some measure of protection."

"I cannot," she murmured. "Find another way."

City by city, they examined the map. Matsurian and Tegel, on the southern coast, both had high transient populations, which worked in her favor. But Raul disliked the distance—a month by ship, two months by fast horses. Klee, another port city, was closer, but its sweltering climate often bred contagion, and Raul had no agents or friends or associates there whom he trusted.

Ilse ran her fingers along the coast, past Matsurian and Tegel and Luzzien, until she came to the province marked *Valentain*.

"That remains a choice," Raul whispered in her ear.

"No," she said softly. "We must not tempt each other."

Back to Tiralien then, to examine the cities nearby. Leniz was a garrison town a week's ride south of Tiralien. Compared to Tiralien, it offered little unless she took up soldiering. North was Idar-Alszen, a market port that served as an interim stop between Melnek and Tiralien. Back south, beyond Leniz to Osterling Keep.

"Osterling," she said, half to herself.

Raul, who had been studying the northern provinces, glanced up. "What about Osterling?"

Ilse touched the gold circle marking Osterling Keep, which lay between Leniz and Klee, on a point of land jutting into the sea. A range of hills covered most of the point, except for a highway along the coast. It was not a large city, but Lord Joannis, the regional governor, had chosen it for his seat, and it served as an important garrison and watch point for the coast.

"Good positions would be plentiful," she said. "And if there's anyone from your shadow court with greater official influence than Nicol Joannis, you never told me their name. I should be safer there than in any other city. Unless you believe Dedrick gave away Joannis."

"Dedrick knew nothing about him. Therefore . . ."

"Therefore we guess that Lord Khandarr has learned nothing since. What about Benno?"

"Benno swears Markus used no magic on him. We cannot be certain, of course, but every choice carries its own risk." He traced a route along the Gallenz River, then southeast, through the hills, to the point next to Osterling's name. "Three weeks by coach, following the highway. Ten days by an adventurous horseman—if that horseman has a change of mounts, and isn't afraid of cutting through swamps and hills and wilderness."

"Are you adventurous?"

"At times." His finger edged closer to hers. "And it would comfort me to know you were not half a continent away. What do you say?"

She drew a long breath, considering the matter. "Osterling. Yes. That would be good."

BY UNSPOKEN AGREEMENT, they left further plans for another week. In between weapons drills and managing the pleasure house, they gave themselves over to the silent exploration of each other's bodies. Something of their mood bled through the rest of the pleasure house. Eduard and Mikka quarreled, Johanna wept between customers, and Nadine turned a closed face to the world. Even Kathe showed signs of prickliness.

"Will you change your name?" Raul asked her at breakfast.

Ilse paused in drinking her coffee. "Should I?"

"I don't know. It might give you some scant privacy. On the other hand, if Khandarr's spies track you down, changing your name implies you wished to hide something."

She considered it a moment. "I'll keep my name. Better if he thinks I'm acting openly."

Raul nodded. "You are Ilse Zhalina, then. Lately of Tiralien and now seeking employment in Osterling Keep. Shall I write a letter of recommendation?"

They both smiled tentatively.

"The next point," Raul said. "Why are you leaving me?"

Ilse blew out a breath. "Because of me. Something I did."

"No," he said roughly. "Not that."

An uncomfortable silence followed. Ilse studied her coffee cup, as though she might find answers in its dregs. What might drive two lovers apart? It could not be a sudden thing, or Khandarr would disbelieve it at once. It would have to be a difference rooted in her nature and Raul's, something they could not overcome with logic or debate or simple passion.

"Children," she said abruptly. "I wanted my own children."

Raul visibly paled. "That's . . . a very good reason. So we start a rumor that you became disgusted with my shortcomings."

"Not disgusted," she said hurriedly. "Frustrated, perhaps."

His gaze flicked toward hers, then away. "I could understand that."

Another silence, while Raul rubbed his hands together. Ilse instinctively reached toward him, but let her hand drop. *We have only got to the truth by telling lies,* she thought, watching his face as his expression grew more remote.

"Raul . . ." she said softly.

He nodded absently. "I am here. Thinking. We must convince everyone in this house as well, or our plans are worthless. Let me spend a few evenings away. Lord Vieth invited us to his estates for the hunting season. I'll go alone."

"A good idea," she said carefully. "When you come back, we can have an argument."

"Very well." Now he glanced toward her. "Shall I take a lover?"

Again that high fey tone.

"Do you want to?"

"No. Never."

He reached across the table and gripped her hands.

"I love you," she whispered.

"Too much," he said thickly. "Why not marry me and forget the world?"

"Because we are Ilse and Raul. Because we must be true to ourselves."

RAUL LEFT THE next morning for two weeks with Lord Vieth and several of the governor's household. During his absence, Ilse moved all her belongings to her old rooms. Mistress Denk said nothing, except to ask if Mistress Ilse wished any assistance.

"None," Ilse said, as calmly as she could. "Thank you. I would rather do the work myself."

She heard whispers, whenever she passed through the public rooms. Stares, quickly averted. Conversations broken off. A sense of unnatural restraint from those she loved the most. Raul had told her they must lie to their friends. She had not realized how difficult it would be.

The worst, the most difficult moments were with Kathe.

"Why did Lord Kosenmark leave without you?" Kathe said.

She had brought Ilse's supper tray herself. But her manner was odd and awkward, with none of the friendly chatter from before.

"He went hunting," Ilse said. "Lord Vieth invited him."

Kathe frowned as she laid out the dishes. "I know that. Why didn't you go with him?"

"He wanted time alone. To think about Lord Dedrick."

"Strange," Kathe murmured. "Not what I expected him to want."

She curtsied and withdrew, leaving Ilse to pick at her food without any appetite. There was some truth in what she told Kathe. Lord Dedrick's death was the reason behind this dreadful charade. If Khandarr had not executed him, she and Raul might be together this very moment.

By afternoon she had recovered her nerve. A courier had brought a packet from Melnek. Ilse reviewed the latest papers from her brother. Her share of the inheritance came to twenty-three thousand gold denier. As she had requested, Ehren had sold off several of their farms and deposited the money with Lord Kosenmark's agent in Tiralien. He had also signed over several other holdings; she would receive the rents and interest quarterly.

I am rich. I could live wherever I wanted.

She had her wish from long ago, when she had lived in her father's house. The thought made her queasy. She sighed and poured herself a cup of strong tea, then reviewed the list of agents Raul had drawn up. There were three whom Raul recommended as the most reliable—Maester Harro Stangel, Mistress Emma Beck, and Maester Felix Massow. All of them had connections throughout the eastern provinces. Felix Massow had offices in Duenne as well, while Emma Beck had associates near Károví.

Ilse wrote letters to all three, asking for more details about their businesses, and how they might help her to invest her holdings. She secured the letters in her letter box—she would post them after she and Raul had had their first public argument.

Restless, she left her rooms for the rooftop gardens. It was a fair autumn day, the skies a clear dark blue. The seas were choppy, however, and low clouds obscured the eastern horizon. A summer's day in Melnek is an autumn day here, she thought. What were the seasons like in Osterling?

She heard footsteps—Raul hurrying toward her. He swept Ilse into a tight and breathless embrace. "I came early. I couldn't wait."

She leaned against his chest, breathing in his scent. Horse and sweat and leather and musk. Him. Exactly him. "I'm glad. What did you say to Lord Vieth?"

"That I was ill with longing for you."

She could almost laugh. "Unwise, my lord."

He buried his face in her hair. "It's the truth. But I was discreet. I told him that urgent family business awaited me. How have you been?"

"Very ... not well," she said. "I wrote to my brother and some agents in Osterling. I lied to Kathe."

Raul drew back and touched her cheek. "I'm sorry for the necessity."

He looked ill, she thought. Dark circles shadowed his eyes, there were faint lines around his mouth—lines of laughter transformed into lines of pain. Her heart ached at the sight, and when Raul touched the corner of her mouth, she nearly burst into tears.

She drew a deep breath. "So. When do we argue?"

"Tonight."

A shiver ran through her. "So soon?"

"Soon or never," Raul said. "I cannot pretend much longer. Besides, I heard talk at Lord Vieth's. The sooner you leave, the better chance we have to avoid suspicion."

"I thought the parole—"

"—is temporary, I believe. I doubt Lord Khandarr trusts me. And I learned years ago not to trust him."

She nodded. Laid her palm against Raul's chest. His heart was beating as fast as hers. If she pretended—

No more pretense. No more delays.

"Very well," she said. "Tonight."

RAUL SENT ORDERS to Mistress Raendl for a private dinner served in the Blue Salon. Ilse waited until the girls were laying out dishes and lighting candles, before she hurried into the room, just a few steps ahead of Raul.

Raul caught up and spun her around. "Why the old rooms?" he asked, in a tense whisper.

Steffi glanced up, her eyes wide, but immediately busied herself with the arranging the wine cups.

"Why?" Raul repeated, louder.

"Not here," Ilse whispered. "Not now."

"Because of them?" He flung out a hand, and Dana jumped. "Why do you care what they hear? You didn't keep it a secret from Kathe."

Ilse pressed her lips together, trembling. "Kathe is my friend."

"So much your friend that you betrayed my concerns to her."

"No!" Her chin jerked up. "I've betrayed nothing. But I'm tired of secrets, Raul. Sick and miserably tired. Do you understand?"

Raul smacked the wall with his hand. "Go!" he said to the serving girls. "We can serve ourselves."

He slammed the door shut after them and rounded on Ilse. "You knew that I cannot have children. Are you blind? Deaf?"

"Neither. I thought—"

"What? You thought what?"

"Let me finish!" Her voice cracked. "I thought we could have children. You said it yourself. Magic crippled you. Magic can heal you. If you truly wanted children, you could find a mage—"

She broke off at his glare.

"Only Markus Khandarr," he said in a harsh whisper. "Only Markus Khandarr has enough magic to heal this cripple. And I will not bear a debt to that man."

Tears gleamed on his eyelashes. Raul brushed them away, paused a moment with his hand over his face. When he finally met her gaze, she saw that his face had smoothed and all trace of his pretended anger had vanished. *I love you,* he mouthed.

And I you, my love. And I you. She glanced pointedly at the doors. *Do we continue?*

Yes.

Ilse drew a long breath and prepared to scream with rage.

FOR THE NEXT two weeks, they divided their hours between scripted arguments and nightly conferences. Their quarrels and their lovemaking took on a desperate edge, until it became difficult to separate the two.

Meanwhile Ilse sent letters by special courier to Mistress Beck and Mistress Adela Andeliess, who owned the pleasure house in Osterling. Mistress Andeliess's steward had recently left her service, so Ilse wrote to apply for the position, saying that her qualifications were similar, secretary to Lord Kosenmark, liaison to the steward here, her upbringing as a merchant's daughter. Five weeks later, she had answers to both.

Yes, delighted, Mistress Beck wrote. Ilse forwarded her name and particulars to Raul's agent, and asked him to transfer her moneys.

Please send me references, Mistress Andeliess replied. Ilse provided those, including a terse but businesslike letter from Raul, and another from Mistress Denk.

She had taken care to let others know about these transactions. Thereafter,

Eduard and Mikka and Johanna and the other courtesans sent her curious glances. Dana and Steffi and Hanne and the rest of the kitchen girls grew very quiet in her presence. Nadine said nothing, but whenever their paths crossed, her gaze passed over Ilse, as though she'd turned as invisible as the air. As for Kathe . . .

Ilse went to Kathe's rooms one afternoon, before she returned to the kitchen for evening preparations. Kathe opened the door to her knock. Her first reaction was a startled exclamation, followed quickly by wariness.

"Do you have a free moment?" Ilse asked. "I'd like to talk."

"Do we have anything to say, Mistress Ilse?"

"I'm leaving. I wanted to explain."

"Explain what? That you—" Kathe broke off with a grimace. "Come inside. We don't need to start more gossip by arguing in the hallways."

She stood aside and stiffly gestured for Ilse to enter. There were books open upon Kathe's small desk, and papers covered with what looked like menus and recipes, all written in Kathe's neat handwriting. Except for a new carpet, the rooms were just as Ilse remembered, from the days when she and Kathe had taken their late-afternoon breaks here. Or later, whenever their work allowed a brief visit. Kathe had taught her and befriended her. Even when Ilse moved from secretary to lord's mistress, she had remained someone Ilse could trust and talk to. But now . . .

"I know you're leaving," Kathe said without preamble. "And I know why. Lord Kosenmark was honest with you. But you—"

"I thought it didn't matter," Ilse said quickly. "But it does. Very much. I'm sorry."

Kathe's lips puffed in silent laughter. "Why apologize to me? I am not the one you wronged. Go to Lord Kosenmark. Beg his forgiveness. Tell him you wish to stay."

"I can't. It's too late."

"Then we have nothing to discuss."

Ilse let her breath trickle out. "I'm sorry, Kathe," she said softly. "I will not trouble you again."

Kathe shook her head. If she grieved for their lost friendship, she hid it behind a remote mask. Ilse hesitated another moment, then silently left.

This moment, too, is part of the scheme. Unplanned and yet unavoidable.

ONE LAST TASK. One last visit.

"Where are you going?" Raul asked a few days later.

"To visit a friend."

His mouth quirked in smile. "One of mine, or one of yours?"

"Yours," she said in a low voice. "I'll make new ones in Osterling."

He opened his mouth, but whatever he meant to say, he didn't. He kissed her softly on the cheek and said he hoped she would return in time for a late private dinner. Ilse suspected he guessed her destination, but he didn't ask and she didn't offer.

She was still divided in her own mind when she arrived at Benno Iani's small elegant house, in the same neighborhood as Lord Vieth's soaring palace. The footman showed a very polite face when she announced her name, but she could tell he, too, had heard of the break between her and Raul. Would Lord Iani refuse to see her? Would he simply announce that he was not at home?

The footman came back with word that Lord Iani would gladly see her. Ilse followed the man to a sunny parlor at the rear of the house. Sunlight streamed through the tall windows. Outside, a profusion of russet and golden flowers made a splash of brilliant color against a gray stone wall.

Lady Theysson was not present, she noticed at once.

Iani smiled at her. It was a brief smile, but genuine. "Emma was here," he said. "She left because she cannot bear to see what happened to two of her best friends."

"And you?"

"You are both my friends. It grieves me to see you argue. It would grieve me more to lose you entirely. Why did you come to me?"

To say good-bye. To see if you and Emma believed our lies.

"To ask a favor," she said.

His smile turned wary. "What kind of favor?"

"It's about magic . . ."

As she explained her request, Iani's eyes narrowed in concentration. It was a question of security. She remembered the spell Benno had used to alter Rosel's memories. It had very specific properties, she knew. With it, a skilled mage could obliterate days or weeks, or he could blur memories from a single hour.

"You wish me to make you forget," Iani said. "Now?"

She shook her head. "I want you to explain the spell. Write down the words and how to use them. In case . . . in case, I need to forget certain important details."

In case Lord Khandarr ever decided to extract a confession from her, as he had from Lord Dedrick Maszuryn. Iani turned gray at the implication, but he was nodding. "Of course. I understand. Let us go to my study. I have some books I could give you on the subject."

They spent the rest of the afternoon in close discussion. Iani gave Ilse three treatises about memory spells, including one describing keys to undo the magic.

"I won't need that spell," Ilse said, trying to hand back the scroll.

"Take it anyway," Benno said. "Please."

Reluctantly she agreed, and he pressed the scroll into her hands.

CHAPTER TWENTY-EIGHT

AUTUMN PASSED INTO winter, marking the end of her second year in Tiralien. Kathe did not speak to her after that last private conversation, the courtesans avoided her as well, and by necessity, her hours with Raul were few and secret.

The last night, Raul came to her rooms after midnight. With a wordless gesture, he led Ilse into the bedroom and locked the door with bolt and magic. His expression made her throat catch—the deliberate way he moved, his intent gaze, as though he were committing every moment to memory.

She reached for him. He stopped her with a gesture. "Humor me."

He set the lamp on the highest shelf, traced the gleam of its light along her cheek and jaw, the outline of her lips. Then he extinguished the lamp and kissed her where the moonlight did. His cheeks were wet with a silent flow of tears that unnerved her more than all the others he'd shed before. "I'm sorry," he said. "I meant this night to contain only joy."

"Then you want the impossible."

"Always." He drew her close, and she felt him shake with silent laughter. "Ah, my love. You are joy itself. Come, we shall make love by sunlight and moonlight together."

"As Lir did with Toc," she said. "For Toc died, and in dying was reborn."

"Because death is but the prelude to life. Who could show us that hidden path but a god?"

He lit all the lamps in the room, making the room blaze with light. *Silver and gold,* Ilse thought, watching him. *The sun and the moon.*

Raul turned. His eyes were wide and dark, the golden irises eclipsed by dark centers. "Now," he whispered.

"Now," she answered.

Keeping her gaze upon his face, Ilse unbuttoned her shirt. She paused a moment, feeling the cool air brush over her skin, then she slid the shirt off and dropped it onto the floor. Her skirt came next, and then the rest of her clothing—item by item—pausing each time that he might memorize how she looked. Once she had finished, he did the same for her, the candlelight gilding his skin with gold, the moonlight reflecting from his eyes.

Their last night—time to employ all their senses. Time to strip away every pretension, every barrier, as they had not dared before. They gave until their bodies collapsed, spent and exhausted. Raul traced patterns upon her breasts and belly; he caressed her thighs, and kissed away the spendings from between her legs.

I cannot refuse you anything, she murmured. *Ask whatever you will, whatever you desire.*

You are the elixir of my joy, he murmured. *With you I am immortal.*

Lir and Toc's words, in their season of love.

"Lie back," Ilse whispered.

Raul obeyed, lying quiescent while Ilse ran her hands over his body, combing her fingers through his hair, brushing her palms over his cheeks, kissing his neck and chest and groin. Wordlessly, she slipped her hand between his legs, urging them apart, and heard the quick intake of his breath as she kissed where the mage-surgeon had operated.

We are one. One heart. One desire.

They made love until dawn stained the sky with silver and white and palest red. "I will love you forever," Raul said. He buried his face against her neck. His cheeks were damp.

"Raul."

"Hush." He kissed her tenderly. Again, softer still, each one an infinitesimal distance further from passion until they were lying apart, not touching.

"Now," he whispered.

Now, she thought, but her throat would not let the word pass.

Silently they rose from the bed. Raul wet a cloth in the washbasin and ran it lightly over her face, her throat, and down the curve of her hip. His expression had left carnal passion behind, and watching his face, Ilse felt a stirring in response—an emotion beyond desire that she could not name.

When he had done, he sat cross-legged on the bed and watched, his expression still intent, while Ilse dressed for her journey. He was a witness to her departure, she thought. He would remember every moment, and thus they would not truly be separated.

"I'll fetch breakfast," Ilse said softly.

Raul smiled pensively. "I'll stay here and make everything ready."

She nodded. They must leave no traces of this last night together.

Down in the kitchen, only a few scullions remained from the night shift.

No one greeted Ilse. No one questioned her presence in the kitchen. Most likely they all knew she left today. For a moment, Ilse wished she could unwind the months to a point between today and her arrival. When she still had friends here. When Kathe smiled and Berthold Hax was alive.

Today isn't yesterday. It cannot be.

Silently she prepared a breakfast tray herself with coffee and freshly baked meat pies. When she came back to her rooms, she found Raul fully dressed and pacing the outer sitting room. He paused. "Trouble?"

"None," she replied. "The house is asleep."

They shared coffee from a single cup, and ate from a single plate. They talked little except to make a few commonplace observations—how good the coffee tasted, a comment about the pastry cook's gift for crusts, whether they heard birdsong outside or someone was whistling in the lane below.

Finally, the dishes lay empty before them. Outside, the bells rang six times. Ilse drank the last of her coffee. She stood, but sat again immediately. *I cannot leave him.*

Raul kissed her. "Until forever, my love."

She stood—she hardly knew how—and walked from her rooms, down the stairs and through the pleasure house's grand front doors, where the coach waited, her baggage already stowed. Ilse waved aside the guards and mounted into the coach herself. A glance at the house showed nothing—only dark windows and a blank facade of dusky red stone.

The guards closed the coach's door and took their posts. The driver mounted to her seat. Ilse shut her eyes. No tears. No sudden weakness. But when the coach rolled into motion, she leaned out the window for one last hungry glance. Far above, golden firelight flickered in a window. Ilse caught the strong dark scent of magic with Raul's signature. *Until forever. That is my promise.*

Magic and light both vanished. Ilse fell back against the cushioned seats. She dared not dwell upon how long forever might be.

The coach wound through Tiralien's streets and avenues, from the elegant neighborhood where Raul Kosenmark's pleasure house stood, through the merchants' quarter, then to the public thoroughfares, already noisy with traffic. At the city's western gates, they halted, and while the driver exchanged news with the guards, Ilse watched several caravans making ready for their own departure. Guards patrolled on horseback and on foot. Crewmembers stacked barrels into wagons. Young boys and girls darted between the wagons, as quick and lively as the dust motes whirling through the sunlight.

The driver finished her conversation. Once more the coach rolled forward. Ilse had the brief impression of the sentries bowing to her, the gates impossibly tall and bright. Then they were through, and leaving Tiralien behind.

ILSE TOOK HER journey in easy stages, stopping at inns or camping at the roadside shelters. Her guards, a woman and a man, doubled as Ilse's servants. Deft and polite, they saw to all her needs—setting up camp, fetching water and cooking meals, and caring for the horses. When Ilse retired to her luxurious private tent, they stood watch in turns. Raul had discreetly checked their references himself. Ilse trusted them. Even so, she wore a knife strapped to her wrist and another in her boot—knives she knew how to wield.

Four days from Tiralien, after settling camp for the night, the senior guard approached Ilse, and presented her with a small wooden box and a sealed envelope. "My lady, a runner came to me right before we left Tiralien. He gave me these, said to wait so many days before I was to give it to you."

The box was narrow and held shut with leather straps with buckles. Ordinary. The envelope was heavy—several sheets thick—and she detected strong magic saturating the parchment and wax seal. Neither of them carried any inscription. "Thank you," she said.

She went into her tent, glad for the privacy, and lit a shaded lamp. The box first, she decided.

She unbuckled the straps and opened the lid. Straw filled the interior. On top lay a small square of paper with the printed words *A Dangerous Gift*.

Raul. Her heart beating faster, she cautiously reached into the straw and pulled out a dagger in a leather sheath. She exhaled in silent laughter as she drew the dagger from the sheath and inspected the dark blue blade. Dangerous, yes. Any gift from Raul Kosenmark would prove dangerous. Dangerous to her resolve. Dangerous if anyone discovered who had given her this very beautiful, undoubtedly very costly dagger.

And yet, it was a deliberately anonymous gift.

I will keep it.

She sheathed the dagger and set it aside. Next, the envelope with its seal. Magic nipped at her fingertips as the wax parted. The letter unfolded into her lap—five pages of closely written script that looked as though it had flowed from Raul's pen without hesitation or correction. Had he written these pages during their hours apart? she wondered. Then she was devouring its words, while the scent and buzz of magic rippled over her skin.

He wrote of his unqualified love, of his admiration for her strength and bravery and intelligence. He wrote of trust in her decision, and of his hope that their lives would reunite without barriers or constraints, just as she wished. There was no word of politics or schemes or their shared beliefs, but she still read those thoughts behind every word he had written. As she read on, her heart lifted with a tenuous joy.

> *Beloved, you might find moments where you doubt my constancy, when you suspect I relinquished you too easily, because my love had faded to ordinary desire. Disbelieve those thoughts. Cherish our past memories only as they give you strength. Like swords tested apart, we will prove that much stronger when joined together.*

He had signed the letter Raul of Valentain. Next to his signature, he had pressed a single rose petal, of a red so dark, it looked black.

Ilse folded the letter carefully and tucked it away. Soon she would have to destroy it. *But not yet,* she thought. *Please, not yet.*

WITHIN ANOTHER DAY, they met the southern highway, which looped between the hills in slow unhurried curves. Soon the Gallenz River disappeared from view, oaks and aspen gave way to scrubby pines, and the hard-packed road changed from dun-colored dirt to dark red clay. The driver stopped frequently to rest the horses and let them graze on the sparse grass, while the guards built a fire and prepared tea for Ilse. Ilse read from her favorite books or watched the guards practice their sword work. At times she simply gazed into the southern hills, remembering her own trek, alone, through their northern counterpart.

At the next valley, a road built of crushed stone and dirt led across the marshes and into the next range of hills. They traveled south and then southeast along a larger highway, where they encountered farmers and itinerant craftsmen, a scribe journeying to her next appointment, and even squads of soldiers marching in formation. There were garrisons all along the coast, set at regular intervals, first built against marauding pirates, then, in later years, to guard against Károví attacks. Spear points, the histories called them.

The longer the journey, the more Ilse's thoughts returned to Raul and Tiralien. As the highway unrolled between the hills and the open seas, her gaze skipped past the foam-dotted swells, and she wondered how Raul had spent these past weeks, hardly noting what passed outside. So it took her by surprise when the coach halted, and a strong voice called out, "Who comes?"

"Mistress Ilse Zhalina of Tiralien," the driver replied.

"Welcome, then," said the man. "Welcome to Osterling Keep."

THE THREE-QUARTER HOUR was ringing when Ilse's coach stopped in front of Mistress Andeliess's pleasure house, which stood at one corner of a busy main square. The house had three stories, built of dark red bricks, with a long veranda and graceful fluted columns. A smaller lane bordered one side; a second faced onto a courtyard with an arched passageway.

One guard held the horses, while the other helped Ilse to dismount. By the time Mistress Andeliess came out to greet her, Ilse had paid her guards and driver their final installment. Together they supervised as servants from the house unloaded Ilse's baggage and carried it inside.

Soon the coach was gone. Ilse stood alone on the veranda with Mistress Andeliess.

"Come and see your rooms," Mistress Andeliess said. "No doubt you're tired and hungry, and a bit dusty from the road. I'll send up food, and a girl to help with your things. Take today and tomorrow to settle in. Look over the house and walk around the town."

Mistress Andeliess, too, was not what Ilse expected. Her voice was higher and sweeter; her gorgeously dressed hair fell in braids around her plump face. She herself showed Ilse to her new rooms, which were on the third floor. There were but two—a large outer room that served as both parlor and study, and a small but comfortable bedroom. They smelled of beeswax and soap and the faint traces of incense.

"I saw your many, many trunks," Mistress Andeliess commented. "You had a much larger set of rooms in Tiralien?"

Ilse felt a brief pang of memory. "Larger, yes. I should have left more behind."

Mistress Andeliess gave her a kindly smile. "No worry. We've plenty of storage behind the house."

She did not chatter the way Kathe did, but her smooth flow of conversation helped Ilse through that first hour. Two girls arrived with hot coffee, cold soup, and fresh bread. Her appetite awakened, Ilse ate, then washed her face and changed into a new linen gown and robe.

See the house and town, Mistress Andeliess had suggested.

Not yet. Too soon.

She wandered from her parlor into her bedroom and inspected its furnishings. The narrow bed looked soft and inviting. A larger wardrobe covered half of one wall—ample room for the clothes she brought. A series of shelves lined a second wall. Her books on magic and history would easily fill the lower ones. She could alternate poetry books with a few of her ivory figurines on the upper shelves. Her new dagger in its elegant sheath could hang over her bed. Perhaps she could buy a new sword to match, and make a display of weaponry. Thinking of weapons, she wondered if she might find a weapons instructor to continue her lessons, or if the garrison permitted outsiders to drill with the soldiers.

Ilse sank onto the bed and covered her face with her hands. *It's true. I left him.*

Dimly she heard the next hour bells striking. Late afternoon. Ebb tide's pungent aroma filled the air. Ilse wiped the tears from her eyes. She was here. She would manage. Day by day.

She walked to the open window, which overlooked the courtyard she had seen from the square. A large prosperous inn stood on the opposite side. To her right, she could just see the governor's mansion where Nicol Joannis lived. Beyond it, she saw the remnants of an old castle keep, which must have existed during the empire days or before, when Fortezzien was an independent kingdom. In the other direction lay the water-filled horizon. The air was warm and the sun as bright as a summer's day in Melnek. Only a faint cast of gray in the sky hinted at winter.

A sudden noise below caught her attention—a group of soldiers were passing through the courtyard on their way to the square. Ilse counted six or seven, men and women both. All were armed with swords and armor; most were dusky or dark-complexioned—southerners—except for one plain-faced girl whose light brown coloring and hair stood out from the rest.

The soldiers were laughing and chatting. One young woman happened to glance up. She saw Ilse and waved. Another companion pulled the young woman to her side, and they were whispering in breathless tones. Gossip, Ilse thought. The same here as everywhere.

Soon the soldiers were gone, leaving only the echo of their presence. By now the sun slanted down between the buildings, casting longer shadows. Ilse turned back into the room and lit a lamp. Automatically she took Raul's letter from her pocket and read it again, trying to memorize every line.

. . . I will love you forever, beloved. No matter what passes during our time apart, my love will not fail. Someday, by grace of Lir and Toc, in this life or the next, we shall find each other again . . .

Someday.

She lit a candle and held the paper to the flame until it caught. Words flared and turned black as she watched. When the flames had consumed everything but one corner, she dropped the paper onto the tiles. Even that corner shriveled into ashes, which she swept up and deposited in her fireplace.

I have burned my past, she thought.

Then she had to laugh. She would burn her past day after day, she could tell. Every time she thought of Raul Kosenmark and her life in Tiralien, she would have to set a match to those thoughts, until the action became rote with her.

Oh, never entirely rote. Someday—

She broke off the thought before she could complete it. *Yes, someday,* she told herself. Someday she would recover Lir's jewels, Raul would forge an alliance with Károví, and they could rejoin their lives. But not today. It was best if she gave herself a task instead of sitting and brooding. Something ordinary. Something tied to her new life in Osterling Keep.

Ilse retrieved her writing supplies from one trunk. There was a desk in her sitting room, another piece of furniture she would probably replace, but for now it would do. She sat down and picked up the pen. Hesitated. What to write? Her thoughts drifted back to her first day as Berthold Hax's new assistant.

A schedule for my first month, she decided. *After that, a catalog of supplies.*

More voices drifted up from the courtyard. Through the plaster walls, Ilse heard soft laughter and a mandolin being played. *My new life,* she thought. *A future whose words I choose.*

She dipped her pen in the ink and began to write.